PETER F. WARREN

Wes,
Hope you enjoy the story I've told. Have many fond memories of our days together at Troop A.

Stay well.
Pete

THE
Parliament
MEN

outskirtspress
DENVER, COLORADO

PETER F. WARREN

THE
PARLIAMENT MEN

The Parliament Men
All Rights Reserved.
Copyright © 2015 Peter F. Warren
v2.0

Outskirts Press, Inc.
http://www.outskirtspress.com

ISBN: 978-1-4787-4839-7

Library of Congress Control Number: 2015902384

Outskirts Press and the "OP" logo are trademarks belonging to Outskirts Press, Inc.

PRINTED IN THE UNITED STATES OF AMERICA

Dedication

To my wife, Debbie, for her continued support and love.

To Rita Margaret Warren,
a mother and grandmother we all love.

To Brian & Kati, and Sean & Lauren,
thank you for being who you are.

And, to the men and women serving as state cops,
local cops, deputies, prosecutors, forensic scientists,
and evidence techs, whether sworn or civilian, who
are charged with investigating the brutal and senseless
murders that occur far too often in life these days.
Stay the course – your efforts are greatly appreciated.

Peter Warren Books

---

www.readpete.com

Other novels by Peter Warren include:

The Horry County Murders

Confederate Gold and Silver

The Journey North
(Written with Roy McKinney and Edward Odom)

Peter Warren often speaks at libraries, book and civic group meetings, and at other events. He has spoken numerous times to Confederate Civil War groups and camps, and at Gettysburg. As well, he often attends, and participates in, Civil War reenactments and other events across South Carolina.

If you would like Peter to speak to your group, please contact him at www.readpete.com or by email at petesbooks63@yahoo.com

For additional information, please visit the author's Facebook pages. (The Parliament Men or The Horry County Murders or The Journey North) LIKE the author on Facebook.

Acknowledgements

In each of my first three novels, several of my characters have been named after family and friends. Doing so is a way for each of my 'characters' to know how much they mean to me. I have again chosen to do the same with several of the characters in this story.

Readers of my books have come to know and like my principle characters, Paul and Donna Waring. Many of those same readers have also told me how much they have enjoyed one of my other principle fictional characters, Bobby Ray Jenkins, as well as a handful of other characters who have continued to be featured in each of my books. On many occasions, during book talks or visits to local libraries, I have been asked if each of these three characters have been named after friends or state troopers I had the pleasure of working with for so many years. The simple answer is that they have not been named after any specific individuals. Like their names, the personalities and traits of Paul and Donna, as well as those of Bobby Ray, come from a number of people I have known for many years. These three characters exemplify the types of people my family and friends are. From the hundreds of comments I have received, it is easy to tell that many of you have taken a liking to Paul, Donna, and to Bobby Ray. I hope you will enjoy how I have portrayed each of them in this novel.

To each of my friends who have kindly agreed to allow me to

use their names for repeat characters, or for new ones this story introduces, I extend my sincere thanks.

I also need to thank friends like Kenneth Zercie, a former cop turned forensic scientist, whose dedication and leadership helped earn the Connecticut State Police Department's Forensic Lab the excellent reputation it still enjoys to this day. His help and expertise in matters regarding firearms for this novel is greatly appreciated. I also need to thank retired state police detective Wes Clark for his help concerning the finer points of interview and interrogation techniques. A new friend, Robert Battista, as well as his brother, Carmine, the owners of the 707 Gun Shop, and the 707 Indoor Shooting Range, in Myrtle Beach, SC, were also a huge help as they spent time showing me the workings of their impressive store and indoor firing range. I also appreciate the time they spent discussing a few of the finer points regarding firearms. Another former CSP detective, Darren Edwards, also was a help in issues related to firearms. I appreciate all of their contributions.

Finally, to Blake Stine, Bob Bonner, and to a few others, THANKS for your input and review of the early drafts of this story.

The writing of any book, whether it's a novel, a biography, or even a technical manual, is often a long and, sometimes, arduous task to complete. It is one that is made far easier when you have so many great friends to help you along the way. I am blessed to have such great friends.

Enjoy your read of *The Parliament Men*.

Contents

About the Author

Peter Warren, a former resident of Connecticut, retired from the Connecticut State Police Department after serving for many years in several command assignments. He is a graduate of the University of New Haven, of the FBI National Academy, and an Honor Graduate of the Connecticut State Police Academy. He is a past national president of the National Alliance of State Drug Enforcement Agencies; a past member of the CT Chapter of the FBI National Academy; a past member of the American Association of State Troopers, and served several terms as President of the CT State Police Academy Alumni Association.

Currently he resides in South Carolina with his wife Debbie.

A Civil War enthusiast, and an avid golfer, the author has combined those interests, along with his law enforcement experience, to write four novels. *The Parliament Men* is the author's latest book, and it closely follows the release of the author's first murder mystery, *The Horry County Murders*. Several characters from his first book, *Confederate Gold and Silver*, appear in both of these murder mysteries which occur along the South Carolina coast. Peter Warren is also the author of *The Journey North*; a novel written with Roy McKinney and Edward Odom. *Confederate Gold and Silver* and *The Journey North* are novels about the American Civil War. They are stories that readers of most books will enjoy.

The author routinely speaks at libraries, social events, book events, Civil War reenactments, and at many other similar types of events. Individuals and organizations interested in having Peter Warren speak at your event may contact him directly at www. readpete.com or by sending him an email at pfw1863@ yahoo. com. See the author's Facebook page, or the Facebook pages for The Horry County Murders or The Journey North for additional information. Twitter : @peterfwarren1

Single or bulk copies of this book may be obtained through the author, through Outskirts Press, or through the worldwide web.

Some of the Characters
Within the Book

The Parliament Men is a story that takes place within Georgetown County, South Carolina. Some of the characters in this story are folks who have lived in the county their entire life. Some speak with the rich flavor that so-many Southerners have in their voices. A few of them, for several reasons in their personal lives, have received little in the form of a formal education; hence, their speech has been intentionally designed to be rough. Those characters, who add so much to the story being told, are designated below with a * next to their names. I hope you enjoy those characters as much as I do. Like most of the others in this novel, they are honest and hard-working folks; just the kind of people I enjoy having as family and friends.

Paul Waring
> First appearing in the author's novel *Confederate Gold and Silver*, and again in *The Horry County Murders*, Paul is the principle character in this book. He is a retired Connecticut state trooper who now resides in Murrells Inlet, SC. One of his closest friends is Bobby Ray Jenkins.

Donna Waring
> Paul's wife. She is a bank manager.

Captain Bobby Ray Jenkins*
> A close friend of Paul's. He is the commanding officer of the Georgetown County Sheriff's Departments Major Case Squad. Like Paul, he is one of the principle characters.

Lt. Audrey Small
> She works for Bobby Ray.

Sheriff Leroy William Renda*
  The sheriff of Georgetown County.

Solicitor Joseph Pascento
  A South Carolina prosecutor.

Kenneth Zercie
  A forensic scientist who works for SLED.

Betty Repko*
  A waitress who is a close friend of Paul's.

Phillip 'Cotton' Horbin*
  He is a neighbor who lives near the victims' home.

Zeke Payne*
  The owner of a lawn maintenance company.

Peter Paul Payne*
  Zeke Payne's father.

Douglas Vane
  The Georgetown County Sheriff's Department Evidence Officer.

Bobby 'Bats' Battista
  A gun shop owner.

The Victims
Carl Diggs, Tyler 'Ty' Johanson, Robert Tanner,
James Robinson, Trevor Gilmour

The Investigators
Sgt. Kent Wilson, Det. Frank Griffin, Det. Blake Stine,
FBI Agent Thomas Scozzafava, Det. Darren Edwards,
Det. Bruce Davis, Sgt. Don Elmendorf,
Det. Ron Levesque, Det. Lonny Mo

One

An Old Man's Dream

In early 1963, when the old man finally purchased the half acre of property that he had found so appealing, the sprawl south from Myrtle Beach was just in its infancy. In North Litchfield, a small community situated between Murrells Inlet and Georgetown which seldom was shown on most maps, less than a handful of lots had been purchased of the two hundred and twenty home sites which had been surveyed as part of the planned beachfront community just off of Highway 17. Of the three homes that had been started, one had been designed for year-round use and two had simply been planned as beach cottages for use whenever their owners and special friends visited the lower end of the Grand Strand.

The old man's lot sat three sandy roads removed from the row of prime lots immediately adjacent to the pristine beaches running north from Pawleys Island up towards Murrells Inlet. Even a casual stroll from the small unimproved lot took less than two minutes to reach the edge of the Atlantic Ocean. Despite their spectacular views, the oceanfront lots were far too expensive for an accountant's meager salary to afford. Even factoring in a small inheritance, and his wife's income from cleaning homes, they were ones he gave little attention to after learning of the hefty prices being asked.

In life, he had been given little, but the knowledge of doing better than his parents had pleased him. It was the same thought his own father had experienced years earlier. In his family, like in many others, each succeeding generation was expected to do better than the one before it. Like his father, the old man was far from wealthy, but the fact that he had been able to purchase a lot close to the ocean to build his summer cottage on made him feel like he owned the world. It was a dream he had harbored for years.

By early April, the warm weather had dried the soft sandy soil sufficiently enough to allow the clearing of the lot to begin. Like the rest of the lots within the planned community, all were locations where the region's early settlers had visited and camped at while escaping not only the hot and humid South Carolina summers, but the deadly viruses carried inland by mosquitoes. Like his, most of the land surrounding it was still virgin territory, inhabited mostly by deer, raccoons, snakes, and birds of various types.

Placing a significant down payment on the lot had placed a serious strain on the old man's budget. Despite his financial woes, he had saved just enough to hire a local tree company to take down several of the Long Leaf pine trees which sat on the space where he planned to build his new cottage. Working on weekends mostly, he and his wife, with occasional help from a couple of friends, spent the better part of two months clearing the rest of the lot of small scrub pines, brush, and other vegetation so construction could begin. Over the next several weeks, the small one-story cottage began to take shape.

Despite his love of both the beach and his summer cottage, Brian Patrick's dream of retiring to his home-away-from-home died with him only two short years later. In the years following his death, and despite his family's love and visits to their cottage, little was done to maintain their cozy little three bedroom bungalow. Less than ten years after Patrick's death, his wife died of a massive brain hemorrhage. With little children of their own to feed and clothe, and with little spare cash available to keep up a cottage that had already started to fall by the wayside, his two sons soon sold it for barely more than what was left on the mortgage and for the taxes that were owed on it.

Over the following thirty years, the small cottage, at the hands of four different owners, underwent a series of renovations and a handful of additions. As those occurred, the remaining few lots around the immediate area of the Patrick cottage were sold to families wanting a lifestyle close to the beach. Soon what was once a small close-knit neighborhood of less than seventy-eight homes was now one with two hundred and twenty homes of all different shapes and sizes. The original homeowners, who had shared so many informal dinners and birthdays with each other, had now been replaced by folks who barely knew their neighbors. Many of the homes were now owned by absentee owners, folks who were only interested in making a buck renting out their homes to wealthy vacationers from different parts of the country. Among those new owners were the owners of the home that had been built by the Patrick family. Now owned by a middle aged couple from Myrtle Beach, they cared more about receiving their monthly rent check on time than they did about the beauty of the neighborhood.

The current owners had purchased the home during the housing recession of 2013. The once small cottage had now been expanded to two floors. While three bedrooms were now housed on the second floor, the four bathrooms were spread across both floors. Like the previous owners before them, they had also made their share of changes to the home that the original owner had dreamed of living in with his family after retirement. Now, no longer being used as their own vacation get-away, it was rented out to help supplement another family's dream about their own future.

* * * * * *

For fifteen months the beach home of Alice and Jerry Zerbola had been the residence of Carl Diggs, Tyler Johanson, and Robert Tanner. They were each in their mid-twenties, and, despite their ages, were still working on a part-time basis to complete their undergraduate degrees at Coastal Carolina University. Like many of their friends who often visited the home they rented, they worked a variety of part-time jobs as they tried their best to keep their heads above water financially. Doing so made balancing a busy schedule of work, school, and their own individual personal lives often difficult. For personal and financial reasons, it was not uncommon for each of them to take turns organizing many of the social activities being held at the home near the beach.

It was during one of these small social gatherings when things went bad very quickly for them. In the past, there had been a few run-ins with him, and while a few heated words had been exchanged, none of the three young men or their friends had ever feared him. Now, by the time their fear had finally surfaced, it was too late for them to defend themselves. It was quickly over with in a matter of minutes.

* * * * * *

Years of grief would follow for the Diggs, Johanson, and Tanner families, as well as for those of two of their friends. Separate from the grief shared by those five families was the grief and anguish that would be shared by one other family. The difference was they had been prepared to expect it. For them, it was simply a matter of time as to when and where it would occur.

Two

Back to Work

It was late on Friday afternoon, and only two days after the summer solstice, when Paul Waring pulled the small metal anchor out of the Waccamaw River's murky brown water. Like the yellow nylon rope that was tied to a dead cypress tree just off the bow of his pontoon boat, the anchor had kept the boat from drifting while its owner spent most of the afternoon fishing in the river's slow moving brackish water.

The tide had just begun to change when he first arrived at his favorite fishing spot, but now, with it being close to five p.m., the level of the river had risen considerably as the afternoon tide rushed inland after entering Winyah Bay from the Atlantic Ocean. It was all part of one of the cycles of life that, fortunately, man could not tamper with.

Paul welcomed the changing tide for several reasons, but mostly he did so because every Sunday he had gotten into the habit of memorizing the times the tide was going to change each afternoon of the following week. High tide on this particular day meant that drinks with his wife; followed by a nice dinner, were not too far away. Like the changing tides, this had become a ritual years ago for Paul and Donna. Friday nights were date nights, and that meant drinks and dinner. Seldom did they let anything interfere with those enjoyable evenings. The higher tide also meant navigating his boat down the small creek leading to his slip at the Waccamaw Boat and Fish Club was going to be that much easier than doing so when the tide was not quite as high. Years earlier a small wooden boat sank in the middle of the creek, and while neither the remains of that boat or the rotted old wooden posts from a former dock had ever caused him too much difficulty in getting back into the marina, he always felt a little more comfortable bringing his Harris FloteBoat in during high tide. Now with nothing impeding his progress, he slowly steered towards his slip. Slip B-12 was located on the east side of the marina's fairly large waterfront.

"Another successful voyage," Paul muttered to himself as he cut the power to his outboard motor, allowing the remaining energy of his forward motion to carry the pontoon boat part-way into his slip. Jumping onto the wooden dock from the right side of his boat, he grabbed the bright yellow bow line and quickly tugged hard on it. Doing so brought the boat close enough so he could easily secure the bow line to a large metal cleat near the front of the dock. Like the others nearby, the large dock had been painted a bright white so it could easily be seen at night and during foul weather. As he secured the boat, three off-white colored bumpers kept it from banging directly against the dock. Soon finished securing the bow line, he then moved to secure the boat's stern line to another cleat.

After collecting his fishing gear and the rest of his personal items that he decided not to chance leaving locked up in the boat's ample storage compartments, Paul headed up the dock's walkway to where his truck was parked. Being a regular visitor to the marina had allowed him to figure out the best place to strategically park his truck each morning. Parking it in the gravel covered parking lot in an area drenched by the cooler morning sun meant by the time he returned each afternoon it would be under the cover of four large pine trees. As he walked to his truck on this hot June afternoon, the shade provided by the trees had helped to keep his vehicle cool.

Quickly finished securing his gear, Paul glanced at his cell phone to get the correct time. What he saw displayed on the phone's screen caused him to realize he had gotten his times mixed up. The military time displayed read 1702 hours. Under the time was the date, Friday, June 23rd.

"Oh, hell! It's Friday, you jackass! Donna does not even get out of work till six tonight." Immediately, Paul realized his screw-up had cost him an hour of fishing on this beautiful afternoon.

A retired state trooper from Connecticut, Paul, along with his wife, had retired to the Murrells Inlet area of South Carolina five years earlier. While two significant incidents had caused retirement life to be everything but what he had planned it to be, he still managed to find time each week to venture out on the river; sometimes spending a day or two fishing and other times just exploring the various creeks and inlets along the way. While many of his friends from work had gone into a variety of other positions after retiring, Paul had chosen not to, declining several interesting offers to manage security firms in Connecticut. He had done so just to enjoy life. A thirty-plus year career in law enforcement, one which caused him to be woken up several nights a week to help manage various emergencies across the state, had caused him to follow a simpler path in life after retiring. It was a choice he never regretted making.

Covering his boat after realizing that Donna would not be home for at least another ninety minutes or so, Paul had a quick chat at the far end of the dock with a casual acquaintance. Soon finished hearing about how poor the fishing had been in the river recently, he made sure he locked his truck before starting the short walk to the marina's small restaurant to kill some time. It was also time to kill the thirst he had worked up before heading home to grab a shower before dinner. The restaurant was located in the back of the single story wood framed building that also housed the marina's small store.

The store itself was slightly larger than the restaurant, and, as expected, it catered to the variety of needs of those boaters who either moored their boats there or those who paid a small daily fee to use the marina's boat ramp. Among the items the store sold were eight different kinds of ice-cold bottled and canned beer, soft drinks, chips, live bait, including blood worms, fishing tackle, and several different shades of sunscreen.

On most occasions when he visited the small restaurant, Paul confined himself to having a cold beer or two on one of the six stools which sat adjacent to a Formica counter. Depending upon what time of the day it was, it served as the restaurant's lunch counter or bar.

Walking into the restaurant, Paul spied Rich Campbell, one of the marina's two mechanics. Campbell had finished work for the day and was now nursing a cold can of PBR as he sat on one of the stools facing a large Sony television that was sitting on a shelf behind the counter. Two other empty cans, along with an empty bag of Lay's barbeque potato chips, sat off to Campbell's right, the cans surrounded by small pools of condensation that had dripped off each of them. Like the restaurant itself, the wooden shelf had not seen a fresh coat of paint since the early days of the Hoover administration. Paul gave the television a brief glance, but paid little attention to what one of the local news reporters was telling his viewers. In the background, he could hear the restaurant's air conditioner as it strained to keep up with the heat of the day. The constant opening and closing of two nearby doors as customers came and went caused the ten-year old unit to work harder than it should have. Sitting down two stools away from where Campbell sat, Paul ordered a bottle of Coors Light. It was a request that Sandy McDavid, the young and attractive wife of the marina's owner, showed little interest in filling right away. On most days she worked behind the scenes, managing the majority of the marina's inside operations while her husband took care of the heavy work involving their customers' boats and dock maintenance. On this afternoon she was forced to fill in at the restaurant when one of her part-time employees called in sick at the last moment. Filing her nails as she talked on her cell phone, while occasionally staring at what was playing on the television, she had reached her limit of multi-tasking for the moment. Soon finished on the phone, and with her emery board placed back inside the right rear pocket of her jeans, she strolled down behind the counter to get the cold beer Paul had ordered.

Setting it down in front of him, she gave him a wink and then a brief smile. "Hi, Paul. You coming or going? If you're going, I'm sorry to see you leave; it's too nice of a day to be heading home so early. Jamie's working late tonight so he can have a customer's boat ready for tomorrow, so I'm headed out in a bit for some fun with two of my girlfriends. Perhaps you and Donna would like to join us for some laughs tonight? Interested?"

"Uh, no thanks, Sandy, we've already got plans, but I appreciate you asking. Besides, you and your friends party far too hard; even on the best of my days I can't keep up with you girls." Paul said after taking his first healthy hit on the cold beer. It helped to quench his parched throat, but not completely.

"OK, I understand. Maybe some other time then." McDavid said with a smile as she returned to where she had been standing at the far end of the bar.

"Yeah, sure. Sounds like fun." Like his wife, Paul had always enjoyed joking with McDavid every time he saw her in the store. While he knew some of her female customers were jealous of her for several reasons, he liked her a great deal. Like other petty people he knew in life, some of McDavid's customers were envious of her good looks, friendly personality, and, most of all, her and her husband's business acumen. The moderate size marina, one handed down through four generations of her husband's family, had provided quite well for them since they had taken ownership of it three years earlier.

Snuffing out the last of his Marlboro cigarettes, Campbell took a hit on his third PBR of the afternoon before acknowledging Paul. A native South Carolinian, he had little use, or respect, for the many northerners who now lived in the area, even those whose boats he often worked on. The exception was Paul. As with many others, he had exhausted Paul's patience several times in the past, but unlike his fellow boaters Paul had not been afraid of giving him an ass-chewing one day when a minor repair to the pontoon boat's motor had not been repaired correctly. That ass-chewing, along with the publicity Paul had received from both the find of the lost Confederate treasury, and for his role in helping to solve several recent area murders, caused Campbell to have a new found respect for one of the marina's customers, a Yankee one at that. Paul had grudgingly accepted Campbell's newly found respect for him, and his quasi-friendship, by sharing a beer or two with him when they occasionally bumped into each other in the restaurant.

"How's the boat running, Paul?" Campbell asked rather weakly as he gave Paul a friendly nod. Not waiting for a response, he quickly turned his head to look back at the news program he was watching on television.

"Running just fine now, Rich. Changing the gas filter and then burning a couple tanks of a higher grade of gasoline seemed to clear up the problem I was having."

Taking another swig of his beer, Paul's ears finally began to listen to what the news reporter was saying. He did so just as Campbell spoke again.

"That looks like a huge shit sandwich right there, Paul. You think your buddy is there helping to sort it out?"

Campbell was referring to one of Paul's closest friends, Captain Bobby Ray Jenkins. Bobby Ray, who was one of the senior members of the Georgetown County Sheriff's Department, was the commander of the department's Major Case Squad. Over the past couple of years, Jenkins had helped Paul not only find the missing treasury of the Confederacy, but he had also recently supervised a multiple murder investigation, one he sought Paul's help on. Like many murder investigations, that investigation had been a difficult one to solve; finally being solved after Paul had come up with the necessary evidence needed to arrest the killers responsible for each of the murders.

Listening intently to what the WFXB news reporter was saying, and looking closely at the crime scene being shown on the dust covered television screen, Paul ignored Campbell's question for several seconds. As he continued to watch the events unfold, he quickly realized whatever had happened was not good. The sight of several marked GCSD cruisers, as well as a handful of Georgetown County Fire Department vehicles, including two from the local Midway Fire Department in Pawleys Island, all of which were parked with their emergency lights flashing, helped to reinforce the seriousness of the scene being shown. Watching for several more seconds, Paul watched as several cops and firemen tried to knock down a side door of the residence that was on fire. As the events continued to play out on the television, he heard, for the first time, the words the reporter repeated for his viewers to hear.

"To quickly recap what little we really know at this time, the scene of this deadly house fire is located at 79 Lakeshore Drive, in North Litchfield. At this time, we know the fire has claimed at least two lives. Both victims are believed to be males in their early to mid-twenties. Little else, including the identities of these two victims, is known at this time. We are also working to confirm the cause of this fire which we are being told burned out of control for roughly forty-five minutes before firefighters were able to get it under control.

WFXB will remain at this deadly scene until we know the answers to the many questions our viewers have."

Shaking his head before taking another swig of his beer, Paul groaned a painful sigh over what he had just heard the reporter talk about. His groan came from his years of having investigated many similar tragic scenes during his career as a state trooper in Connecticut. Despite what little he had seen or heard from the news report, his years of experience told him this was not going to be an easy investigation to conduct.

"There's going to be some awful pain felt by at least two sets of parents tonight. It's terrible, just terrible." Paul said as he glanced at the television for another brief moment. "I pity whoever has to deliver the sad news to those parents about their sons. Been there and done that far too many times back home. It's one of the most miserable tasks any cop has to perform."

As Campbell sat quiet for a moment, he could tell Paul was reliving one or two of the occasions when he had to deliver the sad news to a mother and father that their son or daughter was never coming home again.

"Glad I never had to do that, Paul. Damn glad in fact! Gives me a new found respect for what guys like you have to do at times. You think Bobby Ray is going to have to deliver any of that bad news tonight?"

Again, Paul shook his head before speaking, but this time in a different way. "Not tonight he won't, Rich, not tonight. Bobby Ray is home flat on his back. He just had some minor back surgery on Monday and just got released from the hospital on Wednesday because of an unrelated concern to the surgery. Seems his doctors were worried about his blood pressure being a bit too high, but it turned out to be nothing. He's probably talking to his guys on the phone as he's watching this on television, but he's not going to have to do any of the dirty work tonight."

* * * * * *

As Paul returned his attention to the television for a few minutes before leaving to head home to meet Donna, another person watched the same scene from a different position. Standing in the late afternoon shadows provided by a row of old oak trees, he watched as the Georgetown Fire Department struggled to keep the house fire from spreading to three adjacent homes on the street. A light afternoon wind had caused the once contained fire to briefly burn out of control again. After a few intense minutes, the firefighters regained control of the fire preventing it from reaching the other nearby homes. Their hard work had also kept the fire from consuming the second floor of the home where each of the three bedrooms were located.

As the male figure continued to stand in the shade, he watched as the growing pool of deputies and investigators from the Georgetown County Sheriff's Department began to address the variety of issues now confronting them. They were still too busy around the immediate area of the fire to pay much attention to the crowd of neighbors, passersby, and others who were standing along the road watching the proceedings of the afternoon. Soon the sound of arriving EMS personnel added to the confusion that now existed. As he continued to watch what was occurring, he did so with little emotion. His lack of emotion was not being suppressed to keep attention away from him, but rather it was because he was not one to display his emotions publicly. An angry and emotional person in private, he had learned from his counselors how to control his emotions in front of others on most occasions. Today, a couple of hours earlier, had not been one of them. What occurred that afternoon had happened before on several occasions, his anger nearly causing the blood vessels in his brain to explode, but those were occasions he seldom allowed others to see. He knew in due time the cops would likely find out all that he had done, but as he stood there watching the fire being knocked down he wondered if they would understand why he had done what he had done. "After all," he thought, "cops are people too. Like me, they don't work for free, do they?" Like most criminals, he also held out hope that the cops would not be smart enough to figure out who was responsible for the horror they would soon find.

As he moved further south down the narrow street to where he had parked his truck in a small weed infested lot earlier in the day, he tried justifying his own loss that had also just occurred. Quickly his anger surfaced for another brief but intense few moments, but, unlike earlier in the day, no one was there to witness it. As his anger began to subside, he dismissed his own loss as he justified his earlier actions that afternoon.

"Those freakin' punks . . . those wise-ass sons of bitches . . . I . . . I showed them who was boss, didn't I! Mess with me and you get what you deserve!"

Climbing into his truck, he tossed the two items he had earlier set on the front seat into the rear. One landed on one of the two back seats, while the other bounced off and came to rest on the floor alongside several other tools and crumpled up fast food bags. As he closed the driver's door, a moment of regret suddenly surfaced. Grabbing the steering wheel with both hands, he yelled as loud as he could. "If that one kid had just not said that to me, if he had just kept his damn mouth shut this would not have happened!" Calming down, he tossed his cell phone onto the right front seat and then placed the other item inside the storage compartment of his armrest. Before closing the cushioned top of the armrest, he stared for several moments at the item he had placed there. It had been used less than an hour earlier to deliver a brutal final message.

Taking a moment to light a cigarette, he stared at the cheap BIC disposable lighter in his hand. Stopping for gas shortly after leaving his house, it was one he had purchased earlier that morning along with his coffee and cigarettes. Holding the lighter, he barely recalled using it to start the three fires inside the victims' residence as the inexpensive curtains in both the kitchen and living room had caught fire far faster than he imagined they would. Along with a small pile of papers he stuffed inside a cardboard box, they had been set on fire after the rest of his work had already been completed.

In moments, the Chevy pick-up he was driving slowly pulled out of the weed infested lot so he could begin moving towards his next stop of the day. Like the truck, he would leave the area near the fire as discreetly as he had entered it a few hours earlier.

Three

Horror in North Litchfield

Despite its close proximity to both the beach and Highway 17, a road which closely ran along its western edge, the neighborhood, on most occasions, was a quiet and peaceful place to live and visit. Like other nearby beachfront neighborhoods, it had its share of noise and traffic, but those were generally during the summer months when schools were closed and vacationers were in town visiting. The only other time of the year when the neighborhood got crazy and somewhat out-of-control crazy was on Halloween when parents living in the neighborhood felt it was safe enough to allow their kids to run from house to house in their Trick-or-Treat costumes without having to worry about speeding traffic. But for the rest of the year, this was the perfect neighborhood to live in if you liked a peaceful place to live.

But, on this Friday afternoon, the normally tranquil neighborhood was turned upside down by the sirens of responding police cruisers, fire trucks, and ambulances as they raced from several different directions to the emergency that now existed on Lakeshore Drive.

Further away, the sirens of additional fire trucks could be heard as they responded to the mutual aid call that had been put out by the Midway Fire Department's on-scene commander.

Within the first fifteen minutes of fighting the fire, three firefighters had partially made their way into the burning home as they dragged a one and three-quarter inch attack hose through one of two doors on the home's south side. Supporting each other's movements as they moved a few more steps into the fully engaged kitchen, they found the first victim. Quickly, the lieutenant in charge of the three-man team radioed for medical assistance as two other firefighters half-dragged and half-carried the badly burnt lifeless body of a young adult male out of the home to where they placed him down on the lawn of the side yard. Despite several moments of valiant CPR efforts by EMS and fire personnel, it was soon apparent that he was dead. As others had worked to save him, a GCSD deputy sheriff quickly saw that while the victim had been badly burned around his legs and lower torso, he had not died from the fire or from smoke inhalation. Looking closer at the injury he saw to the back of the victim's head, he quickly realized what the cause of death had been. But, in the chaos of the moment, with his help needed elsewhere as the fire continued to eat away at the downstairs living area, the deputy's observation went unreported for the time being.

As others placed the first victim on a wooden stretcher to carry him further away from the active fire, another team of firefighters were being supported by other deputies near the home's front door. With the use of a halogen tool, and from several strong kicks, they forced open the locked door. Barely making their way inside, they found their second victim on the floor of the front foyer. Unlike their first victim, this male's body had not sustained nearly as much damage from the fire. But like their other victim, it was easy to see this victim had also sustained a significant injury to the back of his head. As fire personnel kept the flames away, two deputies dragged the second victim out of the home, placing him down on the front lawn. Soon his body was carried to the side yard of the residence where it was placed down next to the first victim. Both bodies were soon covered by a single white sheet.

With the fire again under control, and with fire personnel working to make sure that all of the hot spots were sprayed with gallons and gallons of water so they did not flare up again, sheriff's deputies began to take a closer look at the head injuries the two victims had sustained. It was quickly apparent these were not the type of injuries normally associated with a house fire.

Concerned by what he was seeing, and from what his nineteen years of experience was telling him, Sergeant Edward Kindle, the GCSD dayshift patrol supervisor, began barking orders to the six deputies who were present. In a matter of minutes, the immediate area around the scene was taped off with yellow plastic crime scene tape. The wording written on the yellow tape, one seen far too often on news reports and on cop shows, simply read CRIME SCENE – DO NOT ENTER. As this was being done, two of Kindle's deputies began writing down the license plate numbers of all the vehicles parked in the immediate area. Another began using a cheap, but effective disposable camera to record what the exterior scene looked like. Soon finished with those tasks, the deputies then began writing down the names of everyone who lined the street watching the events of the afternoon unfold. Those were among several actions that Kindle did right this busy afternoon after learning and seeing the injuries sustained by the first two victims. Through no fault of his, they were actions that were initiated five minutes too late.

Raised barely four miles from the crime scene, Kindle, a big man in stature who looked and sounded as most Northerners expected a Southern law enforcement officer to look and sound, did one more thing correctly that afternoon. After formally notifying Georgetown County Sheriff Leroy William Renda of what had been found at the scene, he called Captain Bobby Ray Jenkins.

"Hello?"

"Bobby Ray, it's Kindle. How ya feelin', buddy? That back surgery go as well as ya hoped it would?"

Laid out in bed from his recent surgery, Bobby Ray Jenkins, the commander of the Georgetown County Sheriff's Departments Major Case Squad, smiled at the sound of his friend's voice. Quickly he muted the sound of his television so he could hear what Kindle had to say. Unaware of what was going on that afternoon; Bobby Ray had been watching a documentary about Pickett's Charge at Gettysburg on the History Channel.

"I'm alive, Big Ed, but I'm afraid I'm not going to be mowing the lawn or swinging the golf sticks any time soon. I'm still hurting a bit, but I'm getting there slowly. Going back to see the doctor on Monday for my first follow-up. Not sure why that's happening though. Guess he must have a house payment coming up on one of his villas or something like that."

Bobby Ray's joke made Kindle laugh for a brief moment. Like most people, Kindle included, Bobby Ray believed that a large number of follow-up visits to doctors' offices after surgical procedures were a giant waste of time and money.

After a few more moments of small talk, Kindle soon got to the reason why he had called his friend. "Bobby Ray, I thought you might want to know what's going on here this afternoon seeing that it's going to keep your folks busy for some time. You got the local news on by chance?"

Intrigued by what Kindle had just asked him, Bobby Ray's eyebrows raised as he used his remote to bring up one of the Myrtle Beach television stations. As he did, he listened carefully for several minutes to what Kindle was telling him about the investigation that had just gotten underway. Listening to the facts and details being presented to him, as well as watching what now filled the screen of his television, Bobby Ray only interrupted on two occasions to briefly ask for clarifications about the conditions of the two bodies that had been found. Later, when Kindle finished, he peppered the sergeant with several other questions.

"Ed, you sure there's only two victims?" Bobby Ray asked as he began formulating his next question in his head.

"Nope, not sure about anything right now. That's why I'm calling you. My gut is telling me this is gonna get worse before it gets better. Once we start searching what's left of the first floor we may find another body or two in there. The FD is still working inside; too early for us to get in there yet." Kindle said as he stood sweating profusely in the late afternoon sun.

"Audrey there yet?" Bobby Ray asked.

Kindle took a moment to look around as he stood outside of his cruiser to see if Lt. Audrey Small, the deputy commander of the Major Case Squad, had arrived. "Not that I can see, Bobby Ray. I heard her answer Dispatch when they called her about this, and I heard her tell them she was en route, but I haven't seen her arrive as yet. Want me to have her call you when she does?"

"Yeah, do that, Ed. Tell her that I want to talk with her before she gets started doing anything. You call in for any more help on this yet?"

"If she doesn't get here soon that's just what I'm planning on doing, but I thought I'd wait a few more minutes to see if she shows up. With you laid up, it's her responsibility to call out the truck and the rest of your folks. Figured I wouldn't step on her toes too early, if you know what I mean. I've got enough other bullshit to do with keeping traffic and the media far enough away from here so we can work without being under a damn microscope." Kindle paused for a moment to watch two late arriving EMTs rush by. "Bobby Ray, no disrespect intended because I like that girl, but with you laid up like you are, and with this giant mess we've got on our hands and her being fairly new to the murder game, is she gonna be able to handle all of this on her own? Maybe I shouldn't say this, but I know a lot of us would feel a whole lot better if your sorry-ass was down here running the show."

Bobby Ray understood Kindle's concern, but he quickly dismissed it in a joking manner. "Ed, relax. Audrey is good at what she does. She's just not as good at it as you and I are. We're in good hands for now, don't worry."

His joke was meant to give Kindle some confidence in Small's ability to manage a scene of this magnitude, but the veteran cop could not help playing two of Bobby Ray's words over in his head.

"For now? What's that mean?" Kindle asked curiously.

"She's out of here in ten or eleven days. She's getting married and then she's headed to Hawaii on her honeymoon for two weeks. She and her husband are going to visit several of the islands there. I should be able to get back to work by the time she leaves. In the meantime, just give her whatever help you can and everything will be fine."

Bobby Ray's explanation brought another wave of concern to Kindle. "Yeah, but what if you aren't back to work by then. Who's gonna run the show then?"

Before Bobby Ray could answer, Kindle's portable radio brought him the news that another male victim had been found inside the house. This victim, nearly burnt beyond recognition, had been found lying on the living room floor under a badly burnt couch.

"Bobby Ray, did you hear what I was just told on the radio?" Kindle sadly asked.

"Got part of it. Sounds like you now have three victims, is that correct? Did they say if there was any kind of head wound found on the third victim?"

Bobby Ray could not see Kindle shaking his head at the news his radio had just brought him. "They didn't say, Bobby Ray. What they did tell me was that they found the third victim with some kind of rope tied around his ankles and wrists. It sounds like he was intentionally tied up for some reason just before the fire started."

"Damn!"

It was the only word Bobby Ray uttered in response to the latest news he had been given. After quickly processing his thoughts, the veteran investigator finally spoke again. "Make sure Audrey calls me as soon as she gets there. Be there with her when she does. In the meantime, I'll give the sheriff a call."

* * * * * *

Over the next fifteen minutes, Bobby Ray made, and took, several phone calls. Two of those he took were amongst the most important ones he fielded that day as they began to give direction to the labor intensive investigation that was just getting underway. The first of those two calls was one he took from Small. It updated him on a few more details regarding the fire and on the three bodies that had been found.

"Audrey, is the scene ours yet, or is the FD still in control of it?" Bobby Ray asked the person he had personally selected to be second-in-command of the Major Case Squad.

"It's ours now. I just spoke with Chief Sullivan. I've got it noted that he turned it over to us at 1914 hours. He's going to have his fire marshal work closely with us on the cause and origin of the fire, but the scene is ours to start processing. Chief Sullivan has reached out to SLED for some additional help on determining the cause of the fire as well. The FD hasn't detected any signs of an accelerant being used, but we'll know more about that tomorrow. SLED's also on stand-by for any additional help we may need, but for now until I get up to speed with everything that's happened here I'm not asking them for help. If we need it, I'll speak to you first before making that call. That sound OK with you?"

"That's fine. Listen, you know what needs to be done. Start handing out the assignments to our folks as you see fit. Just make sure they get the scene videotaped and thoroughly photographed from every possible angle before you start ripping it apart. Have a copy of the tape and a set of photos run over to me at the house sometime this evening so I can take a look at the mess that's confronting you."

Small listened attentively as her boss gave her the marching orders on the obvious tasks he wanted done. Loyal to Bobby Ray for the support he had shown her in selecting her as his deputy commander, Small knew it was killing her boss not to be at the scene. This was just the kind of scene Bobby Ray excelled at, the very same kind which had caused him to be held in such high regard in the South Carolina law enforcement community. But while she heard every word he said to her, what she heard next was why she had so much personal respect for him.

"Audrey, I'm not going to be much help to y'all over the next few days, so this is your scene to work. You know what to do, so go do it. You call me if you need me, and while I may be calling you with some suggestions, this is your investigation. Go solve it for us. If anyone, including the sheriff, gives you any trouble, you call me and I'll make that trouble go away. Hear me?"

"Yes, sir. Thanks!" Small said with a touch of appreciation in her voice.

Despite being pleased by what Bobby Ray had told her, Small was already doubting her ability to supervise a case of this magnitude. While she had always performed well since joining the Major Case Squad, and had learned a great deal about how to handle such complex investigations, she knew her boss had always been there to have the final say in how they would be worked. As she tried to thank Bobby Ray for the support he was showing her, she fumbled trying to find the right words to express.

As Bobby Ray listened to what Small was trying to tell him, he also heard the words she did not say. Those unspoken words quickly told him the one thing he had hoped not to hear. They were ones which told him his deputy commander needed help. In the back of his mind, he distinctly heard her voice telling him one simple message.

"Please send me help. I cannot do this alone."

Bobby Ray's next call was to Sheriff Renda. It was one he was forced to make so the integrity of the investigation was there from the beginning. While the recommendation he was about to make was done so the investigation would get started off on the right foot, it was one he also made out of concern for at least three other people. He knew that each of the victims deserved their murders to be thoroughly and competently investigated. They also deserved to have someone running the investigation who knew what they were doing. With regrets of having to do so, his fingers placed the call to Renda's cell phone.

* * * * * *

The question was, would that person be willing to get back into the game one more time?

Four

Back in the Game

The fact that his Major Case Squad commander was flat on his back at home had little to do with Sheriff Renda responding to the scene of the devastating fire. An incident of this significance, one which now had three suspicious deaths associated with it, demanded his presence. The phone call he had received from Bobby Ray, one which informed him of his investigative captain's own concern about the investigation getting off on the right foot, caused Renda to arrive at the scene a bit earlier than he might normally have.

Seeing the sheriff's shiny black unmarked Ford Expedition arrive at the scene caused word to spread quickly through the ranks of three different agencies that the boss was present. While others ran their own particular departments across Georgetown County, Renda was by far the one who wielded the most power. In office already for several years, he had recently won election for another term by a fairly wide margin. By the end of his new term, he would become the longest running sheriff to hold office in Georgetown County since the early 1800's. Across the county, no one was better known than Sheriff Leroy William Renda.

Spying his boss as Renda walked from his vehicle towards the still smoldering residence, Kindle walked towards him so he could begin briefing the sheriff on the status of the situation. As he did, others either continued on with what they were doing or began to make it appear that they were busier than they really were.

"It's pretty bad, sheriff," Kindle said as Renda got within a few feet on him. "It's the worst thing I've seen since that Air East plane crashed several years ago just outside the county airport. Just like all of those bodies I saw that day, I'll probably never forget this scene either."

Renda quickly scanned the fire scene from where he stood in the driveway of the residence before speaking. As he did, he saw Small holding a reporter's style notebook in her left hand as she spoke with the fire chief and two of his investigators just outside the front door.

"What's the cause, Ed? Do we know yet? Is it accidental or a torch job?" Renda hit Sgt. Kindle with three quick questions right out of the box. The last one was the one that Kindle thought somewhat strange for his boss to ask.

"We've got three dead kids here, sheriff. There's nothing accidental about it. Some bastard set this house on fire on purpose. I mean . . . isn't that kind of obvious to figure out?"

"Yeah, well I . . . never mind. I guess you're right, it has to have been set intentionally." Renda was now slightly embarrassed by how straight Kindle had put it to him.

"We're not sure of how or where the fire started, too early to determine that right now. But I think it's a safe bet to say it started somewhere in the first floor living room. It's just off the kitchen, and close to where most of the bodies have been found so far. With the exception of a small area around a fake fireplace, most of the really heavy damage is in that section of the house. We just took possession of the scene a short time ago because the FD had trouble with a few stubborn hot spots on the first floor."

Renda nodded impatiently at the answer he heard from Kindle. "I understand we have three victims for now? Is that right or are there more?" The sheriff nervously fidgeted for a brief moment before adding, "Let's hope there aren't any more."

"Three so far, boss, but we've got five cars parked in the driveway and out in the street. We haven't been able to find their owners; been too damn busy since we got here to do that. Not sure who owns two of them yet, but I've got one of the rookies running NCIC checks on them right now. I'm afraid I'm going to have to tell you the same thing I told Bobby Ray on the phone a few minutes ago."

Renda stared at his sergeant for a brief moment before turning to look back at the still smoldering home that Brian Patrick had first built many years earlier. "You think there are more victims in there, don't you?" Renda swallowed hard after asking his question as he had also starting feeling the same way after being told about the number of cars that were found parked close to the home. Then the sheriff asked Kindle his next question. Like the previous ones he had asked, this was also one he felt he already knew the answer to.

"Bobby Ray told me on the phone about the wounds that at least two of these victims sustained to their heads. Based on what you've told him, he's thinking this is no ordinary fire. You share those same concerns, Ed?"

"Boss, it's hard not to. Just so you know, all three of our vics have sustained pretty much the same serious injury to the back of their heads. We have not had time to start looking around in the house, but I'm pretty confident these kids were all shot execution style before the house got torched. There's no doubt about it, at least not in my mind there isn't. The fact that our last victim was also found with his wrists and ankles bound tells us something bad happened in this house this afternoon, something that wasn't an accident. You'd have to be a fool to think otherwise. Somebody shot our victims for some unknown reason as yet, and then set the place on fire. My guess is whoever did this started it on purpose in hopes the bodies would be damaged bad enough that we'd think they had gotten trapped inside after it caught on fire. Unfortunately for that person, that's not the way it played out. This is clearly no accidental fire."

"Damn!" Renda replied as he stepped over a fire hose being dragged across the driveway. "Do you know what this is going to do to this part of the county? People are going to be shocked by what's happened here today. This is going to stay in their minds for a long time. It's going to take an even longer time for those folks to heal from the pain they're going to feel. No one forgets when something like this happens, especially when it happens so close to home."

As Renda and Kindle finished with their thoughts, Small, who had just finished up speaking with the fire chief, started walking to where they stood. Her conversation with the fire chief would prove to be one of many they would have over the course of the next several days.

"Evening, sheriff," Small said as she took note of the time for an entry she was making in her field notebook. Finished documenting the time of her first meeting with Renda at the scene, she spoke again to the person in life who intimidated her more than anyone else.

"Sheriff, I'm sure Ed has briefed you to some degree, and I'm not sure if you have spoken with Captain Jenkins as of yet, but this scene is a mess. As you can probably tell, we're going to be here for quite a spell; several days at least. We've got three male vics already, and maybe one or two or three more inside the home. I'm going to be needing some help with this." It was not what Small said, it was how she said it that made Renda's blood start to boil.

"Help? What kind of help are you talking about, Audrey? Investigative or supervisory, because if it's supervisory I thought you were in charge of this scene." Renda wanted to tell her that her boss would not have presented a request for help to him this way, but he bit his tongue. Upset by what had occurred, and even more upset due to his investigative captain not being there to manage the scene, Renda knew he had to show some patience with his inexperienced lieutenant.

Small attempted to explain what she meant by her previous comment, but only managed to get a few words out before Renda interrupted her again. This time he spoke more calmly to her.

"I did speak with Bobby Ray before I arrived here. Initially he told me that he has all the confidence in the world regarding your ability to manage this scene; he did so quite emphatically might I add. But he also told me he detected some apprehension in your voice when you were speaking with him. That's got me worried some. Like him, I also have that same confidence in you, Audrey, but what I really need to know is this. Was his assessment of you possibly not being able to handle this situation a mistake on his part? Because, if it is, then mine is wrong as well. Do we have a problem here or not?" Renda's red face was starting to display the concern he was feeling.

Feeling as if she was being talk downed to by her boss in the presence of Sgt. Kindle, Small tried digging in her heels by giving Renda a quick comeback, but it did little good. Again she chose the wrong words to use.

"Sheriff, I need both." Small said somewhat agitated, her words growing louder as she continued to speak. "I've got several victims already, and, quite likely, more to come. I've also have a significant case to manage, and a total freakin' mess of a crime scene that's going to take days to process the right way. I need some cops who know what they're doing to assist us, and, if you can remember, you need someone to work this case with me because I'm getting married in two damn weeks!" She wanted to say more, but chose to hold back, biting her tongue as she did. As unprofessional as Renda had been in challenging her in front of Kindle, she was not about to do the same to the sheriff of Georgetown County. Calming down, she looked at Kindle first before speaking to Renda again. "I'm asking for help due to my concern about the integrity of this investigation. I need to feel comfortable when I hand this case over to someone when I leave on my honeymoon. I want that person to be up to speed on it. Maybe we'll have it solved before then, but maybe we also need to give some consideration to us not having it wrapped up by then."

Seeing Kindle nod approvingly to Small's statement made Renda smile at the bluntness of her response. He liked the fact that she had not caved into his pressure, and also liked the fact that she had already given some thought to who would have to manage the investigation in her absence. While he liked her bluntness, her eyes, just like her body language, did not show the degree of confidence he had hoped to see in her. He now sensed her confidence level was far different from how she had conducted herself at previous scenes that he had been present at.

Because Small had never handled a complex investigation of this size, Renda, with some reluctance, asked his last question of her.

"Audrey, I realize what's coming up in your personal life is important, but so is this shit storm we're facing. I need to know two things for right now. First of all, I need to know that this case is going to get your undivided attention. The other thing I need to know is this. I'm going to get you some help, but for now this case is yours. You do whatever you need to do with the resources you have available to you for now. What I want you to tell me, and let's obviously take Bobby Ray out of the picture because of his surgery, who do you feel has the same skills sets as you that I can hand this case off to when you're gone?"

"I've got it," Small said in response to Renda's first question. "My wedding plans are pretty much finalized so there's nothing that's going to get in the way of me working this case hard for the next couple of weeks."

"OK, good!" Renda replied. "What about the second question I asked?"

It was a question Small did not have an immediate answer for. With far too many needs and tasks already confronting her, she could not think of anyone who she felt comfortable leaving the case to manage in her absence. "Sheriff, give me a day or two, and then I'll give you a name."

Then Renda asked the one question he should not have asked as by now Small had already had enough of his condescending attitude. "Are you ready to take charge here and to help get this mess solved, young lady?"

Pissed off by what she heard come from Renda's mouth, Small shifted uneasily on the balls of her feet for several moments as she stuffed her notebook inside the waistband of the light brown cargo pants she was wearing. Trying to suppress her anger over what she felt was a sexist comment unfairly directed at her, she brusquely answered the question with a terse sarcastic response. "Would you have asked that same question to one of the guys if they were about to take this case on just before they got married?" Her eyes now glared hard at Renda.

Small's response made Renda chuckle for a moment as he gave an approving nod to what she had said. He liked the gumption she had put into her response. His next statement allowed some of the existing tension between them to dissipate.

"Fair enough, Audrey, fair enough. If you are telling me that you're on your game, then that's good enough for me. You know I have faith in you, but right now I'm a bit concerned about a few things. One of those concerns is that I'm afraid you're going to find another body or two inside that house." Renda stopped talking as he watched two Assistant Medical Examiners walk with one of Small's detectives to where the three bodies had been placed. Refocusing his attention back to Small, Renda spoke his last few words before heading back towards his vehicle.

"Get working on this mess right away. I have to give a few of the Myrtle Beach television stations a briefing later tonight, so make sure you call me in an hour or two with an update. If you need to keep Ed and any of his people here to help with traffic, or for any other needs you might have, you do so. I'm going to give Bobby Ray a call . . . maybe I'll stop to see him instead, but I'm going to have a talk with him about getting you some help. You get crackin' on this and we'll talk later. Remember, I don't care what this costs or what it takes to get the job done, just get it done. We good?"

Small nodded her head briefly as she gave her boss a token smile. "We're good. I'm on this, no problem."

Then waiting until Renda got to the end of the driveway, Small muttered a comment about the sheriff under her breath. It was said soft enough that even Kindle, standing less than three feet away, could not hear it.

"Freakin' asshole!"

After noting the time that Renda had finished giving her his instructions, Small turned to walk back in the direction of the house. As she did, she saw several of her detectives waiting for her to give them their assignments. By now the department's

Major Case Squad's crime scene truck had arrived and had taken a position close to the rear of the house.

"OK, boys and girls, time to go to work! On me here in the driveway; we're having our first briefing in two minutes. Bring your notebooks and your sorry-asses over here pronto like!" Small shouted loudly for all of her detectives to hear.

Renda, who had paused to speak with Kindle on another matter, was pleased by what he heard Small holler out to her charges. As he unlocked the door to his vehicle, Renda felt satisfied that he had pressed Small enough to get her motivated and focused on what needed to be done. In reality, he had done little. She had never once come to work unmotivated or unfocused, and had always given the sheriff and everyone else she worked with an honest day's work. What Renda and one or two others had interpreted to be her 'deer-in-the-headlights' look had just been her way of digesting what was confronting her. Just as Bobby Ray and everyone else did each time they arrived at a scene, she also had her own way of doing things. The only difference was because they were men working in a man's environment, and working for a dinosaur of a sheriff, they did not have to prove their worth as often as she did.

Now she knew it was time for her to dispel Renda's lack of faith in her forever. What she did not know was that it was not going to be as easy as she had thought it would be.

Five

Sheriff Renda's Decision

Delayed for over twenty-five minutes as he attempted to leave the scene of the fire by the Georgetown fire chief, who felt it necessary to discuss an unrelated issue with him as he was trying to shore up his manpower and supervisory concerns, Renda finally freed himself from the scene. Not blessed with an extraordinary amount of patience to begin with, he fumed to himself as he slowly drove away. Chief Sullivan was now temporarily on his shit list for wasting his time this particular busy evening.

Sheriff Leroy William Renda had been in office for several terms already on the day the fire had been set. Despite his years of service, and his favorable standing with many of his peers in the South Carolina law enforcement community, he was often distrustful of others outside his own department. This was often reflected by his lack of interest in having his personnel work with the FBI, DEA, US Customs, or with agents from Homeland Security. While he reluctantly accepted the roles the feds played in certain investigations in South Carolina, he had little interest in having his deputies work with them unless it was absolutely necessary. This was especially true with personnel from Homeland Security, who he often referred to as 'rent-a-cops' as he believed they added another layer of unnecessary bureaucracy to an already intrusive federal criminal justice system.

Turning his Ford Expedition south onto Highway 17, in North Litchfield, Renda found the number he was looking for and then hit the call button on his Apple iPhone. Listening as the number was dialed; he waited impatiently as it took four rings for the call to finally be answered. Immediately recognizing the voice on the other end to be the person he was calling, the sheriff made his comments brief.

"What'll it be? Lemon lime or cherry?"

Despite still being groggy from falling asleep less than ten minutes earlier, the male voice on the other end of Renda's call understood the question being posed to him.

"Cherry."

"Cherry it is. I'll see you in fifteen or so." Renda replied.

"I'm not going anywhere today. I'll be here. The front door is already unlocked."

Close to fifteen minutes later, Renda found his way into the living room where his investigative captain was half-asleep on his couch. Despite expecting him, the sheriff's sudden appearance startled Bobby Ray for a moment as he had not heard the front door open or close due to the noise from his television. An ESPN 30 for 30 replay of a documentary on Fernando Nation was now playing.

An avid baseball fan, Bobby Ray had previously only seen parts of the story about the sudden rise to fame of Fernando Valenzuela. The former Los Angeles Dodgers pitcher had become an instant star when he first came up the major leagues in the 1980's. This was especially true within the Mexican-American community.

Leaving the television on, Bobby Ray muted the sound as he slowly tried sitting up against one of the armrests of his couch. Catching his breath after completing what was normally a simple movement, he groaned out loud over the pain he felt shooting down his lower back. It was his first time out on the couch after spending the past couple of days in bed from his recent surgery.

"I feel like a tired and beat-up old man, boss." Bobby Ray said as he reached for the cherry flavored Sonic Blast that Renda had set down on the end table next to him. It was one of the many ice flavored drinks Bobby Ray often craved. "In fact," he added as he slurped his cold drink after swallowing a pain pill, "I think an old man could easily take me today with no problem. Being laid up like this sucks!"

Having had a few bouts with his own temperamental back allowed Renda to appreciate the pain Bobby Ray was now feeling.

Putting his drink back down on the table, Bobby Ray watched as Renda's eyes glanced around the room they were sitting in. His boss had been a visitor to his home in the River Club community on several occasions for parties and other events, but it had been some time since his last visit. From previous comments Renda had made about Bobby Ray's home, he knew his boss felt comfortable sitting there in the spacious and brightly lit room. As he watched Renda's eyes, Bobby Ray saw a look of concern cross the sheriff's heavily wrinkled face.

"You came to see me out of concern about Audrey, didn't you?" Bobby Ray asked, already confident in knowing why his visitor had felt it necessary to stop and see him after visiting the crime scene.

Renda took a sip of his Lemon Lime flavored drink before answering. As he did, the loud sucking noise the straw made as it sucked up the remaining liquid in the bottom of his Styrofoam cup told him his drink was nearly gone.

"Yeah, I guess I did. It's that obvious, Bobby Ray?" Renda asked quizzically.

"She's gonna be fine. I know she's probably nervous; probably preoccupied thinking about how I would be handling the scene as well, but she'll do just fine. She's very competent and a very hard worker as we both know. Besides, she's got me to fall back on." Bobby Ray laughed briefly at the play on words he had tossed out. "She knows she can call me, and she already has, twice as a matter of fact. I trust her and so should you. She'll do a good job for us, don't worry."

"I hope she will, Bobby Ray. I've told her that twice, but I'm not sure she, or I, for that matter, believes that entirely. Besides, she's leaving on her honeymoon soon and, please believe me when I say this; I understand that she has needs to address regarding her wedding. I get all of that. What concerns me is that you're not going to be much help to her because of your back problem, so who do I hand this case off to when she leaves for her honeymoon.

She'll be out in freakin' Hawaii someplace enjoying herself while she pounds down fancy umbrella drinks filled with fruit for two weeks while this case falls deeper in the toilet." Upset by the events of the afternoon, Renda was quiet for a moment before adding, "I need someone with some experience, and someone we can trust. I've already put some feelers out to some of the other departments, but they all claim they can't spare anyone right now. I need someone right now who I can get up to speed on this mess that's facing us so I'm not spending every waking moment worrying about how the investigation is progressing. We can't afford to hand this off cold to someone when Audrey leaves as that won't help us either. That's not fair to anyone; it's certainly not fair to our victims or their families."

Bobby Ray's back pain again flashed up and down his spine as he shifted slightly on the couch. He wanted to tell Renda that he would be back to work by the time Small left for her honeymoon, but due to the pain he was still feeling he was not sure that was going to happen.

"I guess your only other option is to ask SLED for help, or talk with Sheriff Thompson up in Horry County again. He's got a couple of guys who worked the Melkin case with us; they're pretty sharp guys."

Renda nodded his head, but he already knew he was not going to check with Thompson again or with anyone else for help. Not yet, at least.

"I told you, Bobby Ray, that I've made those calls already. I'm not begging anyone for help, and I'm not about to have someone from SLED or the feds run this investigation for us. That would be thrown in my face for sure when I'm up for reelection again. I'm not having someone else telling me how to run our investigation. It's our case . . . our investigation . . . it's up to us to manage it, and, most importantly, it's up to us to solve it. If I have to, maybe I'll ask the other departments for some investigative help, but supervision of the case is staying with us. Understand?"

Bobby Ray's brief nod gave Renda the answer he was looking for. "Then I'll guess you'll have to have Wags … I mean, Sgt. David Wagner . . ."

Renda interrupted Bobby Ray before he could finish with his recommendation on who he thought should take over the investigation when Small took leave to get married.

"Think he'd be interested, Bobby Ray?" Renda asked as he fiddled with the straw in his drink cup. As he did, it made an awful irritating noise as it was pushed and pulled up and down through the tiny opening in the cup's plastic lid.

Renda's question confused Bobby Ray. It took him a moment before he asked his boss for a clarification. "Sheriff, I'm sorry, do I think who would be interested?" Bobby Ray was still not sure of whom his boss had been referring to.

Sliding forward in his chair, Renda let a small mouthful of crushed ice tumble into his mouth from his cup. Slowly he chewed the ice for a few seconds before speaking again. "You know who I'm talking about, Bobby Ray." Renda said as he swallowed the few remaining pieces of ice still inside his mouth. Putting his cup down on the nearby coffee table, he looked for any kind of reaction from his investigative captain. Seeing none, he spoke again.

"He's certainly got the experience as both an investigator and as a supervisor, and he was certainly a huge help in helping us solve the Melkin case. No disrespect to any of you who worked on that investigation, but he was the one who made the connection between all of the loose ends we had so we could start focusing on Melkin and that Frazier character. Besides, no one else who's working for us, or working for any of the other agencies around here for that matter, has his credentials. He's the only logical choice we have right now, besides he's your friend. Why would you not want him to help us again?" Then Renda gave Bobby Ray a friendly professional shot. "That's unless you're afraid he's going to make the rest of you look bad again."

Renda's comment caused Bobby Ray to sit up quickly in response to what he knew was a joke; one that had been directed at him in jest. Doing so caused another wave of pain to hit him and he quickly collapsed back into the position he had been sitting in.

"Just so we are on the same page," Bobby Ray said as his pain started to subside, "you are talking about Paul, correct?"

Bobby Ray's question did not need much of an answer so Renda simply nodded his head to confirm that they were talking about the same person.

Paul Waring, a retired state trooper from Connecticut, had been a close friend of Bobby Ray's for several years. They had first met in 1995 while attending the FBI National Academy, in Quantico, Virginia, and had remained friends ever since. After his move to the Murrells Inlet area of South Carolina, Paul had accidentally discovered the remains of a Confederate soldier along the banks of the Waccamaw River. That discovery had caused him, with help from several others, including Bobby Ray, to discover the bulk of the lost treasury of the Confederacy in Charleston. Shortly after that amazing find, Bobby Ray, at Renda's request, asked Paul to assist the GCSD with a multiple murder investigation that had stalled despite the best efforts of a task force of law enforcement officers. It was a task force that Bobby Ray had been heading. As Renda had said, it had been Paul who finally put some of the evidence together that ultimately led to identifying those responsible for the murders. While one of them, a Georgetown banker by the name of Richard Melkin, had committed suicide before he could be arrested, Paul's tenacious work, and his attention to the smallest of details in that case had led to the arrest of the second suspect, Eddie Frazier.

As Bobby Ray thought about his friend being drafted to help Renda and he out again, he ran a couple of questions by his boss.

"You sure about this, sheriff? I know Audrey got along fine with Paul during the Melkin investigation, and while I'm sure she probably would prefer him over someone else, but are you sure you don't want to look for someone else from SLED or Horry County instead? I just don't want to see you get criticized for at least not pursuing that option you have." Bobby Ray's points were all valid, and while he was pleased by Renda's thought of having his friend assist them again, he knew it was his responsibility to run all of the available options by his boss first.

"I get criticized it seems every day for one thing or another, so what's one more round of criticism going to matter? Most times it's by some idiot politician who knows little, if anything, about police work. I'm used to being second-guessed by now; criticism doesn't bother as much as it used to, especially when I consider where it comes from on most occasions. Let whoever wants to challenge my choice of Paul do so, but he's clearly the guy we need to help us out until you get back on your feet."

"I can't argue with you on that, sheriff."

Eyeing the three plastic prescription pill containers sitting on one of the end tables next to the couch, ones containing the necessary pain pills and anti-inflammatory drugs to keep the swelling down in his captain's back, Renda posed his next question. It was posed to the only person in his department who he had any real respect and appreciation for.

"So, when do you think you'll be back to work, Bobby Ray?"

Bobby Ray had seen Renda staring at the containers before he asked his question. As anxious as his boss was to have him back at work, he was even more anxious. Captain Bobby Ray Jenkins was not the type of person to be sitting around the house wasting time watching television. He lived his job twenty-four hours a day, and the thought of not being at a significant scene, one important enough to have caused his boss to feel the need to pay him a visit, was killing him.

"I don't give a damn what those doctors say, boss. I'm giving it another four or five days tops and then I'll be back. I may not be worth much, and I may need to be picked up and driven home each day, but I'll be back in the game before Small leaves on her honeymoon."

While Bobby Ray's determination to return to work pleased Renda, he was not quite sure that his captain would be able to live up to his promise. Bobby Ray's health was just as important to Renda as it was to the person stretched out on the couch in front of him. He was not about to rush his friend back to work.

"That's your call, Bobby Ray. But I want you to know that I'm not rushing you. I want you feeling good for the long haul; not just for this investigation. We'll be happy to have you back when you're ready, even if it's only for a few hours each day. But let's get back to what we were talking about as you haven't answered my question. What about Paul? Do you think he'll be interested in helping us out again?"

Bobby Ray thought for a few moments before speaking. As he did, he tried to quickly figure out a way to ask his friend to come back to work again.

"Tell you what, sheriff. You get Audrey to meet you here at the house tomorrow morning around 0900 hours. I'll call Paul and tell him I need to speak with him about something. I'll have him get here just after you folks do. That will give the three of us a chance to talk before he gets here. But don't worry, he'll do it. Between his own interest in still wanting to work investigations like this one, and you and me tag teaming him, he'll have no other choice but to tell us that he's back in the game. You know, the more I think about your choice of Paul being the guy to help us with this, the more I like it. He'll be a good fit again."

As Bobby Ray finished speaking, his cell phone, as did Renda's, announced a new text message. Looking at their phones, they saw the text had come from Small down at the scene. It was a simple, but painful one to read.

TWO MORE MALE VICS FOUND INSIDE HOME. BOTH
HAVE SERIOUS HEAD WOUNDS SIMILAR TO THOSE
SUSTAINED BY PREV VICS. WOUNDS APPEAR TO BE
FROM SMALL TO MID-SIZED CALIBER HANDGUN.
WILL FURTHER UPDATE YOU SOON. It was signed A.S.

Finished reading the message from where he sat in a chair close
to his friend's couch, Renda set his phone down on his left leg
before speaking. The anger he felt from the horrible news they
had both just learned was clearly obvious to Bobby Ray. Despite
the sheriff's tough exterior, as well as the fondness he had for
his job and the authority that came with it, Bobby Ray knew his
boss was a parent and a grandfather first. The anger he now saw
in his boss' face came from a father who knew the pain the day's
events would soon bring to five other sets of parents. It was a
pain Bobby Ray prayed he would never experience.

Picking up his phone as he stood up to leave, Renda looked down
at Bobby Ray stretched out on his couch. "I hope Paul decides
to help us. From what we've just learned, we're going to need all
the help we can get. Audrey and I will be here by nine tomorrow
morning. Have the coffee on as I'm afraid we're going to need it."

With that said, Renda turned and saw himself out the front door.
As he walked to his SUV, he knew it was going to be a long night.
Starting his drive back to the scene, something he seldom did,
he prayed for two things to happen. He prayed no other victims
would be found, and he prayed Paul Waring would answer his call
for help.

Later that evening, he would realize at least one of his prayers
had been answered.

Six

Paul's Confusion

Donna Waring waited for her husband in the lounge of the Grumpy Sailor while he walked their mutual friend, Steve Alcott, to his vehicle. Paul had first met Steve, their host for dinner that evening, three years earlier. Despite their age differences, they had become fast friends since their chance encounter on a rainy day. As Paul and Steve had become friends, their elderly friend had also taken an immediate liking to Donna, coming to think of her as the daughter he never had. Steve also played a minor role in the Melkin investigation as he had introduced Paul to a friend of his who was a sitting judge in the South Carolina judicial system. It was through Paul that Steve had also first gotten to know Bobby Ray.

Dinner on Friday night was supposed to have been just between the two of them, but due to their friendship with Steve their plans had changed. Like most Friday nights were, it had been designed to be a night to play catch up with each other after another busy and hectic week. Because of family that had been visiting with them the previous week, and because of work commitments on Donna's part, they had been looking forward to having dinner alone on her birthday. On this particular night, their friend had been a last minute addition for dinner. Late that afternoon, just after Paul had left the marina, Steve had called to invite them both to dinner. Not wanting to exclude him from their plans for the evening, as they both knew their friend often ate far too many of his meals alone, they accepted his invitation. Friday night dinner alone would just have to wait for at least one more week.

Waiting for her husband to return from making sure Steve had gotten safely back to his Mercedes Benz, Donna ordered a glass of J. LOHR chardonnay for herself and a Jack and Coke for Paul. For both of them, it was their fourth drink of the evening. Friday nights were for relaxing together and for enjoying a couple of drinks before and after dinner. While Steve declined their offer of an after-dinner drink in the lounge, Donna and Paul had decided to have one last drink before heading home for the evening. It was just before ten when they finally raised their glasses to toast the end of another long week.

Finally alone, Donna had just started to tell her husband the news she had learned earlier in the day about a possible merger her bank was considering with another South Carolina based bank, one smaller than the one she worked for, when Paul's cell phone interrupted their conversation. Looking at his phone, Paul saw the photo of a friend's smiling face staring at him.

"It's Bobby Ray, Donna. He's probably suffering from some form of cabin fever about now due to his surgery and needs someone to talk to. He told me early this morning that Judy was heading to her mother's house late this afternoon so her mom could spend the weekend with the kids. The way he's been feeling since his surgery, he's probably a happy man being a bachelor and having the house to himself for a couple of days."

The frown on Donna's face clearly showed she disagreed with her husband's assessment of Bobby Ray's situation. "What you meant to say is Judy is probably the happy one this weekend. Bobby Ray is just like you when you're laid up like he is. You both are the typical male patients; complaining about everything and needing constant attention. Judy is probably glad just to have the opportunity to get away from him for a couple of days, just like I would be if you were down from the same kind of surgery. I love that boy to death, but he is miserable when he's sick!"

Paul laughed at his wife's assessment of him as a lousy patient, but deep down he knew her description of him when he was sick was a pretty accurate one.

"High maintenance, that's me for sure!" Paul said, smiling to his wife as he patted her hand.

After hitting the Accept button on the screen of his phone, Paul chose not to answer the call in the typical manner as he normally did. "Hey! What's up, Johnny Reb? How's that back of yours feeling? Ready for a game of golf yet?" The greeting drew a chuckle from his friend.

"Not hardly. Still got some pain there, so I'm taking it easy for a few more days. Got another kind of a pain I'm dealing with right now though. Don't have the right medicine handy for that kind of pain, but I might get some relief from it tomorrow."

At first, confused by his friend's comments, Paul did not

understand what Bobby Ray was referring to. A couple of moments of silence existed between them before he caught the meaning of what his friend was referring to.

"I think I know what you're talking about, Bobby Ray. I saw a few minutes of it on the television earlier. Is it that bad? Last I knew you had two victims. Hope the count has not gone up from that."

The mock snicker on the other end of the phone quickly told Paul that it had. "I'm afraid that it's now up to five." Bobby Ray said rather casually; his voice purposely showing little emotion.

"Damn!" Paul softly sighed in response to what he had been told.

"We don't think we're going to find any more, but who knows. We've searched the structure pretty well; at least that's what I'm being told anyhow, so I don't think we're going to find any others. Audrey wisely suspended the search for the night as it's getting too dark to be working in an unsafe structure this late at night. We've got the uniforms holding the scene until we get back there in the morning. She's planning on hitting it hard with our folks tomorrow morning before we start sifting through all of the debris."

One of Bobby Ray's last few words caught Paul's attention immediately. Cops normally did not sift through the ashes of a fire scene unless some kind of foul play was suspected. That kind of work, work normally associated with a fire scene, was generally the responsibility of the local fire marshal and his staff, or an arson team. The word he heard, and the process associated with it, had bad memories for Paul.

"Bobby Ray, obviously there's more to this story than just a tragic fire that claimed the lives of these young men. Something else bad happen there? Something like a murder; perhaps five of them by chance?" Paul's thirty-plus years of being a state trooper told him he already knew the answers to his questions before hearing his friend's response.

"Yep." Bobby Ray's simple response was the one Paul had expected to hear.

"Holy shit!" Paul exclaimed, his loud response briefly drawing the attention of others sitting nearby.

"Paul!" Donna protested, not pleased by her husband's choice of words.

Having forgotten that Bobby Ray was laid up from surgery, it took a couple of moments for Paul to realize someone else was running the scene for a change. Soon he remembered his friend had mentioned a familiar name to him.

"I had a brain fart there for a minute. It sounds like you've got Audrey Small running the scene for you, is that correct? Is she staying in touch with you?" Paul asked as he thought about who he would have assigned to manage a scene of this magnitude if it had been him laid up back home.

"Yep. She's running the show for now." From their years of friendship, Paul could hear the tension in Bobby Ray's voice. He hoped it was related to his friend's recent back surgery and not to what was happening at the crime scene or with anyone in particular.

"You're in good hands then. I like Audrey; I think she's got a good head on her shoulders. You've got a pretty competent second-in-command working for you. She did some nice things during the Melkin investigation."

"Yeah, she's a good investigator."

Paul then realized what his friend had just said moments ago. "Hey, you just mentioned that Audrey was running the show for now. What's that mean? Is she going someplace?"

"She's getting married in a couple of weeks and then she's headed to Hawaii for her honeymoon. It's been scheduled for weeks. I'd never ask her not to go, but it's also a non-refundable trip. She couldn't get out of it even if she wanted to without taking a financial hit. I remember her talking about that at work a couple of weeks ago." Bobby Ray's response to his question made the picture somewhat clearer for Paul.

Aware of the scope and size of this investigation as he had managed several similar scenes during his career with the Connecticut State Police Department, and the fact that Small was leaving soon, Paul realized the several problems his friend was facing.

"Bobby Ray, from the sounds of it from when we talked early this morning, you certainly are not going to be getting back to work too soon. You might be able to handle a couple of hours each day, but not much more than that. Who are you thinking about having manage the investigation for you during Small's absence? Someone from SLED, or perhaps someone from MBPD?"

Silently, as he chose to keep his thoughts and comments to himself for a brief few moments, Bobby Ray smiled at the question Paul had posed. It was one he had expected his friend to ask. "Not likely, partner. Sheriff Renda is on one of his kicks about not letting anyone from outside the department manage it for us. I'm going to help as much as I can, and Audrey is going to get this investigative mess started for us, but the boss only wants someone he explicitly trusts to work the investigation for us. He's good with reaching out to MBPD, or to Horry County, or to some other agency like SLED for investigative help, but that's where he draws the line. He won't let anyone from any other agency manage the investigation for us."

Realizing where the conversation was going, but not positive that he was correct, Paul excused himself from the booth where Donna and he were seated. "I'll be right back, Honey. I just need to talk to him for another moment or two. Sitting here with that music pounding in my ears is making it difficult to hear what he is saying. I'll be back in a few moments." Paying more attention to the three-piece band that was playing on the lounge's small stage, Donna nodded at her husband's comment as she took a sip of her chardonnay.

Walking outside into the restaurant's well lit parking lot, Paul was soon back on the phone with his friend.

"Listen here, Bobby Ray, are you trying to tell me something I don't want to hear? Because if you are, I'm done, you know that. I'm out of the game. I'm perfectly content being out on my boat or playing golf a couple of times a week. Good luck to all of you, but find someone else. I'm done with that kind of work for good." It was not the answer Paul wanted to give, but, due to a promise he had made to Donna after the conclusion of the Melkin investigation, it was one he was obliged to make.

Despite expecting a similar kind of response, Bobby Ray was

still surprised by the fact Paul had already figured out where his comments were headed. He had not even had a chance to tell his friend what he needed by the time Paul figured out the problem Renda and he were being confronted with.

"Paul, just . . . "

Cutting his friend off in mid-sentence before he could finish his thought, Paul again spoke. This time he did so quite forcefully. "Just nothing, Bobby Ray! I'm done! D-O-N-E! Comprende?"

Frustrated by the position Paul had taken, it was Bobby Ray's turn to come back at his friend. This time he started by asking him to reconsider the position he had taken. "Paul, besides five dead young men, we've got another huge mess on our hands. If Audrey wasn't getting married, Renda would have never thought about calling you for help, but . . ."

"Wait a minute, Johnny Reb, this is his idea?" Paul said somewhat emphatically as he pointed his left forefinger in the air several times as he spoke. "You mean you didn't even think of asking me for help after all we've been through together. You're telling me that it was Renda who came up with this idea of reaching out to me? Well, some friend you are! I guess that shows how much you think of me, doesn't it!" Paul's comments, one's made in jest, were simply said to get a rise out of Bobby Ray.

Despite that intention, Paul's words now confused Bobby Ray. He could not tell if Paul still had no interest in helping them with this investigation, or if he really was interested in coming back to work. "Hey, partner, you've got me guessing here. Are you in or are you out?"

"I'm out, Bobby Ray; I was just messing with you. I've had my career, and while it's been fun, and while I still enjoy investigative work a great deal, I've promised Donna that I wouldn't go back to work again. I'm sorry, but I can't go back on my promise to her."

As he listened to what his friend was telling him, Bobby Ray reached for the glass of water sitting next to him on one of his end tables. Before speaking again, he swallowed two of his pain pills. He did so not only to manage the pain he was feeling, but also to buy himself some time so he could think of what to say next.

"Listen, my man, I need a favor here. We've got personnel and supervisory issues like I've already told you, and we've also got five kids who have been murdered. Renda's asked for you, and I'm supporting his idea of bringing you in on this. For what it's worth, I'm pretty sure Audrey and the rest of my folks would like to have your help as well." Bobby Ray paused intentionally for a moment to allow his next point to have the proper emotional effect when Paul heard it. "Sometimes in life we have to put aside our own interests to help others. This is one of those times. In this particular matter, those others are the parents of those kids who were shot and killed earlier today. We need to help them find some peace and comfort by finding out who took their sons away from them. We need to catch the bastard . . . or, maybe its bastards, I suppose . . . who killed their sons."

Paul shifted his phone from his right ear to his left as he continued to walk in a small circle off to one side of the restaurant's parking lot. This section was away from the lot's main parking area and was far quieter than the other adjoining areas of the gravel parking area.

"Bobby Ray, you missed your calling, my friend. You should have been a Pentecostal minister instead of being a cop. You sure know how to deliver a message, don't you? Listen, you are right about one thing. You need to find whoever did this, but when you do, don't forget about the parents and the grieving they are going through. It's important for you to stay in touch with them throughout your investigation. Doing so will make them feel they have not been forgotten. That will at least give them some solace during this difficult time."

Not missing a thing Paul had said, Bobby Ray's response was quick and to the point. "I was kind of hoping you would do that for us, buddy. You in or not?"

Stopping his random pacing, Paul fidgeted with some loose change in his pocket for a moment as he thought about what to do. "Not sure yet, Bobby Ray, not sure. I'll talk to Donna, and then get back to you in the morning. If I'm in, what's next in your plans for me?"

Bobby Ray knew his emotional pleas about needing to find out who was responsible for these murders for the sake of the victims' parents had helped to soften Paul's initial stance on not wanting to get back in the game. "Be at my house by 0930 hours tomorrow morning. Sheriff Renda and Audrey are going to be here to update me on the latest details then. We'll talk a bit and go from there. Sound OK?"

Distracted by a young couple who were having a tiff near their vehicle, Paul ignored Bobby Ray's question until he was confident the minor verbal argument he was watching did not escalate into something physical.

"What's that? Yeah, that's OK, I guess. If I'm not coming, I'll at least give you a call. Get some rest, Bobby Ray. You're not doing yourself any good by being too involved in all of this so early after your surgery."

After they said their goodbyes to each other, Paul made his way back into the lounge where Donna had been patiently waiting for him. As he did, his friend did just what Paul had told him to do.

Before falling asleep on his couch, Bobby Ray tried thinking about how he wanted Small and their detectives to attack the problem confronting them the following morning. But the painkillers he had taken, along with hoping that Paul would again step to the plate and help them out of a jam, kept him from being able to concentrate on a specific thought for long. In less than fifteen minutes, he was fast asleep. As he drifted off, a nap which would last for the next four hours before he woke up and finally went to bed, the eleven o'clock news began to flash on his television. Soon others across the Grand Strand would also learn that the death toll had climbed to five. Fast asleep by now, Bobby Ray did not hear the words the reporter spoke.

"Good evening, ladies and gentlemen. Tonight we start our broadcast with a terrible tragedy that we first began reporting on earlier today. A tragic fire in North Litchfield has claimed the lives of at least five young men." The reporter's comments would only get worse as he continued to tell his viewers about the other details surrounding the fire.

* * * * * *

As Paul moved back into the lounge area of the restaurant, he sat down in the booth that Donna had sat alone in for the past ten minutes. As he reached for his drink, he apologized to his wife for leaving her alone for so long.

Finished taking the last sip of her drink, Donna smiled at her husband as she watched him take a healthy hit on his Jack and Coke. After setting his glass down on the table of their booth, Paul got the attention of a young skimpily clad buxom waitress. Raising his glass, he motioned for her to bring them another round. He had not planned on having another drink, but Bobby Ray's phone call had now brought some confusion to what had been a quiet and pleasant evening. While he knew the night's next drink was not going to make the confusion in his head go away, it would give him another few minutes to summon enough courage to tell Donna what his friend's call was all about. It would quickly prove to be time he would not need.

As she watched her husband twist and bend the red plastic drink stirrer that had come with his first after-dinner drink, Donna could tell Bobby Ray's phone call had upset Paul. He was now clearly disturbed by what their friend had told him. After forty years of marriage, she did not have to hear her husband tell her what was bothering him. She already knew what had upset him.

"So what did you tell Bobby Ray, Paul? Are you going to go work that case for him or what?" Donna asked as she stared straight into Paul's brown eyes. The answer she was looking for was one she pretty much already knew.

Unaware that his wife even knew what had happened earlier in the day, Paul was stunned by the bluntness of Donna's question. Having no way of seeing it coming, he had no answer ready to give her. At least, not one that would make him happy.

"What? What case?" Paul tried acting surprised, but Donna quickly saw through his feigned expression.

"Don't play stupid with me, mister!" Donna jokingly responded. "You know what I'm talking about. I saw the news earlier today. I know what's going on with that fire and about those kids who died in it. What is it now? Three or four kids who perished in it?"

Sadly, Paul updated his wife with the latest news. "Five. Five for now, at least. Let's hope they don't find any more."

"Five kids . . . five young men dead in a house fire? How could they not have gotten out of the house when the fire started?" Donna was now clearly stunned by Paul's latest news.

Now Paul gave his wife the information she, like so many others, had yet to hear on the news. Before he did, he made sure no one sitting nearby could hear what he was about to say.

"The fire did not kill those young men, Donna. It had been set to make it look like it did. They were all probably dead before the fire even started. Someone, or some folks, made it look like an accidental fire. I don't know all the details yet; neither does Bobby Ray for that matter, but it looks like those kids were all murdered. They were all found with gunshot wounds in the back of their heads."

Donna gasped as she began to comprehend what had occurred inside the house before the fire started. "Oh, Paul! That's terrible! Those kids must have been so scared when all that was happening." Donna's eyes began to moisten as they filled with tears. "Oh, those poor parents . . . those poor mothers. I feel terrible for them."

Paul reached out to comfort his wife, taking her hands into his.

"It's terrible, Donna, just terrible. I don't have the proper words to describe it right now either."

Donna sat quiet for several moments as she dabbed her tears with a cocktail napkin. It proved to be a wasted effort. A mother herself, her tears were shed for the inconsolable pain she knew five other mothers were facing that night.

Stemming, for the most part, her flow of tears a few moments later, Donna realized her husband had not answered her question. "Paul, you didn't tell me what you said to Bobby Ray. Did he ask you to help him with this investigation? If he didn't, I'm sure he could use some help seeing the condition he is in."

Despite being surprised by his wife's comment, Paul told her what he had said to Bobby Ray. "He did ask me for help, but I told him I was out of the game. I told him I had made you a promise not to jump back into police work again. I thought that's what you wanted." Totally taken by surprise by his wife's last comment, Paul was not sure what to say next. While he wanted to jump at the chance of helping out his friend, he also wanted to maintain peace on the home front. Now he anxiously waited to see what his wife was thinking.

"Honestly, Paul, how could you not want to help him in a time of need like this?" Donna said, somewhat annoyed with the position her husband had taken. "He's got a horrible mess on his hands. After listening to you talk about these types of cases when you were working, I'll bet he would be glad to have whatever help you can give him. Think about it, will you? He's probably trying to run this investigation from his couch or bed; that's something you know no one can do. Honestly, I can't believe you're not interested in helping him."

Donna's comments continued to confuse her husband as he sat across from her in the booth with a blank look on his face. What he said next reflected his confusion. For the moment, it was all he could muster. "But what about the promise I made you. You know, the promise that I . . . "

Cutting her husband off before he could finish with what he had to say, Donna let him know just how she felt. She did so quite forcefully. "Save it for another time, Paul. Bobby Ray, just like those five young men and, most of all, their parents, all need your help. Go help him find the bastards who killed these kids! I know you're itching to do that, so go do it. Please! I want you to call Bobby Ray and tell him you will be there for him. Tell him whatever you cops tell each other, but go help them. I want you to do this!" Finished speaking, Donna's tears again began to stream down both of her cheeks.

Still surprised by the position his wife had taken, and still somewhat unsure of what it was that Bobby Ray had asked of him a few minutes earlier, Paul was now totally confused on what to do. His confusion led him to do one last thing before they headed for home.

"Waitress! Another round for my wife and I, please."

* * * * * *

Paul knew he was likely going to be facing several long days over the next couple of weeks. He also knew it would likely be some time before he could spend another quiet night like this with his wife. His last drink was one he was going to enjoy before having to face Sheriff Renda and Bobby Ray the following morning.

Seven

Getting Started

Paul was out of the house by seven-thirty the following morning. He had quickly fallen asleep after getting home, but by five he began tossing and turning. Unable to fall back to sleep, except for two brief ten-minute stretches, he quietly laid in bed for several minutes so his sleeping wife was not disturbed. By six-fifteen, he had given up all hope of falling back to sleep. After a quick shower and shave, he spent close to twenty minutes checking his emails and Facebook messages. Then, with Donna still fast asleep, and with far too many thoughts racing through his head about the briefing he was going to have later that morning, he left the house and made the short drive to the Waccamaw Diner for breakfast.

Walking inside the small diner where he occasionally feasted on one of the diner's breakfast specials, a triple stack of large blueberry pancakes which included three links of their different kinds of homemade sausage, Paul spied Bobby Moniz. One of the diner's three cooks, he was seated at the far end of the lunch counter having his breakfast before the Saturday morning breakfast crowd starting arriving. Busy reading the Sports section of *The Sun News* as he ate his Western Omelet, Moniz had not seen one of his favorite customers standing there staring at him.

"Hey, Bobby M!" Paul hollered down to the far end of the counter. "It's always nice to see a chef eating his own cooking! It reassures me that the food is good enough to eat here!"

Paul's comments brought out a few similar barbs from three other men who were sitting at the counter not far from where Moniz sat. The good-natured jabs caused Moniz to give Paul a friendly wave.

"Well, I'll be! I thought I might see y'all here this morning, Paul!"

The loud friendly greeting came from the nearly deserted section of the diner where Paul usually sat. It came from Betty Repko, one of the three waitresses working the morning's breakfast shift. Now in her late fifties, she and Paul had become good friends during the time he had been searching for the lost Confederate treasury as he and some of his friends had occasionally met at the diner to plan their strategy for finding the missing money. Over time, Paul had introduced her to Bobby Ray, Donna, Sheriff Renda, and several others. As he had, the others had also taken an immediate liking to Betty.

Walking towards his favorite booth, Paul bent down to give his height challenged friend a warm embrace as she cleared dirty dishes from a booth where two earlier customers had eaten their morning breakfast. As he hugged her, he realized again what a wonderful friend she had become. As he had with Moniz, he always enjoyed the friendly banter he shared with Betty.

As she placed a cup of hot coffee and his silverware down on the table, Betty looked down at Paul with a smile on her face. Besides being a friend, she had come to like him from the start because of how he had always treated her with respect. It was something many of her other customers did not often extend to her.

"I suppose there's no sense in me giving you a menu to look at, is there?" Betty asked quite confidently. "I'm guessing it's gonna be our blueberry pancakes and sausage again; just like it always is. You want some OJ this morning?"

"Pancakes it is, Betty!" Paul cheerfully replied. "I'll take the OJ also. Keep the coffee coming when you can. I think I'm going to need all the caffeine I can get today." Then looking down the counter to make sure Moniz could hear his next comment, Paul loudly stated, "Perhaps I can even get some blueberries in my pancakes this time!"

Looking around to make sure that none of his other customers were watching, Moniz gave his friend the middle finger salute. His appropriate and friendly response to Paul's sarcastic jab drew a round of quiet laughter from Paul and Betty.

Sitting in his booth as he waited for his breakfast, Paul scanned the front page of *The Sun News*. Situated just off of Highway 17, in Myrtle Beach, the newspaper was one of the principle sources of news for those who lived and worked in both Horry and Georgetown counties. Centered at the top of the front page just above the fold was a photo of the home where the five victims of yesterday's carnage had lived. Paul shuddered as he looked at the photo as it clearly showed heavy smoke and flames extending out of several first floor windows. Off to the side, three firemen and one cop were captured as they vainly tried to control the fire from spreading to another section of the home. Knowing what had happened inside prior to the fire being set caused him to have an unpleasant feeling in his stomach.

"What a waste," he muttered to himself as Betty set his pancakes down in front of him.

Taking notice of what Paul was looking at, Betty sadly shook her head as she finished topping off his cup of coffee. "Pictures like that just break my heart, especially when they're taken so close to home." She had correctly put into words how her friend was feeling.

* * * * * *

Twenty minutes after finishing his breakfast, Paul gave a light rap on the screen door of Bobby Ray's front entrance. Despite the fact that the front door was wide open, and despite knowing Bobby Ray would have had no second thoughts about just walking into his house, Paul waited until his friend hollered for him to enter. As he waited, he took notice of the two unmarked police vehicles sitting in the driveway.

"I guess I know who they belong to," Paul thought to himself just as he heard Bobby Ray holler for him to come inside. Walking into his friend's kitchen, he found him seated around a glass topped breakfast table next to Sheriff Renda and Lt. Audrey Small. A stack of color photographs, each taken from different angles outside the fire damaged residence, sat directly in front of where Bobby Ray had chosen to sit.

As Renda and Small stood to greet him, Bobby Ray smiled warmly at the sight of his friend standing there. "Morning, partner! Seeing your ugly ass is here, I guess that means you've come to join us. Am I right on that?"

Paul smirked, but ignored his friend's question at first, choosing instead to exchange friendly handshakes with Renda and then with Small. Finished with that task, he poured himself a cup of coffee and then sat down at the table between Small and Renda. As he did, he first answered his friend's question, and then spoke to Renda.

"I'm here, Bobby Ray, to lend my hand in any way you kind folks need it." Then he jokingly added, "I'm not here because you asked me to be here or because of the sheriff's interest in having me help out. I'm here because my wife told me I had to come help you." While Paul's comments drew a few laughs from the others, his next comment was the real reason why he was there to help with the investigation. "While Donna's concerned about you because of your surgery, Bobby Ray, her biggest concern is about us giving the parents of your victims some kind of peace. I try not to use the word closure like some people do as I don't believe those parents will ever be able to have closure based on what's happened to them, but as my wife does, I also believe we can give them some peace. Donna wants whoever did this to have to stand and face those parents in court someday; so do I. So that's why I'm here."

Paul's last few words caused the others to turn their attention away from him. Now they each chose to stare blindly at their coffee cups as they silently shared similar thoughts to those of Donna's. Professionally, and personally as well, they each wanted to have a hand in arranging that day in court for the parents of their victims.

Renda then broke the silence that existed by filling Paul in on the events of what had happened at the scene. As he did, he also spoke on some of the evidence that had been found. Soon finished with his brief summary, he then told Paul why he had asked Bobby Ray to reach out to him.

"Paul, besides the mess we've already got on our hands with this horrific crime that's been committed, we've also got a supervisory problem here for a couple of reasons. As you know, Bobby Ray is laid up for a bit because of his surgery, and despite the fact that he still thinks he's a young man, the truth is he's not. So we really don't know when to expect him back. I can't have Audrey and her folks running this investigation through him on the phone every time an issue comes up. I need someone who is capable . . . someone with your experience . . . to be at the scene directing this investigation each and every day until we solve it. I can't manage this scene myself as I'm being pulled in ten or fifteen different directions every day it seems; besides that's not my job any longer." Now changing his focus, Renda stared briefly at Small before continuing. "Paul, Audrey here knows how I feel about her, and that I believe in her, but she's also part of the supervisory problem we're facing."

Renda's comments caused Paul to turn his attention towards Small. As he stared at her, she smiled at him for a brief moment, but then turned her head away to divert the attention being directed her way. Like Paul, she hated being the focus of anyone's attention, and even liked it less when Renda referred to her as being part of the problem they were facing.

"She's leaving us the week after next to get married, Paul. She's gonna leave us standing here high and dry when she goes off to Hawaii on her honeymoon."

Paul knew Renda had been making a joke with his comments, but he could also tell they were making Small feel uneasy.

"Bobby Ray mentioned that to me on the phone last night. Good for her! Congrats, Audrey! I'm happy for you." Paul said in response to the news he heard. It was a response that Renda had not expected to hear.

Shifting his attention back to Renda after glancing at Bobby Ray for a quick moment, Paul directed his next few comments at the Georgetown sheriff. "From what you've told me so far, it sounds like you want me to work with Audrey on this until she goes away and then hold down the fort until she gets back. Does that sound right?"

Paul watched as both Renda and Bobby Ray shifted uneasily in their seats for a few moments. He also noticed that while Small did not move an inch, she did allow a brief smile to cross her face. Then it was gone as fast as it appeared.

Bobby Ray tried breaking the brief awkward silence that existed, but he was quickly cut off by his boss.

"Paul, we . . . I mean . . . I think it's best if we get you sworn in again with us right away, and then you . . . " Renda was clearly struggling to find the right words to use. His face had become flushed, and it was obvious to the others seated at the table that he was now uncomfortable being in a setting he clearly should have felt at ease in. He was clearly out of his comfort zone.

"What the sheriff is trying to say, Paul, and I'm not trying to put words in his mouth," Small said with a surprising degree of confidence, "is that he wants you to run this investigation for us." Despite the anger she was feeling at the decision Renda had made a few minutes prior to Paul's arrival, what Small had wanted to say was that the sheriff had really wanted Paul to run the investigation for him from the start. She knew his decision had little to do with her pending honeymoon, but rather had everything to do with his lack of confidence in her. For now, she chose to be tactful in how she finished phrasing her statement. "Instead of you working for me, I'll be working for you. You'll be the lead on this for us." Finally finished speaking, she then took a moment to shoot a look of contempt at Renda.

Skeptical of what he had heard, Paul quickly responded by directing three quick questions at Bobby Ray. "Is that correct? Did I hear her correctly? You want Audrey to report to me on his?"

Bobby Ray chose to look at Renda for a brief couple of seconds before answering his friend. As he did, Paul noticed Renda simply sat there nodding his head as a way of telling him that what he had heard was correct. He could tell the sheriff was still uncomfortable sitting there and that he had decided to allow Bobby Ray to answer his questions. As he sat there listening as Bobby Ray advised him of Renda's reasons for asking him to take over the investigation instead of leaving it with Small to handle, Paul's mind took him back to an event he had read about many times. Like many historians, it was one he had tried several times to figure out.

A huge Civil War buff, Paul now equated Renda's uncomfortable position to that of Confederate General James Longstreet on the afternoon of Pickett's Charge at Gettysburg. Not totally supportive of General Robert E. Lee's battle plan for attacking the fortified Union position, Longstreet had been unable to verbally respond to General George Pickett's question about whether his attack should commence on that fateful day. As Longstreet had, Renda now sat quiet during a time when he should have been decisive and in command. Clearly the chief law enforcement officer of Georgetown County was not acting as he should have been during a distasteful discussion. Paul could not help thinking how cowardly Renda was acting.

Upset at the words that had come from Bobby Ray's mouth, Paul shook his head in disbelief. As he responded to what he had heard, he looked at Bobby Ray first, then at Renda. As he spoke, he also glanced at Small's face to see what kind of reaction Bobby Ray's words had caused.

"No disrespect, sheriff, but are you and Bobby Ray crazy? You've got an extremely talented cop here in Audrey . . . someone you have spent time and money on grooming so she could handle investigations like this for you . . . so why should I be the one to run this particular investigation for you when you've got her? What you're asking me to do, at least to me it is, it's a huge slap in the face to her. I'm glad to help, but I should be reporting to her, not vice versa."

"Well, Paul, it's just . . . "

Small politely interrupted her boss again as she had also detected the sheriff's discomfort at having to sit through an unpleasant situation.

"Paul, I appreciate your comments, but Sheriff Renda and Captain Jenkins discussed this with me before you arrived here this morning. I'm OK with their decision on this. If I wasn't getting married I might feel different, but I understand why they're doing this. We need to have some continuity with our supervision of the investigation, so I have no problem reporting to you. You and I got along great during the Melkin investigation and I have no reason not to believe the same will hold true in this one. I like to think that I'm a team player, and I've already checked my ego, so let's just put all of this behind us and get back to work. We need to focus on the issue at hand and that's nailing the bastards responsible for killing these poor kids. Again, I appreciate your kind words, but I'm ready to do whatever it is you want me to do."

Paul smiled at Small's words. He was proud of her for the way she handled herself during the ugly discussion that was taking place.

While not totally supportive of the decision that had been made, Paul realized he had little chance of changing it. Now it was time for him to speak his piece. "Sheriff, I'm not giving Audrey any orders or telling her what to do. I've got too much respect for her to do that, but after listening to what's been said I'll run your case for you. But there are two things I'm putting on the table right now. As far as I'm concerned, Audrey's my equal . . . she and I are going to be partners during this investigation. We both will keep you and Bobby Ray informed on how the investigation is progressing each day. Secondly, if you want my help, then that help comes with a few conditions." While money meant very little in life to him, Paul knew he was in the driver's seat. Making Renda feel a little more uncomfortable for how he had treated Small meant much more to him. "In return for my help, I need a few things from you. These are all non-negotiable; I get them or you can find someone else to run your case for you. First, I need another ten dollars an hour on top of what you paid me during the Melkin investigation. I don't want you to think I've got this big ego that needs stroking, but my management skills alone are worth those few extra bucks. Throw in the experience I have from working investigations like this one and I'd say you're getting a pretty good deal. Second, I'm probably going to need a few more warm bodies to help us run things down. With five vics, you can imagine how much leg work there's going to be. Each of those kids has family members, friends, employers, and others who will need to be interviewed by someone; forget about everything else that needs to be done, those interviews alone are a huge task that needs to get done so we can move on to other needs of the investigation. I'll leave that up to you and Bobby Ray to arrange for us. In addition, I want Sergeant Kent Wilson from MBPD, Detective Frank Griffin from NMBPD, and, perhaps most importantly, I want Detective Blake Stine from MBPD assigned to this investigation. I want all of their assignments to be for the duration of it; no matter how long it takes us to solve it. I also want Scozz . . . you know, FBI Agent Thomas Scozzafava working with us as well. He did a great job when we all worked together on the Melkin investigation, so I want him with us on this one also. He has some special skills I plan on taking advantage of during this investigation; skills the others don't have. Those guys, along with Audrey, and a couple of others, are going to be my go-to guys. I don't care what it takes, but those folks get assigned to this investigation or I'm out. Each of those folks, Audrey included, are far more important to me than the few extra dollars I've asked for."

Paul's demands caught Renda totally off guard as he had not

expected Paul to place any conditions on him. While demands were not usually placed on Sheriff Renda, these were ones that caused brief smiles to appear on the faces of Bobby Ray and Small.

"Good for you, Paul!" Small thought as she waited to hear Renda's response.

Realizing his options were limited, Renda had no choice but to agree to Paul's conditions. "OK, OK, I'll see what I can do. But for now we need to get to work. I'd like you and Audrey to follow me down to the scene so we can all do a walk-through of the victims' residence. Later this morning, Solicitor Pascento, from the Fifteenth Judicial Circuit, is going to meet us there for a discussion on how the investigation is going to be conducted. I'll ask him to help me put some pressure on a few of the other departments for this additional help you're asking for. It may take some doing, but I'll get those four assigned to the investigation as you asked. Is there anything else?" Renda hesitantly asked.

"No, sir." Paul responded. "Just swear me in, give me my credentials and a car to drive, and Audrey and I will start hammering away at this problem of ours."

Relieved that the stressful part of the morning was finally over, Bobby Ray breathed a sigh of relief.

"Bobby Ray, up to now I guess you've been in charge of this investigation, correct?" Paul asked.

"Well, Audrey's certainly kept me up to date so far, so I guess I have been in charge until now. Why do you ask?"

Standing up to leave, Paul smiled to himself as he knew he had his best friend just where he wanted him. "So I guess it's your fault that this has not been done as yet."

"What's that?" Bobby Ray curiously asked as Renda and Small turned to look at Paul. Like Bobby Ray, they had no idea what Paul was referring to.

"Is there any reason why the Medical Examiner has yet to be told to make sure that x-rays are taken of each of the five victims so we know how many bullets are in their bodies? That will tell us how many bullets we still have to look for once we collect all of the shell casings at the scene. Why hasn't this been done yet?" Paul looked at his friend for the proper answers.

Packing up the photos that had been spread out on the kitchen table, Small smiled as she saw Bobby Ray trying to come up with a plausible answer to Paul's valid questions.

"Well . . . Audrey was the . . . "

"Stop trying to pass the buck for this not getting done, Bobby Ray. We're all part of a team here. Right now, Audrey and I are the cops, and you're, well, seeing the condition you are in, you're a paper pushing desk jockey for now. She and I are headed out to make sure the scene starts getting processed the right way. You take care of getting the other arrangements taken care of for us. Call me after you talk to the Medical Examiner's office so I can assign a couple of detectives to be there when the x-rays take place. I want tight control on all chain-of-custody matters involving our evidence." Taking a moment to collect himself, Paul asked one last question of his friend. "You are familiar with the term Chain-of-Custody, correct?"

Frustrated by the friendly, but sarcastic position his friend had taken with him, Bobby Ray jokingly answered Paul's question. "Damn Yankee! Get your ass out my house and get to work!" To his credit, Bobby Ray knew Paul was correct. Those were arrangements which should have already been discussed with the Chief Medical Examiner's Office.

Pushing his chair in at the table, Renda, now more relaxed than he had been before, smiled at the interaction between Paul and Bobby Ray. What he heard Paul say gave him the satisfaction of knowing he had been correct in recommending that Bobby Ray's friend handle this investigation for them. As he walked to the front door with Paul and Small, Renda gave his lieutenant a friendly pat on the back. He knew she had taken one for the team. He also knew she had not embarrassed him in front of the others when she had the opportunity to do so earlier. Her actions now caused him to hold her in a more favorable light.

As he pushed open Bobby Ray's screen door, Renda hoped his decision of having Paul manage the investigation for them had not damaged his relationship with Small too much. Unfortunately for him, it already had. In making his decision, he had failed to consider one important point; that a woman scorned never forgets those who have scorned her. Sheriff Renda was someone Audrey Small would never forget. Not even to the day she died.

Eight

The Sheriff and Solicitor Pascento

Electing to leave his truck in Bobby Ray's driveway, Paul made the fifteen minute ride to the crime scene in Small's vehicle with her. With Renda driving at a leisurely pace out in front of them, it gave Small a few minutes to talk and to update her passenger on what steps she had already taken to get the investigation underway. It was an opportunity for her to speak freely without Renda or Bobby Ray being a part of the conversation.

Before their conversation went too far, Small posed a question to Paul. "Hey, how did you know that neither Bobby Ray nor I had spoken with the Medical Examiner's office yet about having x-rays taken of our victims?"

Her question caused Paul to enjoy a quick laugh. "You liked that, huh? Well, I did that for you. I didn't like how you were being forced to listen to all of that BS they were trying to run by me about your upcoming wedding. No offense, but it's pretty clear the sheriff did not want you running this case alone for some reason. I also knew from talking to Bobby Ray last night that not much had been done on the case due to the late hour that you finally took over the scene from the FD. The fact that you were still recovering bodies during your preliminary search of the residence also told me you likely hadn't had time to talk with the M.E.'s office either. I kind of guessed that it hadn't been done. Besides, it sent a message to both of those guys, perhaps a subtle one at best, that I don't like seeing a friend of mine being embarrassed like that."

Pulling up to a red light at the intersection of Willbrook Boulevard and Highway 17, Small told Paul how she felt about what had happened as they waited for the light to change.

"Paul, I want you to know that I really appreciate what you said back at Bobby Ray's house in my defense. The truth is, I'm not really pleased about what's been done, but it has nothing to do with you. You and I are going to get along just fine, so please don't think that I'm upset with you, because I'm not." As the light changed, Small paused for a brief moment as she turned north on Highway 17 right behind Renda's vehicle. "I'm totally pissed over some of the sheriff's comments, especially some he made to me yesterday, but I'm not going to mouth off about what's happened. Doing so would only serve to give him more reason to believe that he's made the right decision about bringing you on board for this. I'm . . . I mean we . . . we're going to catch whoever did this, and then I'm going to rub the fact that we did in his freakin' arrogant asshole face!" Having grown more agitated as she thought about how Renda had dissed her over parts of the last two days, Small finally calmed down enough to give her passenger a brief look before speaking again. She was about to tell him something she had not shared with anyone except her fiancé. "Paul, please don't tell Bobby Ray about this, but I've recently received two job offers from other departments who are interested in having me run their Major Crime units for them. I've put both of them on hold until after my wedding, but seeing how Renda has treated me I may decide to move on if one of the salary offers is right." Despite her toughness, Small's eyes began to water from the stress she was dealing with from several fronts; most notably, from Sheriff Renda.

Paul listened intently as Small told him about the job offers she received. As he did, he easily sensed the frustration and disappointment in her voice over how she had been treated. Like her, he had also experienced similar frustrations during his career as well. But unlike hers, his frustrations were never about his abilities being questioned. Instead, his had always been about others often meddling in investigations he was managing.

"Just don't do anything impulsively, Audrey. Like you said, wait until your wedding is by the boards and then see how this case is going before you act. I'm sure you know this, but burnt bridges are sometimes tough to repair. Don't let your emotions come into play when you are thinking this out. Make your decision based on what's best for your career."

Small nodded as she shot her friend a quick smile. "Good advice, Paul. Thanks!"

As they turned onto Trace Drive, Paul got the conversation back to the matter at hand. "OK, Audrey, tell me where we stand with this investigation. I want to hit it hard today so I'm hoping your people are ready to go to work. We'll get together with them as a group after the sheriff and Mr. Pascento leave. Oh, one more thing. If you thought Renda appeared uncomfortable back at Bobby Ray's house, just wait till you see what I'm going to make him do before he leaves. I'm going to tell him he has to be the one to break the news to your staff that I'm in charge of this investigation for now. That ought to make him sweat a little bit more!"

Paul's comment brought a wide grin to Small's face as she pulled up in front of the scene. As she did, she gave a wave to the uniformed deputy who was making sure no one tried climbing under the yellow crime scene tape to get a closer view of the damaged home.

From where they sat in her vehicle outside the fire ravaged home, Small gave Paul a brief run down on what had happened, where the bodies had been found, what the condition of the inside of the home looked like, and the steps she had taken since assuming command of the investigation.

"It was really not until after the second body was found that we knew it was more than just a house fire which had killed those kids. When we kept finding bodies with the same kind of head wounds, we knew what we had first suspected was really true. Shortly after we took over the scene from the FD, I had two of my guys sit down and write Mincey warrants for us so we could start processing the house and the vehicles that belonged to each of the victims. But, despite my intention to do so, we never really got started in either area as I had concerns about my detectives working inside an unsafe structure late at night. As those warrants were being obtained, I had two of my other detectives start working with the local coroner so we could confirm the identities of our victims. That took some time because we didn't have a good handle on who two of our vics were until sometime after midnight. The worst part was tracking down each of the parents to tell them the bad news. In fact, we just made contact with the last set of parents about three hours ago. They've been out of town visiting relatives in Michigan's Upper Peninsula. The Michigan State Police made the formal notification for us around six or so this morning. They've been a big help to us as they are also getting those parents to the airport in Traverse City later today so they can get here. I'm having them picked up in Myrtle Beach late this afternoon."

"OK, sounds good." Paul said in response to Small's comments about the victims. "As long as you're confident we have a positive ID on each of the victims, that's good enough for me." Paul saw Small nodding her head at what he said as she stared down at some notes she had made earlier. Her doing so told him she was confident all of the victims had been properly identified.

Walking to where Renda stood waiting for them in the driveway, Paul noticed Solicitor Joseph Pascento had just arrived at the scene. He had met Pascento briefly during the Melkin investigation and had found him to be a very hard-working aggressive prosecutor. From talking to others in the past, he also knew most of the cops in Georgetown and Horry counties respected Pascento for the no-nonsense approach he took in dealing with criminals and their attorneys. Originally from New York City, the tall and well-built prosecutor had recently been elected to his fourth term in office.

As it often happens between people of similar personalities, Pascento and Renda had banged heads in the past over a variety of issues. Most of these occasions related to a handful of significant criminal investigations the sheriff's department had investigated over the years. While they were never the best of friends, they had tried mending fences a couple of years earlier and now they at least did their best to tolerate each other's company, especially in the presence of others.

As Small and her new boss walked to where Renda and Pascento stood, Paul noticed two uniformed Georgetown deputies staring at him from near the front of the damaged home. His casual friendly wave was returned by both of them. The thumbs-up he got from one of them told him his presence was a welcomed one. That simple gesture helped relieve some of the anxiety he was feeling at the moment.

"Hello, Paul!" Pascento said as he reached out to shake hands. "The sheriff just told me you were coming to help us with this case. Glad to have you with us again."

"Thanks, Joe," Paul said, dismissing the formality of using the solicitor's title in his greeting to him. Then, just as frankly as he had spoken earlier, Paul spoke again with little regard for who he upset. "Just so you know, I've spoken my piece with Sheriff Renda, and with Bobby Ray, about my role in this investigation. I still think Audrey should be running this investigation, but I guess the decision's been made on that. I hope you're good with me being asked to help, because if you're not then I'm out of here. I'm not looking to cause any friction between anyone; especially between your office and the sheriff's." Paul watched as Pascento deliberately took a moment to weigh what he was about to say.

"Paul, as long as Sheriff Renda has gotten you the proper credentials to be able to work as a law enforcement officer in the fine state of South Carolina, and as long as he feels comfortable with you being in charge of the investigation because of your past experience in matters like this, then I'm good with you working this case with his department." Pascento paused to give Small a quick look before he qualified his initial comments. "Don't take what I'm about to say the wrong way, Paul, and while I do know of your extensive background in running investigations like this, I would not have asked you to run this investigation if it was up to me. It's nothing against you; I just believe we have some talented folks working in this area. We need to assist them in developing their own skill sets so they can handle cases like this in the future when they arise. But if Sheriff Renda wants you to be the lead dog on this, then I'm good with the decision he's made. All I ask is that you keep my office informed of where the investigation is headed and that you call me if you need any legal help. Fair enough?" After scribbling both his private number at work and his cell phone number on the back of it, Pascento handed Paul one of his business cards.

"Fair enough, Joe. Thanks for being honest with me. I like that in a person, someone who's not afraid to speak what's on his or her mind. I completely understand, and completely support, your position. Just so you know, one of the things I plan on doing during this investigation is to tell the investigators, especially the younger ones, why I want certain things done before they go and do them. Having them doing the work without having an understanding of why certain tasks need to be done doesn't help them become better cops. That's my way of making them even better cops than they already are."

Paul's comments pleased Pascento. "Sounds good, Paul. I hope you're successful in finding out who murdered these young men. You call me when you need to tell me something that I need to hear, OK?"

"Yes, sir." Paul said as they again shook hands with each other.

Before Pascento could leave, Renda spoke to him about a need that had been raised earlier. "Joe, just as Audrey has done, Paul has also asked for some help on this investigation." Then Renda told Pascento of Paul's demand that Griffin, Wilson, Scozzafava, and Stine be assigned to the investigation. "Can you lend me a hand twisting some arms with their departments? We sure could use their help in this."

Pascento nodded as he began to process what he had been told. Squinting due to the day's extremely bright clear sky, he looked down at Renda who was at least four inches shorter in stature than he was. An avid fan of American folklore, the solicitor was built just like the lawmen he often read about from times past. Tall and lanky, with a waist size that most men his age no longer enjoyed, Pascento put a hand on Renda's left shoulder before speaking about Paul's request. He did so to reinforce what he was about to say. It was also done to infer this was not an issue that normally fell within his area of responsibility. In this particular matter, just like in all of the criminal cases he prosecuted, his responsibility was to prosecute those who had broken the law. In this case, it was whoever had committed the murders. It was Renda's responsibility to solve both his manpower problems and to get the investigation underway.

"Tell you what, Leroy, you've got as much pull in this county as I have, maybe even more. You speak to whoever it is you have to speak to so you can get those guys assigned down here. Call me if you run into any trouble. If you have to, you can tell whoever it is you're talking to that I want those guys assigned to this investigation as well. Those four cops are very good at what they do, so let's get them on board."

Turning to leave, Pascento looked at Paul for a quick moment. "You're a good judge of talent. I would have asked for them myself if you hadn't beaten me to it. Don't worry; we'll get them down here for Audrey and you to put to work."

"Thanks, Joe!" It was a simultaneous response from both Small and Paul.

As Pascento walked the short distance to his vehicle, Renda lingered behind for several minutes to speak to Paul and Audrey on matters related to the pending autopsies for each of the victims. With those needs soon addressed, the sheriff made one last tour around the exterior of the residence. As he did, he acknowledged the work being done by those he saw.

Finished inspecting the progress being made on getting the investigation underway, Renda was hit with his last surprise of the day. As Paul had promised, he made the sheriff address everyone as a group. It was not only done to make the sheriff feel uncomfortable again, but rather Paul made him do it so everyone knew where the investigation now stood. Open lines of communication from the top to the bottom were just as important to the investigation's new commander as they were from the bottom to the top.

Nine

Assignments

"OK, Audrey, it's time for us to get to work," Paul said as his eyes followed Renda for several seconds as he walked back to his vehicle. Turning to look at Small, he could not help but notice that she also had her eyes glued on the sheriff as he walked away.

"Good riddance!" Small mumbled softly, pleased by the fact that Renda was no longer at the scene.

Dismissing her comment, Paul then advised Small how he wanted the investigation to get started under his watch. Most importantly, he told her what he wanted her role to be.

"Now that we've gotten all of the preliminaries taken care of, I'd like you to show me the entire scene. Don't leave anything out as I need to know where each of the bodies were found, and where any other evidence was located. I need to have a clear understanding of what took place here." Then looking at the person he considered his partner in this investigation, Paul addressed the subject that, strangely, no one else had thought to bring up as of yet. He did so as they started walking towards the front door of the residence.

"Got it figured out yet?" Paul asked with a friendly smile on his face. The simple but unexpected question caught Small totally off guard.

"You . . . you mean with the fire?"

Small regretted her response as soon as the words left her lips. She knew she had whiffed with her answer. She also knew what Paul was asking her, even if he had just been joking by asking that question. Immediately she began to wonder if he was thinking that Renda had actually made the right choice in bringing him in to work with her. To her regret, her nervousness was beginning to show.

"Yeah, I guess, but what I really meant was the murders," Paul replied matter-of-factly. "Do you have any thoughts on who might have killed these kids?"

"No, not yet we don't. We really haven't had time to look for any guns or any other evidence yet. By the time we were ready to start looking at the scene last night it was too dark; too unsafe as well. I decided to wait until this morning to start the search of the residence. I knew we were going to have a long day in front of us, so I wanted everyone to have a good night's sleep before we started hitting it hard. I don't know if you agree with that decision, but I have no regrets about doing what I did."

"I might have done the same thing, Audrey." Paul said, trying to boost his partner's confidence with his comment. Deep down he knew he would have run his guys back in Connecticut hard all night running down the various leads available. With the hours immediately after a crime like this often being the most important, he also knew she had wasted several hours of precious time. Now he wondered if those precious hours had allowed their shooter time to flee.

"Based on what we began to learn as the body count grew last night, you'd have to be a rookie right out of the academy to think that this was just a simple house fire. These kids were killed for a reason. I'm not sure what that reason is right now, but that's why they all died here. At least, that's what several of my detectives and I all believe at this point. Each of our vics was shot at least once in the back of the head, execution style. A couple of them were shot more than once, but the significant wounds were all found to be located in the back of their heads. This is one of the worst murder scenes I've been at; it's made even gorier than most because of what the fire did to some of these kids' bodies. It's bad enough that all of these parents are never going to see their sons again, but it's even worse when you think that at least two of the mothers are not going to have the opportunity to kiss their son's cheeks one last time before they bury them because of what the fire did to them. Just the thought of seeing their son's casket closed during his funeral is going to give at least a couple of those mothers a terrible lasting impression of what some no-good bastard did to her boy."

Small was not a mother, but Paul could sense the pain she was experiencing at that moment as they paused in the front yard. Even for him, a veteran cop who had seen far too much sadness already during his career, it was hard not to feel the pain that still existed in and around the damaged home. Standing there, he recalled a handful of cases back home that had bothered him as much as this one now bothered Small. Like she was seeing now, he had seen firsthand the senseless pain and sorrow tragedies like this one inflicted upon so many other parents in the past.

For the next twenty-five minutes, Small walked Paul throughout the residence and the property that surrounded it. As she did, she occasionally referred to two rough sketches that had been made the night before. One had been drawn to plot the locations where each of the bodies had been found, and the second had been drawn to show the positions where each of the victims' vehicles had been located. Even as they spoke, each of the vehicles had been left parked where their owners had left them in the driveway or along the curb in front of the residence. As he looked at the sketch of the interior of the residence, Paul saw several measurements triangulated the locations where each of the bodies had been found. He was pleased by the obvious time and detail that had been put into making sure everything was properly documented. Doing so, if needed at a later time, would make recreating the scene fairly easy to accomplish.

As he alternated looks between the interior sketch of the first floor and of the inside of the home itself, Paul saw where each of the yellow plastic tent-like evidence stands were located on the sketch. Inside the home, the five yellow stands were still in place from just inside the front door to near the rear of the residence. He knew each of these stands, ones numbered one through five, represented the locations where each of the victims had been found. While his next thought would turn the stomachs of people unfamiliar with the needs of processing a crime scene, for veteran investigators like he and Small, it was a correct one to have. It was one he quickly shared with his partner.

"Audrey, from the looks of what I see on this sketch, we should have no problem recreating the scene if we have to. Based on where I see the stands on the sketch, and from all of the measurements that have been taken, we should be able to put the bodies right back where they were found. I'm hoping that doesn't have to happen, but if it does your folks have made it easy to accomplish."

Soon finished making two trips around the exterior of the residence, Paul paused near the damaged front door to make a couple of notes in a notebook that he had been given earlier by Small. Finished writing, he asked her his next question.

"So what you're telling me, despite the diagrams you've shown me, and despite the one shell casing that some fireman thought he saw lying on the floor in plain view in the living room, is that the processing of the house has yet to start. You really haven't started searching for any evidence as yet, is that correct?"

"That's correct." Small answered.

"And we don't have any suspects or any weapons that we can connect to this mess we're facing either, correct?"

"Correct. That's it in a nutshell, Paul. Outside of getting the search warrants that I've told you about, and after getting the place sketched and photographed before it got too dark last night, we haven't had time to do much of anything. In fact, the only thing we've done on the second floor was to make sure we did not have any more bodies up there. It was photographed like everything else, but no processing of any of the rooms up there has taken place yet. I was planning on starting the processing of the first floor early this morning but we both know how that worked out, don't we?" Small was referring to the meeting that had taken place at Bobby Ray's house earlier.

Surprised by the lack of investigative work that had begun, Paul could not help thinking how differently things back home would have been handled by his sergeants and detectives. He knew the current pace of this investigation was something he would have never tolerated back in Connecticut. Wanting to challenge Small on what he perceived to be some inaction on her part, Paul decided to bite his tongue. While he understood the decision she had made on not starting the processing of the residence due to concerns about darkness and the safety of her detectives, he could not understand why the processing of the victims' vehicles had not been started or, for that fact, completed. "I suppose it's too early to start off on the wrong foot," he thought to himself. "I'll get this investigation up to speed soon enough when the guys get here."

As they talked for several more minutes regarding evidence that had been observed in plain view inside the scene after the bodies had been removed from the residence, Small told Paul about something unusual.

"When the EMTs and our guys were trying to get a quick fix on each of the kids' identities, they obviously looked through their wallets. But after jotting down some of the relevant information from each of the operator's licenses, they began to notice that none of the wallets had any cash in them. What's the chance of five wallets not having any cash in them? That's kind of strange, isn't it?"

Paul thought for a moment before replying. "The obvious answer is that it's very strange, but when you mix murder into the equation it's really not that strange at all. The easy answer to your question is that it was the end of the week and each of the kids were short on cash; who knows, maybe they hadn't had time to cash their paychecks. The other answer I have is more difficult to accept. But maybe, just maybe, it's the correct one. Maybe whoever did the shooting emptied the wallets of any cash before or after the kids were shot. Who knows, maybe one or two of the vics owed someone some money. Could be this whole mess is just about a crime of opportunity, one that went remarkably bad."

"Could be that, I suppose," Small said as she processed what Paul had said. "Could be that whoever did this just took the money to make it look like a robbery."

"Maybe, but I doubt it." Paul said confidently as he stared inside the fire damaged home.

Small detected the confidence in Paul's response. She wanted to question him further about it, but decided against it for now. "Let's just let this investigation play out. Then we'll see who is right." She thought to herself. Like her new boss, she was also quite confident in her read of the situation.

Soon finished with his own thoughts, Paul gave Small her first marching order. "OK, Audrey, let's get this investigation into high gear. Round up your staff and let's have a meeting with them under those pine trees I saw out in the backyard. There's no need for any of us to be doing business standing out in the hot sun today."

As Paul finished speaking, he noticed Douglas Vane, the GCSD's Chief Evidence Officer, driving up to the scene in a pick-up truck owned by the sheriff's department. The truck's bed was filled with an assortment of different sized wooden boards, three different sizes of metal screening, four sheets of half-inch plywood, and several boxes of assorted nails and wood screws. Lying next to those items were a variety of hand tools and one Black and Decker Skilsaw. As he waited for Vane to climb out of the truck, he also noticed two metal detectors leaning against each other in the right front seat.

After exchanging pleasantries with someone he considered a good friend, Paul jokingly spoke to Vane. "Looks like someone is planning on building a sifter for some reason. Trying to find something, Doug?"

Realizing the enormity of the task in front of him, Vane stared several times at the fire damaged residence as he spoke. "I'm hoping we can start to piece together what took place here. Hopefully we'll find a few spent bullets and some shell casings as well. That's if the casings weren't picked up before the shooter left. I doubt it, but maybe we'll even find a gun or two. That'd be nice, right?"

"Sounds like a plan. To tell you the truth, I half-expected to see you come driving up here with all of this stuff. You're one of the people I'm counting on to get this investigation headed in the right direction."

Vane smiled as he nodded at the compliment sent his way.

"Doug, leave this stuff here for right now. I've got Audrey

rounding everyone up so we can talk for a few minutes. It's important that everyone is working off the same sheet of music and doing what I need them to do. It will only take a few minutes and then you can get back to building your contraption."

* * * * * *

In the backyard of the victims' residence, several members of Small's unit sat on the ground while others stood in the shade as Paul spoke to them. Their new boss had chosen to take a seat on a blue and white Igloo cooler that a thoughtful next door neighbor had carried to the scene earlier that morning. It contained two bags of ice and several bottles of cold water for later in the day. Small sat nearby on an old wooden bench that once had been part of a picnic table.

"OK, folks, I want to start processing this scene as fast and as hard as we can for the rest of the time we have here today. I'm not interested in mistakes being made, or things being overlooked, but we should have at least another eight or nine hours of daylight left before it gets too dark to work. In that time period, we should be able to put a big dent in what needs to be done. Oh, and just so I don't forget to tell you . . . yes, we are working tomorrow." While they had already expected to be working the following day, the assembled group of cops and civilian employees sitting in front of him let out a collective groan to welcome their new boss with.

"I know, I know, it's Sunday, but we've got five dead bodies on our hands. We need to hammer away at processing this scene as quick as we can before we get hit with any rain in the next few days. We've already got enough problems facing us without having to worry about what Mother Nature might throw at us. We cannot afford to have a rainstorm compromising the integrity of our scene, so we need to get as many of the answers as we can to the questions facing us before any bad weather wreaks havoc on us. Understand? Good!" While he knew they did, Paul did not give his new charges a moment to respond.

For the next several minutes, Paul spoke on how he wanted the investigation to proceed. When he was finished, he told everyone who was present what their assignments were going to be over the next day or so. Each of them, he told them, was going to have a specific role in one of the many facets of the investigation.

"For now, I'm breaking this investigation up into three parts. The first part is the scene itself. I've tasked Lt. Small, with Doug's help, and with those of you who work for Sergeant Elmendorf, to get the interior scene processed as soon as possible. Tomorrow I'm expecting two arson investigators from SLED to come down and help us for at least a day or so with their expertise. Obviously we're also going to be relying on some much needed input from the Medical Examiner's office, but right now we need to try and figure out what kind of gun was used to kill these kids. Later today, Doug is going to build a sifter so we can start sifting through the debris from inside the house. Doing so will hopefully help us find some spent bullets, some shell casings, and whatever else might be in there. It's going to be hot and dirty work, but it has to be done. Once we ID the kind of gun that was used to shoot these kids, then we'll start looking for the bastard who pulled the trigger. Questions?"

With Small's help, Paul answered a few questions from those who were being charged with processing the residence. As they did, her cell phone rang. Moving away from the others, she allowed Paul to finish answering the questions being asked. As he did, he gave everyone a bit of good news.

"With the amount of work that needs to be done here, as well as in who knows how many other places the investigation is going to take us, I've asked Sheriff Renda for some additional warm bodies to help us. While I believe we need their help here at the scene right now, we're going to need it even more, God forbid, if something else happens in the county and Lt. Small has to divert some of you away from here to handle something else. Let's pray that does not happen."

"So who's coming to help us?" One of Small's younger detectives asked. "Hopefully not the feds!"

Paul smiled at the detective's concern about the feds coming to help. Like most cops did, including his own detectives from back home, this detective shared the same worry. The concern was one shared by many others who were present. No one liked it very much when a federal law enforcement agency came strutting in and adopted a case the state police or a local agency like theirs had worked hard on for weeks. Or, like in this case, one that had been worked on for only a few mere hours. It was a practice that often alienated cops who, in theory, should have been working together for a common cause.

"I've specifically asked for people who most of you already know and respect. I've asked that Kent Wilson and Blake Stine from MBPD, Frank Griffin from NMBPD, and FBI Agent Thomas Scozzafava be assigned to the investigation. Many of you worked with these guys during the Melkin investigation, so you know they're as good as you are at what they do. Believe me, when this is over and done with, you're going to thank me for getting you this additional help."

"Paul, is that going be true about Scozz too? You know, us thanking you for bringing him down here and all." Detective Bruce Davis' joke gave everyone, Paul included, a good laugh.

"He's a good fed, guys." Paul said, still laughing somewhat at Davis' joke. "He's a good cop too!" Pausing to let the last few laughs die down, he then let those around him know that he valued their opinions. "Any of you folks have any objections to the names I've just mentioned?"

No one in Small's collective group, including Small herself who had returned from taking a call, voiced any objections. Several now nodded their heads in silent approval of additional help being sent their way.

"Paul, I guess the cavalry is on the way. That was Sheriff Renda on the phone," Small said, somewhat pleased by the timing of his call. "He's arranged for the two SLED investigators, as well as the others you've mentioned, to be here by seven tomorrow morning. Stine might even be here later today for a spell so he can get a lay of the land, but they will all be here tomorrow for sure." Small's words brought good news to Paul's briefing.

"OK, good. Listen up, folks, because I want you to know about something Lt. Small worked out earlier this morning. Later today she is meeting with the parents of one of our victims after they fly in from Michigan. This involves the second part of the investigation. She's going to take one of you with her, so whoever it is, be supportive of those parents when you're dealing with them. Tomorrow, Tommy Scozz, with a few of you helping him, is going to start heading up all of the needs we have with the parents. That includes interviewing them about whatever they might be able to tell us about what happened here. Please, and I cannot stress this enough, please be mindful of the horror they are dealing with right now. Treat them as you would expect to be treated if this had happened to your son or daughter. If they need time to mourn, let them have that time, but at some point get them to talk to you. I'll talk with Scozz in the morning and then he'll give you your assignments on who you're going to be interviewing. Just remember these mothers and fathers need you to become their best friend right now. You have my permission to do whatever it takes to help them get through this difficult time in their lives. In the end, they will all have a sincere appreciation for the help you've given them. Trust me on this, OK?"

Paul saw a couple of heads drop as he finished speaking, but several others had already been staring at the ground in front of them. From the facial expressions he saw, as well as from some of their body language, it was obvious the cops in front of him were already thinking of the pain that five sets of parents were now dealing with.

Standing up from the cooler he had been sitting on, Paul opened it and took out a cold bottle of water. The busy morning had caused his throat to become dry from the heat of the day and from talking. He also drank the cold water to wash away the acrid stench of the fire that lingered a mere few feet away. The unpleasant smell of burnt wood, furniture, and carpeting had crept inside his mouth and nostrils with every breath he took.

Two quick gulps of cold water soon made him feel somewhat better.

"The last part of the investigation that some of you are being assigned to are all of the interviews and background checks we're going to have to get done. I'm taking charge of this aspect of the investigation. Like some of you, Wilson, Griffin, and Stine will be helping out in this area as well. We have enough other work to do today regarding several other tasks, so I'll hand out those assignments to you in the morning after Audrey and I talk some more later today."

* * * * * *

Paul had little way of knowing this, but the time he spent talking with everyone and telling them what their roles were going to be in the investigation was more than what they had each been told since the GCSD assumed responsibility for the scene. The confidence that Small's detectives now had, especially in their new boss, would mean a great deal over the next few weeks. For Lt. Audrey Small, the lack of confidence she had in herself would prove to be another obstacle in her career. It was something she would have to learn to overcome very quickly.

Ten

A Burglary Gone Bad

*"Little surfer, little one, Made my heart come all undone,
Do you love me, Do you surfer girl, Surfer girl my little surfer girl . . ."*

Despite being a huge Beach Boys fan, the ringtone on Paul's cell phone was not something he appreciated hearing at twelve minutes after three in the morning. The large red digital numbers he saw displayed on the clock next to his bed confirmed the ungodly hour he was being woken. Looking at the number displayed on the phone caused him to first think that it was someone who had mistakenly dialed his number. Groggy, and still half-asleep, it was not a number he recognized.

"Hello?" Paul said as he forced himself to wake up from the sleep he had been enjoying.

"Paul, sorry to wake you, it's Audrey. Something just happened at the victims' house that I thought you should know about. I'm walking to my car right now; I'm headed over there."

The news he heard immediately cleared the remaining cob webs from his tired brain. Quickly he sat up on the edge of his bed for a brief moment before walking out of the bedroom. He did so in the hopes of not disturbing Donna more than she already had been.

"What's going on, Audrey?" Paul said as he flipped on the light over his kitchen table.

"The deputy on-duty at the scene, his name is George Bontya, had gotten out of his cruiser to stretch his legs when he saw two figures trying to hide in the tree line of the victims' backyard. Unfortunately for them, not only does George have good eyesight, but the full moon that's out tonight cast their shadows across the lawn as they were trying to hide. Luckily for us, George had his K-9 with him. When he challenged them on what they were doing, his dog, Woodsy, took off after them when they tried running away. From briefly talking to him, it sounds like his dog got a few bites of one of the suspects; supposedly in the guy's butt cheeks. We're still looking for his buddy."

"Ouch! What the hell were those two idiots doing at the scene at this time of the morning? Do we have any idea if they were actually involved in the murders?" Paul asked as he processed a mental picture of Bontya's canine taking a few bites of the suspect's backside. Sitting at his kitchen table, he made a few brief notes of what Small was passing on to him.

"Not sure, but the one interesting thing I've been told already is that the asshole we've got in custody had a Smith & Wesson .38 snub-nose revolver on him when they arrested him. He's claiming he and his buddy, who he won't identify by name as yet, heard about the murders; says they went there because they thought the place would be vacant. Figured they'd come and see what they could boost out of the house."

Despite comprehending what he was being told, Paul was still half-asleep as he sat shaking his head at what Small was telling him. "You know, it's just amazing what some people will do. Some idiot comes and murders these young men in their own home, and then some other creeps come up with the bright idea that the vacant murder scene presents a great opportunity for them to score some electronics and whatever else they can get their hands on. Probably for no other reason than just to fence whatever it is they can steal for a few quick bucks. Despite being a cop for thirty-plus years, I'm still amazed by how some people act. Tell you what, tell Bontya to have that dog of his bite that no-good son of a bitch a few more times, that will teach our wannabe burglar a lesson or two about taking advantage of other people's misfortune."

Small couldn't help laughing at Paul's request as a similar thought had crossed her mind several minutes earlier. "I've got a better idea. When we get done interviewing this jerk, I'm going to give my guys the OK to take the bastard across the street and hang him from one of those Live Oaks I saw there. You OK with that?"

"Yep, sure am," Paul said as he exchanged laughs with Small.

"From what I'm hearing, this doesn't sound like murderers coming back to the scene to look for something; it sounds just like it looks. It's a burglary attempt that just went south." Small said, still chuckling over the comments she and Paul had just exchanged with each other concerning the two burglars. "I'm being told the guy in custody, Jessie Maynard, has a lengthy arrest record, burglaries mostly, but nothing associated with any violence. I'm just calling you to give you a heads up, that's all. After I get there, I'll call you if it turns out to be anything more than that. If you don't hear from me soon it's because our guy in custody isn't being looked at for any of the murders. I'll fill you in with the rest of the details in the morning. That OK with you?"

Already on his way back to bed, Paul nodded at what Small told him. "Yeah, that's fine. I'll have a length of rope ready if you need it. Talk to you when the sun comes up. Thanks for the call."

As he crawled back into bed, Paul again shook his head at what Small had told him. "The parents of these five young men have barely had time to start grieving over their sons' deaths, and now some bastard and his friend are trying to break into the home where they were murdered." As he pulled the sheets up close to his face, one last conscious thought entered his head before he fell back to sleep. "Maybe I should bring that rope down there after all."

Eleven

Partners

As it would be until the GCSD finished processing the entire crime scene, the immediate area around the victims' residence was held overnight by the patrol division until the detectives and crime scene techs returned back to work each morning. The same was true for the first Sunday of the investigation.

With the sawhorses and yellow crime scene tape taken down at the sight of the Sabbath's first light, items which had been used to block off the road in front of the crime scene, traffic, although light, moved slowly through the neighborhood. For the next several days, carloads of onlookers would drive by the scene in hopes of satisfying their morbid curiosity.

After Paul's talk on Saturday, three detectives and two crime scene techs executed the search warrants on the victims' vehicles. Not to the surprise of anyone, no items of any real evidentiary value were found. One of the vehicles was found to have several partially smoked marijuana joints, roaches as they are commonly called, inside a plastic cup that had the wording *I Love Myrtle Beach* written on it. The cup had been left in one of the vehicle's cup holders by its owner. While the roaches, as well as an opened pack of E-Z Wider rolling papers which had been found between the two front seats, were seized as evidence, none of the investigators believed for a moment that the small amount of grass was remotely connected to any of the murders. The GCSD's Possessed Property Report for the items seized from the black 2005 Dodge Neon listed those items simply as numbers five and six of the nine exhibits seized from the vehicle. After being processed, the victims' vehicles were removed to the GCSD's secured impound lot for safekeeping until they could be claimed at a later date.

Paul allowed everyone to sleep in on Sunday morning as they had all put in a fifteen hour day on Saturday. Besides wanting to give his detectives time to go to church with their families, or to spend some time having breakfast with their spouses and children, he knew the extra couple of hours of sleep would help his people through what was more than likely going to be a week full of equally long days. Prior to them all going home on Saturday, he had told them to be back at the scene by nine the following morning.

As was his custom, especially when something hot was on the burner, Paul arrived back at the scene shortly after six on Sunday morning. For him, sleep had been a wasted effort for a good part of the night, especially after being woken up by Small. Focused on far too many possible scenarios of what had caused the murders to occur, and how he was going to attack the problems facing him, sleep was something he had given up on shortly after five.

Arriving at the scene, Paul noticed the GCSD's Major Case Squad's crime scene truck had been left parked in the driveway overnight. Unlike Vane's unmarked pick-up truck that had also been left parked at the scene, the crime scene truck was easily recognizable to all who saw it. Besides the electronic roof rack that was mounted on the cab, both sides of the large gray and blue box style truck had been professionally stenciled in big letters to let others know what its purpose in life was. The large top line of lettering read 'Georgetown County Sheriff's Department'. Underneath that, a second line of smaller lettering read 'Crime Scene Processing Vehicle'. Like Vane's, the large truck was equipped with an array of tools and other needs required for processing a variety of different kinds of crime scenes. The self-contained vehicle, equipped with a variety of portable radio and other hand-held communication devices, as well as three laptop computers and a combination fax machine and printer, made the processing of any type of scene far easier than when Paul and Bobby Ray first became cops. A variety of electronics, lasers, portable GPS devices, and many other modern forensic tools now replaced the ordinary pens, pads, string, and tape measures that so many veteran cops had relied on for years.

Adjacent to the driveway, Paul also noticed work had nearly been completed on erecting a large olive drab colored army surplus tent, one belonging to Renda's department. The tent's presence brought a smile to his face as he knew it would come in handy over the next several days. At one end of it, detectives and crime scene techs would soon begin work there as they used Vane's sifter to process debris through it. Having performed that task on several occasions back home, he knew those performing this tedious dirty work would be far more comfortable while standing out of the hot sun or afternoon rainstorms as they sifted through what would likely prove to be yards and yards of debris looking for bullets and shell casings left behind by their shooter. As he stared at the tent, Paul nodded approvingly at the crudely built sifter Vane and his crew had nearly finished building before leaving the previous day.

"Whatever that material cost us was money well-spent. That sifter is going to pay us back tenfold by the time Doug and his folks get done using it." Paul thought as he gave Vane's creation one last look before moving on.

Walking towards the backyard from where he had parked his assigned vehicle in a small vacant lot across the street from the scene, Paul gave a wave to one of the uniformed deputies parked in the driveway of the crime scene. Along with Deputy Bontya, he had been responsible for securing the scene overnight. The weak, but friendly wave he got in return told him the deputy's night had been a long and boring one outside of the brief encounter with two inept burglars. To most civilians, protecting the integrity of a crime scene might sound glamorous, but to the cops who drew those assignments it was like drawing the short end of a stick for a job no one wanted.

Further down the driveway, Paul stopped to speak with Sergeant Kindle for a few moments. They had briefly gotten to know each other during the Melkin investigation as Kindle had not only been at one of the scenes where one of the bodies had been found, but he had also helped a South Carolina state trooper box Richard Melkin in on Front Street so he could not escape. Six weeks after that case had come to a conclusion, Kindle was promoted to sergeant.

Now working as a patrol sergeant, Kindle, who was filling in for the night for another sergeant, had stopped at the scene that morning to make sure all was well. He had also done so to give the two deputies stationed there a chance to make a quick pit stop at a nearby gas station for a much needed cup of coffee.

"Paul, it's nice to see you again." Kindle said as he glanced at his watch. "I heard the boss brought you back to work this case with us, but what the hell are you doing here so early for? I thought you folks were not coming back until around nine or so. Kind of early, ain't it?"

Shaking hands with the recently promoted sergeant, Paul offered him his congratulations. "Someone told me yesterday that you had been promoted. Congrats! Well-deserved I'm sure! As for me being here early, you're right, I am. Don't know why, but I've never been able to sleep much when there's work to be done."

After a few more brief minutes of conversation, mostly small talk about life in general, Kindle spoke about the investigation at hand.

"This one is bad, Paul. It's terrible when anyone gets killed, but five young men at one time, well, that's just sinful. The media, even the big boys, you know, CNN, MSNBC, Fox News, all those folks, they've been bugging us since this happened. As far as they're concerned, the shock of the murders is old news to them, now they're demanding to know when we're going to catch the asshole who did this. I tried telling a couple of them that investigations like this one, just like the recent one in Pennsylvania where the troopers searched for weeks for the bastard who shot and killed one of their brother troopers, that it often takes time to catch the bad guys, but they didn't give a hoot about what I was telling them. They're just looking for immediate gratification, you know, something they can put up on the screen to satisfy their viewers. Bunch of demanding no-good bastards, that's what those folks are. Get this thing solved for us, will you? We need all of these so-called journalists to stop calling our Dispatch Center every five minutes. I can't wait to see them and their pain-in-the-ass satellite trucks move on to the next crisis in the world. Let's just hope it happens outside of Georgetown County."

Paul smiled at Kindle's personal take on the media. It was one that was not too far off from his own, but having too much on his mind already, he elected not to prolong the conversation on the fourth estate. He was about to change the subject to something more pleasant when he was startled by the sight of a figure dressed in black clothing and wearing a black bandana. Almost immediately, the figure slowly began walking towards him from near the rear of the residence. Kindle saw the same figure moments after Paul first had.

"Hey!" Kindle yelled. "What the . . . "

It took a moment for it to register, but when it did it caused Paul's face to break out in a big smile. Quickly he interrupted Kindle's challenge of demanding to know what this person in black clothing was doing within the crime scene.

"It's OK, Ed, relax. It's Stine from MBPD. He may not look it, but he's one of us." Paul said as he began walking towards the south side of the house.

"Good to see you, Blake!" Paul said as he closed the distance between the two of them. "You trying to sneak up on us?"

Detective Blake Stine stood waiting for him with a big grin on his face. Like his friend, Stine was as early riser on most mornings.

"Nope. Not at all." Stine answered in response to Paul's question. "I parked down the street as I didn't want any reporters to see me if they were still hanging around. I've been doing some UC work and I don't care to have my pretty face all over the evening news. That wouldn't be good for business, would it?"

After shaking hands with each other, and after introducing Stine to Kindle, Paul slowly walked his newest investigator around the exterior of the property. A quick summary of what the first responders had found at the scene followed.

"It still smells like death here, Paul." Stine said as he peered inside the residence from just outside the opened back door. "The smell of a fire you can kind of get used to, but the smell of burnt flesh, well that's a whole different story. It's a smell that seems to linger for far too long."

As he finished up with his brief description of what had been found within the residence, Paul looked to see what kind of reaction it had gotten from Stine.

"Sounds like you . . . ." As he paused to gather his thoughts, Stine took a moment to collect himself as well. "I guess I should have said it sounds like we have a lot of work to do here."

Looking around the yard as they walked towards the driveway side of the residence, Stine saw that several pieces of burnt furniture had been dragged out of the residence during the time the firemen were knocking down the fire. In the backyard, not far from where the furniture now sat, he saw a disgusting sight that had yet to be cleaned up. Piled up on the lawn nearby were several blood stained sheets, used gauze pads and their paper wrappers, latex gloves, and other spent medical supplies. They had been used by the firemen and EMTs in their attempts to render first aid to a couple of the victims. Seeing those blood soaked items caused Stine to ask his friend a question.

"Paul, why am I here?" What is it that you're looking for me to help you folks with?"

"Tell you what, Blake, let's wait until the others get here before I answer your question. I expect Kent, Tommy Scozz, and Griff will likely be asking me that same question. I'd rather answer it once when you're all here together. But, for now, I'll simply tell you're here because I asked for you. You're good at interviewing people and you're even better at getting them to tell you things they don't want you to know. All of you are here for that same reason. We need information and we need it fast. I'll explain the rest of it to you later."

Stine smiled, shook hands with Paul again, and then started another tour around the exterior of the residence so he could take it all in again on his own. He would wait patiently for Paul to clue him in with the rest of the details when he was ready to do so. Unlike so many others he had worked with during his time as a cop, Stine knew Paul had his act together. Part of that act included having a plan on how he wanted this case investigated.

******

At 0850 hours, with everyone present and accounted for, including those who Paul had asked Renda to have assigned to the investigation, Small conducted a brief update on what had occurred at the scene, and what had occurred during the first thirty-six hours of the investigation. Besides the law enforcement personnel present, also attending this briefing was Walter Barber, the deputy coroner for Georgetown County. He was present representing the South Carolina Chief Medical Examiner's Office. Unlike Barber's, Small's update was primarily being done for the benefit of those who were visiting the scene for the first time that morning. As she spoke, Vane, who Paul had asked to sit in on a briefing for the second day in a row, sat impatiently in a metal folding chair. With his staff already at work inside the residence, he was itching to get to work himself. Paul smiled to himself when he noticed Vane's obvious discomfort of having to waste part of his morning listening to what he had already heard discussed the previous day. While not big on people wasting their time attending meetings that were not productive, Paul believed having Vane present for the first meeting that Wilson, Griffin, Stine, and Tommy Scozz were at was important.

Finished with her five-minute presentation, Small called on Barber to advise everyone present of the preliminary findings from each of the five autopsies. Performed by three Assistant Medical Examiners, they had all been conducted late on Saturday. Not use to working on a Sunday, and tired from several other autopsies they had been forced to complete the previous day, they had reached out to Barber to represent them. Like he had on several other occasions in the past, Barber was there to present their findings to the investigators working the investigation. Armed with a green file folder that was nearly filled to capacity with a variety of reports which had been emailed and faxed to him during the night, Barber stood and walked to where Small had given her presentation.

Opening his folder to take out a few of the reports he had received, Barber quickly changed his mind and closed it without retrieving anything from it. He already knew what needed to be said from having carefully read everything he had been sent. Like some of the detectives he was about to address, he had also viewed each of the bodies shortly after they had been pulled from the burning house.

"I've received the preliminary reports that relate to each of the autopsies. I'll get with Paul and Audrey when we get done here, and later today I'll make a couple of working copies so you have them for your needs and reports." Normally composed when interacting with others, Barber stopped talking for a few moments to catch his breath. As he paused, it became apparent to the others gathered under the large tent that what he had seen done to each of the victims, and from reading each of the autopsy reports, had bothered the veteran coroner significantly. Taking two additional deep breaths, he soon continued with his presentation. "Like most of you know already, these five young men did not die from the fire or from smoke inhalation or from anything else related to the fire. They each died from gunshot wounds to the back of their heads. Some died from more than one gunshot, but each of the shots were fired from a close distance . . . execution style is the best way to describe it, I guess. Each of their deaths will soon be ruled a homicide, and their causes of death will all read the same; death by gunshot. Just so you know, I spoke with one of the Assistant Medical Examiners by phone last night about the type of weapon that might have been used. While we all know that's not their job to determine what particular kind of weapon was used as that's the job of our friends at SLED, he did tell me his best educated guess was it was some type of a small caliber firearm." Barber paused briefly to look at Paul for a moment. "The bad news I have to tell you is that while they retrieved a lot of metal from the victims' bodies, only one of the bullets is in somewhat decent condition, but I'm afraid even that one may not be good enough for any comparison testing. The others are in real bad condition, fragments mostly, probably unusable for any forensic testing from what I'm being told as they were badly damaged from striking a variety of bones. Maybe when you folks process the scene you'll find one or two spent cartridges in a wall or in some furniture, but I'm not too confident that's going to be the case. I was also told you need to look for around eight to nine shell casings as what was retrieved from the victims' bodies looked to have come from that many rounds being fired into them."

Barber saw the disappointed looks on the faces of Paul, Audrey Small, Vane, and several others. He knew not having any spent bullets to match with any shell casings found at the scene was going to make their work that much more difficult.

Then looking at Paul again, Barber added, "Just so you know, each of the bodies was x-rayed before and after their autopsies were performed. Any bullets or bullet fragments that were in them have now been recovered." Then Barber directed one last comment to him. "You and Audrey may know this already, but the fragments that were taken out of the victims' bodies were given to two of your investigators last night. My understanding is Mo and Carlson are planning on taking that evidence to SLED today. They reached out to someone they know there and got them to agree to take the evidence in for you even though it's a

Sunday. Apparently everyone knows how important this case is, so that's why they're going to be able to drop the evidence off today."

Investigator Richard Carlson, a former cop from New York, had moved to South Carolina after retiring from Yonkers PD. He had first found work with the Horry County Sheriff's Office before transferring to the GCSD after working on the Melkin investigation. He had been lured further south by Bobby Ray based on the promise that he would not have to work the road any longer. The modest raise that came with the transfer had made Carlson's decision an easy one to make. While he and Paul had butted heads when they first met during the Melkin investigation, Paul's management style, along with a tongue-lashing from Bobby Ray, soon won Carlson over.

Detective Orlando Mo, a twenty-two year veteran of the GCSD, had recently taken his first promotional test in over ten years, scoring near the top of the list of in-house applicants seeking promotion to the rank of detective in Bobby Ray's Major Case Squad. Well-respected by all of his peers, Mo had been welcomed to the squad with open arms by everyone.

Paul nodded at Barber's remarks about the bullet fragments and who they had been given to. "Audrey already spoke to Mo this morning about them. He and Carlson should be delivering them to SLED right about now. Mo's contact there is going to have them photographed for us after the evidence gets signed in so we can have a couple of working sets of photographs to use for our needs here. Hopefully we'll know in a couple of days or so what kind of rounds they are. That will at least give us an idea of what kind of gun they were fired from."

After finishing up with a few brief housekeeping issues regarding work assignments and keeping track of the hours they each worked over the weekend, the meeting was adjourned. As it broke up, Paul could not help but laugh when he saw Vane nearly trip in his haste to get back to work with his evidence techs. The techs had just brought out a garbage can of debris from inside the house and were preparing to use Vane's sifter for the first time. As the others left to get to work, Paul held back Stine, Griffin, and Wilson, as well as three of Audrey's detectives. Now he explained to them what their roles were going to be in the investigation. Also present was FBI Agent Thomas Scozzafava. While he had been the last person to arrive for the briefing, he was the first to be told what his assignment was going to involve.

"Scozz, I want you to be the principle contact for each of the victims' parents. It's not going to be easy work because of their grief, but make sure they each get interviewed as soon as possible. Everyone assigned to this investigation knows before any parent gets contacted, they run that through you first. I realize things are going to overlap during this investigation, but I want you to be the guy who sets things up with the parents." Looking at the others present, Paul directed his next comment at them. "Guys, these parents are important to us, so I want to make sure we're all working on the same page. No one talks to the parents without Tommy Scozz's approval. Got it?"

Then Paul spoke to Griffin, Stine, and Wilson about the significant number of interviews that needed to be completed. Like so many cop shows on television, ones like Dragnet, Starsky and Hutch, Miami Vice, and so many others, the chemistry that existed between partners was often critical in the success of closing cases, especially ones as tragic and violent as the one they were all about to start working on. Knowing that Small knew the strengths and weaknesses of her detectives better than he did, Paul turned to her for help.

"Let's put Detective Bruce Davis with Blake," she first announced. Davis quickly stood up from where he was seated so the others could put a name with a face. "Bruce has only been with the squad for about three months now, but he's learning fast. I think Blake and he will make a good solid team, especially after he's shown the Stine way of doing things." Stine and Davis exchanged friendly nods with each other as Small finished speaking.

Paul nodded approvingly at the first pairing Small had made. "Bruce, I hope you're ready to learn. Blake's a hard charger who sets a pace most people cannot keep up with. Good luck!" Turning to look at Small, he asked, "Who do you want to pair up with Griff?"

"Let's put the big red-headed guy, his name is Darren Edwards, let's pair him up with Griff. He's been with our unit for the past eight months after working the road for nine years prior to that. Darren's proving to be a good detective; he's quite knowledgeable about firearms as well. I'm sure we'll put that knowledge to use once or twice during this investigation."

"OK, sounds good. Welcome aboard, Darren!" Paul said as smiled at Edwards. "OK, so who is left? Who gets to work with Kent?"

"We're going to team Detective Ron Levesque up with Kent." Small said as she motioned for Levesque to stand up. "Ron transferred over from the Charleston County Sheriff's Office after he recently moved up our way from Mt. Pleasant. He was a road deputy, and later an investigator, with them for nearly seven years." Then Small let out a quick laugh. "Kent, your new partner has a unique nickname. His friends call him Jaws. I'm going to let you figure out why they call him that."

Paul thought for a moment about Small's laugh, as well as her subsequent comment about Levesque's nickname, as he stared at the short and stocky detective standing off to his right.

"Jaws? What kind of a nickname is that? You have to either be a big talker or a big eater with that kind of a nickname."

Small laughed again briefly before moving to where the others now stood under the tent. As she spoke to them about their assignments, a female GCSD uniformed deputy walked up and paused near the edge of the tent. She was one of the deputies performing traffic control out in front of the residence. Taking off her sunglasses, she called to Paul who was standing several feet away.

"Excuse me, Paul. A guy who claims to be the owner of the property here just arrived a few moments ago. Says his last name is Zerbola. He claims he was out of town on vacation when this happened; told me he cut it short so he could get back here. Says one of his neighbors down the street called and told him what happened. I've got him sitting in his fancy new Lincoln for now. You want me to escort him back here so someone can speak with him?"

Paul exchanged a brief glance with Small before he answered the deputy's question. This was one of the most important people they had been looking for since the day the murders had taken place. The fact that he had shown up without them having to try and find him again pleased Paul.

"Do me favor, will you, deputy? It's Carol, right?"

"Yes, sir." Deputy Lemieux's smile told everyone who was now staring at her that she was pleased by the fact that Paul knew her first name. Paul had only briefly met her during his first assignment with the GCSD, but name recognition had always been one of his strengths. It was a skill he refined after attending several Interview and Interrogation courses as a young trooper, and later during an advanced class at the FBI National Academy.

"Carol, please keep close tabs on Mr. Zerbola for a few minutes. Do not allow him to leave under any circumstances. I'll have a couple of guys out to interview him in a few minutes."

"Yes, sir, no problem."

Lemieux started to walk back down the driveway, but suddenly remembered she had one more thing to pass on. "Paul, excuse me again, I almost forgot. There's a pick-up truck out front; it's towing a small flatbed trailer that's got a fairly large ice machine on it. The driver says his name is Chubby; claims you know him. He says the ice machine is for you. He just needs to know where you want it set up. You know anything about this?"

Despite standing under the camouflaged tent where he was out of direct contact with the sun's bright but harmful rays, it was still extremely warm. Now, as he stood listening to what Lemieux was telling him, Paul pulled a white handkerchief out of one of his back pockets. It was the only thing he had available to wipe the sweat off his forehead and face. The perplexed look she soon observed on Paul's face told Deputy Lemieux that he had no idea of what she was talking about.

"An ice machine?" Paul asked.

"Yep. The driver . . . that Chubby fellow, he said he'd like to speak with you about it. What should I tell him?"

Annoyed by having to address another problem on an already busy morning, Paul told Lemieux to have the driver sit tight for a few moments until he could get out to see him. He did so in irritated voice that told the deputy he really did not have time to deal with this unexpected interruption.

"Tell him to find some shade until I get there." Then, to no one in particular, Paul said, "Dang, it's too freakin' hot out here already this morning." Another wipe of his sweaty forehead quickly followed.

As he turned his attention back to the task at hand, Paul's focus was momentarily interrupted by the sound of another wheelbarrow full of debris being dumped onto a large blue tarp that had been spread out on the ground next to Vane's sifter. Like the other piles that would soon follow this one, the debris would be scanned twice by two metal detectors before being run through the sifter. It was basically a duplication of effort, but one which increased the chances of finding anything of evidentiary value. As he briefly watched Vane's crew at work, Paul said a silent prayer. "Let's hope our shooter used an automatic and not a revolver. At least that way we might stand a chance of finding some of the shell casings. That would at least give us some type of a direction to proceed in."

After gazing at the work being done around the sifter, Paul

returned his attention back to those investigators who were still waiting for the rest of their marching orders. "I've picked you folks to help us get started with all of the interviews we need to get done. I can't emphasize this to you enough; we need information and we need it now. We're flying kind of blind right now. As I told you, Scozz and his folks are going to start working with the parents; you folks have got everything else. The first thing I want done is for you to start working the neighborhood. Get a canvass going as soon as we get done here." Pausing for a moment to locate where Wilson was seated, Paul then directed his next comment at the veteran cop. "Kent, you and Griff are heading this up for us. Put a plan together amongst yourselves and get it done as soon as you can. See what people living in the area know, and see who they think might have done this to those kids. It has to be someone with a bitch, a beef, or a grudge of some kind with one or more of these kids. Get going guys! I want a call in an hour or so with an update."

Paul turned to look at Stine while the others started making their way to their vehicles. "Blake, you've got the homeowner. Take Bruce with you and show him how a good interview gets done. We need everything this guy can tell you about his tenants. He's obviously an important witness, that's why I gave him to you. Go find him. Then have him tell you something that we don't already know so we can get this case moving. I'll be waiting to hear back from you."

Standing up from his chair, Stine nodded in response to the instructions he was given. He was pleased by the confidence that Paul had in him to handle such an important witness. Looking over at Davis, he hollered over the noise Vane's crew was making as they sifted through another portion of the growing pile of debris.

"Davis! On me! Let's go, we've got work to do."

Eager to make a good impression while working his first homicide case, Davis quickly fell in alongside his new partner as they walked towards the street. As they did, the two new partners barely had enough time to shake hands with each other. A more formal introduction would have to wait until later. Reaching the end of the driveway, they saw Lemieux babysitting their homeowner.

* * * * * *

As soon as Small finished with a few other minor tasks, she put together a list of names for each of Paul's three teams to interview once the neighborhood canvass was completed. These were names of people who had been found during the search of the victims' vehicles. Some of the names had been found written on scraps of paper, others on pay stubs and other pieces of paper, while others had been found during a search of each of the victims' Favorites list. A list stored inside each of their cell phones.

* * * * * *

Like it would be for the victims' parents, what the cops would soon learn, especially Paul and Bobby Ray, would be something they never would have expected.

Twelve

Steve's Gift

Before walking out to the road to see what the delivery of the ice machine was all about, Paul took a moment to finish off what had once been a cold bottle of water. The day's excessive humidity, along with a quickly rising temperature, had warmed the bottle's remaining contents considerably in a short period of time.

Throwing the plastic bottle in a trash can located just outside the tent, Paul paused to wipe the perspiration off his forehead again. He had already done so several times that morning and by now his handkerchief had become quite damp. Placing it back inside his right rear pocket, he walked to the far end of the tent to briefly check on Vane's progress.

"Morning, Don," Paul politely said as he greeted Sergeant Don Elmendorf. "I've been busy this morning, just as it looks like you have been. Sorry I didn't get a chance to say hello earlier. Everything going OK?"

A sixteen-year veteran of the GCSD, Elmendorf was the senior member of the department's Major Case Squad. His primary assignment was that of serving as the supervisor of the squad's crime scene processing truck. This morning, while several others were busy handling the debris from inside the damaged residence, it was his responsibility to document what occurred around the sifter. Like Vane, his civilian counterpart, Elmendorf was highly educated in both forensics and crime scene documentation. Prior to signing on with his department, he had graduated cum laude from Clemson University with a double major in Microbiology and Accounting.

"Morning, Paul. Yeah, everything is good so far." Elmendorf said as he stood next to Vane's sifter with a Canon .35mm camera dangling from around his neck. Taking pride in how he approached and thoroughly documented every crime scene he worked, the veteran detective had stationed himself by the opening of the tent where Vane's crew was working. Because of the soot and other airborne particulates that had been stirred up when the debris was dumped onto to the tarp or into the sifter, Elmendorf, like the others working close-by, had donned an air-purifying respirator to protect himself. From where he stood, he documented the sifting process through a series of photographs that would later be added to his report on how the scene had been processed. In addition to documenting what was taking place outside, over the two previous days he had worked with three crime scene techs to photograph, measure, and sketch each of the rooms on the first floor of the residence. While he had thoroughly photographed each of the rooms on the second floor, neither he nor anyone else had done much of a search in any of the bedrooms.

"Probably too early, but have you folks found anything yet?" Paul asked, his voice inferring that he was hoping to hear some good news from Vane and Elmendorf's efforts.

"Nothing that we've been hoping to find, not yet anyways." It was Vane's turn to answer one of Paul's questions. "We did find one very small piece of metal, not sure what it is yet. It's over there on the table in one of our plastic evidence vials. It could be part of a bullet's jacket, but it's hard to tell by just looking at it with the naked eye. We'll send it up to SLED with everything else we find. I'm sure they'll be able to tell us what it is."

Paul looked over at the small vial sitting on one of Vane's work tables, but made no effort to go and inspect it. It was not a find that was going to tell them much, so for now he chose to ignore it.

After watching Vane and a couple of his evidence techs work the sifter for a few more moments, Paul turned and started walking towards the mouth of the driveway. As he did, he saw Stine and Davis talking with the homeowner. A middle-aged white male with thick graying hair, Zerbola appeared to be in his mid-sixties. The three of them stood talking in the front yard in the shade provided by two large maple trees.

"Hey, partner! How y'all doin'?" The loud and unexpected voice startled Paul at first, but turning to confront it, he quickly connected the voice to the large round and unshaven face he saw smiling at him.

"Chubby! Chubby who works for Steve Alcott down at the marina," Paul said, somewhat embarrassed by the fact that he had not realized who it was that had been asking for him.

Paul could not help noticing that Chubby was dressed in his usual attire, a white sweat stained tee shirt and a pair of worn and faded bib overalls. Due to Chubby's girth, the shirt had four X's on its label to indicate its size. Like his dirty tee shirt, it was quite apparent his overalls had not seen the inside of a washing machine for some time.

Paul and Chubby had initially met when Paul purchased his first pontoon boat from his friend, Steve. It was Chubby who had cleaned the boat up, and made a few minor repairs to it, before Paul took ownership of it.

Walking up to where Chubby stood resting his large frame against the ice machine as it sat on the trailer, Paul smiled warmly as he extended his right hand. It was quickly swallowed up inside Chubby's large and somewhat dirty hand. Despite that, the two men shook hands for several seconds as they warmly greeted each other.

"Good to see you, Big Man! You doing OK these days?" Paul asked the person he had first taken a liking to months earlier.

"Doing fine, doing fine! How about y'all? I heard about that new boat them fellas gave you. You enjoying it?" Then nodding his head in the direction of the fire ravaged home, Chubby asked, "Them dead boys still in there?"

Dismissing Chubby's question about his new boat, Paul answered his friend's other question concerning the whereabouts of the victims. "No, they're not, Chubby. They're all at funeral homes now. Three of them are being buried the day after tomorrow. The other two funerals are taking place later in the week." Paul's response to his question caused the big man to nod again. This time it was done slightly more deliberately and much more respectfully.

"So what's this ice machine business all about?" Paul asked as he stared at the large commercial grade red and blue cooler sitting on the trailer. It was similar to the ones he had seen located outside several gas stations and convenience stores in the area. Lying next to it was a yellow extension cord that, in Paul's estimation, was least fifty feet in length. The small Lowboy style trailer sat low to the ground and had a mechanism in the front of it that allowed it to be cranked by hand so the back of the trailer could be lowered even closer to the ground. Doing so allowed the trailer to be slightly tilted from front to back, making it easier for whatever it was carrying to be off-loaded.

Seeing the confused look on Paul's face as he continued to stare at the ice machine caused Chubby to let out a brief laugh. "Steve sent it down here for y'all to use. We use it on occasion down at the marina when we're busy as all get-out, but most of the time it just sits in one of our storage rooms as a spare until we need it. He realizes you folks are gonna likely have some long hot days in front of ya so he had me load one side of it with some Gatorade and bottled water; the other side has ten or twelve bags of ice in it. The cooler doesn't make ice, but it will darn sure keep whatever y'all put in there real cold like. We just need to get it plugged in so it starts cooling down before the ice melts."

Taking a moment to wipe his forehead, Chubby, whose nickname accurately represented his size and weight, also took a moment to catch his breath. The hot humid morning was already taking a toll on him. "In case y'all ain't figured this out yet, it's dang hot out here today."

Since they had first met, Paul had already been on the receiving end of several gifts from his wealthy friend. The one that had meant the most to him was the deal Steve had given him on a pontoon boat as it helped fulfill a longtime dream of owning a boat. Besides that gift, Steve had also arranged for his friend to have a part-time job at *The Links of Pawleys Island*, a golf club he owned with a few of his friends. That job had given Paul the opportunity to play golf on a regular basis at one of the finest courses on the Grand Strand for free. While the job was fun to have, it often caused conflicts with Paul's busy schedule and he had given it up a few months earlier.

Standing in the road, Paul stared at the latest gift from his friend, one he was happy to share with those working the crime scene with him. "It's just Steve being Steve," Paul thought to himself as he opened one of the cooler's doors and saw the drinks it contained. "He's always thinking of ways he can help someone else. What a guy!" Steve and Paul had developed their friendship from the first day they met, often sharing meals and lazy afternoons with Donna and Bobby Ray.

"OK, Chubby, back this rig of yours down the driveway and I'll show you where to put it. We can plug it in to the generator we've got running in the backyard. I'll make it a point to call Steve later and express my thanks for his thoughtful gift."

* * * * * *

Despite the cold drinks, the heat and humidity, like several other issues, would continue to play havoc on Paul, Lt. Small, and the rest of the personnel working the case. Part of this havoc would include one frustrating obstacle that would consume far too much of their precious time.

Thirteen

The Victims

The hot morning had finally started to calm down for Paul after getting his personnel updated on the events of the fire and the shooting. It had taken longer than he wanted, but now each of the detectives knew what needed to be done. As the others left to either start the formal canvass of the neighborhood or, in Stine and Davis' case, to begin the interview with the owner of the home where the murders had taken place, Paul had met with Chubby. The drinks and the ice machine had been an unexpected, but thoughtful gift from a very generous benefactor.

"Too bad the world doesn't have more people like Steve Alcott in it. It certainly would be a better place to live." Paul thought as he set a file folder down on one of three long rectangular tables that had been set up at the opposite end of the tent from where Elmendorf and Vane were busy at work. The green colored file had steadily grown thicker and thicker since he had been asked to manage the investigation. It was now crammed with various intel print-outs, including copies of GCSD Calls for Service to the neighborhood, and several DMV print-outs related to the victims and their vehicles. Other information, including various reports generated mostly by the First Responders to the scene, was also included in the folder. Slowly, he slid out a stack of papers from inside the thick folder. They were held together by a large black paperclip, the kind Office Depot and Staples each sell by the thousands. While he had been told snippets about each of the victims, it was now time for him to finally get a look at who they really were. Far too many other tasks over the past day and a half had prevented him from doing so before now. They were tasks that should have been started far better, and far earlier, than they had been, but until recently he had no control over those concerns. The fact that they had not been started as they should have been was now a concern of his. It was not the way a multiple-murder investigation should have gotten started. That was a discussion he knew he would have to have with Bobby Ray in the coming days. Now he simply chose to take a healthy swig of Gatorade to quench his growing thirst before sitting down on a white plastic chair. Then, for either the tenth or twelfth or fifteenth time that morning, a quick wipe of his forehead followed. Like the heat he was learning to cope with, he was also learning to deal with the self-induced pressure of trying to solve a difficult murder investigation. It was pressure he always put on himself in situations like this one; pressure to fulfill obligations he felt he owed to those who had died.

Sitting back in his chair, Paul began studying the faces of the five young men who had been senselessly murdered. He did so at first by studying several digital photos that had been stored electronically by the South Carolina Department of Motor Vehicles. The photos had been used to create each of the victim's operator's licenses. These photos, known as Blow Backs in cop jargon, also contained the victims' dates of birth, their operator's number, and each of their respective addresses. Studying the info contained on each of the Blow Backs, he noticed that three of the victims, those who had the lease of the home in their names, had never taken the time to notify DMV of the current address where they had been living. Each Blow Back still displayed the address where they had lived in Myrtle Beach prior to moving to North Litchfield.

"That's kind of strange," Paul thought as he continued to scan each of the Blow Backs. "They've been living here for some time now and none of them took the time to notify DMV of their address change. Was that an act they simply gave little thought of doing, or were they planning on moving sometime soon?" It was a brief thought that only a veteran street cop would have. It was caused from years of trying to track down people who no longer resided at addresses they had provided to the Department of Motor Vehicles at one time or another. It was also a thought he soon paid little further attention to.

After looking at each of the Blow Backs for several minutes, and at a couple of other photos of each victim which Small and her investigators had obtained from friends and family members, Paul began reading the brief bios that had been prepared. What he read had been put together especially for him as he had come into the investigation well after the bodies had been removed from the scene. The photos, while useful for his needs of being able to put a face with a name for each of the bios he was reading, had primarily been obtained for identification needs at the scene during the early hours of the investigation. The intentionally set fire, just like some of the gunshots the victims had sustained, had done significant damage to three of the victims' facial features.

Victim #1 – Carl Diggs

A star in three different sports during each of his four years in high school, twenty-two year old Carl Diggs had lived in several small towns across South Carolina during his young life. The Diggs family had moved six times by the time Carl had completed eighth grade due to his father's career in the automotive business.

After severely injuring his left knee playing baseball the summer after his senior year of high school, Carl took a year off from school in the hopes that his injury would heal from the rehabilitation program he was participating in. The following year, he tried making it as a walk-on at the University of South Carolina after enduring a long and painful rehab period, but during his second day of practice with the football team's incoming freshmen, and with the other players who had been red-shirted the previous year, his knee buckled and he had to be carted off the field. An MRI two days later, as well as several consultations with two orthopedic surgeons over the course of the next month, confirmed what Carl already knew. His athletic career at the collegiate level was over before it really began.

Deciding to become a part-time student at the end of his freshmen year, Carl moved to the Myrtle Beach area with two of his friends after being accepted at Coastal Carolina University. First living in Myrtle Beach itself, in a tiny two bedroom apartment at the eastern end of Mr. Joe White Avenue, he and his friends, Tyler Johanson and Robert Tanner, soon signed a two-year lease to rent a home on Lakeshore Drive in North Litchfield. Their new monthly rent was significantly higher than it had been for the apartment they had been living in, but they were committed to living near the beach and in a neighborhood far nicer than their previous one.

Of all the victims, Carl was by far the most ambitious. Despite working two part-time jobs, ones which caused him to work over sixty hours each week, he had recently decided to change schools. Five weeks before he was murdered, he had started taking computer classes at Horry-Georgetown Technical College, in Conway. A gifted student in high school, he had decided to change majors in the hopes of becoming a computer engineer.

Like it did for the other sets of parents, the news of their son's murder devastated Jill and Timothy Diggs. The loss of their only son would cause them to be inconsolable for months.

On both the rough sketch and the finished drawings of the crime scene's interior rooms, each would simply refer to Carl Diggs as number one. He would become the first victim listed in all of the reports submitted regarding this investigation.

Victim #2 – Tyler 'Ty' Johanson

A year younger than Carl Diggs, and not nearly as gifted an athlete, Tyler had first met his friend the year they entered high school together. Called Ty by his family and friends, Johanson was also a gifted student who had skipped seventh grade after testing revealed his scholastic capabilities, especially in the field of mathematics, were much more advanced than most of his fellow students.

After graduating from high school, and despite receiving a handful of scholarship offers to attend other more prestigious schools, Johanson decided to continue his studies at Coastal Carolina University. Unlike most of his friends, he planned on going to graduate school to get an advanced degree in mathematics. His goal in life, besides living close to the beach with his friends, was to become an electrical engineer. He had set that goal for himself during his sophomore year in high school. His dream was to someday work for NASA.

While a gifted student in college as well, Johanson had experienced a few minor brushes with the law. Despite being relatively minor in nature, they were ones which greatly disappointed his parents, both of whom were physicians with busy practices in the Conway and Myrtle Beach areas of South Carolina. As doctors and parents they frowned heavily on their son's use of marijuana, and liked it even less when his occasional binges were mixed with heavy alcohol consumption. But despite their concerns, Ty continued to excel academically.

Johanson had signed the lease as one of the renters of the home for two reasons. While they had already been living together, for years Diggs and he had talked about living close to the beach before career and family obligations caused them to settle down in life. He had also done so to further distance himself from having to live under the close scrutiny of his parents. While they had great plans for their son's future, their plans were not the ones Ty had chosen to follow. Unlike his parents, he had little interest in becoming a doctor.

Johanson's body was found in the living room area of the home he had rented. His ankles, just like his wrists, had been bound together with rope. A single piece of grey duct tape was found covering his mouth. The final case report would later conclude that he had likely been the first victim the shooter had encountered. The same report would also state that it was quite likely the tape had been placed over his mouth to prevent him from being able to warn his friends about the danger existing inside their home.

Tyler Johanson's body was found with a single gunshot wound to the back of the head. Like his friends, he had been shot execution style.

Victim #3 – Robert Tanner

Close to six foot three inches in height, the blond haired twenty-three year old Robert Tanner had first met Diggs and Johanson at one of the two bars he worked at. Regular customers at several of the bars lining the waterfront in Murrells Inlet, Diggs and Johanson, like several of their other friends, had been drawn to Tanner because of his friendly personality, and for the number of pretty girls who were attracted to him on a nightly basis.

Over a three-month period, Tanner had introduced his newest friends to several of his female admirers. It was during this time that Tanner, Diggs, and Johanson, often accompanied by an assortment of pretty blonds and brunettes, would burn the midnight oil several nights a week partying together.

A lifelong Pittsburgh Penguin fan, Tanner had relocated to Myrtle Beach from Pennsylvania after deciding college life was not for him. While still technically considered a part-time student at Coastal Carolina University due to two courses he had taken there, he had not enrolled in any others during the past two semesters. Shortly after meeting his new friends, he learned they had started to look for a new place to rent. With his own lease soon about to expire, Tanner had pitched an offer to join them in renting a place together. It was an offer Diggs and Johanson found too attractive to pass on.

With two steady paychecks, and an even steadier supply of good tips coming in each night due to both his good looks and the stiff drinks he poured, Tanner had a regular source of income that significantly exceeded what his friends generally took home each week. Needing a place to live, he proposed to his two new friends that he would pay half the rent each month, as well as his share of the utilities, in exchange for the largest bedroom and the best parking spot. His other contribution, he promised them, would be a steady supply of pretty girls for the parties they would occasionally host. They were terms Diggs and Johanson eagerly accepted.

Like the body of his friend that lied not far from his, Tanner's body had also been found with his wrists and ankles tied together. Like his friend, a single piece of grey tape covered his mouth. The only difference was that the EMT's, as well as the cops who had helped to remove his body from within the still smoldering residence, had noticed his face and hands had fresh cuts and scrapes on them. These same wounds would also be strongly noted in the Medical Examiner's final report concerning Tanner's autopsy. It was obvious to everyone who viewed his body that he had fought with whoever had killed him before being shot.

Unlike Johanson, Tanner had been shot twice; once in the back of the head and once between his shoulder blades.

Victim #4 – James Robinson

James Robinson was different in several ways than the other four victims. Born and raised in poverty in Georgetown County, he had come from a broken home. Until he reached his mid-teens, the twenty-three year old had never experienced living in a stable and caring family environment. Never knowing his real father, his mother had died when he was only three years old after years of heavy alcohol and drug abuse. Shuttled between family members for much of his early life, he escaped that difficult life only after the state of South Carolina finally realized he needed a better environment to live in than what his extended family had been able to provide.

Later, from the age of twelve to fifteen, James lived with two sets of foster parents who provided a somewhat better life for him. It was during this time that he finally had a bed to call his own. It was also the first time that he was fed on a regular basis. These foster parents were the first people in his life who really cared about him, exposing him to what life as a family was supposed to be about.

At the age of sixteen, James, despite all of the issues and problems he had experienced far too early in life already, was finally placed with his last set of foster parents. It was here, in Pawleys Island, that he began to blossom. For the first time in his life, this set of parents would give him his first real taste of how parents genuinely love and care for their children. Despite his long ordeal, James had never been anything but a happy child and, surprisingly, a gifted artist.

During and after high school, James continued to develop his skills as a self-taught artist. Several libraries, as well as a handful of small art galleries across Georgetown and Horry counties, began exhibiting his work. At the prompting of several of his teachers, he had also begun displaying his work at local fairs and festivals.

To make ends meet, James had become a waiter after graduating from high school. A free spirit in life, he often changed jobs whenever the mood struck him. It was during one of these moves that he met Robert Tanner. It was through his new friend that he also became fast friends with Diggs and Johanson, and later with their mutual friend, Trevor Gilmour.

James had been a frequent visitor to the home rented by his three friends. He often spent time there by himself while the others were working or off with their girlfriends, as the quiet neighborhood allowed him a place to paint without being disturbed.

Found on the kitchen floor, James' body had been badly burned in the fire. While a large serrated kitchen knife was found lying on the floor next to him, there was nothing found at the scene to indicate that he had been successful in using it to defend himself. He had been shot once in the chest and once in the back of the head. In the kitchen sink, investigators found six paint brushes that he had apparently been cleaning when he was first confronted by his murderer.

Victim #5 – Trevor Gilmour

Trevor Gilmour had come to Myrtle Beach four years earlier in hopes of finding a way to the PGA Tour. Twenty-two years old at the time of his death, he had moved to South Carolina from Michigan. In high school, he had been the best golfer on both his high school's golf team, and in the Upper 'A' Division of the league his school's sports teams competed in. In both his junior and senior years, he had been ranked as Michigan's best junior golfer.

Gilmour had first met Diggs, and then the others through his new friend. The two had met when Diggs first started taking golf lessons from him at the golf academy where he worked. Sharing the same interests in sports, and in pretty girls, they had hit it off from the start. Soon he began socializing with Diggs and the others during visits to area bars and dance clubs.

Unlike Robinson though, Gilmour was an infrequent visitor to the home his friends shared. While he liked to have a good time in life as often as possible, Gilmour was focused on both his job and his career goals. He had been wise enough to realize that late nights of partying with his friends would likely lead to problems with his early morning job at the golf academy. Recently moving up to the First Assistant's position due to his skill as a golfer, and because of his ability to interact with players from all age groups, he had also recently qualified to start playing on both the PGA Latinoamerica Tour, and the Coastal Player's Tour. While his new friends had set goals in life for themselves, Gilmour was the closest of them to finally being able to realize his.

Gilmour's body had been found under several pieces of overturned furniture in the living room. To the cops and firemen who found him, it was clear that he had put up a struggle before being shot. He was found clothed in the same golf attire he had worn to work that day. Unlike some of his friends, neither his wrists or ankles had been bound by rope, nor had his mouth been covered with tape. He had died after being shot twice in the back of the head.

✳ ✳ ✳ ✳ ✳ ✳

Paul shook his head in disgust as he finished reading what little he had been given on each of the victims. Outside of what he read about Johanson's minor drug problem, and about a couple of moving violations that Tanner and Gilmour had each received years ago, there was nothing to suggest the victims had been involved in any sort of illegal activity of any kind. Placing the large black paperclip back on the papers he had read, Paul realized something else had caused these young men to be murdered.

"This has got emotion written all over it." Paul thought as he angrily jammed his hands inside his front pants pockets. As he did, he stared down hard at the file folder lying on the table in front of him. The papers inside it, some of them graphically describing how each of the victims had died, were ones he thought he would never have to read the likes of again after retiring. "This is personal . . . it has to be about a girl . . . or a slight of some kind perhaps, but it's something along those lines." As he continued to think about what he had just read regarding how the victims' bodies had each been found, one last thought entered his mind. "Whoever did this has likely been thinking this out for some time now. The rope and duct tape were obviously brought to the scene by the shooter as part of his or her plan. No one comes to someone else's home carrying those kinds of items, as well as a weapon and who knows what else, unless you've got a plan to use them. In this case, a very sick plan to kill some innocent kids."

Moving back away from the table, Paul took a swig of the Gatorade he had started to drink just before sitting down to read his folder of painful notes and paperwork. The once cold drink had now turned warm due to the day's rising temperature. Despite the less than pleasant taste it now had, the warm liquid still served a purpose. It quickly washed away the bad taste that had been left in his mouth from what he had just finished reading.

"Hey, Paul!" Stine's loud voice suddenly broke the tension Paul was feeling from reading about the victims and how they had died. "We might have something to get working on. Meet us over there!"

Paul could not help noticing the brisk manner in which Stine was walking as he made his way towards one of the far corners of the victims' backyard. Then, as Stine turned to look back at him, he saw his friend pointing to what looked like an abandoned flower bed. As he moved towards the spot Stine was pointing to, he heard orders being barked to a uniformed deputy who was walking several steps behind them. Out in front of the deputy, and walking at a slightly slower pace, was Detective Davis. With him was Zerbola, the property owner.

"Ray, get Mr. Zerbola something cold to drink. Have him take a seat under the tent. I'll call you when we're ready for you." Stine's comments, along with the briskness of his stride, aroused Paul's curiosity immensely. Quickly he fell in behind Stine as they made their way across the backyard.

"What has he found? What does he know?" Those were several of the questions racing through Paul's mind as he closed in on the position where Stine now stood. He hoped the answers to those questions, and to others which would soon follow, would help them get started on learning who their shooter was.

Fourteen

The Shed

"See here, Paul!" Stine said as he pointed to a slightly raised pad of crushed three-quarter inch black stone. "This is what our homeowner was telling us about."

Staring down at the pad of stones for a few seconds, Paul noticed it was roughly twelve by twelve feet in size. Around three sides of it he saw that an equally thick layer of brown mulch, one roughly three feet in width, was now being invaded by a variety of weeds. Several flowers and three small shrubs, long since dead, had been planted within the mulch bed at one time. It was obvious they, like several other nearby plantings, had not been cared for in some time. As he continued to stare at what Stine had pointed to, Paul noticed Small had joined them in the backyard.

"What's up guys?" Small curiously asked as she tucked her reporter's style notebook into the small of her back. "You guys find something?"

"I'm not sure, Audrey. I'm waiting to be enlightened by Blake. I'm hoping there is more to know about this pile of stones and dead flowers than what we're seeing right now." Looking at Stine rather cautiously, Paul added, "Please tell us there is, Blake."

Stine smiled at the confused looks he saw on the faces of the two cops standing with him. "Davis and I were interviewing the homeowner about everything we could think of regarding the kids living here. We asked him questions about the house, visitors they had here, the neighborhood . . . you know, all the usual stuff we normally ask. We weren't learning a heck of a lot from him, but then Bruce asked him about anything unusual that might have taken place here recently. That's when Zerbola told us about this." Stine again pointed at the pad of stones near their feet.

Paul stared down at the ground again before looking over at Stine. He still had no idea of what he was supposed to be seeing. "Just what did he tell you about this pile of stones and dead flowers, Blake? Something interesting, maybe even useful, I hope."

Standing quietly off to the side as the others listened to what his partner was telling them, Davis found humor in Paul's comment. Quickly he let out a brief laugh, one that also caused Small to chuckle as well.

"No, Paul, he didn't." Stine replied somewhat sarcastically. "That's unless you want to know about a shed that caught fire here about three months ago." Catching himself, Stine then added, "It didn't catch fire because of anything that was stored inside of it; it was intentionally set on fire. At least, that's what this Zerbola guy told us."

"OK, now you've got my attention. Tell us more." Paul said as he started walking around the pad of stones where the shed had once stood. As he did, his eyes focused directly on the pad, and then on the mulch surrounding it. Twice he gently kicked at the layer of brown mulch with his right foot. Doing so revealed a layer of pine straw under the mulch, one that still had the telltale signs of having once been burnt. Seeing the burnt layer of pine straw caused Paul to drop to one knee to inspect it as he listened to what Stine was telling him.

Stine, the veteran detective whose face was showing the stubble from three-days of not shaving, spent close to ten minutes describing what Davis and he had learned from Zerbola. As he spoke, he told Paul and Small about a small cookout the victims had hosted for several of their friends the weekend after St. Patrick's Day. He further explained that during the day's warm temperature, two of the victims, joined by three of their guests, had been playing Frisbee in their backyard when a neighbor's dog ran over and began chasing them as they were playing catch. Stine continued to describe how Zerbola had told them this incident with the dog lasted for several minutes. "Mr. Zerbola told us he heard about this from two of the vics a couple of days after it happened. He was also told that this aggressive dog, who had been barking quite loudly as it chased after the kids, nearly bit a couple of them before running off with their Frisbee."

Pointing to it at first, Stine then told the others how two of the kids, Johanson and Tanner, had finally gotten up the courage to walk through the tree line, one jammed with pricker bushes and other similar types of vegetation, to the neighbor's backyard so they could retrieve their Frisbee. Once there they were rudely challenged by the dog's owner as to why they were on his property. "According to Mr. Zerbola, the kids told him the dog, which had been tied to a tree by the time they got there, continued to bark loudly while they were trying to explain to its owner what had happened, and that they were simply there to retrieve their Frisbee. Supposedly the homeowner got pissed off by their presence and after a few more words were exchanged, he tried escalating the matter by pushing and shoving them. The kids allegedly told Zerbola they didn't go there looking for trouble, just their Frisbee. After they found it, they tried leaving but the dog's owner kept threatening them, telling them he'd treat them even worse if he ever saw them on his property again." Then Stine spoke about one more thing Zerbola had told them. "Supposedly later that afternoon while the kids and their friends were having their cookout, this neighbor of theirs walked into their backyard and started yelling at them for a few minutes, again threatening them with physical harm if they ever came back on his property."

As Stine finished speaking, Paul exchanged looks with Small before looking back at Stine and Davis.

"Anything else?" Paul asked. "When did this shed go up in flames, do we know?"

"Less than a week after the Frisbee incident," Davis replied. "According to our homeowner, the Midway Fire Department down in Pawleys ended up responding to the fire. Two sides of it were burning pretty good by the time they got here."

Still down on one knee, Paul began to poke around in the mulch and pine straw with his fingers. As he did, he spoke to Davis without looking up. "Bruce, you're the local guy here. Get in touch with the FD, and get a copy of their report. Get whatever they have on the fire, and then see if your department responded as well. I want to know if the FD made a determination on how the fire started."

"OK, boss. Anything else?" Davis asked before being surprised by Paul's next comment. It was one which caught Small and Stine by surprise as well.

"Yeah, you better get Elmendorf and Vane over here just to be safe." As he finished speaking, Paul looked up at the others standing around him. In his right hand, he held up a partially smoked Parliament cigarette for them to see. "Any of our vics smoke? There's at least five other butts mixed in with this pine straw. They're all the same flavor as this one. We better have Don and Doug take a few photos and then have them take the butts as exhibits until we know for sure what we have here. Best they sketch this area as well. Who knows if these butts have any connection to what took place inside the house, but let's play it safe for now and assume they do."

As Paul stood up, he looked to see Stine staring through the tree line in the right rear of the victims' backyard. Several nearby homes were partially visible through the dense foliage.

"Which house is it, Blake? The one with the green roof?"

"Yep. That's it. That's where Mr. Zerbola says the guy with the dog lives."

Paul thought for a moment before speaking to Small. "Audrey, I think you told me Griffin and Edwards were doing the canvass on the street where our new best friend lives. Dial them up on

Griff's cell and tell them what we've just learned. Tell Griff I want them to try and find out if our guy smokes Parliaments. After they talk to this guy, I want them to call you with an update on what they've learned. You know . . . his name, address, arrest history, and whatever else they can find out. Tell them the dog owner is their main focus right now." Turning to Stine and Davis, Paul gave them their next set of marching orders. "Finish up getting your statement from Mr. Zerbola. See if he knows if any of our vics smoked Parliaments or, for that matter, if he does. If he doesn't know the answer to that question, call Tommy Scozz and have him find out from the kids' parents if any of their sons smoked. If they did, we obviously need to know what kind of cigarettes they liked. Make sure you get hot on this cigarette issue ASAP!"

As he finished with his instructions, Paul watched as Elmendorf began photographing the immediate area around where the shed had stood. With help from Vane and two evidence techs, the small area was then sketched for any evidentiary needs that might later arise. Then they began to search through the mulch and pine straw for cigarette butts or anything else that might have caused the shed to catch fire. When they were done, they had collected seven partially smoked Parliament cigarettes and one used match.

* * * * * *

What Elmendorf and Vane found, along with what Griffin and Edwards would also find out, would start the investigation moving forward very quickly. They all would be very surprised by what they would soon learn.

Fifteen

Cotton

The neighborhood canvass being done on Bobcat Drive by Detectives Frank Griffin and Darren Edwards was methodically being completed just as they had done so many other times during their careers. While they now had a possible suspect to focus on, they gave no outward signs to anyone who might have been watching them that they were anxious to interview the single male occupant who was living in the house with the green roof.

Detective Frank Griffin, a stocky but well-built narc from the North Myrtle Beach Police Department, was one of the cops Paul had asked Renda to have assigned to the investigation. He had first met Griffin, a no-nonsense in-your-face kind of cop when he had to be, during the Melkin investigation. It was Griffin, along with Sgt. Kent Wilson, a narcotics supervisor from the Myrtle Beach Police Department, who had conducted the interviews with Ricky Frazier. The critical points of information they had sweated out of Frazier had significantly helped to solve that investigation. It was also because of Griffin's work ethic and, perhaps most importantly, because of his interview and interrogation skills that Paul had wanted him working this investigation as well.

Griffin's partner, Detective Darren Edwards, twelve years junior to him in years of service, was someone who had quickly earned a good reputation as being a cop who never gave up on a case. A large man with reddish hair who stood well over six feet tall, Edwards had previously demonstrated his investigative skills to Bobby Ray when he briefly filled in on the Major Case Squad, covering vacations and other leaves taken by squad members. Whether working as a uniformed deputy or as a temporary fill-in on Bobby Ray's squad, he had earned a reputation as someone who possessed the ability to dig through the minutiae of a tough case he was working on to find the facts needed to solve them. Because of that, he had affectionately been tagged with the nickname of Digger by his fellow detectives.

After speaking with Small about what needed to be done prior to concentrating their efforts on the dog owner, Griffin and Edwards accidentally came across a mailman whose route included the North Litchfield neighborhood they were working. In a ten-minute conversation with Larry Bishop, a Pawleys Island resident who had been delivering mail in the area for the past fourteen years, they learned who the sole occupant was that had been getting his mail delivered to 287 Bobcat Drive for the past several years.

"I don't know the guy very well," Bishop told them from behind the steering wheel of his small red, white, and blue postal truck. "He's signed for a few packages over the years and once in a while I'll see him picking up his mail, but that's about all I know about him. I can tell you the guy is not the friendliest person in the world. Almost everyone else around here gives me the occasional wave now and then when they see me, but not him. He never waves. I had some words with him a couple of years ago about that damn Doberman Pinscher of his . . . damn thing tried getting into my truck that day . . . but that's really the only time I've ever spoken with him. I believe he works for some type of a construction company up in Murrells Inlet as I see one of their trucks parked in his driveway once in a while. About the only other thing I can tell you is that I refer to him as the smokestack guy. He always seems to have a cigarette in his mouth . . . you know, seems like his mouth always has smoke coming out of it, just like a smokestack. Disgusting habit, if you ask me."

"Thanks for the info, Larry, you've been a big help. Just do us a favor, will you?" Edwards asked as he and Griffin shook hands with Bishop. "Don't let him know we talked. We owe you for this."

* * * * * *

The loud noise of his dog barking as soon as it heard the two men walking in the street out in front of his home caused Phillip 'Cotton' Horbin to abruptly open his front door. As he did, he saw both of them as they approached from his right.

In his mid-thirties, Horbin was known to his family, as well as to his few friends and co-workers, as Cotton. Years earlier, at a fairly young age, his hair had prematurely turned completely white, causing his maternal grandmother to start calling him Cotton. It was a nickname that he did not particularly care for, but it was also one he never told people not to use.

As they walked closer to Horbin's driveway, first Edwards, then Griffin, both noticed several cigarette butts lying along the edge of the curb in front of their suspect's mailbox. A quick look at the mailbox number showed it corresponded with the number displayed to the left of their suspect's front door.

Both cops also quickly noticed that unlike the other homes on the street, their suspect's yard, like the Palmetto bushes which lined most of his property, had not been taken care of for some time. At the far end of the driveway, they also noticed a large limb had fallen off a nearby pine tree. Its brown and dead needles were an indication it had been left lying there for some time. Next to it sat four overflowing black garbage cans and three old truck tires. Stacked next to the garbage cans, the tires appeared to have been left sitting there for an extended period of time as wind had caused a large pile of pine needles to accumulate up and around the bottom tire.

Walking slowly down the steps outside his front door as he saw the two men approaching, Horbin flicked a cigarette onto his front lawn before cutting Griffin and Edwards off before they could reach them. Then he greeted them rather rudely. "You fellas looking for something? Because if it's trouble you're looking for, I'm here to give it to ya! So why don't you both get the . . . " Spotting the badge Griffin displayed on his belt, and then the Sig Sauer pistol strapped next to it, the burly Horbin stopped talking before he could finish with what was on his mind.

"Lost? Is that what you were about to say, Buddy Boy?" Griffin asked sternly as he glared back at the fat unshaven wise-ass who stood on the cracked concrete sidewalk directly in front of him. The veteran cop was already less than pleased by the welcome he and his partner had received. Now he took a moment to set the tone for the rest of the discussion he was about to have with their suspect. "You may talk to the bible thumpers who come calling on you like that, but you're not talking to my partner or me like that. Understand?"

Pausing alongside his partner, Edwards flashed his badge to Horbin. "Just so there's no misunderstanding over who we are, or who it is you're talking to." Finished making his point, Edwards clipped his shiny badge back on his belt.

"Whatever!" Horbin replied, clearly not impressed by the presence of two cops standing in front of him. "What's the beef today, or are you two jerks out selling tickets for some kind of asshole cop party? Because if you are, I'm not buying! So why don't you two morons just beat feet and leave me alone."

Horbin turned to leave, but Griffin caught him by the arm and spun him around before he could take another step. Like his partner, his dislike for their suspect was growing by the moment.

"Just a minute, Chief!"

Already doing a slow burn over Horbin's attitude, Griffin did his best to keep from exploding. Repeatedly he reminded himself of why they were there and of the information they needed. "I'll get even with this shithead some other time," he thought as he forced himself to calm down.

"Mr. Horbin," Griffin asked, trying to be the professional cop he was, "have you heard about the five young men who lived on the next street over? They were murdered the other day." As the question was posed, Edwards' eyes tried peering through the two bed sheets that served as curtains in the front window of Horbin's home.

"I heard about it. Why? You think I did it because I had a run-in with a couple of those jerks a few months back?" Horbin's response was an angry one, spit and saliva flew from his mouth as he answered Griffin's question. Still angry as he finished speaking, he roughly wiped his mouth with the back of his right forearm.

"I didn't say that, nor are we implying that. We're just doing a canvass of the neighborhood to see if you or any of your neighbors saw or heard anything that day." Griffin could tell his words had a slight calming effect on their suspect, and he paused for a brief moment before speaking again. "How about it, did you see or hear anything suspicious that day, Mr. Horbin?"

"Didn't see a thing. Didn't hear anything either. Can't say I'd tell you even if I did. As you can probably tell, I don't care too much for cops; you two included. Besides, that damn dog of mine barks all the time. You two jerks must have heard him barking when you walked up here, didn't you? Freakin' dog is getting to be a pain-in-my-ass, just like my ex."

Edwards smiled briefly at what Horbin had said. "I know what you mean, Chief. I've got one of them myself, an ex that is, not a dog." Then realizing their suspect had just given him an opening, Edwards asked, "You mind if I go take a look at this barking dog of yours?"

Horbin eyed Edwards suspiciously for a moment but then gave him permission to do so. "Just stay clear of him by about ten to twelve feet, that's how long his leash is. I ain't paying for no torn clothing or bites."

As Edwards walked away, Horbin hollered one more warning to him. "Remember, this is private property. Don't go looking in my windows or touch anything you ain't supposed to be touching. Get a warrant if you want to do anything more than look at my damn dog."

Independent of each other, Griffin and Edwards immediately made mental notes of the words Horbin had just used.

"Mr. Horbin, do you own any guns?" Griffin asked as his partner moved towards the backyard where Horbin's dog was tied to a pine tree. Excited by the presence of two strangers standing in the yard, the black colored Doberman had already worked himself into quite a lather by the time Edwards first saw him.

"Yeah, I do." Horbin glared hard at Griffin now, but offered little in the way of any additional information.

"Mind telling me what kind they are?"

"Yeah, I do." Horbin answered as he folded his arms across his chest defiantly. "I've got a permit for them. They're all registered like you assholes require. Go look them up if you want to know what I own."

Finished answering Griffin's question, Horbin watched as Griffin now took off his sunglasses and gently placed them down on the sidewalk on top of his notepad.

"Listen, Buddy Boy, I've got a job to do, and I'm going to do it whether assholes like you like it or not. Part of that job means asking questions to shitheads like you, understand? I don't like being here anymore than you like me standing here asking you these questions you consider stupid. But I'm going to ask whatever questions I have to ask to find out who killed those kids, and you're going to answer them for me. Hopefully more politely than you have been. If you're looking for a problem, then let's go out back and have a go at it, but if you'd rather just answer my questions, then let's get this over with. It's your choice, answer them for me or let's go out back, but I'm not leaving until I get the answers I want. Then I'll be out of here and I'll move onto the next shithead on my list that I have to ask these same stupid freakin' questions to. That will make both of us happy, won't it?" By the time he finished, Griffin's face was less than three inches from Horbin's. He was pissed, sweating heavily, and red in the face, but he had made his point with his suspect. The truth was he was also hoping Horbin would accept his invitation to continue their discussion in the backyard. A boxer in his younger days, Griffin was anxious to have a few minutes alone with their suspect, hoping those few minutes would teach Horbin to be more respectful of cops like him.

Horbin flashed a brief smirk at the cop who had just talked to him like no other cop ever had. In life, he had zero respect for authority, including his parents, had even less for cops, but Griffin had just earned a token amount of his respect. "I've got a few . . . three .22 caliber pistols, a .380 H & K pistol, a Beretta 9 millimeter, and a couple of shotguns. Maybe I've got others and maybe I don't. You figure the rest out, but I'm telling you none of my guns killed them kids, and neither did I. I'd like to be able to tell you that the thought of killing them smart-ass punks never crossed my mind, but one thing I'm not is a liar. Them kids pissed me off plenty that day, but I didn't kill them."

"Know who did?" Griffin calmly asked as he wiped beads of sweat off his forehead.

"Nope!"

"Know who burned down the shed they had in their backyard?"

For a brief moment, Horbin smiled wryly in response to Griffin's question. "I've been waiting for one of you two cops to ask me that stupid question, officer. Sadly, for you, I don't. But like I've already told you, it wasn't me that did anything to them kids."

As Griffin bent down to pick up his sunglasses and pad off the sidewalk, Edwards came walking around from the rear of Horbin's home. As he did, Griffin noticed the brief, but barely noticeable wink his partner quickly flashed at him. It was one that said, *"I've got what we need. Let's get out of here."*

"That's a nasty dog you've got there, Mr. Horbin. Thanks for letting me take a look at him."

Horbin stared at the two cops for a brief moment before waving them off with another of his rude comments. "If you cops are done asking me your stupid-ass questions, I've got to go. I'm due at work later on and I haven't had my lunch yet."

"Yeah," Griffin answered sarcastically, "we're done for now. Thanks for all of your hospitality. We *really appreciate* the support you've given to your local law enforcement professionals."

Horbin easily detected the sarcasm he heard in Griffin's last statement. Stopping part-way up his front steps, he flipped the two cops walking down his driveway the middle finger salute.

The fact that neither of them saw it meant little to him. He had flipped off the cops he hated and that meant more to him than anything.

* * * * * *

Stopping at the end of Horbin's driveway, the two detectives compared notes as they watched their suspect walk inside his house. For a brief moment, they saw him watching them as he stared out from behind the sheets he used as curtains in his living room window. Soon the sheets were pulled tightly back together. Tight enough so prying eyes could not see in or out of them.

"Well? What'd you find?" Griffin eagerly asked his young partner.

"You mean besides the piles and piles of dog crap in the backyard?"

Griffin laughed as he looked down at Edwards' shoes. "Come on, Darren, you know what I mean. I saw the wink you gave me, what did you find?"

As his partner started walking towards Horbin's mailbox, Griffin followed him. Stopping not far from the single mailbox, Edwards extended his right arm and then opened his tightly closed fist.

"Just this," Edwards said as he waited for a response from Griffin. "This and fifty or sixty more just like it. They're all over the backyard."

Griffin stared at the partially smoked Parliament cigarette butt that Edwards now held in his hand. The same markings were on it as the ones Paul had found on the ground next to where the victims' shed once stood. While he knew its importance, he also knew how that one partially smoked cigarette could have had a negative impact on their investigation.

"Darren, you should know we can't use that, toss it away. We'd need to have a search warrant in order to seize that or any of those other butts you saw out there. If we tried using them against him we'd have Horbin's attorneys screaming about them being seized during an illegal search. We're not going to jeopardize all of our hard work by using those, besides there's no reason to." After giving his partner a quick refresher course on the rules of proper search and seizure techniques, Griffin surprised Edwards with his next comment as he started walking along the curb in front of their suspect's residence.

"Let's use these instead."

As Edwards tossed the butt he found in Horbin's backyard out into the middle of the street, Griffin pulled a handkerchief out of his back pocket. The young detective then watched as his partner unfolded it as he dropped to one knee on the side of the road. Rather quickly, Griffin picked up four partially smoked Parliament cigarettes that were lying in the road close to Horbin's mailbox. Soon they were secured within the white handkerchief.

"While there's no doubt we need a warrant to pick up the ones in our buddy's backyard, we don't need one for these. These we found lying on a public street; they were obviously thrown away by whoever smoked them. In the eye of the law, that means they fall under the rules of abandoned property. It also means whoever smoked them, and then threw them away, has no expectation of privacy or any other rights associated with them. They're ours now. Score one for the good guys!"

Edwards smiled at his partner's quick thinking and resourcefulness as they moved further away from Horbin's residence. "I never argue with someone who knows what they're doing."

"When you were in the backyard, did you find anything else besides the butts you saw?" Griffin asked as he finished securing their new found evidence within his handkerchief.

"Asshole's pick-up truck was locked up tighter than his brain is, but I managed to see two hard packs of Parliaments inside it. One was in plain view on the dashboard and the other, the one that looked to be unwrapped, was in one of the cup holders between the front seats. Not bad, huh?"

Griffin nodded at the good news his partner told him. Quietly he ran several pieces of information through his brain. Among that information was what he had learned about Horbin owning a handful of guns, as well as the other incriminating evidence that Edwards and he had found. His years of investigative experience were now telling him they had found enough to start the next phase of the investigation.

"Darren, let's go see Paul and Audrey about what we've just learned. We'll get back to the canvas later."

Sixteen

Bobby Ray's First Visit

Waiting on the front porch of the victims' home, Paul and Small watched through the opened front door as Elmendorf and three evidence techs processed the living room in their hunt for any evidence. Unlike the investigators they were watching, Paul and his partner were simply trying to stay out of the way as they waited to hear word on how the canvas was progressing.

As they stood there watching, two large portable exhaust fans vented air contaminated with a variety of particulates out two side windows of the residence. While heavily charred from the fire, especially the area close to the kitchen, the side of the room by a decorative, but fake fireplace had only been scorched roughly three feet off the floor. While some suspended matter from the fire continued to linger in the air, a great deal of it had been disturbed when the techs swept the floors in the nearby kitchen, front hallway, and living room of accumulated debris. The remaining furniture in each of the rooms, including partially burnt pillows and blankets found on two large chairs, had all been hand-searched for signs of shell casings and spent rounds. Those efforts had revealed nothing of any evidentiary value. Now as Elmendorf's crew filled two large black garbage cans with the remaining debris, one of the techs suddenly reached into one of the cans that were destined for Vane's sifter.

"Hey," the female tech's excited voice yelled out, "I found one! I found a shell casing!" Quickly the casing was held up between the dirty white thumb and forefinger of the glove she was wearing for others to see.

After the casing had been set down on a piece of clean white paper that sat on top of one of Elmendorf's small work tables, a vinyl six-inch Sirchie evidence ruler was placed next to it. The small ruler had a tape measure printed on it by the manufacturer to allow items of evidence to have a scale next to them when they were photographed. After photographing the casing from every angle possible, Elmendorf, with Vane assisting him, carefully studied it through a handheld magnifying glass.

"It needs a good cleaning from being caught up in the fire, but we need to leave that to the Firearms Examiners up at SLED to do for us." Vane stated as he continued to look at the casing through the magnifying glass. "It looks to be a .380 caliber casing that's in relatively good shape. Let's hope our friends at SLED can tell us more about it."

Paul heard the comments Vane offered from where he continued to stand by the front doorway, but his focus was now on what else might be inside the two garbage cans. "Let's hope there's more of the same in there," he said as he pointed at the cans nearby.

As Small and two of the evidence techs speculated on how many other casings might have gotten mixed up with the debris sitting in the garbage cans, Paul asked a question loud enough for everyone to hear over the noise of the two fans. It was one that was not directed at anyone in particular.

"I know you've swept the kitchen floor clean, but have any of you bothered to roll the refrigerator away from the wall, or have any of you pulled out the stove's bottom drawer? Have we checked those two locations yet for any shell casings?"

The blank stares his question received from everyone standing around the small table in the living room quickly gave Paul his answer. It was not the type of response that he had hoped for.

"OK, boys and girls, let's do that then. I mean now." Paul said, his raised voice clearly reflecting the frustration he was feeling at the moment. "Instead of playing a damn guessing game on what's going to turn up when we run the debris from the cans through the sifter, let's get back to work and process the kitchen like we should be doing." Pausing for a moment to let his anger die down, he then continued with his instructions. "Let the crap in the cans wait until tomorrow. It's not going anywhere overnight. Get the kitchen done tonight; *like right now*. Take whatever photos you feel you need and do whatever else you need to do to get the job done, but get it done right this time. I don't want anything missed."

As Vane and Elmendorf finished their Chain of Custody needs with the first shell casing that had been found, the techs, with Small following them, walked to the kitchen to complete Paul's instructions. It took less than three minutes, but soon Small's excited voice confirmed what Paul had suspected.

"Oh my goodness! We found one! We found another one!" In another short moment, she cried out again. "We found another one!"

Walking quickly back into the living room, Small updated Paul and the others on what they had found in the kitchen. One shell casing had been found under the refrigerator, and the other had been found after the drawer to the stove had been pulled completely out. "They must have rolled there after being ejected from the weapon our shooter used." She said rather excitedly.

"Think so, Audrey," Paul sarcastically muttered as his anger returned. He now knew the evidence techs had failed to properly search the kitchen as thoroughly as they should have. He also knew the finding of these three casings now confirmed the shooter had used an automatic and not a wheel gun to shoot his or her victims. "If they missed finding these two casings here in the kitchen, what else have they missed during their search of the house?" Paul wondered to himself. As he stood watching the techs continue their search of the kitchen, he could not help shaking his head in disgust. As he did, he also forced himself to bite his tongue, not wanting to say what he was thinking at the moment. Finally calming down, he looked over to see Vane shaking his head at him.

"What's wrong, Doug?"

"Nothing really, nothing at all. It's just that you continue to amaze me, that's all. The techs have been working in here all day, and until a few minutes ago they had found nothing. Now you come in here and find two casings in a matter of a few minutes. It's just like the Melkin case, you see things that we mere mortals don't."

Paul quickly waved Vane's compliment off as he moved outside to get a breath of fresh air. While he appreciated his friend's kind words, the tech's lack of attention to detail still continued to bother him. "How could they not have thought to check under those two appliances?" He knew that any good evidence tech's routine included moving furniture and rugs, as well as some appliances, during their hunt for evidence.

Paul's thoughts were quickly interrupted by the sight of his good friend struggling to make his way down the front sidewalk of the residence. At first, it had actually taken him a moment to realize that the person he saw walking with such difficulty was Bobby Ray. Even though he now held one in each hand for both balance reasons and for use later, it was his friend's first time walking without crutches since his surgery. While it felt good to be able to do so, Bobby Ray was being careful as he slowly moved to where Paul was standing.

"You're walking like an old man, Bobby Ray!" Paul jokingly said as he walked to greet his friend. This was also Bobby Ray's first visit to the crime scene.

"Feel like one too! Not sure if this damn back surgery helped me out at all or not. The pain is not nearly as bad as it has been," Bobby Ray said as he paused to catch his breath, "but as you can see, I still can't walk very well. My doc has told me to give it time and to just rest, but what the hell does he really know. As everyone knows, back surgery comes with no guarantees. I just needed to get out of the damn house so I could get some work done. By the looks of this mess, I'm thinking y'all could use some help."

With Audrey soon joining them on the front porch, Paul gave his friend an update on where the investigation now stood. His update included the news they had learned earlier in the day about the shed fire, about the argument between the victims and one of their neighbors, and about the three shell casings that had just been found minutes earlier.

"Wish I could do more to help," Bobby Ray said as he moved from a standing position to a more comfortable sitting position on the front steps. Doing so took some of the pressure off his back.

"Bobby Ray, I can understand your frustration, but you didn't know this was going to happen when you decided to have your surgery. Your health is your priority right now; Audrey and I have got this covered, so don't worry. Besides, we both know as soon as we get this mess all figured out that will be the time you'll come back to work and arrest whoever's responsible for this. I can already see your ugly face on the front page of the papers taking all the credit!" Paul's humor, which was meant to cheer his friend up, caused Bobby Ray to flash a brief smile. Standing in front of a group of reporters and crowing about what he had done to help solve an investigation was everything but Bobby Ray's style.

As the three of them continued to speak about where the investigation was headed, Griffin and Edwards suddenly appeared in the driveway.

"Hey, Bobby Ray!" Griffin called out as he climbed out of the unmarked Chevy Impala that Edwards was driving. "Good to see you, my friend! You doing OK?"

As they walked to where the others were seated on the front steps of the residence, Edwards, who had only worked for Bobby Ray for a short period of time prior to his boss' surgery, stood respectfully off to the side after giving him a quick salute and a friendly handshake.

"Not doing as good as you are, Griff, but I'm doing. Should be back on my feet in a week or so, I hope." Then pointing a friendly finger at one of his newest detectives, Bobby Ray asked, "So, how's the rookie detective working out?"

"Good, real good. He did real well today. In fact, he and I have something to show y'all in a minute." Griffin then filled Paul, Bobby Ray, and Small in with the details of their interview with Cotton Horbin.

"The guy's a first-class jerk the whole way. I know I wanted to rearrange his face a couple of times due to his smart-ass remarks, but I held off for the sake of my job and this investigation. I may not next time, but I did today."

Griffin's comments caused Paul and Bobby Ray a brief laugh, but they brought no form of a reaction to Small's stoic face.

"After Darren gave our guy a bullshit reason for wanting to go look at his pain-in-the-ass dog that was barking up a storm in the backyard, I asked Horbin if he owned any guns. It was an effort for him to do so, but finally he told me that he owned a few pistols and a couple of shotguns. I think the prick was lying to me when he claimed that was all he owned, but we'll find out when we start checking to see what he's got registered."

"Did you see anything, or find anything at the house that caused you any concern? Anything that might connect him to our investigation?" Paul asked as he looked at Griffin, and then at Edwards.

Griffin smiled before nodding to his partner. "Paul, you mean something like this abandoned property we found?"

Now joined by Elmendorf and Vane, who had come outside to say hello to their boss, Paul, along with the others, stared for several seconds at the Parliament cigarette butts that Griffin and his partner had collected earlier in his handkerchief.

"These are the same brand as the other fifty to sixty butts I saw in our guy's backyard. The ones you're looking at now we found lying in the road right in front of his mailbox. I also saw two Parliament hard packs in Horbin's truck." Edwards proudly announced. As he spoke, he wisely followed Griffin's earlier advice about not saying anything about picking up one of Horbin's discarded butts from his backyard. They were ones that would not have been admissible in court as they had been seized without a search warrant.

Hearing what Edwards said, Paul spoke before Bobby Ray or Small could manage to muster their thoughts. "This is very interesting news based on what we've already found here this morning in the backyard. I'm sure Mr. Pascento will agree with your thoughts, Griff, about the butts being considered a case of abandonment. I know I do. Once they've been tossed away, especially on a public street where there's no expectation of any privacy or continued ownership, they're there for whoever wants to pick them up, cops included. The courts might have ruled against us if we took them from his yard without a search warrant, but you found them in the street and you were legally there. You can't be faulted for making observations of items, even those of evidentiary value, that are lying in plain view on a public thoroughfare. I'll call Pascento later to get his take on this, but I'm confident we've got no problems." Looking at Griffin and Edwards who were standing next to each other on the sidewalk, Paul added one last comment. "Nice find by the way, good job by both of you." The comment he directed at them caused a smile to crease Edwards' face. Then he added one more.

"Darren, what you and Griff did, not only by recognizing that these butts were the same brand as those we had found earlier, but by also seizing them is a classic example of how cops solve cases like ours. Hard work is one thing, but being aware of your surroundings and being aware how certain things are related to other evidence or other leads, that's what solves cases more often than not. Seeking Horbin's permission to look in his backyard was a great move on your part as well as it allowed you to make the connection of the cigarette butts you found in the street to the ones you guys found in his yard. We're going to use what you guys found to our advantage. Good work!"

Unlike his veteran partner, Edwards continued to smile at the compliments directed at them. For Griffin, while he was pleased by what they had found, it was just another day at work. Pats on the back meant little to him, arresting bad guys was what meant something to him.

Looking next at his friend, who was sitting to his left, Paul began to give out his next set of orders. He did so diplomatically as having both Bobby Ray and Small there with him was not how he normally did business. He could not help thinking this particular moment was another example of too many chiefs and not enough Indians.

"Bobby Ray, I know I'm the so-called boss of this outfit while you're out of the picture, but I also realize that you are still in charge of these folks. I also realize the strong role Audrey has within your unit. With your permission, and with Audrey's help, this is what I want to do next. Besides Doug and Don taking possession of the cigarette butts the guys found, I want them to run the last two garbage cans of debris through their sifter first thing tomorrow morning. If they don't find what we're looking for, then we're going to run that entire freakin' pile of debris through the sifter one more time to make sure we have not missed anything. It's going to take time to do that, but right now we cannot afford to miss anything. We need every bit of evidence we can find to put this case together. If it means Audrey and I have to help shovel some of that debris into the sifter, then so be it, but we're going to get it done. Obviously we'll use the metal detectors again as well."

"The entire pile?" Vane asked, his voice somewhat surprised by the fact that Paul wanted the entire sifting process to be repeated. "You do realize that's going to take at least four of us . . . maybe five if you want it done in one day . . . to accomplish, you do realize that, correct? That pile, as you call it, is quite large now. I just want you to understand that it's going to take the better part of an entire day to run all of the debris through the sifter again."

"Yep, that's right, Doug, the entire pile; but only if we have to. No disrespect intended, but from what we just learned a few minutes ago from what your techs missed in the kitchen, we cannot afford not to. I realize it's going to take some time, but time is the one thing we seem to have plenty of right now. It's evidence that we seem to be in short supply of."

Vane looked over at Elmendorf for a confirmation on the amount of time it would take to process the debris again, but his look was just met with a blank stare. Like his partner, Elmendorf had little interest in completing the dirty, but necessary process a second time.

Paul looked briefly at Edwards, but then directed his next comment at Griffin. He knew and trusted the veteran detective better at this point in time; valuing Griffin's years of experience in dealing with cases similar to this one.

"Griff, this Horbin guy, is he our guy? Is he the one you like for these murders?"

Griffin shifted uneasily on the sidewalk as he thought about what had been asked of him. As he did, he repeatedly clicked the ballpoint pen he had been taking notes with earlier. It was a habit he often performed when deep in thought about some issue, and one that often annoyed others around him. The answer he soon gave showed why Paul respected his years of experience so much.

"Do I like the creep for the murders? That's a question I don't have an answer for, you should know that. It's far too early for any of us to say that he's our guy for what's taken place here. Just like most of you, I'm trying not to speculate on who our killer is; just like I try not to speculate on who committed whatever crime it is that we're investigating. It's hard to do sometimes, but I do my best to try and wait until we know most of the facts about what happened before I start thinking about who the guilty party is. But Horbin's certainly a guy we need to look at real close. The fact that he basically lives in the victims' backyard, plus the argument we know he had with the vics, plus the fact that he smokes the same kind of cigarettes as the ones we found around the site of the shed fire, all are reasons for us to take a close look at him. To be honest, all of those concerns I just mentioned intrigue me more than the guns he owns." Griffin paused for a moment as Stine and Davis walked up to where he and the others were talking. "But the other two reasons we need to take a look at this guy is because he's admitted that he owns a few guns. Horbin clearly demonstrated to Darren and I that he's got a temper, and we all know guns and bad tempers aren't a good mix. To answer your question, Paul, I think we have to take a hard look at him until we either decide we like him or we don't. With what we're going to find out about him in the next day or so, and with the evidence we've got so far, we should know soon enough if we like him or not."

Looking at his friend, Stine asked him one question. "Griff, I just got here, but unless I missed something, you said there were two reasons we need to take a close look at Horbin. What's the second reason?"

Griffin smiled like only a veteran cop can as he looked at Stine, and then at the others. "Because he's a first class freakin' asshole, that's why!" Griffin's comment caused those around him to clearly understand what he thought of their suspect.

"I guess that's a good enough reason as any for us to take a look at Horbin then, Griff." Bobby Ray said as he tried to keep from laughing too hard so he did not aggravate his back. Like the others, except for Small, he liked Griffin's bluntness on most occasions. This was one of those occasions.

"OK, Griff," Paul said, "you and Edwards find out everything you can about Horbin tonight. I mean everything. We need to know what he drives, where he works, what guns he owns, and whatever else you can find out about him. The whole shooting match, that's what we need to know. Tomorrow morning, let's say at 0730 hours, we're all going to meet back here and then we'll start our surveillance on him." Pointing to Stine and Davis, Paul added, "These two are going to be your back-up team when we start looking at him tomorrow." His comments caused Griffin and Stine to exchange nods with each other, and they quickly agreed to talk, along with their partners, once Paul was done covering all of his points.

Then Paul looked over at Elmendorf and Vane. "Boys, I hate doing things like this, but we need some answers to some questions. I don't care what time you get started in the morning, but by mid-afternoon at the latest I need to know how many shell casings you've found. With Bobby Ray's help, maybe that of Sheriff Renda's as well, we're going to relay all of the casings you've found up to the folks at SLED. We need to know what kind of gun or guns were used to kill these kids, and if the shell casings have any prints on them. Got it?"

"Got it." Elmendorf and Vane stated in unison.

Paul then looked at his friend again. As he did, he noticed Bobby Ray had propped his crutches under his legs to relieve some of the discomfort he was feeling in his back. The steps that several of them had been sitting on were not the most comfortable place to being sitting, especially for someone who had recently undergone back surgery.

"Bobby Ray, I need two things from you. Audrey's going to help you with one of them. First thing, you heard what I said about the shell casings. Can you make a call, or have the sheriff make a call, so these casings get pushed to the front of SLED's list of things to do? I can't imagine they have anything more important to work on than a quintuple murder investigation. Like I said, we need some answers, as well as some information, to keep us moving forward."

"No problem. I'll do it myself. A good friend of mine, his name's Ken Zercie, is SLED's go-to guy on most firearms issues. He'll help us out with whatever we need. He's a former cop so he knows what we're looking for and why."

"OK, good. Next thing we need to do is to get the public involved in helping us solve this case. Doing so will hopefully put some pressure on our shooter once he or she knows we've got people talking about this case even more than they already are. I'd like to start putting our own pressure on the shooter as well. You know, make him or her start sweating a little more than they likely are already."

Bobby Ray understood where Paul's comments were headed. "I agree. I think what you're asking me to do is to have a talk with Renda and to have him authorize a reward for information that might lead us to our shooter. Is that correct?"

"That's it, Bobby Ray. Let's start with ten big ones and see how that works. That work for you?" Paul asked.

Despite slowly standing up from where he had been sitting, Bobby Ray grimaced at the pain he felt running down his lower back into his legs. It took a couple of moments for it to subside enough so he could speak. "Consider it done. I'll call the sheriff when I get home and get his permission to use some of our Case Prep funds for the reward. One more thing we might want to consider is asking the parents if they want to pony up some of their own money so we can raise the amount of the reward even higher. You know as well as I do, the more the reward, the less loyal people are likely going to be to even the best of their friends. That goes for bad guys as well."

"That sounds like a good idea, Bobby Ray. When I talk with Scozz later, I'll have him tactfully bounce that thought of yours off them. I need to get an update from him on how each of the parents are doing, so I'll bring it up to him then."

Small, who as usual was writing down most of what was being discussed, finally looked up at Paul when she finished. When she did, she asked him what the task was that he wanted her to help Bobby Ray with.

"Following up on the idea of getting a reward for information approved by Sheriff Renda, I'd like you to work with Bobby Ray and your Crime Prevention folks, and with your PIO staff as well, so we can have some fairly large reward posters made up. Let's get them made, let's get them posted wherever we can, and let's get your PIO staff to start working with the local television and radio stations so word gets out about the reward. We need to get these posters in the public's eye as soon as we can as doing so is only going to benefit us."

Finished with what had to be said, and after a few minutes of chatter amongst themselves, they all prepared to head off to either finish the day's tasks or, for some of them, to start planning the next day's tactics. While Griffin and Edwards had a lot to do in order to be ready for the start of the surveillance, Elmendorf and Vane had their own work to finish before they could even begin to start thinking about heading home. As they all were about to start heading off in different directions, a question from Detective Davis caused them to pause for several moments.

"For some of you, this investigation is what you folks have been trained to work on. That's certainly the case for Paul and Bobby Ray, but for me, possibly for Darren as well, I'm new to the murder game. I'd like to know your thoughts on one thing. Why did this happen? I mean, we've got five young men who are dead, but there's no forced entry we've been able to find, and each of the victim's wallets, cell phones, and car keys have all been accounted for. What . . . what happened here?"

Bobby Ray nodded at the logical question the inexperienced Davis had asked. It showed him his young detective was trying to grasp what had truly caused the murders to occur. Knowing the reason would only benefit him as he proceeded along with the tasks assigned to him in this case and with others in the future.

"It's personal, Bruce." Bobby Ray answered as he looked at the young detective standing a few feet away from him.

"Personal?" Davis quizzically asked.

Bobby Ray could see that Davis had not comprehended his answer. "Based on the time frame of when the shed was burned to the ground, something likely happened a few days prior to make this a personal attack against one or more of the victims. My guess is someone felt they had been wronged, you know, disrespected, and it grew into a hatred . . . or perhaps a grudge . . . that couldn't be resolved except by killing whoever the target or targets of the hatred was. I'm guessing that one, but maybe it was two, of our vics was the intended target and the others just happened to be in the wrong place at the wrong time. Just like you, I don't know any of this for sure yet, but I'll bet next month's pay on it."

Turning his head towards Paul, Davis looked for his take on it.

"Bobby Ray's right. This wasn't a robbery or a burglary gone wrong, this is a personal dispute that probably grew out of something small and just escalated from there. It's certainly something that didn't have to end up like it did."

"You really think that's why this happened? Because someone was pissed off about something?" Davis asked.

Paul nodded his head before speaking again. "Yep, I have no doubt that's the reason. Like Bobby Ray said, I'm not sure that all of the vics were our shooter's targets, but one or two of them were for sure. Once the shooting started the shooter couldn't take a chance of leaving behind any eyewitnesses, so he shot them all. That's the same reason for the house being set on fire. It wasn't set on fire to make it look like an accidental fire, it was set on fire with the purpose of destroying as much of the evidence as possible."

Davis was fairly stunned by what he had been told. "You think the killer, perhaps more than one of them, may have gotten into the house through an open door and then was waiting inside when our vics arrived home? If that's what you are thinking then I guess those kids could have been caught off guard like it appears they were. That's probably just how it occurred now that I think about it. They were surprised, or maybe even overpowered by whoever did this. That's why they didn't put up more of a fight or why none of them were able to escape. Wow! I hadn't thought of those possibilities."

Turning his attention back to Small, Paul gave her one more task to do. "Audrey, I know it's going to take some time for the final autopsy reports to come out, but do me a favor. Call the ME's office and see what they found, if anything, when they checked the kids' fingernails. Let's find out if they found anyone else's skin, blood, or hair follicles when they did the scrapings. It would be nice to know if the kids caused any scratches or injuries to whoever shot them."

Small's nod told Paul that she understood what he was looking for. "First thing tomorrow, Paul. That OK?"

Out of frustration from what he heard, Bobby Ray did not give Paul time to answer Small's question. "Tonight, like right now, would be better, Audrey."

"Understand." Small responded, somewhat embarrassed by the frown she saw on Bobby Ray's face. "I'm on it. I'll go call them right now. After I do that, I'll give Kelly a call regarding what you want done." Quickly she turned and started walking to her car as she pulled her cell from her pants pocket.

"Kelly?" Paul asked with a confused look on his face. He had no idea of who Small had been referring to.

"She's referring to Kelly Glover." Bobby Ray explained. "Kelly's in charge of our Crime Prevention Bureau. She's a civilian employee who Renda hired about a year and a half ago; she does a great job for us. She just came back to work after being out on maternity leave. I know she's been itching to get started on a project like this. I'll call her myself later and run a few things by her."

"Sounds good, Bobby Ray. Make sure you tell her we need those posters as soon as possible. I want them sent to all of the area police departments, including the highway patrol, and the FBI field office down in Charleston. Let's get it posted on your department's website as well."

* * * * * *

As the others walked to finish up what they needed to get done, Paul noticed a uniformed deputy was parked out front of the victims' residence. "Good," he thought as he waved to the deputy whose job it was to protect the scene until the following morning, "I'm still not sure we've found everything we need to find inside this house."

* * * * * *

The following day the search of the victims' home would turn up a few unexpected items. It would take days of hard work to figure out if those items were the reasons why five young men had been so brutally murdered.

Seventeen

A Cop's Gut Feeling

Perhaps it was the noise caused by Vane and some of the evidence techs as they worked processing the last two cans of debris, or perhaps it was because he was lost in his own thoughts while mentally documenting what had been found the previous day that caused Paul not to hear Sgt. Kent Wilson as he approached the tent.

Like Griffin, Stine, and Scozzafava, the bespectacled thirty-seven year old Wilson had been one of the handful of cops that Paul had demanded be assigned to the investigation. On the previous case he had worked, the Melkin investigation, it had been Wilson and Griffin who had developed some of the critical information needed to solve it. For that reason alone, Paul had taken a strong liking to both men because of their relentless approach to working that particularly gruesome investigation.

A fourteen-year veteran of the Myrtle Beach Police Department, Wilson, a slim gray haired cop, was a tenacious investigator who excelled in two areas. Not only was he an excellent interviewer, one who often got people to tell him more than they wanted to tell him, but he was even better at just listening to what crooks and perps, victims, and plain old ordinary people told him. An accepted expert in linguistics, by both the South Carolina courts and the federal court system, he had earned his reputation as an expert in that field after destroying a high-priced defense attorney's challenge of his knowledge of psycholinguistics and neurolinguistics during a well-publicized trial involving a serial rapist four years earlier. A graduate of the University of Georgia, Wilson had completed his graduate studies in Health Systems at Georgia Tech, and was currently working towards his doctorate degree in Language and Literacy at the University of South Carolina. Unlike many other well-educated academics who had a tendency to be full of themselves, he was a simple down to earth Southerner who still loved to hunt and fish when he could find the time to do so.

"Hey, Paul! Back at it again early this morning I see," Wilson said as he walked to where his boss was seated under the tent. Detective Ron Levesque, Wilson's occasional partner during the investigation, followed several steps behind him.

Like his good friend Edwards, Levesque was a fairly new detective; promoted to his current rank less than six weeks earlier. As Wilson had, he also gave his boss a brief but friendly wave. Somewhat out of character, Levesque said nothing as he sat down at the end of the same table where Paul was working.

"Morning, boys! Didn't plan on seeing either of you here this morning. Everything OK?" Paul said as he reached for his cup of coffee, one which had sat untouched on the table for the past ten minutes. Despite the day's already warm temperature, the black coffee had turned lukewarm; the unpleasant taste quickly caused him to spit the remaining liquid in his mouth onto the grass by his feet. Cold coffee was not a taste he had ever gotten used to as it seemed to always leave a bitter taste in his mouth. Quickly the remaining black liquid in his cup was poured onto the grass.

"Yeah, it's all good, just like I told you last night." Wilson's rich South Carolina drawl brought a warm smile to Paul's face. "I do have one surprise to tell you about though. I've already talked to Scozz about this; he told me to stop and see you this morning about it."

"I'm all ears, Kent." Paul said as he pushed his pad and pen off to the side after tossing his Styrofoam cup into a nearby garbage can that sat close to where he was seated.

"As you know, one of our victims, Trevor Gilmour, is originally from Michigan. His folks have come down here to claim his body as they're planning on burying him back home in a town called Manistique, it's someplace in the Upper Peninsula. Because of their personal grief, they've chosen not to attend any of the other kids' funerals. That's a personal decision of theirs, and it's one the other parents completely understand." Wilson's cell phone interrupted him from speaking for a brief moment as he checked the number of the incoming call, but realizing it could wait he let the call go straight to his voice mailbox instead of answering it. "The reason I'm mentioning this is because Mr. and Mrs. Gilmour have told Levesque . . . he's been their primary contact during the investigation . . . that they want to come by here later today. They have the need to see the place where their son died. Mr. Gilmour told Ron that he and his wife need to do this to help them sort this tragedy out in the heads. Their flight home leaves Myrtle Beach late this afternoon so they plan on stopping here sometime later this morning."

Paul gave Levesque a quick glance before leaning back in his chair. "Ron, did you tell

them the house is still a crime scene?"

"I did," Levesque answered with a doleful look now displayed across his face. "They understand that completely. They're not looking to get inside the house or his bedroom or to cause any problems. They just want to take a walk around the house, maybe say a prayer or two in the backyard, but that's about it."

"That's good. I certainly don't have any problems with that, and I also understand their reasons for wanting to do so, but just make sure they know we cannot allow them into the house at this time. Elmendorf and a couple of his techs actually just started processing the rooms on the second floor about an hour or so ago. I'm going to have Mo and Carlson, and maybe a couple of the others, start searching the bedrooms after Don lets me know he's done up there. The other reason I don't want them in the house is because of all the dried blood that's still on the floors of the main level. Christ, can you image them seeing their son's blood on the floor where he died? That would be a lasting impression they would never get over."

Wilson and Levesque both nodded over Paul's unpleasant comment about any of the victim's parents seeing where their sons had died.

"If they want me to, I'll be glad to spend a few moments with them.

If not, you boys handle this, but please extend my condolences to them. Give them whatever support they need. We can work out the details of getting their son's belongings back to them at a later time. If they ask about his vehicle, tell them I spoke to Solicitor Pascento about all of the victims' vehicles the other day. He wants them held as evidence until we know something more definitive about why the kids were murdered. Rightfully so, as I know I wouldn't want to release any evidence prematurely either. That might be tough to explain once this case goes to trial."

"OK, boss." Levesque replied.

As Wilson filled Paul in with a few other important details from the interaction with several of the parents, he soon told him one other very important piece of information. "To the best of their knowledge, none of the parents ever knew their sons to be cigarette smokers. Maybe a cigar once in a while during a round of golf, or when they were out having a few cocktails with their buddies, but none of them could ever recall seeing their sons smoke even one cigarette. We also asked the parents if any of them smoked, and the only one who does, the Tanner kid's father, doesn't smoke Parliaments. Besides, he's never visited the house where his son lived. "

Paul was not surprised by the news he heard. "That helps to some degree, I guess, but it doesn't point us to who did smoke those cigarettes we found. We didn't find any cigarettes in any of their vehicles, or in the house so far, that's why I had the feeling someone else tossed them there and not the kids. We're just going to have to keep working on that issue, won't we? Have anything else you need to tell me?"

Wilson's next few comments helped to clear up a few unresolved issues. "I agree with what you just said, those cigarette butts you found over by where the shed had stood obviously were tossed there by someone else. I'm not sure why, perhaps because I haven't seen any signs of ashtrays in the house or cigarette butts being discarded in the lawn or driveway, but I've thought that all along. Oh, I almost forgot, I've got one more thing for you. Those plantings that you saw around the area where the shed stood, they were planted there by Carl Diggs' mother; same is true for the pine straw and the mulch. She had visited the home a few times and thought the backyard needed some color so she added all of that during two of her visits. She added the mulch to the flower beds after the shed had been set on fire; she told us she didn't like seeing the sight of the burnt pine straw. Said it was easier to cover up than having to pay someone to take it away. After she told us all that, I confirmed it with her husband just to be sure. He told us the same story."

"OK, all of that's good to know. Thanks!" Paul quickly jotted down what he had just been told by Wilson. As he did, Griffin, then Small, and then the others, began meandering into the tent. As they did, they each took note of Vane hard at work on the other side of it.

"Paul, I think we've got a way to handle our surveillance of Horbin." Griffin said as he handed his boss several printouts of information about their suspect.

"Like I told Kent a few minutes ago, I'm all ears, Griff. Let's hear what you've got to say." Paul said as he tried making sense of the papers Griffin had handed him.

With some help from Edwards, Griffin explained to Paul and everyone else what they had found out about Horbin the previous night after running his name through several federal and state databases. Mentioned in his summation was the basic information about Horbin's pedigree, including his date of birth, tax information about his home and vehicles, his work and arrest histories, and, most importantly, information on what types of firearms their suspect had registered with the state of South Carolina.

"When we checked with SLED last night about the guns he had registered, they confirmed to us that Horbin has properly registered several weapons with them; he also has a valid concealed weapons permit. Later, we verified what they told us through a couple of NCIC checks as well." Then Griffin added a personal comment into the conversation. It was one he had no supporting evidence to base his comment on. "Besides the fact that Horbin's a complete asshole, and besides my own gut telling me I'm right, I have little to rest my next statement on. But I'm pretty confident he's got another gun or three that he hasn't told us about; ones he likely hasn't bothered to register either."

Taking into account Griffin's experience of working criminals like Horbin, Paul nodded at the veteran detective's intuition. Despite knowing that Griffin was probably correct, he also knew a cop's gut feeling mattered little to the court. "We can't get a search warrant based on speculation, Griff. I wish we could, but we can't. I'm not saying you're wrong, but you know we need more than mere suspicion or a cop's hunch to convince the court to issue us a warrant so we can search his home for guns we think may be there."

"Yeah, but we can get into the prick's house one other way. Look at Horbin's DMV printout regarding his CDL license." Griffin said as he handed Paul one last document to look at.

Looking at the document for a moment, Paul then looked up to see Griffin smiling at him. Soon he noticed what Griffin wanted him to see on the printout. Amongst other routine information, it showed their suspect's license had been suspended due to two recent tickets he had failed to take care of with the courts.

"I like it, Griff! A very simple and neat way of doing it. Good idea." Paul's years of experience told him what Griffin had planned. For the others around them, who had yet to be clued in on what the DMV records reflected, they had little idea of what was about to be put into motion. Before he had Griffin explain what was going to take place, Paul made one last comment. It helped the others to quickly get a sense of the direction the surveillance on Horbin was about to take.

"Pretty tough for a truck driver to work if his CDL is under suspension, huh?"

Griffin then laid out his plan for the others regarding the surveillance that was about to start. The plan would involve stopping Horbin for a motor vehicle violation regarding his suspended license after he arrived at work. As he did so, Griffin directed part of his comments to Paul.

"Look, I think it's best if we let our surveillance play out for a couple of days. If we go ahead and stop him today, we might not get what we need. Let's have a few of the guys sit on his house for a day or two. That will give us some time to follow him wherever he goes; whether it's for work or someplace else. Either way, we'll be there with him. This way we can see where he goes and who he talks to. Who knows, maybe we'll get lucky somehow." Turning, Griffin looked at Small for a brief moment before directing his attention back at Paul. "That OK with you, boss?" Unlike several of the others, Griffin was not a fan of Small's. A veteran cop who thrived in stressful situations, he detested her inability to make decisions on the fly like Bobby Ray and Paul. His snub was meant to be intentional.

Paul nodded before diplomatically answering Griffin's question; making sure he included Small's rank, as well as Griffin's, in his response. "That's fine. Lt. Small and I don't have a problem with that, detective. We'll give you today and part of tomorrow to do what's needed with the surveillance. Sit on him or follow him wherever he takes you, but tomorrow afternoon after he gets to work, or perhaps tomorrow evening at the latest, you stop him. Come to think of it, stopping him in one of his company's trucks might be your best option as it would give us something else to hold over his head."

Griffin, as did Small, smiled at Paul's thought of stopping their suspect as he drove someone else's vehicle.

"Got it, boss!" Griffin excitedly replied.

Managing an investigation involving five murders was a difficult enough task for anyone, but having to manage a variety of vastly different personalities at the same time made the first task even harder. It was akin to managing a professional baseball team with twenty-five different large egos. Tactfully, Paul continued to do his best at stemming the personality differences which confronted him, especially the strained relationship between Small and Griffin.

"Griff, you keep Audrey informed as your plan develops. I'll call Scozz and tell him I'm reassigning Wilson to work with you for the time being. Levesque, you'll stay with the parents for now. I don't want them thinking they've been forgotten about."

"OK, boss." Levesque's face clearly reflected his disappointment in not being a part of the surveillance on Horbin.

"Audrey, after you and Griff finalize the surveillance, get us a uniformed deputy or two to help with the takedown of Horbin tomorrow. I don't want him being able to say that he didn't know who it was if he takes off on us and doesn't stop. Using a couple of marked units will also make it easier for us when the time is ready to pull him over."

Then looking at Edwards as he spoke to the others, Paul told them about a call he made to Solicitor Pascento the night before.

"I spoke to him about the Parliament cigarette butts you saw in Horbin's yard and the ones you found in the road near his mailbox. I explained how you had gotten Horbin's permission to be in his backyard before you observed them. Pascento's got no problem with what we seized as evidence even though we didn't have a warrant. He told me he'll be ready in the event someone tries to pitch a bitch about any right-to-privacy issues or about any illegal seizure concerns. As far as he's concerned, both of you were legally there in both places. You had gotten Horbin's permission to visit his backyard, and you saw the butts lying there in plain view by the mailbox and in his yard. He doesn't have any issues with us taking possession of the butts that were in the road."

Paul's comments caused a large smile to appear on Edwards face. It grew even bigger when he heard the next comment directed at him as well.

"Digger, nice job! You too, Griff! Who knows if Horbin's our guy or not, but the fact that you guys had the sense to see what kind of cigarettes he smokes is a testament to the kind of cops you both are. Paying attention to even the smallest of details helps to solve cases like this one. Paying attention to those details is what earns cops like you guys, and like everyone else who's sitting here, the reputations of being a good investigator. Now I understand how you got your funky nickname."

The conversation taking place under the tent was quickly broken up by the sound of an excited voice.

"Paul! Audrey! You folks might want to see this!" Vane's loud voice yelled out from across the other side of the tent. "We just found three more shell casings!"

* * * * * *

Later that afternoon the six shell casings that had been found, along with the Parliament cigarette butts found in the road close to their suspect's mailbox, were sent to SLED's forensic lab. Tipped off by Small that the evidence was headed their way, two Firearms Examiners, a Fingerprint Examiner, and two DNA scientists were told to clear their schedules for the next two days. The evidence Vane, Elmendorf, and the others had found was now being given top priority. Calls from Sheriff Renda, Small, and one from Governor Dixie Messer had made sure the evidence in this particularly gruesome case was moved to the head of SLED's list of priorities.

Two days later, the results of SLED's examination of the evidence they had been sent would have immediate ramifications on the direction Paul's investigation was headed.

Eighteen

Mistakes

The finding of the three shell casings early that morning interrupted the search for any new evidence on the second floor of the crime scene. Sergeant Elmendorf had been directing the efforts of three detectives and two crime scene techs when he was forced to go outside to document the discovery of the new evidence.

Like he already had done with the other evidence that had been found, and like he had with the entire house before and during their search for any items of evidentiary value, Elmendorf now did what he did best. Carefully he spent several minutes using both his video camera and a Canon .35mm camera to document the shell casings Vane and his crew had just found.

The findings of these shell casings, while important to the investigators for several reasons, now would cause them one additional problem to have to solve. It would take days for them to finally figure it out. The new problem was first identified by

Elmendorf when he began to take close ups of the shell casings as they sat in Vane's sifter where they had first been found.

"Hey, Doug," Elmendorf yelled to his co-worker, "the casings we found yesterday were all .380 caliber rounds, correct?"

"Yes, they were. They were all Winchester .380 casings."

Scratching his head, Elmendorf stood up from where he had bent over looking at the newly found casings. Like always, his ever present camera dangled from around his sweaty neck. Quiet for a brief moment, he then turned to look at Vane who was standing a few feet away making notes in his evidence log book. "Not sure if you noticed this, Doug, but these aren't the same size shell casings, these are larger. These bad boys you just found are 9 millimeter caliber casings; if I had to take a guess, I'd say they look to be 9x19 Parabellums."

What he heard startled Vane. Quickly he moved to take a second, and a more thorough look at the casings his techs had found. "I, I didn't notice that, but you're right. When we found them I left them lying on the screen so you could photograph them where we found them, just like we did when we found all of the others. I just thought they would . . ." Vane went quiet for a moment as his mind recalled the many other scenes he had worked. "I'm surprised by this. Does this mean we now have two shooters to try and identify?" It was a rhetorical question Vane did not expect an answer to.

Paul had just come out from under the tent when he saw the commotion around Vane's work area. Realizing something important was taking place, he moved to where the others were standing.

"We find something else, guys?" Paul anxiously asked.

Vane and Elmendorf looked at each other briefly before pointing to the casings that still rested where they had been found. As he moved to take a closer look, Elmendorf explained to Paul what the issue was.

"Wow!" Paul said, obviously surprised by what he had been told. "I have to admit, I didn't expect to hear that." Now many of the various possibilities began to race through his mind as he thought about the two different caliber casings that had been found. "I guess we either have two different shooters, or we have a shooter who brought more than one gun to the fight. We might even have a shooter who fired different caliber rounds from two or more magazines. Sounds strange, but I guess it could have happened. You boys agree with that?"

Busy with their own thoughts, Elmendorf and Vane chose to answer Paul with simple nods of their heads.

Out of concern about other problems that might arise, as well as fear about mistakes that may have already been made, Paul asked his next question.

"Guys, besides the issue of now having two different calibers of shell casings, how did we not find these casings when they went through the sifter before? I'm asking you this question because if we missed them during the first go-round, what else have we missed?"

Somewhat defensively, Vane addressed Paul's concern. "What we're doing with this sifter can hardly be called an exact scientific method of trying to find evidence we can use to build our case around. In fact, we're using a rather rudimentary process to try and find evidence, in other words shell casings and spent bullets, to help identify what took place when our vics were murdered. Obviously we started this process for several reasons; one of those was to help us identify what kind of a firearm was used to kill those kids. Instead of looking at what we've been doing as a failure, I think you need to look at it as being a success. I say that because we've found two different calibers of shell casings as a result of using our sifter. If we hadn't found anything then this effort of ours could be considered a failure … a huge waste of time …but it's not. It's a success because we've identified the fact that two different weapons may have been used to kill those kids. That's far more than what we knew the day this happened . . . hell, it's more than we knew an hour ago. I would also suggest you look at what we're doing in a different way than you currently are and, if I might add, in a more open-minded way at that."

"Yeah, but . . ."

Upset by the criticism he thought was unfairly being directed at his techs and the use of his sifter, Vane cut his boss off before he could say what he wanted to say. "Yeah, nothing, Paul! The simple answer to your question is quite obvious. The casings themselves are smaller than the holes in the screen. They somehow managed to fall through the three levels of screening when they were run through it the first time. If we used screening with holes too small we'd never get anything through them because they'd all be clogged with different kinds of crap. I don't know how this happened, but obviously they also got by the metal detectors as well. I'm not making excuses, nor am I defending my folks for not finding them earlier, but things like this happen. For what it's worth, you made a good call when you decided to have us run the entire pile of debris through the sifter a second time. Now, if we're done trying to figure this out, I've got work to do." Finished with what he had to say, Vane stood impatiently for a moment as he waited to see if the conversation was going to continue. As he did, he turned to look over at his techs as they worked on finishing the processing of the debris.

Despite being less than pleased about the casings avoiding detection until now, Vane's simple but vigorous explanation satisfied Paul for the moment.

"Alright, Doug, keep working at it. I know you're all doing your best. We'll deal with this new issue just like we deal with everything else. Let me know what else you find." Paul was about to walk away so he could call Bobby Ray with an update, when another problem suddenly popped up. Like the shell casings, this new issue added more speculation to what had caused the murders to occur.

"Hey, Donnie!"

Detective Jeff Brandau's loud voice yelled out from one of the residence's upstairs bedroom windows. "We found something you're gonna want to take a look at. You might want to bring Paul with you, maybe Dougie as well."

"What now?" Elmendorf said out of frustration as he began the short walk to the back door of the residence. Like the others, he had too much on his plate already. He had little time to deal with another problem.

******

"It's in the closet over there." Brandau said pointing to a closet that had no doors on it as Elmendorf and the others entered the small upstairs bedroom. The smallest of the three bedrooms, it was the one Johanson had called home. "We just found it. No one's touched it."

Moving closer to the closet, the three cops Brandau called up to the bedroom that he had been working in quickly saw what he was referring to. Sitting on top of a small wooden bureau that had been placed inside the room's single closet were three large clear plastic bags of marijuana. Unlike others who had briefly been in the room previous to his search of it, Brandau had found the bags after pulling a large blue colored towel and several soot covered shirts off the top of them. Each of the plastic bags had been marked by their manufacturer as being the gallon size variety. Also on top of the bureau, one which had obviously been placed in the closet to allow for more living space in the bedroom itself, were four packs of rolling papers and a strange looking orange colored bong. A quick visual check of the bong's bowl showed it appeared to contain residue from being heavily used. On the walls to either side of the closet, two pro-marijuana posters were held in place by colored thumb tacks.

After seeing what Brandau found, and after being told how it had been found, Paul sensed his anger growing by the second. His anger was not in regards to another issue being added to the mix; one that possibly was a reason why the murders had occurred in the first place, but rather it was about evidence not being found before now. While it was not Brandau's fault that it had not been, he quickly became the target of Paul's wrath.

"Damn it, detective, this is not acceptable! This whole freaking room reeks of marijuana. If an old cop like me could smell it coming up the damn stairs then everyone who's come within ten feet of this room should have smelled it as well. The pungent odor that stuff gives off should have been enough of a clue for even a rookie cop to realize what was in here. The smell of it is even stronger than that of the damn fire! Why has it taken four or five days for this to be found?" Paul tried calming down as he finished speaking, but could not. He was pissed, pissed because he knew he could have had someone working the drug angle from the start. While it was not his job to search the house for evidence, he was now upset with himself for not making sure Small and her detectives had completed an adequate cursory search of the upstairs bedrooms.

"Donnie, Doug, get this stuff photographed, seized, labelled, and whatever else needs to be done with it. Then get it packed up and ready to be sent to SLED with the rest of the crap we're sending them. Just like the casings you found earlier, we'll deal with this new problem later on, but I'm pissed. Let me know if you find any other surprises." Paul angrily said before quickly walking out of the room. It was time for him to make a phone call, and time for him to ream someone's butt over what had just been found.

* * * * * *

"Paul, do you think the Johanson kid was selling weed, or do you think it was just for his personal use?" Bobby Ray asked his friend from the comfort of his couch. He had hoped to get down to the scene that morning, but his back had tightened up considerably over night and now he elected not to push it.

"Don't know yet. I also don't know if it's the reason these kids were murdered or not. Brandau's search of the bedroom also turned up a couple hundred dollars in a pair of socks in one of the bureau drawers, but who knows if that's drug money or if the kid used the drawer as his bank. We'll get those answers soon enough, I guess."

Paul had called Bobby Ray a few minutes earlier to update him on what had been found during the search of the second floor of the residence. It was not a call he wanted to make, but sloppy police work for the second day in a row was something he could not tolerate any longer. Especially at the scene of multiple murder investigation.

"You're absolutely right, Paul. I'm as disappointed to hear that as you must have been when you were told about it. Between the slow start this case has gotten and now this weed being found days later, I'm not too pleased by what's been going on either. I don't have an answer; maybe it's her wedding, but I don't know. It's certainly not the first murder scene she's worked. You want me to rip her a new ass or what?" Bobby Ray asked his friend, disappointed by what he had been told about issues with the investigation, and with Small's supervision of it.

"Nope, not now. She's got a lot on her mind, including her wedding. I'll deal with it later, perhaps when I write the After Action report, but I'll handle it. I don't ask others to do my dirty work for me. She only has another few days of work before her wedding; I deal with it when she comes back."

Finished with that issue, Paul gave his friend an update on the three shell casings that had been found in the sifter, and on his plans to get them up to SLED later in the day. The other casings, as well as the marijuana, would all be part of the evidence the lab would receive. As they spoke, he also updated Bobby Ray on a few new twists to the surveillance that had just recently gotten underway.

* * * * * *

Like the start of the day, the surveillance operations would also bring a whole new set of issues that needed to be overcome. Those issues would take several more long days of work to address. Like most murder investigations, this was one that now had begun to take on a life of its own.

Nineteen

Surveillance of a Suspect

The surveillance of Horbin's home on Bobcat Drive started at 1045 hours. In planning the details of the surveillance, ones which included who was going to comprise the primary and back-up teams for both the day and evening shifts, what the hours for each shift were going to be, and who would remain sitting on the house in the event their suspect went mobile, Griffin got lucky with one particular need.

When Small made the arrangements to have a uniformed deputy assigned to each shift, she learned one of the deputies being assigned to her had an aunt and uncle who lived four houses north of Horbin's residence. With their approval, each shift now had a place to sit and watch who came and went from their suspect's home. During the planning of the surveillance, it was decided the marked GCSD cruiser assigned to each shift would be parked out of sight closer to the beach so its presence did not tip anyone off on what was occurring near their suspect's home.

As Paul had mandated, the surveillance of Horbin's home was to end sometime during the afternoon or evening hours of the second day. Based on that, Griffin had put a plan into place that once their target arrived at work, and later drove away from the concrete plant he reported to at the start of each work day, he would be stopped by at least one uniformed deputy for operating a motor vehicle with a suspended license. This would meet the necessary requirements - the probable cause - to stop his vehicle for a known violation.

On the morning of the second day of the surveillance, Detectives Stine and Davis obtained Search and Seizure Warrants for Horbin's brick style home and for each of his vehicles. The well-articulated warrants, ones quickly approved by Superior Court Judge Jefferson Davis Douglas, sought the court's permission to search for guns, ammunition, rope, duct tape, as well as other similar types of tape, for any type of written documents alluding to the victims, and, surprisingly, to the reviewing judge when he read the warrant applications, Parliament cigarettes and cigarette butts. The warrant for Horbin's residence also sought permission to search the grounds of the property for the same items, especially those items that had been discarded or abandoned. It was permission the court quickly granted.

Griffin's plan to stop Horbin, a plan Paul approved after being told how and where the stop would be made, called for the search warrants to be executed shortly after the traffic stop of their suspect occurred.

* * * * * *

Tucked between two vehicles owned by Deputy Ken Erwin's

204 | PETER F. WARREN

aunt and uncle, Wilson, and his partner for the evening, Detective Timothy Baughman, had a clear view of Horbin's driveway. Helping out with manpower needs for the operation, Baughman was an eight year veteran of the GCSD who was assigned on most days to an FBI Joint Terrorism Task Force based in Charleston.

At 1845 hours, Wilson reached for the Motorola microphone in his undercover vehicle; it was connected to the same kind of radio that all GCSD vehicles were equipped with.

"All units on channel seven, Mr. Cotton appears to be locking the front door of his residence at this time. It looks like he is getting ready to head to work. All units copy?" Wilson asked as he finished his first broadcast. Not wanting to use their suspect's last name over the radio, Griffin had directed the members of the surveillance teams to use Horbin's nickname during their radio transmissions. Unlike the patrol deputies routinely did, the detectives, who were operating on a secure and scrambled radio channel throughout the investigation, spoke in plain English on the radio. This was such an occasion as Paul, like some of the detectives assigned to the investigation from other agencies, had not had time to learn all of the radio codes employed by the GCSD. For this important traffic stop, using words instead of codes would reduce the risk of any mistakes occurring.

"Copy." Small said as she listened intently for Wilson's next transmission. Next to her in the front seat of her undercover vehicle, Paul tried to anticipate what Wilson would broadcast next.

"Copy that." The unfamiliar voice Paul heard on the radio was that of Deputy Erwin. Like the others, he now waited patiently, albeit nervously, for more information to be sent out over the radio. This was the first time the young deputy had been assigned to assist with a high profile case like this one.

Further north, just off of the Highway 17 By-Pass, Griffin and Edwards learned of Horbin's actions by way of a call Baughman made to Griffin's cell.

"OK," Griffin responded upon learning of Horbin's movements, "keep us posted. Darren and I are right down the street from where he works. We're ready for you when you get here."

* * * * * *

For the next twenty-five minutes, three unmarked GCSD vehicles, with two marked units following them at a safe distance, followed their suspect's slightly banged up Dodge Ram pick-up as he headed to work north on Highway 17. Another unmarked vehicle, one driven by Stine and Davis, was roughly a half-mile in front of Horbin's truck. Their assignment was to stay out in front of their suspect's vehicle in the event the others were cut off in traffic or held up by a red light.

As the surveillance of Horbin's truck proceeded north through Murrells Inlet, Wilson called out each of the major intersections they cleared. He did this so Stine and Griffin, as well as Paul and Small, continually knew the exact location of their target.

Then Wilson began the important updates, ones which followed previous transmissions in rapid fashion. These were ones that no longer required the others to acknowledge hearing. With the exception of Erwin, each of the cops participating in the surveillance knew enough to let Wilson have sole use of the radio.

Acting as their quarterback, he knew what vehicle they were each in and who to call if a problem popped up. For the others, they each knew their job now was just to listen.

"OK, folks, Mr. Cotton just turned left onto Highway 707." Wilson radioed on the secure channel they were operating on. "He's less than a mile from work. We'll stay with him until he turns into the driveway of the concrete plant. Then we'll take an observation post nearby so we can see him when he leaves in his company truck. Stand-by for a few."

Horbin's vehicle, like those of the surveillance teams, was forced to slow down due to the presence of slow moving traffic shortly after entering Highway 707. Painfully they moved slowly in a westerly direction for several hundred yards until clearing the highway's intersection with Old King's Highway, a busy residential side cut. Once past this intersection, traffic resumed to a more normal flow. Moments later, Horbin's truck briefly displayed its left turn signal before turning into the driveway of the plant he reported to.

For eighteen minutes, the surveillance teams anxiously waited for their target to reappear. To their relief, he soon did. Driving a service truck equipped with a variety of tools, lubricants, and spare parts used to maintain the company's cement mixers and other vehicles working at a nearby construction site, Horbin turned left out of the driveway. In moments, he was picked up again by the surveillance vehicles as he headed west on Highway 707.

"Target's moving!" Wilson excitedly put out over the radio. "He's all alone in a white Chevy service truck. It's got a large oil tank in the back of it, and the truck has several compartment doors on both sides. It's easy to pick out. He's coming right at you, Griff. Paul, you copy?"

With Edwards driving their unmarked Chevy Impala, Griffin acknowledged the transmission he heard from where he sat parked in a CVS parking lot. Parked in the same lot, Small also acknowledged Wilson's latest broadcast.

"Loud and clear, Kent. Give the uniformed deputy time to make the stop and to confirm that Horbin's license is suspended; then we'll move in. Seeing that we just crossed county lines a few hundred yards back, I'm going to have Dispatch give Horry County a courtesy call so they know what's going on. We don't need any problems later if someone pitches a bitch about us not calling them."

✶✶✶✶✶✶

The stop of Horbin's company truck went just as it had been planned. In minutes, Deputy Erwin, after confirming their suspect's license was still under suspension, had Horbin out of his truck and was patting him down for any concealed weapons. Like it was in most states, operating a vehicle with a suspended license warranted, on most occasions, a custodial arrest. This was one of those occasions.

With a South Carolina state trooper standing by as back-up, Horbin was soon handcuffed without incident. The trooper, who had been on patrol in the area, had overheard Erwin calling in the stop of Horbin's company truck. Like Horbin, the trooper was suddenly surprised by the appearance of several unmarked vehicles.

"What the hell is this all about?" Horbin asked rather loudly as he watched the area around him being flooded with plainclothes cops wearing dark blue raid jackets. Large gold colored lettering on the back of each jacket easily identified who the wearers of the jackets were. Most were marked POLICE, but in Scozzafava's case it read FBI. Horbin then watched as Griffin, followed by his partner, walked up to him with smiles on their faces.

Without directing any greetings or questions at their suspect, Griffin got right to the point. As he did, Paul, followed by Small, walked up behind him. Their experience told the others not to crowd the area where Griffin stood talking with their suspect. Stine, with Davis in tow, now began walking back to their vehicle so they could prepare for the execution of the search warrants at Horbin's residence.

"As this deputy just told you, Mr. Horbin, you're under arrest for driving with a suspended license. In a minute, my partner is going to read you your Miranda Rights. For now, I just want you to listen to what I have to say . . . *don't say a word*." Pausing for a brief moment, Griffin made sure their suspect was listening to what he was being told and not paying all of his attention to the flurry of activity taking place around him. "Earlier today the Georgetown County Sheriff's Department obtained search warrants for your home, the grounds it sits on, and for your vehicles. This, as you may have figured out by now, has to do with five of your neighbors recently being murdered. You are currently a suspect in those murders."

"That's bull . . . " Horbin attempted to speak, but Griffin quickly cut him off.

"Mr. Horbin, like I said before, for now I just want you to listen. I'll give you the chance to talk later, but for now I suggest you just keep quiet. I'm ready, just like my partners are, to start ripping your home and vehicles apart for what we're looking for. But we're going to give you a chance to cooperate with us. You can play it smart, and by that I mean you can choose to cooperate with us, or you can choose to make it difficult for us, but either way we're going to find what we've set out to find. If you choose to cooperate with us, we won't tow this company truck you're driving, nor will we tell your boss you've been driving it with a suspended license for the past four months. That way you get to keep this wonderful job you have of being an overpaid grease monkey. That's our way of being nice to you." Griffin said sarcastically to Horbin. "Your cooperation also means you likely won't have to pay for any accidental damage that occurs while we're searching your home. Catch my drift? Tell you what . . . think on it for a moment while your rights are read to you."

Despite the hatred he had for cops, Horbin quickly realized the precarious predicament he was in. Loudly he began complaining to everyone near him that he had not killed anyone, but as he expected no one paid the least bit of attention to his brief rant. With little choice, he quickly decided not to be the total asshole he normally was.

"OK, OK, this is pure bullshit, but I need my job. What the hell do you guys want from me?" Horbin said, staring at Griffin with angry eyes that flashed hatred.

＊＊＊＊＊＊

With help from Elmendorf and Vane, as well as from a tired group of evidence techs, most of whom had worked with little sleep over the course of the past few days, Stine and Davis executed the search warrant on Horbin's home. As Wilson and Griffin drove their suspect back to the GCSD facility in Georgetown, Paul briefly stopped at Horbin's home with the keys to the front door and his vehicles. He had promised their suspect that he would not allow any of his detectives to kick in the front door of his home if he elected to cooperate. Paul's promise had satisfied Horbin to some degree, but it had greatly disappointed Stine. As a second sign of good faith, and with their suspect's written permission to do so, Paul arranged for Horbin's Dodge pick-up to be driven back to his home instead of having it towed. Doing so also made it easier for Stine's crew to process it under the search warrant.

"Blake, I'm not here to tell you how to do things, but I've already told Don I want one thing done before it gets too dark out here." Paul said as he stood in their suspect's driveway watching Vane and several others entering Horbin's residence just before leaving to drive down to Georgetown.

"What's that, boss?"

"I want the backyard photographed, sketched, and whatever else done that Don thinks is necessary to do, but I want those Parliament cigarette butts out there seized. Most of them have probably been exposed to the weather for far too long already for us to get any DNA from, but who knows. Seize them before you do anything else. Make sure you also seize any butts you find in ashtrays or cups or wherever else you find them inside the house."

"Got it, boss." Stine replied, still mildly disappointed over not having the opportunity to kick Horbin's front door in. Then seeing Elmendorf standing by the front steps, he turned and hollered, "Come on, Donnie Boy, we've got work to do out back."

As Paul walked to where Small was waiting for him in her vehicle, he began the series of calls he needed to make to give Bobby Ray, Pascento, and Sheriff Renda updates on where the investigation now stood.

* * * * * *

As the search of Horbin's home began, soon afterwards so did the start of Wilson and Griffin's interview with their prime suspect. Earlier that afternoon, because of their past experience in conducting high-profile interviews, Paul had instructed Wilson to assist Griffin with Horbin's interview. Earlier in the day as well, he had also assigned Edwards, because of the observations he had previously made at their suspect's home, to assist Stine with the searches that were being conducted. He did the same with Davis as well. Because of the importance of Horbin's interview, Paul knew he needed to have two of his 'A' players where they were needed the most. They would be the ones who would grill Horbin on what he knew about the murders of five young men; ones that occurred not far from his own backyard.

* * * * * *

Like the results of Horbin's interview, the results Paul soon received from SLED's comparison testing of the DNA found on both the cigarettes seized from the victims' backyard to those butts found in and around their suspect's home would surprise him. He would also be similarly surprised by the results of the comparison tests involving the shell casings found at the scene to those test fired from their suspect's guns.

But then again, murder investigations never came with any promises of evidence being easy to interpret.

Twenty

Horbin's Admission

The small Interview Room chosen for the interview of their suspect was only slightly bigger than the one they had used at MBPD for the interviews of Ricky Frazier during the Melkin investigation. Like that room, this one, painted a dull and depressing light gray color, was also equipped with a video camera and two listening devices. One fed directly into a VCR mounted in a small room immediately outside in the hallway, while the other fed into a small speaker in the adjacent, and equally small, Observation Room. There others could listen and observe, through a one-way mirror mounted on one of the walls, to what was being said during each interview conducted in the room specifically designed for interviews. For now, Horbin sat alone, quiet for once as he awaited his fate.

"Comfortable, Mr. Horbin?" Griffin said rather caustically as he led Wilson into the room where they had intentionally kept their suspect waiting for the past ten minutes.

"Yeah, it's great to be back. Looks just like I remember it; pretty shitty." Horbin said as he glanced about the small room, taking an extra moment to again stare at the video camera looking down on him, and then at the one-way mirror mounted almost directly underneath it. It was not his first time being interviewed in a room like this for some sort of nefarious illegal conduct. Four years earlier another set of detectives had interviewed him and two of his friends regarding a series of strong-armed robberies that had taken place in different parts of the county. Looking down at the concrete floor from where he sat handcuffed to a gray metal desk, Horbin made one more wiseass remark. "Looks like you assholes had the floor painted since I was here last. Wonderful job!"

Standing next to his partner, Wilson put a hand on Griffin's right shoulder as a means of keeping him calm. He knew quite well his partner's propensity for losing his cool when dealing with idiots like Horbin. He also knew it was far too early for the Good Cop – Bad Cop game to start as well.

Wanting to capture this on both the audio and video tapes, Wilson asked their suspect an easy question. "Mr. Horbin, you were read your Miranda Rights earlier, correct?"

"Yeah, I was. So freakin' what!"

"You understand those rights?" Wilson asked.

"Do I look like a moron to you, detective?"

"Actually it's sergeant, not detective," Wilson said as he chuckled at the opening their suspect had given him. "And that's a question my partner and l will both be glad to answer some other time for you."

Horbin angrily responded by viewing the two cops in front of him with even more contempt than he previously had.

Wilson continued to smile at the several ways he could have answered Horbin's remark about himself, but said nothing more as he gave Griffin a quick look. As he did, he sensed his partner was growing more and more pissed off at Horbin's snide remarks.

"Mr. Horbin, one more thing before we get started. That sign right there by the door tells everyone who comes in here that all interviews being conducted are being videotaped and recorded. You understand that?"

"Yeah. But I think its bullshit that it has to be printed in English and Spanish. If them freakin' illegal assholes want to live here they should learn to speak our language. It's also bullshit that I have to Press One when I make some of those phone calls to certain places. Screw that, I ain't pressing any buttons to speak English; make them assholes press the buttons 'cause I ain't doing it any longer."

Shaking his head, Wilson answered their suspect's brief outburst. "That's a discussion we'll also have to save for another time, Mr. Horbin. Let's just deal with the matter that's on the table for today, OK?"

Over the next several minutes, Horbin was questioned about his residence, about the firearms he owned, and about his involvement in the shed fire. He was also questioned about his role in the incident involving his dog, the Frisbee, and a couple of the murder victims. Despite their best efforts, the two veteran cops learned little more than what they already knew. It soon became clear to them that Horbin was not intimidated by the facts which seemed to connect him as being the person responsible for the murders of five of his neighbors.

Now clearly bored and even more pissed off by what he saw as a huge waste of his time, Horbin repeated a statement that he had made twice already. "Like I've told you two cops a bunch of times already, I admit I own a couple of guns, but they sure weren't used to kill them kids, and neither did I!"

Frustrated by Horbin's attitude, and by the lack of progress they were making, Wilson angrily lashed out at their suspect's statement. It was now time to increase the pressure on their only suspect.

"We know you own several weapons, Mr. Horbin, that's one of the reasons you're here. What we want to know right now is whether you've told us about all of them. Because if you haven't, and if we find any that you haven't told us about, then we'll have the state of South Carolina, and maybe the feds as well, prosecute your sorry-ass like they've never prosecuted anyone before!" Normally the emotional one in the handful of interviews they had conducted together, Wilson's uncharacteristic outburst caught his partner by surprise. Proud of how Horbin had been dressed down, Griffin allowed a wide smile to cross his face.

As Wilson forced himself to calm down, Griffin's cell chirped softly as he stood in the corner of the room entering a few notes in his Apple iPad. Taking a moment to look at his phone as Wilson began to follow up with their suspect on a few points that had already been raised caused Griffin to flash a grin at his partner, and then an even larger one at Horbin, before speaking.

"Blake just sent me a text from Horbin's home. I'm going to step out into the hallway for a moment, I'll be right outside if you need me." Opening the door to leave, Griffin paused to throw a comment in Horbin's direction before closing it behind him. "I'm thinking you best talk quick before I get back. It may be too late to help yourself once I come back." Wilson's eyes remained focused on their suspect as he nodded in agreement to the warning Griffin had tossed out.

"Like he said, Mr. Horbin, if you want to help yourself then you'd better say what needs to be said before my partner comes back. I'm not going to be able to help you much after he comes back in here with something you haven't told us about yet. It's your choice, I guess." Wilson said as he put his pen down on the desk next to a pad he had been writing on. After doing so, and with Horbin staring at the floor and momentarily lost in his own thoughts, Wilson flashed a thumbs-up to those watching him from the other side of the one-way mirror.

Horbin's still defiant attitude started to soften as his chin dropped down against his chest. He now realized that time, just like the cops he hated, was running against him.

"I might own a gun or two that I ain't yet told you about." Horbin weakly offered as he stared hard at the floor. "I've got a couple of pistols your boys have probably found by now. I'm guessing that's what that message was probably about." Shaking his head as he continued to look down at the floor, Horbin offered up a few more points to Wilson. "They're my guns, and they ain't registered like the others I own. I bought them about a year or so ago; got them from some biker dude I met in a bar down in Pawleys Island one night."

"OK," Wilson answered as he picked his pen up, "keep talking."

Horbin looked up at Wilson before speaking, clearly upset at the predicament he was in. "Listen, please, Mr. Wilson. Listen to me when I tell you that I knew my license was under suspension, and please believe me when I tell you that I got them unregistered guns just like I told you, but please believe me when I tell you that I didn't kill them kids. Test all of them guns I own like I see cops do on television; you'll see they weren't used to shoot them kids. Do what you've got to do about me not registering them guns like I was supposed to, but . . . please don't arrest me for killing them boys. I don't need that kind of trouble. I didn't do that, and I didn't help anyone else do it either, you'll see." Finished with his emotional plea, Wilson's once insolent suspect was now quiet as he looked down at his work boots.

"If you didn't kill those kids, do you know who did? Have you heard anything about those kids being killed?" Wilson asked as he stared across the desk at their suspect.

"No . . . no, sir. I sure don't." Horbin answered without looking up.

"What kind of pistols are we talking about?" Wilson asked.

"One's a Beretta 9 millimeter and the other's an H&K .380." Horbin quickly offered.

As his partner walked back into the Interview Room, Wilson's facial expression remained stoic as he tried hard not to react to the news Horbin had just told him. Pleased by what he had just learned, especially the news about the calibers of the two unregistered weapons, Wilson wondered how his fellow cops in the Observation Room were reacting to the same news.

Knowing he had little to lose, Griffin announced some of the news he had learned from Stine. He also did this so Paul and the others, listening in from the adjacent room, could hear what he had just learned. "The guys found two pistols inside the house that we hadn't been told about. They also found several boxes of ammunition. They were all found on top of a rather dusty cabinet. One's a 9 millimeter and the others a .380. Supposedly they both are in real good shape, but neither of them are apparently registered. When they get around to it, the boys are gonna check to see if they're stolen or not."

Wilson then tried one last time to pry a confession from their suspect, efforts his partner soon began helping him with. They were efforts that quickly failed. Taking a short break so they could talk in private outside the small room, Wilson and Griffin soon conferred with Paul in the hallway.

"You've made some progress by getting Horbin to admit to owning a couple of guns that aren't registered, but if he's not going to confess, which it doesn't seem that he's about to do, then we're going to have to ship the guns up to SLED so they can perform some comparison tests on the cartridges and shell casings." The mention of shell casings caused Paul to realize that while several damaged bullets had been recovered from the victims' bodies, only six shell casings had been found at the scene. It was not a thought that pleased him. "Obviously we still have some more work to do at the scene," he thought to himself.

"What now, boss?" Griffin asked, his question snapping Paul out of his thoughts about evidence that may or may not still exist at the scene.

"Get all you can out of him, Griff, including a written statement. Kent, you really need to focus in on the guns and the deaths of those kids, then let's see how your boy stands up to a game of Good Cop – Bad Cop. Maybe he'll hurt himself by lying to us again. I'm going to call Pascento as soon as you get done with your next round of questioning. When you finish interviewing him, and unless something drastically changes, I guess we'll have to cut him loose for now. Hate to do it, but we've got no choice right now. Even a first-year law student would be screaming at us if we tried holding him for much longer. I guess we could hold him on the weapon violations, but he's not going anywhere soon. We can pick him up on a warrant after we get everything sorted out. We've got more pressing needs to address tonight. We're going to have to sit tight until we hear back from SLED, so make sure Horbin knows that he's not to leave South Carolina without the court's permission."

Standing there with Wilson, Griffin gave Paul a confused look after hearing his last few words. "I didn't know the court had issued that kind of an order restricting his movements."

"They didn't. What your guy doesn't know won't hurt him, will it?" Paul responded, displaying a shrewd smile on his face.

* * * * * *

The following morning Lt. Small detailed Detectives Brandau and Baughman to transport Horbin's firearms, as well as the other evidence seized under the search warrants to SLED for examination. Despite the pressure the lab had already received to expedite the processing of the previously submitted evidence, especially the comparison testing of the shell casings, it would take several more days for all of the test results to be relayed back to Paul and everyone else.

What they would soon learn from SLED would not be the results Paul and Bobby Ray hoped for. The rest of the cops working with them would be equally as disappointed by the news they would soon learn.

Twenty-One

Disappointment

Over the next two days, as Paul and the others anxiously waited for SLED's findings to be made known, Audrey Small worked her last day of work. Despite the many investigative tasks which still needed her attention, she had a host of last minute wedding needs to attend to. She would be gone from work for the next sixteen days.

On the day after Small had finished work, at Paul's request, Solicitor Pascento, as did Judge J.D. Davis, signed off on an extension for the term of the principle search warrant. Doing so gave everyone associated with the processing of the victims' residence several extra days to complete their tasks without having to rush. While the house had been thoroughly searched, Paul, with Bobby Ray and Pascento concurring with his thoughts, saw the need to extend the life of the warrant so additional searches of the entire property could occur. The magnitude of the violence that had occurred there, as well as the enormity of the investigation, easily convinced Pascento and Davis that the request was based on legitimate needs.

One day later, Paul and Bobby Ray, who had returned to work for a few hours each day due to Small's absence, spoke early in the morning on the efforts being made to interview all of the witnesses a second time. It was a conversation taking place near where the shed had been intentionally burnt to the ground.

"We're still not finding that one clue or that one piece of evidence we need. Now we're hammering away here again looking for something that may not even exist." Like his friend, Bobby Ray was more than frustrated by the lack of any real progress being made to identify who had been responsible for the murders. As he finished speaking, his cell phone rang.

"Bobby Ray, its Ken Zercie from SLED. How's it going down there? Making progress, I hope."

Kenneth Zercie, a friend of Bobby Ray's for the past several years at the professional level, was SLED's Chief Firearms Examiner. A nationally recognized expert in all areas of firearm examinations, he had offered testimony in well over five hundred criminal cases across the country involving violence associated with a wide range of firearms. He had done so at the request of a bevy of both federal and state prosecutors, as well as for a number of high-priced defense attorneys.

"Hey, Ken! We've been anxiously waiting for your call. We need some good news for a change; hope you've got something good to tell us. Hey . . . I'm going to put my phone on speaker mode so a friend of mine who's working the case with us can hear what you've got to say. His name is Paul Waring." Bobby Ray took a brief moment to change his phone to speaker mode before speaking again. "OK, Ken, we're ready. Tell us what you've found."

A brief silence on the other end of the phone was Bobby Ray's first hint that the news they were about to hear was not going to be good.

"Wish I had something good to tell you, Bobby Ray, but unfortunately I don't," Zercie disappointedly said. "I'll get my report down to you soon, but I wanted to call you with my findings because I know you've got a huge problem on your hands down there. To make it simple for you to understand, I test fired all of Horbin's weapons, and then I compared each of those shell casings to the ones you found at your scene. Unfortunately for you, when I was looking at each of the casings I noticed significant differences between them. In a nut shell, the casings you found at the scene were not fired from any of your suspect's firearms."

"Ken, Paul Waring here. As you've heard, I'm working with Bobby Ray on this investigation. I'm sorry to interrupt you, but what differences are you talking about? Are you talking about differences in the ejector markings on each of the casings?"

"Yes, I am. I can't say this with a complete degree of certainty, but I'm fairly confident that the casings you found at the scene were either fired from a H&K pistol or from a Mauser. This may not make sense to you, but the casings I've examined from the scene have similar, but vastly different markings to those that I fired from your suspect's guns. But what I really need is the gun that fired the casings you found at the scene, or I need some other casings that we know were fired from your shooter's gun. If I had either, I could do some additional testing on them to determine if the firing pin impressions are a match. I could also do the same to determine if either the breech face marks or the ejector marks matched." Catching himself, Zercie added, "Obviously if one's a match, then they're both going to match. Without them, I can't say with any degree of certainty what kind of firearm was used to shoot your victims with."

Like Bobby Ray, Paul was silent for a few moments as he digested Zercie's disappointing news. "Mr. Zercie, forgive me for being a bit too informal before. In the excitement of the moment, I forgot that we haven't met as yet, so I should not have called you by your first name. I apologize for doing so."

"I'm an informal kind of guy, Paul. No offense taken at all."

"Thanks, Ken." Somewhat old fashion in how he greeted people for the first time, Paul was relieved to hear he had not offended Zercie. "Let me ask you a couple of more questions if I may. If the extractor markings were that different, then I'm guessing the impressions made by each of the firing pins were just as different, is that correct?"

"Afraid so, Paul. If one is different, then they're both different. No exceptions." Then Zercie surprised Paul and Bobby Ray with his next comment. "I told you that the comparison tests I ran didn't match your suspect's weapons, but I didn't say the impressions on the casings you found didn't match each other. Even though they're different calibers, the firing pin impressions matched perfectly."

Zercie's news startled Bobby Ray, but it did not receive the same reaction from Paul. "Ken, correct me if I'm wrong, but what you're saying is the same gun . . . our shooter's gun . . . fired all of those casings we found at the scene?"

"Yep, I sure am. Your shooter obviously used a firearm that can fire more than one caliber. Many firearms, even some revolvers, allow for one gun to fire different calibers of rounds. In your case, it was an automatic. The firing pin impressions are an exact match on the casings you found at the scene; so are the ejector markings."

"OK, I understand all of that." Paul said as he processed the news Zercie had given them. Then he asked about the one badly damaged bullet that had been sent to the lab.

"The bad news, which you obviously already know, is that it's in bad condition. The good news is that I think I can still use it. I'd have to be able to compare it to one that's in better shape, and one that's been fired from the same gun, then I'd have a better idea if I can use it. So don't give up the ship yet."

Zercie's news brought a half-smile to Paul's face. "We'll work on keeping the ship afloat, and on finding that gun for you."

Collecting his thoughts on the news Zercie had told them, and reigning in his own disappointment about their suspect's firearms not being a match, Bobby Ray asked a question that meant little in the way of importance regarding the conversation taking place.

"Ken, those differences you noticed. Did you make them with the naked eye or under a microscope?"

Zercie laughed at his friend's question for several seconds before answering. "SLED may not have the biggest equipment budget going, Bobby Ray, but they do buy us microscopes these days. We even have electricity in the building too!" Zercie's comment was meant to poke fun at his friend's question. "I used a compound dual stage comparison microscope to conduct the tests. For what it's worth, I've also taken a sufficient number of photographs of each casing I tested. I'll have them here if you need them."

Frustrated by the bad news regarding the casings, Paul moved the conversation to the next issue. "Ken, what about the cigarette butts? How did the DNA testing work out? Hopefully better than the other news you've given us."

"Guys, I'm sorry, but it didn't. I was told the cigarette butts you found in the victims' backyard were not in good enough condition to get much of a DNA sample from. We got some, but not much. Those butts had been outside and exposed to the elements for far too long. The same was somewhat true with the ones I believe you found in the road in front of your suspect's home. The scientist running the tests found more DNA on that sample, but not as much as she would have liked. The ones you seized from his house are the best samples we have; we've successfully typed Mr. Horbin's DNA from those. But no matter how good or bad the DNA was or wasn't, we've now got his DNA on file. The bad news is that your suspect's DNA did not match the DNA on the cigarette butts you found in the victims' backyard. The other bad news is no one else's does either. We even compared the DNA we found on the cigarette butts to the samples taken from each of the victims during their autopsies. We didn't find their DNA on any of the butts either. Your backyard smoker is either someone who has never been arrested or someone who has never volunteered a DNA sample for us to use. I'm sorry."

"You folks sure about all of this, Ken? I mean . . . like positive?" A defeated Bobby Ray asked.

"Positives and negatives are all that I and the other scientists here deal with, Bobby Ray. We're like a baseball umpires; we just call them as we see them. I can appreciate your disappointment, but I can't invent a positive match for you. DNA is a far more exact science than firearms testing, but the principles are the same. The samples either match or they don't."

Despite the bad news he told them, Zercie did have one small piece of good news to share with them.

"After I finished my testing, I entered the digital images of the casings' ejector marks, firing pin impressions, and the breech face markings into ATF's NIBIN System that we have here at the lab. While what I'm about to tell you doesn't help your case much, NIBIN, after it scanned my images against the thousands that are on file, found two matches to the casings you found at the scene. The casings that match yours come back to a shooting which took place two years ago just outside of Wilmington, North Carolina. I've already contacted my counterpart up at the North Carolina Bureau of Investigation and made arrangements to have their evidence sent down to me so I can compare the casings microscopically. I have yet to do this, but have either of you checked yet to see if your suspect's guns were stolen?"

Paul let Bobby Ray answer Zercie's question for them. "We did that shortly after we found them inside his residence. Two of them came back as having been stolen during a burglary of a residence in Raleigh, North Carolina in late 2012. I've had one of my guys reach out to RPD already. Our suspect is telling us he paid a guy a few bucks for them at a bar in Pawleys Island last year. Who knows if he's trying to bullshit us or not, but I'm having it all run down with RPD and WPD. You're right about this not helping us much with the mess we're facing, but at least we have something to hold over our suspect's head for now. We may not solve what we're facing down here, but maybe we can lend a hand in helping to solve the burglary and the shooting those two departments had. At least someone is benefitting from the NIBIN technology; wish we were too."

"Ken, thanks for all of your help. Do us a favor, will you? Please send a copy of your findings to Bobby Ray's attention just in case something else pops down here." Paul politely asked.

"Will do. Good luck, guys! Call me if I can be of any help."

* * * * * *

The news Zercie's phone call brought them was a huge disappointment to Paul and Bobby Ray. The one thing it did confirm for them, besides Horbin no longer being a viable suspect, was that they now had a significant amount of work to do in order to be able to start focusing their attention on a new suspect.

It was not a task they relished undertaking.

Twenty-Two

Paul's Hunch

After running into more dead ends than he could count in the days following Zercie's bad news, Paul held a mandatory meeting on a Thursday evening for everyone assigned to the case. It was held in one of the meeting rooms inside the recently opened Murrells Inlet Community Center. It was the perfect place for it as one of the GCSD sub-stations was located in the same building. Besides the cops actually working the case, Paul made sure Bobby Ray and Audrey Small were there as well. Despite her wedding being less than two days away, Small agreed to come listen to what was going to be discussed. A similar invitation had also been extended to Sheriff Renda as well, but a prior speaking engagement now caused a conflict in his schedule.

Inside the room, Paul, with help from Elmendorf and Vane, staged various photos of most of the evidence that had been seized, including blow-ups of each shell casing. Other photos, including those which had been taken of the victims before they had been removed from the scene, were also posted for everyone to refer to during the meeting. On the other side of the room, several finished diagrams of the crime scene had been taped to three large chalkboards for reference needs. On a table in the front of the room, various notebooks containing every report that had been written by anyone who had done anything to help with this investigation sat waiting to be leafed through.

"Folks, obviously we're here because we are not having much luck in identifying who's responsible for the murders we've been investigating. All of your hard work has brought us only one suspect so far, and we all know how that recently played out. Like many of you, I liked Horbin as our suspect for a while, but then when I read his statement I began to realize he was not our guy. So now we need to move on. Bobby Ray, Audrey, and I have spoken about this, and I'm afraid we are going to have to start all over at square one again. That means we need to talk to every person we've already spoken to. The only people we are not going to talk with right now are Horbin and all of the parents. Tommy Scozz, just like some of you who have been working with the parents, has told me these folks need some time to mourn. So because of that, and because Scozz believes we've already asked them every question we should, we're not going to bother these folks unless we have to. Unless you tell me different, and I want all of you to look at these reports, as well as the photos and any of the evidence that we've got here tonight so you can tell me if we've missed something, we are going to start re-interviewing everyone we've already interviewed. That's going to start happening tomorrow." Paul paused for a moment before pointing to several of the items spread out across the room. "I can't tell you why I think this, but, personally, I have the feeling that we already have what we need to identify who's responsible for killing those kids. Maybe that's not the case, but I think it is. The problem is I'm not seeing what that is right now; neither are you. I really don't want to waste our time interviewing all of these people again, so please take a good look at everything tonight, especially those areas you may have not worked on. Cross-checking each other's work is one way for us to possibly see what we might have missed. Any questions?"

From the back of the room, one of Small's detectives asked Paul a question about some of the evidence found inside the victims' residence. "What about the marijuana that was found in the Johanson kid's bedroom? Has that been ruled out, as some of us are hearing, as a possible reason why these kids were killed?"

"Good question, but I'm sorry you had to even ask that," Paul said as he stared hard at Bobby Ray, and then at Small. "The marijuana that was found was ruled out shortly after we found it. It was ruled out after we spoke with that kid's parents, and with a few of the other parents, as well as with some of his friends. That should have been passed on to you by now. If it wasn't, that's not acceptable as I'm not interested in having any of you wasting your time working on something we've already ruled out. That's also not doing our victims, or their parents, or even us any good. The weed we found was for that young man's personal use and not for anything else. I won't call it an addiction, so let's just leave it as the victim had a problem with that kind of stuff. Don't spend any more time on that issue, OK?" Finished with his answer, Paul again stared at Bobby Ray and Small. The look they saw reflected Paul's displeasure in one of them not getting the word out to all of their people about the marijuana no longer being considered a reason why five young men had died. It was another in a series of mistakes and omissions which others were responsible for that again frustrated him.

"OK, if there are no further questions, please get to work. Take your time looking at whatever you want, or take your time asking questions of others, but find whatever it is that we've been missing. We need to give these parents some solace by finding those responsible for murdering their sons."

As the others got to work, Paul walked to the back of the room. Bobby Ray soon joined him there while Small stayed near the podium that Paul had been speaking from. Her job was to answer questions for her staff as they reviewed all of the reports and exhibits.

"Hey, good to see you two boys! Thanks for coming here to help us out!" Paul said as he greeted two old friends with a big smile.

Tony Cummings and Mark Foster, two veteran cops who were longtime friends of Paul and Bobby Ray's, stood up from where they had been seated to shake hands with their buddies. Arriving in town less than an hour earlier, they had come to the community center after checking into their hotel, a nearby Hampton Inn, in Pawleys Island.

Convinced that a couple of fresh sets of eyes would do the investigation some good, Paul, with Bobby Ray's support, had convinced Sheriff Renda to allow him to bring in two seasoned cops to look at what had been done on the investigation so far. They had been surprised by Renda's support of the idea, and had been even more surprised when he quickly agreed to pay their expenses for coming in to help.

Tony Cummings, who had recently turned sixty years of age, was a former commander with the North Carolina Bureau of

Investigation, based primarily in the Wilmington area. His principle areas of expertise were in conducting homicide and narcotic investigations as a major portion of his career with NCBI had been spent in those two areas. During his time as the Narcotics Commander, he had hosted a NASDEA meeting in Atlantic Beach, and it was there Paul and Bobby Ray had first gotten to know the person they often referred to as TC. After retiring, Cummings was hired by the sheriff of Brunswick County as his Under Sheriff. While Cummings was a good friend of the sheriff who hired him, his reputation as an excellent investigator had been the primary reason he had been appointed to that position. Holding that position for nine years until he grew tired of county politics getting in the way of being able to do his job, for the past three years he was the principle owner of Cummings Investigations, a well-respected security firm based on the outskirts of Wilmington, North Carolina.

Earlier in their careers, Paul and Bobby Ray had first met when they attended the FBI National Academy, in Quantico, Virginia. It was at this advanced law enforcement training center that they had also met Mark Foster. At that time, Foster was the Narcotics Commander for the Charleston County Sheriff's Department, in Charleston, SC. After graduating from the academy he was later promoted twice, rising to the rank of Major. Recently retired after a thirty-two year career in law enforcement, he now ran his own business, a highly successful firm which assisted law enforcement agencies up and down the east coast with their hiring and promotional needs. His development of Assessment Centers, a practice which used veteran law enforcement professionals to help state and local police departments when it came time for them to conduct promotional examinations, was one of his biggest accomplishments since retiring. His list of clients was a long and impressive one. On several occasions in the past, after securing a handful of lucrative municipal contracts, he had asked Paul, Bobby Ray, and TC Cummings for their professional assistance.

As the others in the room worked on trying to find something that may have been missed, Paul and Bobby Ray spent the next forty minutes walking their two friends through the investigation. As they did, and with Small's assistance at times, they used the photographs and diagrams to show Cummings and Foster how they had found the scene, and where most of the evidence had been located.

Without any prompting from Paul or Bobby Ray, Cummings began focusing on the incident involving the shed that had burned to the ground. "I know you've told us that SLED's examination of your evidence has ruled out the neighbor as being a suspect in this mess y'all have, but I can't help thinking this shed fire is connected to your murders. If there wasn't anything combustible in the shed, and if there wasn't an ignition source and a source of fuel, such as a gasoline or anything like that, then it was intentionally set on fire for a reason. Most likely it was done to send a message to at least one or two of your victims. The fact that you found those cigarette butts mixed in with the pine straw seems to confirm my feeling on how the fire started, at least in my opinion it does. I think we need to focus on that one issue some more."

Foster quickly agreed with the points Cummings had raised. "Just because the neighbor's DNA was not found on the cigarette butts doesn't mean someone else's wasn't. From what you're telling us, SLED's findings have already confirmed that for you. I'm guessing there's a whole bunch of folks around here who smoke Parliaments; we just need to find the person connected to the butts you found."

"I'm thinking that's obviously easier said than done." Bobby Ray offered in response to Foster's comment. It was one that caused Foster and Cummings to both nod their heads in agreement.

For the next ninety minutes, Cummings and Foster took the time to study most of the material available in the room. During that time they also spoke to Stine, Griffin, Wilson, and to some of the others, including Elmendorf and Vane. They spoke to them about areas of the investigation that each of them had been a part of. After doing so, and after sensing the others in the room had already put in a long day, Foster made a suggestion to Paul and Bobby Ray. It was one they quickly agreed to.

"Guys, why not send your folks home so they can get some rest. They're going to be back at it again tomorrow, so, if y'all will allow me to make this suggestion to you, why not send them home and let us stay here for however long it takes us to give this stuff a closer look in private. When we're ready to leave, we'll let the deputy in the sub-station know he can lock the room up." Then pointing to the photographs, diagrams, and other material present, Foster added, "We'll take all of this with us when we leave and give it back to you in the morning when we meet you back at the scene."

Tired himself, and knowing Bobby Ray's back was beginning to give him some discomfort, Paul quickly agreed to Foster's suggestion.

"Have fun, boys! See you around eight at the house." Fatigued from far too many long days and nights, Paul waited for everyone else to leave before walking out to the parking lot with Bobby Ray. Overcast for most of the afternoon, a light rain began to fall as Paul started his car. With his friend's back beginning to act up, he decided to play it safe and drive Bobby Ray home. Paul knew doing so was the right thing to do, but at this late hour he also knew it meant delaying the little time he had left in the day to enjoy a Jack and Coke or two at home before grabbing a few hours of precious sleep. Dinner itself would have to wait until tomorrow. A couple of drinks and a few hours of sleep now took precedence over a cold ham and cheese sandwich or whatever it was that was in his refrigerator.

* * * * * *

Accidently dropping his keys on the tile floor in his kitchen as he took them out of his pants pocket woke Donna up from a sound sleep. She had fallen asleep on a couch in the living room as she watched television while waiting for Paul to arrive home. On the stove, one of her husband's favorite meals, a now cold meatloaf dinner sat waiting for him to enjoy it for the past three hours. Ignoring the food, Paul quickly made himself a tall Jack and Coke, one with plenty of ice. Finished making his drink, he watched as Donna rose up off the couch and slowly made her way into the kitchen. Quietly they shared a long and warm embrace.

"Care to join me?" Paul asked after taking a healthy swig of his drink. "Be glad to make you one."

"A glass of wine, please, that'll be fine. I'm going to bed soon, so make it a small one. I'll sit down with you for a few minutes, but then I'm making my way to the sheets. I'm exhausted," Donna said as she looked over at her tired husband. "I don't know how you cops keep going for so long day after day. All of your folks have to be exhausted by now."

As his wife sat down at their kitchen table, Paul poured Donna a glass of J. LOHR chardonnay. Handing it to her, he immediately sensed he had given her too much from the frown on her face. It was one that was far too large for her liking at this time of the day. Sitting down next to her, Paul asked about her day at work, but she was more interested in learning what had happened during his day. As the one who had given him the OK to go back to work to help solve this case, she grilled him each and every night he came home, hoping to learn the person or persons responsible for committing these heinous murders had been caught. As a mother herself, she had taken on an almost personal interest in the case. A quiet and peaceful person in life, one who despised arguments and confrontations of any kind, this matter was an exception to her. She wanted the son of a bitch, and whoever else was responsible for murdering five young men, to die a long and slow painful death.

"Sorry, honey," Paul said as he took his third healthy swig of his drink, "I wish I had something good to tell you, but I don't. I still feel like we're close to solving this, but then I also feel like the wind has been knocked out of a few of the folks since our first suspect was ruled out."

Draining his drink, his first in several days, Paul made himself another Jack and Coke. It was just as large as the first one, but made with a slightly heavier splash of Jack Daniels this time. He easily justified doing so as he told himself that he had earned it after several especially long days at work. Walking back to where Donna was still seated, Paul pushed a bowl of Fritos in her direction. For him, this was going to be dinner. The cold meatloaf dinner would have to wait until tomorrow.

After answering a handful of additional questions for Donna as she occasionally munched a few Fritos, Paul told her about the meeting he had earlier that evening with everyone assigned to the investigation. He told her about the photos that had been blown up, told her about the crime scene diagrams which had been posted for everyone to see, told her about all of the reports that had been written by all of the detectives assigned to each of the various tasks, and then he finally told her about why he had asked Tony Cummings and Mark Foster to be there as well. Donna knew Cummings fairly well, and had met Foster on a handful occasions over the past twelve years or so.

"I think that's a good idea you had, Paul." Donna mumbled through a handful of Fritos she was polishing off. "Having those guys come in to conduct a review . . . you know, to spot-check what everyone else has done makes perfect sense. Hopefully by doing so nothing falls through the cracks, something, perhaps, that maybe is too obvious for you and the others to see."

Paul smiled as he nodded at Donna's interest in the case. The fact that she understood completely why Cummings and Foster had been called in to help with the investigation pleased him.

"Donna, I know we're going to get this solved, but when? The local politicians, just like the media has been doing all along, have started breathing down Sheriff Renda's neck demanding to know when we're going to catch whoever's responsible for this tragedy. Bobby Ray's now feeling some heat from Renda, and so is Audrey to some degree, but we're doing everything we can. I've lost track of how many people we've already interviewed, but it has to be close to one hundred."

Donna sat quiet for a moment, but then asked her husband about any evidence that might have been overlooked.

"I've had Donnie and Doug go over the house, the yard, the location where the shed stood before it was burned to the ground, and the victims' cars three times. They didn't find a thing that we had missed. We even brought in some of the Myrtle Beach and Horry County crime scene techs to see if our guys missed anything. They didn't find anything either."

Donna had not heard much about the shed fire and asked Paul a few questions about it. After hearing all that he had to say about the small fire, and realizing her eyes were getting heavy, she stood up so she could place her glass in the kitchen sink.

"I'm going to bed, Paul. I'm sorry, but I'm tired." Patting her husband on the top of the head after giving him a goodnight kiss, Donna turned to make her way to their bedroom. As she did, she paused to look briefly over her shoulder at her tired husband. "Don't stay up too late, you're tired too. Tomorrow's another day to sort this mess out. Who knows, perhaps Tony or Mark will figure something out for you tonight. But you'll figure it out, I'm sure. Maybe the clue you need is with someone those kids knew, someone your guys just haven't spoken with yet. It could be someone who might have gotten pissed off at them after attending a party at the house or someone who did some work there. But I know one thing for sure, I'm going to bed. Love you!"

Paul gave Donna a tired wave as he watched her make her way to the bedroom. Sitting at the table for several more minutes, he ate the rest of the Fritos and finished his drink. As he did, he tried scanning the day's paper, but the articles he read were making little sense to his tired and now alcohol impaired brain.

"Donna's right," he thought as he stood up to clean up the small mess he had made in the kitchen. "Tomorrow's another day. Hopefully we'll get it figured out somehow during the day."

Walking into their Master Bedroom suite, Paul took care of a few personal necessities, including brushing his teeth. As he did, he tried again to sort out some of the details which continued to flood his head, but he was beyond tired. In moments, he was fast asleep in bed next to his wife.

* * * * * *

His sleep was even more restless than it normally was on most nights. Even the two large Jack and Cokes just before bed had not helped Paul sleep like they usually did. Like most people having a restless night's sleep, he tossed and turned repeatedly, never really falling into a deep restful sleep. Dozing off and on, he realized he was thinking of the many tasks that still needed completion. As his thoughts raced through his mind, he silently cursed himself for not being able to fall asleep.

Rising early after a long night of restless sleep, Paul gave Donna quick kiss on the cheek as he tried not waking her. It was one that was barely acknowledged. Unlike her husband, she had spent a restful night in bed, hardly noticing Paul's inability to sleep much during the night.

Leaving his home in the warm morning air, Paul drove the short distance to the Waccamaw Diner. It was just before five when he pulled into the nearly deserted parking lot. As he walked towards the diner's front door, he caught Betty waving to him. She had just started the diner's day by unlocking the door.

"You look like hell! Looks like you either couldn't sleep or your wife made you sleep in your car." Betty chuckled at the sight of her tired friend.

Settling down into his favorite booth, Paul took a moment to catch his breath. It was far too early in the day to be tired, but several long days with little sleep had worn him out.

"It's the former, Betty, not the latter." Paul said in response to her previous statement as she soon followed him to the booth.

"The what?"

"Never mind," Paul weakly replied, "just bring me the usual and some really hot coffee, please. I could use some sleep, but I need some chow even more."

In a matter of minutes, Paul sat eating warm blueberry pancakes in his booth which overlooked a section of the diner's parking lot. They were pancakes he had a craving for on most occasions as no one made them thicker and stuffed full of blueberries like the diner did. As he ate and read the morning paper, he began to feel somewhat better. Sitting there, he tried hard not to think about the problems associated with the investigation. But just like his efforts at trying to fall asleep during the night, his efforts of trying not to think about problems failed as well. Soon he was again far too focused on work to notice Betty approaching.

"Hey, ya want some more coffee?" She asked as she began refilling his cup without giving him time to respond.

"Thanks, Betty. Sorry I'm not much of a conversationalist this morning. Too damn tired, and too much on my mind, I guess. When you have a second, make me a coffee to go, will you? I'm going to need all the caffeine I can get to help me make it through the day today."

Finished refilling Paul's cup, Betty set the glass coffee pot down on the booth's table. "Still trying to figure out who killed them poor kids, huh?"

"Yep." Paul mumbled through a mouthful of pancakes.

"Catch whoever done it, will ya? Me and a whole lot of folks from around here want to see whoever done it hung for doing what they did. Them poor parents must be beside themselves over this." Betty said, shaking her head as she thought about the tragedy that occurred not that far away from where she now stood talking with Paul.

As she started walking away to make Paul's coffee to go, and to greet another customer who had just come into the diner, Betty stopped to look back at her tired friend for a moment. "Paul, don't fret none about not talking to me this morning, I understand. Besides, in a few minutes all of them boys who cut lawns for a living will be in here for their morning coffee. Most mornings they're worse than old women; those boys love to talk. By the time they leave here each morning my ears are tired!"

His mouth once again filled with pancakes, Paul could only nod at what Betty said. Soon finished eating, he began washing down his breakfast with his second cup of coffee. As he sat in the booth looking out the large window to his right, he noticed several pick-up trucks being parked in the parking lot. Each was towing a trailer packed full of commercial grade mowers of all kinds, as well as leaf blowers, rakes, weed whackers, and other lawn equipment. He watched as several men, some still half-asleep, emptied out of the trucks to start making their way to the diner. "Looks like Betty's talkative morning customers have arrived." Paul thought as he nursed the remaining coffee in his cup.

Within minutes, nine young men in their early to mid-twenties entered the diner. As they made their way towards several vacant stools aside the lunch counter, each of them loudly greeted Betty and the two other waitresses with friendly comments.

"What a life," Paul thought as he watched the men sit down at the counter several feet away from where he sat. "What kind of worries could those guys have each day? Certainly it's nothing close to what we're trying to figure out about who killed those kids."

Soon finished with his breakfast, and after giving Betty a friendly wave, Paul was out the door a few minutes later. Climbing into his own personal truck, which he had elected to drive that morning instead of the GCSD vehicle he had been assigned, Paul stared at two of the pick-up trucks parked close to his. The first one, a red Ford Super Duty F350 XLT, and the other, a navy blue Chevy Silverado, both had the names of their respective lawn services painted on the front doors of the trucks.

While the rising sun had begun to brighten the sky as Paul drove south on Highway 17 towards the crime scene, there was still enough darkness left to warrant leaving his headlights on. Most of the other motorists travelling in both directions chose to do the same, protecting themselves from some local idiot who might later tell a cop that they had not seen their fellow motorist's car or truck approaching as they tried pulling out from one of the many side streets lining the busy road.

As he drove past the busy intersection where traffic headed south on Highway 17 Business merges back together to form one road with Highway 17 By-Pass South, Paul noticed three vehicles trying to merge onto Highway 17. The vehicles, two passenger cars and a Dodge Ram pick-up, were trying to merge onto the highway from his left. Moving from the left lane to the right to allow them an easier opportunity to enter the highway, he noticed that while the pick-up's lights were properly displayed, the rear lights of the trailer it was towing were not. Despite the little amount of daylight that was now available, it was easy to see the trailer was carrying a significant number of lawn tools. Amongst them were a large commercial mower, two push style mowers, several leaf blowers, as well as a handful of rakes and shovels.

Seeing the trailer being towed without any lights being displayed caused Paul to wonder what the South Carolina legislature had been thinking when they decided not to require lights having to be displayed on certain size trailers during hours of darkness. "No running lights, and probably no brake lights on that thing either. That's an accident waiting to happen." Paul thought to himself as he glanced back at the trailer through his rear view mirror.

As he looked back one last time, Paul caught a brief glimpse of the large lawn tractor sitting on the trailer. The sight of it caused

246 | PETER F. WARREN

his brain to immediately react to what he was seeing. It also caused him to momentarily lose focus on his driving. It was not until the tires on the right side of his truck ran over the rumble strips on the side of the road that he regained his focus. The bumps he felt, as well as the noise generated by his tires running over the depressions intentionally cut into the surface of the road, made him quickly realize how easily he had been distracted, and how close he had come to striking a section of guardrails off the right side of the highway.

Once safely back in traffic, Paul continued to head south towards the crime scene. As he did, his thoughts again returned to the tractor being towed. It had been the sight of it that caused him concern. The more he thought about what he had seen, the angrier he became.

"I know I've read all of the reports on the interviews we've done, so why haven't I read that one?" Paul interrupted his thoughts so he could try and sort out what he was thinking, but he could not. Not being able to do so, he asked himself a question. "We've interviewed the mailmen delivering mail in the area, we've interviewed all of the neighbors, and I know we've interviewed the UPS and FedEx drivers who service the neighborhood, as well as everyone else we could think of, so why in hell have we *not* interviewed whoever took care of the victims' lawn?"

Turning onto Trace Drive, one of the two main roads leading into the crime scene, Paul tried to think of the list of names that he and Small had put together for her detectives to interview. "I know we talked about needing to speak to those folks who had done work at the house, but why I haven't seen the report that summarizes the interview with the lawn service folks?" Then an upsetting thought caused him even more concern. "I thought Audrey was staying on top of these interviews, making sure they had all been addressed. Apparently that might not be the case though." Silently he prayed that no others had been missed as well.

Looking at his watch as he pulled in front of the victims' residence, Paul saw that it was quarter after six. Bringing his truck to a stop alongside the edge of the road, he saw Stine standing in the driveway holding a cup of coffee while he talked with the uniformed deputy who had safeguarded the scene overnight.

Despite the early hour of the day, and his lack of sleep, Paul was now focused on a hunch he had. Putting down his driver's window, he hollered to Stine, giving a quick wave to the deputy as he did. "Blake, let's go!"

"What's up, boss? Kind of early to get going, isn't it?" Stine asked as he buckled himself into the right front seat of Paul's truck.

"It's too early for most people," Paul said as he pulled away from the side of the road, "but not for idiots like you and me who can't sleep."

Stine laughed at Paul's accurate description of their shared sleeping problems.

"To answer your question, I'm not sure anything is up, but I've got a hunch we've missed something." Paul said as he steered his truck out onto Highway 17.

During the short drive to the nearby Hampton Inn, Paul filled Stine in with his thoughts and concerns, ones focusing on the lawn service responsible for cutting the victims' grass. Despite having a good idea of who had been told to conduct that interview, like Paul, Stine was also unsure if it had been done or not.

"You thinking that maybe one or two of the guys who cuts the grass might have killed those kids for some reason?" Stine asked as he climbed out of Paul's truck at the hotel.

"If you've got a better idea on who did this, tell me, 'cause I sure in hell don't." Paul said as he pushed the button for the third floor on the elevator. Walking to the hotel from his truck, he phoned Cummings telling him to anticipate two unexpected guests within less than two minutes.

"I guess I don't." Stine admitted.

* * * * * *

Groggy-eyed as he opened his hotel room door, Cummings, who had only gotten to bed a few hours earlier, watched as Paul and Stine walked inside his room. Moments earlier he had been roused out of a deep sleep by his friend's early morning phone call. With Foster's help, they had spent several hours reviewing most of the documents pertaining to the investigation before retiring for the night. Not knowing why Paul was coming to see him so early, Cummings had not bothered to wake Foster up from where he slept two doors down the hallway.

"This had better be important," Cummings said through a rather loud yawn as he closed his hotel door.

Laughing at the sight of his friend standing in front of him wearing nothing but a pair of lime green and pink boxers that he had worn to bed, Paul's next comment made Stine laugh. "You look mighty impressive standing there in your colorful skivvies, TC! Mighty impressive! Did you actually buy those skivvies or did you lose a bet to Foster?"

Cummings tried to stifle another yawn as he answered Paul's remark about his sleeping attire. "Is that what this is all about? You're here to break my chops about the color of my underwear?"

"Good thing no one pulled the fire alarm last night, huh, Paul?" Stine offered, jumping into the banter about Cummings' colorful sleeping attire. His comment caused Paul to let out a loud, but brief snicker.

Composing himself, Paul brought the conversation to the reason why he and Stine were there. "OK, enough about your attire, TC. Where are the reports and photographs that you and Mark were looking at last night?" His eyes now quickly scanned his friend's neatly decorated hotel room for the boxes of documents.

"Over there . . . on the sofa. They're under that comforter right there. I took the damn thing off the bed last night; it got too hot in here to leave it on the bed. We put everything back in the boxes after we finished looking at them early this morning." Cummings said as he put on the tee shirt he had worn before going to bed.

Walking over to the sofa, Paul began pulling the notebooks full of reports out of the bigger of the two white-colored cardboard boxes. Finding what he was looking for, he quickly began thumbing through the pages of a large black notebook that been titled PHOTO REPORTS. Inside the notebook, he searched to find one specific photo report, it was one written by one of the first uniformed deputies who had arrived at the scene on the day of the murders. That deputy, Deputy George Bontya, had filed the report after being directed to take some real estate type of photos by Sergeant Edward Kindle. He had directed his deputy to do so as he wanted the exterior of the residence photographed to show what the scene looked like before it was trampled by other arriving cops, EMS workers, ambulances, and others. Soon finding the report he was looking for, Paul sat down on the edge of Cummings' bed to take a look at the accompanying photos.

As Paul began examining the photos, Cummings sat down in an office style chair that went with the desk sitting near the foot of his bed. Despite his lack of sleep, he easily detected the intense look on his friend's face; it told him Paul was looking for something important.

"Paul, I'm not sure what's got you so fired up so early this morning, but seeing what notebook you're looking through has got my attention."

"Oh, yeah." Paul said as he finally found the two photos he was looking for. "Why's that?" His own attention was focused on the photos more than on what his friend had just said.

"Because when Mark and I were looking through all of these reports you've got crammed into these here boxes, we noticed that no one has mentioned anything about interviewing anyone associated with the lawn company responsible for mowing the victims' lawn. One or two of the reports talk about the yard being maintained by a lawn company, but no one ever followed up on that by interviewing any of the workers, or even the company's owner. Seems like everyone else who did work at the house has been interviewed, so why haven't the lawn folks been interviewed as well? We found that kind of funny, if that's really the right way to describe it."

Cummings' comments caught Paul by surprise at first. Quickly he stopped looking at the photos he had found; his eyes noticing the stare that Stine directed at Cummings.

"I guess I should have called you boys in earlier to help us, TC. You could have saved us a whole lot of time." Paul said as his eyes focused back down on the photos Deputy Bontya had taken. After a few moments of staring at them, he showed the photos to Cummings and Stine.

"These are photos that Kindle had taken shortly after he realized the scene was more than just a house fire. Kudos to him for doing so." Turning to look up at Stine and Cummings, Paul spoke again as he pointed directly at the photos. "Like the others that Deputy Bontya took with a bullshit disposable camera, these two here are just as important as the casings we've found. See anything in this particular photo that attracts your attention?"

After briefly studying the photos, Stine spoke first after taking an extra moment to look at the photo Paul had been pointing to. He, like Paul and Cummings, had been looking at two photos Bontya had taken while standing in the road in front of the victims' front yard. "Looks like the lawn has just been cut as I can see the tracks the mower made when it made its way up and down the lawn."

Paul nodded approvingly at Stine's observations. "See anything else?"

"Well," Cummings said as his tired eyes continued to bounce

back and forth between the photos in question, "to take Blake's comment a bit further, I'd have to say it looks like the lawn was cut with a fairly large commercial mower of some kind. By the looks of each of those passes the mower took, they're not the size or shape of a mower that someone buys at Home Depot or Sears. The width of each of those passes tells me the lawn was cut with some kind of a commercial grade mower."

"You're getting warmer, boys. See anything else that's important in this one particular photo?" Paul asked as he again pointed to the photo that Bontya had marked as Photo #7 of 12 in his report. Stine and Cummings remained quiet until Paul pointed to the one feature that had stood out in the photo to him.

"Look at the right side of the driveway in the photo, it's obvious, at least to me it is, that the lawn was cut early that morning. The mower has left tracks of cut grass clippings on the surface of the driveway. That means wet grass was caught in the mower's tires. It also means each time the mower was turned around to make another pass it left wet clippings on the concrete driveway."

Stine looked at Paul, and then back at the photo for a brief moment. "Yeah, so?"

His friend's comment caused Paul to smile. "Look at the far right side of the photo." Paul said as he pointed to a different set of tracks that the mower's wet tires had left. "These tracks go off in a different direction than the others. This wet set of tracks is from when the lawn to the right of the driveway was cut. The tracks cross the driveway horizontally, just like the others from the left side of the driveway do. But this other set of tracks are different. They run the length of the driveway;

they're vertical in their direction, and there are only one set of them. Why's that? Can you two so-called detectives figure this important clue out?"

Cummings had listened carefully to everything Paul said, but still had not totally grasped the full meaning of what his friend had pointed out. "OK, so perhaps those tracks mean the guy got done mowing the lawn and was moving his mower out to the end of the driveway, so what? I'm not seeing the meaning behind this set of tracks that you think are so important."

"Look at the tracks, Tony," Stine said as he now pointed to them. "I think Paul's trying to tell us the mower headed south after it left the driveway. See how they turn slightly to the right at the end of the driveway and aren't seen again in the photo?"

"And?" Cummings asked.

"It was moved south as it left the driveway because there was another lawn to mow nearby or, perhaps, a truck and trailer parked further down the road." Stine's interpretation of what his boss had first seen in the photo again caused a smile to cross Paul's face.

Cummings now quickly caught on to what needed to be done that morning. Dressing as he moved about his small hotel room, he looked at Paul for confirmation.

"We need to find out if anyone else on that street had their lawn mowed that day. We also need to see if anyone saw a pickup truck, possibly one towing a trailer, parked on the street. We also need to get in contact with your homeowner to see who he or the kids used to maintain the yard. Those kids certainly didn't mow the lawn because the inventory of the garage that your folks conducted didn't list any mowers or tractors being present. As a matter of fact, and I can look this up on the inventory sheet if I have to, but I don't recall any gas cans being listed either. That means someone hired a lawn service to mow the lawn." Pausing to tuck his shirt in, Cummings soon spoke again. "If the homeowner tells us it was the kids' responsibility to have the lawn taken care of, then I guess we'll need to check their bank statements to see who they paid to mow the grass. Hey . . . we better get cracking on this. I'll call Foster and wake his ass up so he can get moving. We're gonna need that boy's help."

"TC, you would have made a helluva detective, you know that?" Paul's comment drew the hearty laugh from Cummings that it was meant to do.

* * * * * *

During his time as a young detective with NCBI, Cummings had seen it all; murders, rapes, kidnapping cases, and much more, but none had been as violent of a scene as the one he was now a small part of. But just like Paul, Stine, and all of the others soon would be, he was already chomping at the bit. He was anxious to help capture the bastard responsible for the carnage that had been left for the cops and firemen to find inside the small cottage Brian Patrick had carefully built so many years ago.

Twenty-Three

A New Direction

The sleepy sounding voice on the other end of the phone caught Paul by surprise. It was already close to seven, and far too late for anyone to still be sleeping on a weekday morning, especially a cop who still had a mass murder to solve.

"Hello?" The gravelly female voice said as she tried clearing her throat. Still full of sleep, her eyes remained shut as she waited to hear what the caller had to say.

"Audrey, you're not awake yet?" Paul asked his partner rather surprisingly.

"Uh, no, I'm not. Paul, why are you calling me so early on my day off? Did something happen that I should know about?"

In the excitement of uncovering a possible solid lead to work on, Paul had lost track of the fact that Small was through with work for the time being due to her upcoming wedding. Embarrassed by what he had done, he quickly apologized. "Audrey, I'm sorry,

I forgot you are off for a while. That's my mistake. I'm sorry I woke you."

"No problem." Small muttered through a yawn. "I need to get going anyhow. Too many details to take care of and not enough time to get them all done. Let me tell you, this bride work is hectic stuff."

Apologies taken care of, Paul pushed on with the reason he had called.

"Audrey, I called you because I believe we might have found something this morning that we've previously overlooked. I'll explain it to you when I see you. For now, I could use a huge favor. Can I get you to get on the horn with the guys and tell them I need them to meet me at the scene like ten minutes ago? Tell them there are no exceptions this morning; I need all hands on deck for this." Then, realizing there was not any new evidence which needed processing, Paul qualified his previous statement. "Besides their techs, the only folks I don't need for right now are Don and Doug, but I need everyone else down at the tent ASAP. Just so you don't try calling him, Stine is already here with me. I'd appreciate it if you could be there also. It's that important."

"Yeah, OK, sure, I guess I can get down there. I'll make the calls and then grab a quick shower. I'll meet you there, but I've got things to do today, including getting ready for my wedding rehearsal later this afternoon. I can't stay for too long."

* * * * * *

As soon as his collection of cops had gathered under the tent, and after being told that everyone had arrived, Paul began explaining what his concerns were about the lawn service staff not being interviewed. They were people, he further explained, that had been responsible for caring for the same lawn the tent now stood on. Scanning the faces in front of him as he spoke, he noticed Davis was not present. Immediately he sought to know why.

"Audrey, I thought you said everyone was here? Where's Bruce?"

"He'll be here soon. He's meeting with an informant of his. He told me when I called him that he had just received a call from his CI and that it was rather important. I thought it was best to let him go ahead and meet with his snitch. Might be something we can use."

While some of those present exchanged puzzled looks with each other, looks which questioned who amongst them had screwed up by not interviewing the lawn service, Paul was not interested in knowing which of the cops in front of him was responsible for that omission. At least, for now he was not.

"Look, I can see that several of you are already wondering how this interview got missed. It's something that happened, but for now I really don't care how it occurred. We're not here to play the blame game or to point fingers at each other; we're here to get some work done."

Collectively each of the cops standing and sitting under the tent nodded their heads at Paul's statement. What they heard their boss say not only pleased them, but it made them realize Paul was not looking to make any of them the scapegoat for the screw-up that had occurred. It also made them start to appreciate Paul's management style even more than they already had.

Turning to look at Small, Paul set the tone for how they were going to start correcting the mistake that had been made. A mistake, if not detected in time, was one that might have allowed a possible murder suspect to have never been identified.

"Lieutenant, I need four detectives to start a new neighborhood canvass for us. Pick four names as I want them to get this started before people start leaving for work or play."

Small scanned the faces staring at her for only a brief moment. "Edwards, Brandau, Baughman, and Levesque. You're up!"

Paul quickly gave the four detectives their marching orders. "Darren, you coordinate this. Get it done as soon as possible. Take Levesque with you; Tim and Jeff will work the other side of the neighborhood. We need to know which of these residents has their lawns cut by a lawn service and who doesn't. We also need to know if any of them might have seen a pick-up truck, one possibly towing a trailer, parked south of the victims' home on the day of the murders. Unless any of you have any questions, get going so you don't miss anyone before they start venturing out for the day. Call me as soon as you boys know something. One more thing, you can forget about stopping at Horbin's home. We're probably not on his list of favorite people these days."

Looking back at the others, Paul directed his next set of orders at Stine and Detective Mo; Stine's partner for now due to Detective Davis being busy with his CI. "Blake, take Lonny with you and go find our homeowner. Get him back down here so we can have a talk with him. I don't care how you do it, but get him down here as quick as possible."

Stine gave a quick nod to Detective Mo, and then started to make his way out of the tent. "No problems, boss. I'm sure he'll be glad to help us. If he's not, I'll take the appropriate steps necessary to correct that deficient attitude of his real quick!" Stine's comment brought a quick, but brief smile to Paul's face.

As the short briefing finished, Small, like a few others, noticed Davis walking to where they had gathered under the tent. Each of them easily noticed the wide smile on their fellow detective's face.

"You learn something good this morning, Bruce?" Small asked as the others moved closer to where Paul and she now stood.

"Yeah, maybe. My informant, well . . . she's actually not one of our registered informants; she's just someone who likes to tell me things now and then. She's a local gal I know from around town. She's also a pretty reliable source of information most times she calls me."

"What'd she tell you this time, Bruce? From that smile you're wearing it must be something good." Small's curiosity was starting to get the best of her.

"She told me last Friday night she was out with some of her friends bouncing back and forth between a few of the bars in Murrells Inlet when she heard a group of folks talking about our murders. They were sitting at the bar next to her and her friends at the Dead Dog Saloon. She overheard those folks having a general conversation amongst themselves about how terrible it must have been for those kids right before they were shot. The way she described it, these people were pretty upset . . . actually she used the term pissed off . . . by what had happened. But what really got her attention was when some other guy sitting at the bar by himself jumped into the conversation uninvited and made an inappropriate comment. From what she's told me, that comment led to a few moments of heated words between several members of this group and this asshole who piped in with his two cents."

"What did this guy say that ticked everyone else off?" Paul asked as he took a seat at one of the tables under the tent.

Davis disgustedly shook his head for a few moments before speaking. "This knucklehead said the kids probably had it coming. Meaning they deserved to be murdered. Can you imagine someone actually saying that?"

"What a ridiculous thing to say!" Small loudly shrieked. "Was this guy cocked out of his mind or what?"

"Sandy . . . I mean, she didn't say. The only other thing she told me was that she's seen this guy around Pawleys Island on occasion. She doesn't know his name, but she remembered staring at the work shirt this guy was wearing when he got up to leave. It was a dark blue tee shirt with white lettering on the back of it; claims she didn't see anything written on the front of it as far as she can remember. She said the lettering on the back was for some lawn service company. She couldn't remember the name of it, but she's going to try and find it out by looking in the phonebook. Said she'd get back to me either today or tomorrow with what she finds out. I expect she'll call me, she's pretty good at keeping her word."

"A lawn service?" Small asked incredulously as she shot a look at Paul.

"I know you said this CI of yours is reliable, but just how reliable is she, Bruce? You know her . . . Sandy, I believe you called her . . . you know her well enough to trust what she's telling you to be the truth?" Paul asked, obviously surprised as well by the coincidence of what Davis had learned that morning and his own earlier hunch.

"Yeah, I trust her, and I trust what she's telling me to be the truth. There's no reason not to. I've known her for years, and over that time period she's given me too much good information not to trust her now. She and her husband are folks who grew up here; they've lived in Pawleys Island their entire lives. They're also owners of a well-established business in town."

Nodding his head at Davis' response, Paul took a guess at the CI's last name. "Bruce, this gal who likes to tell you things, her last name isn't McDavid by chance, is it?"

Seeing Davis' jaw drop told Small and the others around her that Paul had correctly guessed the informant's last name.

"How'd . . . how'd you know that?" Davis asked, dumbfounded by Paul's correct guess. Small, like the others, now stared at Paul with their eyes wide open. Like their partner, they also wanted to know how someone relatively new to the area could have figured out the CI's last name.

"Just a lucky guess, that's all. What do you say we just get back to work for now. Maybe I'll tell you more about what I know some other time." The smirk on Paul's face told everyone who was staring at him that he knew far more than what he was telling them.

"Bruce, make sure you document what this alleged CI of yours told you. We may need to have a talk with her, or have her talk with Pascento, at a later time. For the rest of you, when you're out beating the bushes over the next couple of days, keep your eyes open for any lawn service company that has their employees wearing blue tee shirts like Bruce described. Let's use the CI's info to our advantage." Small said as she released everyone so they could get to work on what needed to be done.

Looking to see who was still in need of a task to work on, Paul saw Griffin and Wilson had taken seats next to each other. Both of them sat nursing large cups of Dunkin' Donuts coffee they had picked up during their ride to work.

"Griff, you and Kent sit tight for now. As soon as we hear from Darren, that's if he gives us something to work on, you guys have the lawn guys to start working on. I'll get you some help if you need it, but I want you to get on whoever the boys identify as soon as possible. I want a full-court press put on any and all of the bastards who work for that lawn service, the owner especially."

"No problem there, Paul, we'll be on them as soon as we get the word," Griffin responded. "As you know, I suck at waiting so I hope Darren and his boys find something for us to get going on real soon."

Paul ignored Griffin's statement as a partially opened bedroom window on the second floor of the victims' residence had gotten his attention for the moment. As he continued to stare at it, he knew the bedroom should have still been occupied by one of the victims, someone enjoying the last few moments of sleep before having to rise to face the challenge of a new day.

"Griff, let's take a short walk. Kent and Don can join us as well."

After retrieving a flash drive for one of the computers he was using to document the scene with, Elmendorf had just walked back to where Paul had been standing when he heard his name mentioned. Not sure of where he was being taken, or for what reason, he followed the others as they walked closer to the back of the house. Like the others who fell in behind their boss, a bewildered look now crossed his face. As he walked, Elmendorf's eyebrows arched high above his dark brown eyes as he tried figuring out Paul's thoughts.

Stopping directly under the bedroom window, Paul pointed up to it as he looked back at the three cops who were walking several steps behind him.

"Maybe one of those kids left us a clue in one of their bedrooms about the lawn service. That clue has likely been there the whole time; until now we didn't know what to be looking for. You boys catching my drift at all?" Paul asked as the others stared at the opened window.

Wilson and Griffin, just like Elmendorf was doing, stood quiet for several moments as they tried to figure out what Paul was referring to. It was Wilson who finally grasped what clue their boss had been referring to.

"Their checkbooks!" Wilson stated very loudly. "They would

have likely paid the lawn service with a check each time the lawn was mowed. If we find the right checkbook which recorded the payments that were made then we also find the name of the lawn service . . . that's who we start working on next."

Paul smiled at Wilson's understanding of what they needed to find in order to identify who their next suspect might be.

"Well, there are three bedrooms to search on the second floor, and there are three of you. Kind of makes me wonder why you boys are still standing around here doing nothing. Let's get to work!"

* * * * * *

As the search of the bedrooms got underway, Paul retired to one of the three large wooden picnic style tables under the tent. Like the tent they sat under, the tables had been placed there by the Georgetown Public Works Department for use during the investigation. After grabbing a cold drink from Steve's ice machine, he spent several minutes on the phone updating Sheriff Renda with the latest twist the investigation was headed in that morning. Moments after finishing his call, he heard two distinctively different voices call out his name at the exact same moment. They also came from different directions.

Standing up so he could walk outside the tent, Paul first saw Bobby Ray slowly making his way towards him from the south side of the residence. It was the first time he had seen his friend walking without the use of crutches in several days. He barely had time to give Bobby Ray a quick greeting when he heard the other voice call out his name a second time.

"Hey, Paul!"

Hollering to get Paul's attention, Griffin leaned part-way out of the same window Paul had noticed earlier. As he did, his palms rested on the edge of the window sill; his left hand now holding two small packets of paper in it. "We found something in the Tanner kid's bedroom. I think it's what we're looking for. Give us a couple of minutes and we'll bring it down to show you." As he began to move back inside the bedroom, Griffin saw Bobby Ray as he finally made his way into the backyard.

"Hey, boss! Good to see you up and about! You doing OK?"

Squinting due to the bright sunlight, Bobby Ray shielded his eyes as he looked up at Griffin standing in the window. "I'm doin', Griff, I'm doin'!" Having heard what he had said to Paul, Bobby Ray was now interested in learning what Griffin and the others had found.

"Let's go wait for them in the shade, Paul. It's too damn hot out here already this morning for us to be standing in the sun." Bobby Ray said as he made his way to one of the folding chairs sitting just inside the tent. Nearby a fan that had been strung up on one of the tent poles tried its best to circulate some of the tent's stale humid air.

Minutes later, Paul looked up to see Griffin, followed by Wilson, and then by Elmendorf, walking to where he and Bobby Ray were seated. As they did, he could see Griffin and Wilson were each looking at something in their hands.

"We think we've got what you wanted us to find, boss." Griffin said as he and Wilson each handed Paul the paperwork they had been examining. Without taking a moment to look at what had been handed to him, Paul gave it to Bobby Ray to examine.

"Griff, why don't you save us some time on this hot morning and just tell us what you've found. OK?"

"What we found that's important was not one of the kids' checkbooks, but rather it was what we found in two of the Tanner kid's most recent check registers. We looked twice in each of the bedrooms, but we couldn't find any checkbooks in any of them."

Hearing what Griffin said caused Paul to think back to what had been seized from each of the victims' vehicles. While he could not remember seeing any checkbooks listed on the inventory of items seized, he made a mental note to speak to the detectives who had conducted the searches. "That's kind of odd that they weren't in the bedrooms because I don't remember anyone saying anything about finding any checkbooks in the kitchen or the living room areas either. If their checkbooks weren't found in their vehicles, or in the house itself, where would they be? Could they have been destroyed in the fire?" Paul thought hard about this as he replayed previous discussions he had with both Vane and Elmendorf about evidence seized from inside the residence.

Thumbing through the check registers, Bobby Ray had been paying little attention to Griffin's comments until now. "OK, go on. Tell us what's so important in these registers."

"Besides the one that's likely still in his checkbook, these two registers appear to be the most recent ones the Tanner kid used. If you look through them, it appears the kid kept a pretty good track of the checks he wrote, and the times he used his debit card as well. Each entry has a date, an ending or current balance, a brief notation for what the expense was for, and, in some cases, he actually listed the check number as well. These registers you're looking at appear to cover the past fourteen months as the first entry was in April of last year and the last entry was written in about ten days before the murders. If and when we find the kid's checkbook, I bet we find it with a relatively new check register inside of it. Now for the good news. From the quick review we gave them, there appears to be four entries made out to someone with the name of Zeke Payne. Each of those amounts, and they each have a check number written alongside the entry, are for forty dollars. They were also written during months when people normally have their lawns mowed."

Bobby Ray quickly found each of the entries that Griffin was referring to. "Found them, Paul. They're check numbers 208, 222, 279, and 298. They're all for forty dollars just like Griff said."

Looking at Bobby Ray, but saying nothing in response to what his friend had said, Paul then looked back at Griffin. "You said some of the entries did not have check numbers listed for their individual entries, why's that? Were those occasions when he may have used a debit card instead of writing a check?"

Finishing a quick swallow of Gatorade, Griffin nodded at what Paul had offered up as an explanation.

"Probably so, but who knows for sure right now. From the brief look we gave the entries, it appears those were occasions when a debit card was easier to use than writing a check. You know, for when he purchased gas for his car or purchased a meal some place. No one writes checks for purchases like that anymore. I know I don't."

Looking for an answer to his next question from anyone, Paul asked, "Do we know what bank Tanner had his checking account with?"

Griffin and Wilson exchanged blank looks with each other for a moment, obviously caught off guard by Paul's question. It was one that neither of them had an immediate answer to. The brief moment of silence was soon broken by a comment from Elmendorf, and then by one from Bobby Ray.

"I saw a couple of pieces of unopened mail in Tanner's bedroom that had the return address of a bank on it. They looked like they might have been bank statements or something like that." Elmendorf offered rather casually before adding his most important observation. "I'll double-check to make sure I'm right, but I think they were from the Murrells Inlet National Savings and Loan."

Looking through the check registers again, Bobby Ray confirmed the observation Elmendorf had made. "Yep, that's probably right. There's an entry right here for a late fee the kid had to pay to that same bank. The description listed for that entry is listed as *Late Fee - MINSL.*"

A large smile quickly lit up Paul's face after he heard what bank the checking account was from. "I think I might know someone who's a manager of one of their branches. She should be able to give us some additional information about these checks. She may even know who this Zack Payne character is as well. I guess I'll have to go pay her a visit. You coming along, Bobby Ray?"

His friend was the only one at first who knew who Paul was referring to. "You kidding me? I never miss a chance to visit with that pretty wife of yours." Bobby Ray said as he gingerly raised himself up from the chair he had been sitting in.

Paul was about to give Wilson and Griffin some follow-up work to do inside the residence when he received two phone calls nearly simultaneously. The first was from Detective Edwards. He was calling to give an update on what the second neighborhood canvass had turned up. Answering the call, Paul sensed a touch of excitement in Edwards' voice as soon as he heard his first few words. He quickly decided to let him talk without interrupting him.

"So far it seems like most of the folks who live on the same street as our victims all mow their own lawns. The bad news is no one recalls seeing a truck parked on the street the day the murders occurred. That's because most of them leave their homes by eight each morning for work; there's not any stay-at-home moms with kids until you get further away from the scene we're working. The good news is we did find one guy, a guy by the name of Clemons who lives four houses south of the victims' residence. He's the only one we've found who has his yard maintained by a lawn service. He told us the guy who owns the service is a one-man operation. The interesting part of our conversation with this Clemons guy was that he told us his lawn guy can be difficult to deal with at times, especially when you're late in paying him. He also told me his lawn guy often wears a shirt similar to the one Davis was telling us about earlier. The only reason he stays with him is because he's a few bucks cheaper than most of the other guys mowing lawns around here. Not that this matters much, but this Clemon's guy is an older gentleman. I have the feeling money might be tight for him at times. That's probably why he puts up with our lawn guy's antics."

"Did he tell you what his guy drives?" Paul anxiously asked.

"He drives the NRA truck." Edwards laughed as he answered Paul's question.

"He drives what?"

"Our guy calls it the NRA truck because the lawn guy's pick-up is supposedly plastered with a variety of pro-NRA stickers on the back bumper and on a couple of the windows as well. It's an older model white Chevy pick-up truck of some kind; he's not sure of the exact model." Edwards paused as he thumbed through the notes he had taken while speaking with Clemons. "Paul, the other good news I have for you is that our lawn guy is a smoker as well. Not sure what kind he smokes, but according to this witness we're talking to he always seems to have a smoke in his mouth. I'll try to find out more about that, but for now I just wanted to give you an update of where we stand with the canvass." As he finished speaking, Edwards realized he had forgotten to tell Paul his most important piece of information. "You'd probably like to know this lawn guy's name, wouldn't you? His name is . . . " Paul quickly finished the sentence for his detective.

". . . Zeke Payne."

"How . . . how'd you know that?" A puzzled Edwards asked.

"Darren, keep the rest of the guys working on the canvass. I need you back here. I'll explain why when I see you. I've got another call coming in so I have to go."

Terminating his call with Edwards, Paul looked at his phone to see who the second call was from. The digital display read *BLAKE*. Quickly the call was answered.

"Hey, boss, we're on our way back there with the homeowner. He's being very cooperative, but his boss was a complete jerk about letting him leave work. It took me a few minutes of creative thinking, but I had a quick 'Come to Jesus' talk with him. That showed him the error of his ways. I told him I was going to tell each of the victims' parents, as well as the local press, that he was the sole stumbling block in our murder investigation. He tried calling my bluff, but when I put the Johansen kid's father on the phone, well, let's just say that caused him to come around to our way of thinking. I should have our homeowner back to the scene in about twenty."

Like the news he had heard from Edwards, Stine's good news also pleased Paul. "Sounds good, Blake. Hey, did our homeowner happen to tell you whose responsibility it is to have the lawn mowed? Is it his or the kids?"

"He just told me a few minutes ago that it's the responsibility of his tenants. He's told me that issue is clearly spelled out in all the leases he has his various tenants sign. He also told me he reminded the kids at the beginning of the year that they had to again take care of the lawn this summer. From what he's told me, they've apparently held up their end of the bargain by hiring someone to take care of that for them."

"Blake, can you ask your guy if he knows who cuts the lawn here?"

"Hang on, I'll ask him." Paul heard Stine put his cell phone down so he could ask his passenger the question he had been asked. In a matter of moments, Stine was back on the phone. "He doesn't know the guy's last name, but he says his first name is Zeke. That help?"

"More than you can imagine! Hustle your guy back here and then I'll fill you in. Nice job, Blake. Thanks!"

* * * * * *

Having a good suspect to again look at, Paul waited until Stine and Edwards returned to the scene until he gave out his next set of marching orders. When he did, the loose ends of the neighborhood canvass, like the second written statement being obtained from the homeowner, had just been wrapped up.

Now Paul set into motion the task of finding out everything they could on who Zeke Payne was. As the others began to do that, he, with Bobby Ray tagging along with him, went to pay a visit to his favorite bank manager.

* * * * *

As she had in the Melkin investigation, Donna Waring would also soon have a hand in identifying who the murderer of five young men had been.

Twenty-Four

Donna's Help

At least once or twice a week prior to being asked to help the GCSD with the current investigation he was assisting them with, Paul would stop in to see Donna at work. Sometimes it had been to take her out to lunch, while other times it was just to say hello and to have a quick cup of coffee with her when her schedule allowed. Today's visit was for a far different reason.

Having called Donna to tell her that he was stopping by to see her had caused her not to be surprised when she saw him walking into the bank's lobby less than an hour later. The surprise she experienced was seeing Bobby Ray follow her husband into the bank. She immediately saw that he had chosen to use his cane as he made the walk in from the parking lot. His presence quickly brought a smile to her face as she stood up from her desk to greet him. Bobby Ray and his wife, Judy, were part of a small group of people in her and her husband's lives who they considered among their closest friends.

"Bobby Ray, it's nice to see you!" Donna said as she greeted her unexpected guest. Gingerly they shared a warm friendly embrace. "Paul's told me you're doing better each and every day. I'm pleased to hear that."

"I'm getting there, girl. I hope to take you out for a night of dancing soon. I'll steal you away from that old man of yours at the same time." Bobby Ray said smiling as he slowly lowered himself into a high back chair that sat in one of the corners of Donna's office.

"Forgive me for not calling your lovely wife over the past week or so, but I've been working late a few nights while Paul's been trying to help your folks out with this case you both are working on. I'll make sure I call Judy today or tomorrow; we'll make plans to take the boat out this weekend."

"Sounds good, Donna. I know she could use a relaxing afternoon out on the river. For that matter, I guess we all could." Bobby Ray said looking over at his tired friend. Worrying about the investigation even when he was home, he knew the many problems confronting them had made it hard for Paul to get much sleep recently. "Just tell her what to bring and when to be there, and we'll make it happen. We all need a day just to do nothing."

Wanting to make sure the rest of their conversation was not going to be overheard by others; Paul stood up and walked over to shut the door to Donna's office. Doing so quickly got his wife's attention.

"I'm guessing this isn't a social call you two are making, is it?" Donna's eyes followed her husband as he walked the few steps back to the chair he had been sitting in.

Without giving his wife every little detail about the events of the morning, Paul told her about his latest hunch regarding the victims' lawn service company and about the search that had taken place in three of the victim's bedrooms. As he finished speaking, he slid the two check registers across the desk to her. They were the same ones Griffin and the others had found in Tanner's bedroom.

Looking at her husband, and then at Bobby Ray as she picked up the registers, Donna quickly scanned both of them; her eyes flashing rapidly across several of the pages. After doing so for several seconds, she set them back down on her desk.

"Boys, I already know where this is going so don't get your hopes up. I'm assuming what you're showing me belongs to one of my customers, so that means they are someone's *personal* check registers for their *personal* checking account. That also means they contain confidential and *personal* information that I cannot, and will not, release. I love you both to death, but unless you two ace detectives bring me something you boys call a search warrant then it's my job to protect my customer's privacy. Both my customer and the law expect that from me, and that's what I'm going to do. I'm sorry, but unless there's something more to the story than what I'm seeing here, I'm not discussing the contents of these registers with you." While Donna wanted to help, she was passionate about her job and about protecting the privacy of her customers' accounts. She did her best to emphasize that with the words she had chosen to use.

Already expecting his wife to take the position she had, Paul then tried explaining his position to her. "Donna, the owner of these registers is Robert Tanner. He was one of your customers.

He's no longer one of your customers because he's dead. He was shot and killed by some no-good son of a bitch murderer. Unfortunately that means, at least to Bobby Ray and I it does, that Tanner no longer has any expectation of privacy regarding his bank records or, for that matter, for any other confidential records he might have had. Along with four of his closest friends, Tanner was murdered in his home by someone we're trying to apprehend." Equally as passionate about his work, Paul did his best to reinforce to his wife what he and Bobby Ray were up against. "If we had more to work on we would not be here bothering you, but the fact of the matter is we don't. These registers, along with another clue we uncovered this morning, are our best hopes of identifying who killed those kids. These two clues go hand in hand with each other; we just need to make the connection between them. That's why we need your help."

While Paul understood his wife's duty to safeguard all of her customers' personal information, he knew, as she did also, that most murder victims would want their personal information released to the cops if it helped to identify who had killed them.

Now he chose to play the sympathy angle with his wife, hoping to touch the feelings that only a wife and mother possessed. It was an angle he had to play in order to get the help they needed.

"You do remember that it was you who told me to go help Bobby Ray solve this case. You told me that because you were so upset when you learned about these kids being murdered, right? I'm doing what you wanted me to do, and I'm here because I'm trying to help Bobby Ray identify who it is that killed those kids. Tell me if I'm wrong, but that's how I remember the conversation we had about all of this."

Picking up one of the registers without looking at either of her visitors, Donna asked her first question. After doing so, she forced herself to look across her desk at Paul. "OK, now that you've nearly caused me to start crying in front of Bobby Ray, what do you want?" Then catching herself before her husband could speak, she tried digging in her heels again. "I'll give you some of the answers you need, but I'm not telling you everything. Get our customer's beneficiary to sign a release or go get your search warrant; then I'll tell you everything you need to know about this account. Understood?"

"Yes, ma'am." Bobby Ray politely answered through a large smile that now graced his face. He was pleased Donna had agreed to help them find some of the answers to their many questions.

"Donna, just who is the beneficiary for the Tanner kid's checking account?"

Several clicks of her mouse, as well as a few keystrokes, brought up the information Donna was looking for on her computer. A few more strokes soon gave her the answer to Bobby Ray's question.

"His father, Earl Tanner, is listed as the sole beneficiary of that account."

Bobby Ray nodded at the response he heard, and then sat quiet for several moments. "Donna, I'm going to let Paul ask you a few more questions we have. Please remember that we have five dead kids on our hands when you answer his questions. Also, please remember who the beneficiary is to the account we're talking about. Right now that beneficiary is grieving pretty badly over the loss of his son. As you can imagine, he and his wife have had their hearts broken by their son being murdered. If we have to, and I certainly understand your position on having to protect the rights of your customers, but I'm quite positive we can get Mr. Tanner to sign whatever form is necessary to protect you so you can release his son's information to us. We're not here to pry into his son's personal life; we just need a few answers to help us with Paul's hunch. I'm confident that any help you can give us today will move us that much closer to nailing the no-good son of a bitch who killed these kids. OK?"

Processing what Bobby Ray had said to her, Donna sat quietly for several moments as she stared blankly at the registers that again were resting on the top of her desk. Personally she would have liked to have been able to give Paul any information he needed to help identify who had murdered the young men who were close to her own children's ages, but for ethical and legal reasons she could not.

"Ask me whatever it is you need to know. I'll tell you if I can answer the question or not." Donna's lightly veiled statement was meant to tell her husband to 'ask away and I'll tell you as much as I can without getting myself into too much trouble'.

Inching forward in his chair, Paul looked directly into his wife's blue eyes. It was easy to see that she was upset and nervous, but he also saw a look of determination, one of wanting to help catch the bastard responsible for these murders.

"Donna, if it makes you feel more comfortable doing so, just nod your head yes or no to my questions when it's appropriate to do so, OK?" Paul said as he tried his best to keep his wife relaxed.

Close to tears, as she had become upset over thinking how each of the victims had been brutally murdered, Donna gave a slight nod to what Paul told her. Speaking slightly above a whisper, she finally managed a few words. "OK . . . just ask me what you have to, and I'll try to help. I just want this to be over with so I can get back to work."

Paul's first question was an obvious one, a ground ball in baseball terms, but one that still had to be asked. It was also meant to help calm his wife down. "Donna, our victim, Robert Tanner, he does have a checking account with your bank, correct?"

"Yes, he does. I mean, he did. I . . ." More and more tears began to flood Donna's eyes.

"It's OK, Donna, we know what you meant." Paul recognized that his wife's tears had also begun to affect him as well. He hated seeing his wife experiencing the pain she was feeling.

"Those two registers on your desk, do they look like they belong to Tanner's checking account? By that, I mean are the entries in the registers similar to the entries your computer screen is showing as far as deposits and withdrawals from his account?"

Donna fidgeted in her chair as her eyes bounced between the transactions she saw displayed on her screen to those of the handwritten entries that Tanner had made in each of his registers. "Yes, they are. Most, if not all of the dates, names, and check numbers seem to match."

Paul then got to the questions that were the most important. "Donna, those two registers show four checks, ones written over a period of time, were each made out to someone by the name of Zeke Payne. Each was made out for the same amount, forty dollars. Do you see those entries on your screen?"

Using her mouse, Donna scrolled through the numerous entries that had been posted against Tanner's checking account. "Yes, I see them. Like you said, they each were made out for forty dollars, and each of them was made out to Zeke Payne."

Donna then told her husband something unexpected. "Zeke is also a customer of the bank. I don't know him very well, but I can tell he's one of our customers by the account number that's listed on the back of each of the checks under his signature. The number listed is one of ours." Punching Payne's account number on her keyboard, she quickly brought up the account listed on the checks.

Despite being surprised by his wife's comment, Paul quickly countered her answer with another question. "Besides that one account of Payne's that I'm guessing you are looking at, does he have any other accounts with the bank; perhaps at another branch or two?"

Looking at the screen displayed on her computer, Donna then brought up two other screens to help determine if Payne had any other accounts with the bank. She soon had the answer to Paul's question.

"No, he doesn't."

As his wife continued her search of the records displayed on her computer, Paul asked his next question. "On the day of the murders, a Friday, did Payne make any deposits?"

Switching back to Payne's records, Donna found what she was looking for. "Yes, he did. The transaction occurred at . . . um . . . 4:52 pm; it was an eighty dollar cash deposit."

Donna's response caused different expressions to form on the two faces across the desk from her. While a smile immediately crossed Paul's face, one Bobby Ray saw but did not understand, the look of confusion on his partner's face told Paul he had not grasped the importance of the cash deposit made that day.

"Just so you know," Donna said as she punched a few more commands on her keyboard, "Payne's account is an active one with us. I probably shouldn't be telling you this, but what the hell. There's not much in it. From the looks of it, based on the number of deposits and withdrawals he's made, he may just be using this as a small business account to pay some bills from. You know, for bills related to his business. Strangely, there's not one withdrawal or deposit he's made that's for more than two hundred dollars. He may have another account or two someplace else, but it's not with us."

Paul's curiosity was now aroused even more than it had been. "Donna, can we get you to print us a copy of Tanner's and Zeke's account histories?" Paul already knew the answer to his question before he asked it, but it was one that was worth asking anyway.

"No, you cannot!" His wife's brief but emphatic answer was the one Paul had expected to hear.

"OK, no problem. Let me ask you one more thing then. In the Note section on each of those four checks, is there anything written there?"

Donna easily brought up each of the four checks on her computer. After a quick visual scan, she looked across the desk at her husband. Knowing he was anxious to hear what she had found, she decided to make him wait for just a few seconds longer. His questions had become annoying, and now it was time for her to annoy him, even if it was for only a brief moment or two.

"Yes, there is."

Paul waited patiently for his wife to tell him what was written in each of the Note sections, but she said nothing. He watched for several seconds as she sat quietly at her desk; the small smirk he saw displayed on her face slowly began to grow larger as she stared at her computer.

"OK, Donna, I get it. From the smirk I see displayed on that pretty face of yours, I understand the game you're playing. Information is king. You want me to beg for the information, don't you?" Paul said, rather annoyed at the game being played against him. From where he sat in his chair, Bobby Ray exchanged smiles with Donna.

"Lawn Maintenance." Donna simply said, still smiling over successfully annoying her husband.

Dismissing his wife's humor, Paul thought for a moment as he looked over at his friend. Then he asked his next question. "Donna, just out of curiosity, did any of those four checks bounce? You know, get returned to this Zeke character due to insufficient funds in Tanner's account?"

As Donna searched to find the answer to Paul's question, Bobby Ray spoke to Paul. "You thinking that a check or two or three being bounced might have pissed old Zeke off, and that's maybe a reason why he did what he did?"

"Yep."

"Paul, for someone who doesn't know the first thing about balancing a checkbook, that was a good guess on your part," Donna said as she moved her mouse several times in order to look through a file displayed on her computer. "Three of the checks, numbers 222, 279, and 298, were all returned to Mr. Payne after he tried depositing them. Two of them, 279 and 298, were redeposited two days after they were first deposited, and 279 cleared with no problem. Check 298 took almost three weeks to clear Tanner's account. The last check, number 222, I'm not seeing that again being deposited or cleared on my screen. I'm sorry, but I don't know what happened to that one. Maybe Zeke was later paid in cash for the amount of that check."

"Yeah, but not by Tanner's choice he wasn't."

"What's that mean, Paul?" Donna asked.

"Nothing. Don't worry about it." Paul said rather abruptly. "It's just another hunch of mine, that's all."

"I can see our boy Zeke getting pissed off about these checks. I know I would've been pretty ticked off myself if I had to continually chase those kids down so I could get paid. But being pissed off enough to kill them over it, well that's a whole different story. I guess that's why we're sitting here. Isn't it?" Bobby Ray's comments were not meant to invoke much of a response, but they did. While Donna and Paul simply nodded their heads in agreement to what he had said, Bobby Ray followed up by asking another question.

"I'm not sure if this matters or not, Donna, but if the checks bounced, did Mr. Payne incur any redeposit fees, or maybe some type of late fee, due to the checks being bounced?"

Donna already knew the answer to the question, but gave a quick scan of the records displayed on her computer before answering. "Only Mr. Tanner, the issuer of the checks, was charged overdraft fees, Bobby Ray. It's the issuer's responsibility to make sure there are sufficient funds in their account before writing any checks."

"Donna, we're almost done here, I promise," Paul said, reassuring his wife that the two intruders who had ruined her day were about to leave. "Three more questions and Bobby Ray and I are out of here. Do you know Mr. Payne at all? And, if you do, what's your impression of him. Lastly, do you know him to be a cigarette smoker?"

Donna laughed for the first time since Paul and Bobby Ray had started asking her their questions. "How would I know if he's a smoker? We don't allow people to smoke inside the bank. Duh!"

Paul smiled at his wife's sarcasm, but simply chose to follow it up with a comment that quickly made Donna think.

"I thought maybe you might have seen him at the drive-thru window once or twice when he was here to do a transaction." Then Paul added his own touch of sarcasm. "Tell me if I'm wrong, but as far as I know it's still legal to smoke inside your own vehicle, even when you're sitting at a bank's drive-thru window." Paul's comment caused Bobby Ray to briefly snicker.

"Paul, you're right!" Donna said as she forced herself to flashback to a time she had seen Payne at the drive-thru window. She sat quietly for a moment, her elbows resting on the desk as she rubbed her head trying to recall an obscure mental picture of Payne; one that had been filed away as being unimportant at the time it had been made.

Watching Donna as she sat at her desk trying to recall a brief observation she had made of Payne, Paul and Bobby Ray watched as her eyes bounced from looking straight at them and then up to her left. Trained in Neuro-Linguistic Programming like many cops, they both knew her eye movements up and to the left meant Donna was trying to recall a visual memory she had made in the past. It was an attempt at trying to correctly answer her husband's questions.

"I want to say that I have seen him smoking while he waited in his truck at the drive-thru window. I can't tell you what he was smoking for sure, but I do believe it was a cigarette and not a cigar."

"Any idea what kind it was? Perhaps you saw a pack of smokes sitting on his dashboard when you saw him that day?" Bobby Ray asked, hoping Donna would be able to give them another important piece of information they needed.

"Sorry, but I just told you that I didn't."

"OK, no problem. Just thought I would ask."

"Donna, how about my other question?" Paul asked, trying to get his wife's focus back. "What do you know about Mr. Payne? What's your opinion of him?"

Now clearly understanding what Paul's line of questioning had been all about, Donna told him her opinion of Payne. But first she added a quick comment of her own, one that scared her.

"From the questions you've asked me about Mr. Payne, I can't help thinking back to when you asked me similar questions about Mr. Melkin. I don't even want to think that in a relatively short period of time I've gotten to know two people who've been accused of killing so many innocent people. It scares me to think there are people like that out there . . . people who you think are normal until cops like you guys say otherwise."

Paul saw the pain his wife was feeling. Quickly he tried reassuring her.

"I know, hon, it's scary, isn't it? Listen, you've helped us out a great deal here today. Your help is going to move us that much closer to helping us figure out if Payne's our guy or not. But listen, I'm not trying to pressure you on this, but we need an answer to the question I just asked you."

Dabbing her eyes with a Kleenex in an attempt to try and stop them from tearing up any more than they already were, Donna took a moment to compose herself.

"I've only seen Mr. Payne inside the bank on a couple of occasions; the only other time I've seen him here was when I told you I saw him at the drive-thru. I think I've only spoken to him once; that was when one of those checks he deposited got returned to him due to insufficient funds. He was being rather rude to one of my tellers when he tried to redeposit the check; I had to tell him to knock off his boorish behavior as he was scaring a couple of our other customers. I remember him glaring at me for a couple of seconds after that, but he didn't say anything. That's about all I can tell you about him. I can ask the girls at the teller line what they think of him, but I'm not sure if you want me to do that or not."

Picking up the check registers off of his wife's desk, Paul looked at Bobby Ray for a moment but quickly decided against taking Donna up on her offer.

"No, not now, maybe some other time though. We need to work on finding out as much as we can about Payne ourselves right now before we start asking too many questions about him. If we decide we like him as a suspect, Bobby Ray or I will send a couple of detectives back here to speak with the girls. Speaking of that reminds me of a couple of other things we're going to need. We're going to need a copy of the bank's videotape that was taken when Payne made his eighty dollar deposit on that Friday, and besides needing a copy of the four checks that we've already talked about, we're also going to want a copy of all of the transactions posted against Tanner's and Payne's checking accounts. We'll need them from the day the two accounts were opened. Bobby Ray will send a couple of his guys over here tomorrow to pick those items up from you. Don't worry about getting into any trouble; they'll have a search warrant with them. Just try and make us the necessary copies before they get here. Doing so will save us some time, and time is something we don't have enough of right now."

After saying their good-byes to Donna, Paul and Bobby Ray walked back to Paul's assigned GCSD vehicle. While pleased by what they had learned, they each still knew there was a great deal of work to be done before Payne could be considered a truly viable suspect. For now, they were just happy to have another suspect to look at.

Twenty-Five

Good News

It was just before noon as Paul and Bobby Ray made their way back to the scene in North Litchfield. To fill a craving his partner had for a Chick-fil-A chicken sandwich, and to quiet Bobby Ray's loud growling stomach, Paul pulled into the restaurant's parking lot for an early lunch. Located just off the west side of Highway 17, in Murrells Inlet, the normally busy restaurant sat barely three miles north of the crime scene.

Within minutes of placing his order, Bobby Ray, who barely had taken time to get settled in his seat, heartily dug into his sandwich. Sitting across from his friend in a booth designed for four people, Paul watched in awe as his friend began to make quick work of his lunch. As he sat there, Paul took the first sip of his liquid lunch, a Sweet Tea that Bobby Ray had purchased for him. Far too sweet for his taste, it was soon replaced by a Coca-Cola.

"Bobby Ray," Paul said as he placed his first drink out of range of being accidentally knocked over, "I think Donna helped us out tremendously with some solid information."

Wiping a small gob of mayonnaise off the left corner of his mouth with a paper napkin, Bobby Ray soon agreed with his friend's assessment. He did so in a very confident manner.

"He's our guy, there's no doubt about it. We've still got a bunch of work to do on him, but this lawn guy, he's our guy. I'm betting dinner on it for anyone who wants to take that bet!" Finished with what he had to say, Bobby Ray began drowning his Waffle Potato Fries in ketchup.

As he smiled at Bobby Ray's confidence, Paul's cell chirped to announce an incoming call. Looking at the screen on his phone, Paul saw the call was from Elmendorf.

"Hey, Don. What's up?"

"Paul, is Bobby Ray with you?" Elmendorf asked.

"Yes, he is. Right now I'm sitting at a Chick-fil-A watching him stuff his face. He told me his stomach was upset from the meds he's taking for his back pain, but I think he just used that as an excuse to make me stop here."

Elmendorf laughed at Paul's comment as he knew firsthand the reputation Bobby Ray had of being both a constant and perpetual eater. Working together for years had also given him the opportunity on several occasions to witness his boss' ability to inflict some serious damage to any buffet table he came across.

"Hey, I'm calling you because we found something after you guys left the scene. I wanted you to know about it as soon as possible."

Elmendorf's statement quickly got Paul's attention as he sensed the excitement in the sergeant's voice.

"We're already having a pretty good day, Don, as Bobby Ray and I found out some good info regarding those check registers you boys found earlier. But feel free, go ahead and make our day even better. Tell us what you've found."

"Paul, Dougie and I know you want to release the scene back to the homeowner tomorrow, so he and I decided we'd do one more walk-through of the interior of the residence just to make sure we hadn't missed anything. Well, we decided to start in the living room and then work our way out to the other rooms. I'm still not sure how this happened, but Doug and I were standing right in the middle of the living room where two of the victims were found when my eyes, and again I don't know how this happened, but my eyes caught something reflecting sunlight."

"Reflecting sunlight from where? Reflecting off what? I'm not getting this, Donnie." Paul's voice anxiously asked as he waited to hear more about what had been found.

"Try this . . . think of the false fireplace that's in the living room. There's a mantel above it, remember?"

"Yes, I do. Don, just tell me what you've found. Then we'll go on from there." Paul said as he stared at his friend polishing off the rest of his large order of fries.

"OK, sorry, I just wanted to make sure you knew what I was

talking about. Well, I'm standing there and I see this reflection coming from a basket that's sitting on the mantel with some dust and soot covered dried flowers in it. Being the curious type of guy I am, I walked over to check out what was causing the reflection and that's when I saw it. It was . . ."

Standing up from the booth he had been sitting at, Paul quickly cut Elmendorf off before he could finish telling him what he had found. "Don, please tell me you found the last shell casing we've been looking for. The one we haven't been able to find."

"That's just what we found, boss! Damn thing must have got caught up in the flowers after it was ejected from the shooter's gun. I guess no one ever thought to look there before."

Excited by what he was being told, and not wanting the few other customers eating their lunch to hear what was being discussed, Paul motioned to Bobby Ray that it was time to go. His excited gestures quickly told his friend that something important had just happened.

Once outside, Paul, who was holding his drink cup in his left hand and his cell phone in his right, asked a few specific questions about the casing that had been found.

"What caliber is it, Don, and is it made by the same manufacturer as the others?"

"It was made by the same manufacturer. It's also in great condition, far better than the others. It's a .380 caliber casing."

Continuing his increasingly fast pace back to his vehicle, Paul spoke again to Elmendorf. "Donnie, great, great job by you and

Doug. What you guys did to try and find this . . . you know, making sure we've looked at everything more than we already had . . . that's how good cops solve cases. Great work!"

By now, Bobby Ray had caught up with his partner as he opened the door to his vehicle. Sitting down inside the already hot interior, Paul quickly turned the air conditioner setting to high after getting the unmarked police vehicle started. Placing his still cold drink in one of the cup holders, he switched his cell to speaker mode so Bobby Ray could hear the rest of what Elmendorf had to say.

"There's more good news, Paul. Because the fire never reached the top of the mantel or the dried flowers, the casing is in pristine condition. There's no damage to it at all. Doug's already out in the van with it giving it the once over. He's going to take a look at it with one of his magnifying glasses to see if he can determine if there are any prints on it. I've also taken several photos of it; including a few of where we found it."

"Outstanding! Good work, brother!" Like Paul, Bobby Ray was just as excited by the news they had just learned.

As the three of them continued to talk about what had been found, Elmendorf remained standing in the victims' living room as he prepared to tell Paul and Bobby Ray what he wanted to do next.

"I've got a suggestion that I think you both need to consider, OK?"

"Fire away, Don, we're listening." Like his friend, Paul was always willing to listen to the suggestions his or any other cops made, especially those being made to help solve a murder investigation.

"This is really Doug's idea, but it's one I agree with. We think we need to hold the scene for another day or two so we can do some further testing here. Our experience is telling us that we're likely going to have to explain in court how we found this casing and how the casing could have gotten caught up in the flowers like it did. It's really a no-brainer if you think about it because the casings are ejected out the right side of pistols after they've been fired, and from where our shooter was likely standing it's easy to see how the casing could have landed inside the basket. The others either bounced off the wall or fireplace as they were being ejected, and then harmlessly fell to the floor. In this case, this casing got caught up in the dried flowers and stayed there. You boys with me so far?"

"Yep, keep talking, Don." Bobby Ray somewhat hollered into Paul's cell from where he was seated in the right front seat.

"Doug thinks we should find a fairly large plastic or metal tub of some kind, set it up at the same approximate height that our victims' heads would have been if they had been forced to kneel on the floor like we think they were before being shot. After we do that, we'll fill it with water. Then we'd like to take a couple of automatic pistols and fire a few rounds into the tank. Whether it's Ken Zercie from SLED who fires the shots or it's someone else who does, that really doesn't matter. But we'd like to have Ken here when we do the testing as he's got the national credentials to give credibility to our testing. We also want his help so we can pinpoint where each casing hits the wall or fireplace after being ejected from the pistols. That testing will document how it was possible for the casing we just found to get caught up like it did. We'll take the proper steps to videotape what we're doing, and to photograph it as well. Both of us are of the opinion this testing will help to strengthen our case when it goes to trial."

Paul did not take long to weigh the merits of Elmendorf's suggestion. "Solid suggestion, Don. Those points you've raised are all valid ones. Tell Doug to process the shell casing as much as he can without damaging any fingerprint points that might be on it. I'll get on the phone with Solicitor Pascento and have him obtain another extension for us so we can hold the scene for at least two more days. He'll have no problem doing that for us after I tell him what you boys found there today. I'll have Bobby Ray call SLED and arrange for Ken to get down here early tomorrow morning. He'll try and make it for around nine or so. You go find us that tub we need so we have it ready for when we need it."

Elmendorf was quite pleased to hear the recommendations Vane and he had thought up were ones that were readily accepted by Paul and Bobby Ray.

"OK, I'll find one someplace this afternoon. Consider it done."

Before hanging up to call Pascento, Paul took time to reinforce one important point. "Don, I want you to know Bobby Ray and I appreciate what you two guys did this morning. You went the extra mile for us. We'll make sure Mr. Pascento, Sheriff Renda, and, most importantly, the victims' parents know what you boys did to move us that much closer to finding their sons' killer." Pausing a moment, Paul then spoke to Elmendorf one more time. "OK, enough of this effusive back-slapping rah-rah nonsense. Get back to work!"

"OK, boss, see you soon!" Elmendorf said as he disconnected the call laughing.

* * * * * *

As they began driving back to the scene, Paul and Bobby Ray spoke on the importance of the small piece of evidence Vane and Elmendorf had found at the scene. That good news, coupled with what they had learned from speaking with Donna, had them already discussing what needed to be done in order to follow up on their new leads.

They had just decided which of their cops would follow up on what lead when Paul's cell rang to bring them more good news. This time it would come from FBI Agent Thomas Scozzafava.

Twenty-Six

Surveillance

"**T**ommy, what's up? If you're calling to tell us more good news then I guess we'll have this case wrapped up by the end of the day." Paul said as he shot a wink across the front seat at Bobby Ray. His friend, already busy working his own phone, missed Paul's happy wink. Having already contacted Sheriff Renda with an update of what had occurred during the morning, he was now on the phone with SLED trying to arrange for Zercie, their firearms expert, to be at the scene the following morning.

"Paul, while the others have been out searching for Payne, I've had Levesque running our suspect's name through every database we have at our disposal." Scozzafava said from the front seat of his vehicle. He had been following up on a lead in Georgetown and was now on his way back to the scene.

"Find anything good for us to run with, Scozz?" Paul curiously asked as he sipped his still cold drink.

"No, not really, nothing that stands out, if that's what you mean. Payne's got a valid South Carolina Operator's License, a CDL in fact, and, surprisingly, no arrest record. His vehicles, two pick-up trucks and two trailers, are all properly registered under the name of his business. One truck is an older model Chevy, and the other's a newer model Dodge Ram. He's even up-to-date with the county on all of his vehicle and residential taxes. His business, which goes by the name of Perfection by Payne, is properly registered with the state of South Carolina. If he's our guy, I've got to tell you, he sure isn't fitting the mold of a mass murderer."

"OK, maybe I'm surprised by what you've told me and maybe I'm not. Not every killer is a jerk with a long rap sheet when he starts murdering people; even idiots without previous arrests commit crimes. The country's full of people like that. Sounds like Payne is such an example. We'll just have to work a bit harder to get what we need, that's all. Hey, what about firearms? Does he have a valid pistol permit, and does he have any guns registered with SLED?"

Scozzafava flipped through the notes he had taken after being briefed by Levesque earlier. It took him a couple of moments to find what he was looking for, but soon he found the answer to Paul's question.

"He's got a valid Concealed Carry permit from SLED; it's good until 2019. He's got several guns registered, including a couple of Smith & Wesson 9 millimeters, a SIG P226, a Sig 1911 .45 caliber, a Walther PPK .380, and a H & K pistol of some kind, but for some reason the records don't list the model or caliber for that gun. That's very strange; I'll have to have Jaws follow-up on that later today."

Paul was disturbed by what Scozzafava told him regarding the kind of weapons Payne had registered. "None of those, with the exception of a few of them, including that H & K you're going to check on further, fire the same caliber of casings we found at the scene. Get Levesque on the H & K issue ASAP. I want an answer on that as soon as he can get one. Call me when you know something."

* * * * * *

As Paul finished speaking with Scozzafava, Bobby Ray took a call from Wilson. Like several others that afternoon, he had been out trying to locate their newest suspect.

"Bobby Ray, we've been pulling our hair out trying to find our guy for the past couple of hours. We've had a car in his neighborhood watching his house in case he came home early, and we've had three other teams beating the bushes trying to find him down in Pawleys Island. That's where we believe he does most of his lawn business. It's been a frustrating process, but the good news is Griff and I just found him. We got lucky as Griff just happened to spot his Dodge pick-up parked at one of the Kangaroo Express gas stations on Highway 17. It's got a small lawn trailer with a fairly good size tractor on the back of it. As we speak, it's still parked here at the gas station."

As Paul had done earlier, Bobby Ray now switched his cell to speaker mode. "What about Payne? Where's he at?"

"Right now he's at one of the gas pumps filling up three of his gas cans. We're parked on the other side of the lot so he doesn't see us. So far we're good; he hasn't even bothered to look over at us."

"Kent, it's Paul. Our surveillance on Payne starts right now. You and Griff stay with him until later tonight; Bobby Ray will make arrangements for a back-up team to join you real soon." Paul was about to say something to Bobby Ray when a more important thought entered his mind. "Hey, can one of you guys do a casual stroll by his truck when he goes inside to pay for the gas or to pick up a drink? We'd sure like to know if you can see any packs of Parliament cigarettes on his dashboard or on the front seat."

"That shouldn't be a problem, Paul. Payne's truck is parked on the far side of the lot so if he goes inside we should be able to eyeball what's inside of it with no problem at all." Before he could say anything else, Wilson saw their suspect finishing up at the gas pump. "Hey, I've got to go. Our boy is on the move back to his truck. Get us some help up here just in case he makes us. I'll call you when we know more." Wilson said as he abruptly ended the call without giving Paul or Bobby Ray time to say another word.

* * * * * *

On most occasions cops do not have days like Paul and Bobby Ray were having. In a short period of time, they had learned the name of their newest suspect, where he did some of his banking, a fair amount of information regarding his pedigree, and several other important points about him. Soon their day got even better.

Twenty minutes after hanging up on Paul and Bobby Ray, Wilson called Bobby Ray's cell a second time. Immediately it was switched to speaker mode. What they would learn would keep their streak of good fortune intact. Wilson's news would also cause many of the cops assigned to the investigation to have several more long days of hard work.

Twenty-Seven

More Good News

Making one brief stop after leaving the Chick-fil-A restaurant, Paul and Bobby Ray had just arrived back at the scene when Bobby Ray answered the second call from Wilson. As he did, he asked Wilson if their back-up team had arrived as yet.

"Yes, sir. I've got them parked across the street in some insurance company's parking lot. They've been watching Payne's truck while Griff and I were inside the gas station eyeballing Payne after we checked out his truck like Paul asked."

"OK, good." Bobby Ray said, pleased to know that Wilson and Griffin had another set of eyes to help them with the start of Payne's surveillance. "Got anything else to tell us, Kent?"

"Yeah, I do. What are Donnie and Doug up to? They busy right now?" Wilson's questions were ones neither Paul nor Bobby Ray had expected to hear.

"Why are you asking about them?" Bobby Ray demanded to

know. "What do they have to do with the surveillance you're conducting?"

As he watched Payne drive out of the Kangaroo Express parking lot with Stine and Davis following him behind two other vehicles, Wilson laughed at Bobby Ray's question. He knew it was impossible for either of his two bosses to know what he meant by the questions he had asked.

"I thought they might like to drive up here and seize the evidence we have." Wilson's comment surprised Paul as he turned his car off outside the victims' home. Quickly he realized they were about to be told something important.

"What evidence is that, Kent?" Paul asked cautiously.

Hearing the anxious tone in Paul's voice caused Wilson to laugh all over again.

"To start with, after our guy put his gas cans back on his trailer, he walked inside the gas station. When he did, Griff went to check out Payne's truck while I stayed with our guy." Wilson stopped talking on the phone for a moment to answer a question from his partner about the evidence they had seized. "OK, sorry about that. Here's the good news we have for you. Griff says he saw two packs of Parliaments in plain view inside Payne's truck. Griff never entered the truck in any way and never touched the smokes or opened the truck's doors. He simply saw what any other person would have seen if they had walked up to his truck and looked inside."

"Good! That's real good news, Kent. Nice job!" Bobby Ray was clearly excited by what they had just been told.

"Bobby Ray," Wilson said rather excitedly, "to be honest, that's the least important part of the good news I have for both of you."

Paul and Bobby Ray, still seated inside Paul's vehicle outside the victims' residence, exchanged surprised looks with each other as they waited for Wilson to tell them more.

"I followed our guy inside the gas station, and as I did I saw him go up to the soda fountain; you know, one of those self-serve dispensers. Well, he fills a twenty ounce cup with Coca-Cola and ice, and then walks up to the counter to pay for it. Maybe I took a chance doing this, but I wanted to watch him as he paid for his drink, and to see if he purchased any smokes, so I grabbed two cold drinks from one of the nearby coolers and followed him up to the cash register. I grabbed the drinks just in case he turned around and saw me standing there; I didn't want him to think that I was following him. I wanted him to think I was just another customer waiting in line."

"Good thinking on your part, Kent. Did he buy any more smokes?"

"Yep. Two soft packs . . . and the Coke."

"Do you have anything else to tell us then?" Paul asked as he continued to try and figure out why Wilson wanted the two evidence experts sent to the scene.

"Yeah, I sure do! When Payne got done paying for everything, he walked outside and sat inside his truck for about five minutes drinking his Coke and having a smoke."

"So what's Payne doing right now?" Bobby Ray asked.

"Not sure, boss. He drove off about three or four minutes ago. When he did, that's when I called you."

Wilson's statement perplexed Paul and Bobby Ray. It also caused them to exchange nervous stares with each other for a few brief moments as they wondered where Wilson was taking them with his story.

"So if Payne's not with you, are we correct in assuming Stine and Davis are following him? And, if that's the case, what the hell are you and Griff doing?" Bobby Ray was nearly at wits end from the conversation they were having with Wilson.

Finished teasing his two bosses, Wilson finally gave them the rest of the good news. "Bobby Ray, after our boy got done smoking his cigarette, he flicked it out the driver's window. From where Griff and I were standing in front of the gas station, we could still see smoke coming from it for another few seconds after it landed in the parking lot. Then the dumb-shit did us another huge favor. Instead of throwing his cup away in the garbage like most people do, or throwing it on the floor of his truck, the lazy littering shithead he is just opened the door of his truck and placed the empty Styrofoam cup on the ground. Then he closed the door, started his truck up, and drove off. Stine's following him while Griff and I stayed behind to seize the cigarette butt he discarded and the soda cup. You know what I'm trying to tell you, right?"

As a smile slowly began to fill his face, Paul shook his head at the good fortune they had just been handed. "Kent, you're sure you've got the correct cigarette butt? I'm sure there is more than one butt that's been discarded in that parking lot; could you guys have identified the wrong one?"

"Nope! Not a chance. I never took my eyes off of it. It was the only one that was still smoking, and still warm to the touch when we got to where it had been discarded by our guy. No worries, boss, it's the right one. Besides, it's a Parliament as well." Wilson's voice brimmed with confidence as he brushed aside Paul's concern.

"That means we've now got that SOB's DNA on both the cigarette butt and the soda cup. It's obvious this guy had no freakin' clue you guys were watching him. Wow!" Like Bobby Ray, Paul was elated by the news they had just learned.

"Thought that news would make you two happy." Wilson offered. "Oh, just one more thing. His DNA is likely not going to be found on the cup itself. The lab folks are going to find it on the straw he was drinking from."

It was now Paul's turn to laugh. As he did, he could tell from the look he saw on his friend's face that Bobby Ray was rather pleased as well by the good news they had learned.

"Kent, for me personally, I don't care where we get it from." Bobby Ray nearly screamed from where he was still seated. "As long as we have his DNA, I don't care where it's found."

"Does this mean that Donnie and Doug are on their way?" Wilson asked, a large smile now crossing his face as well. It was one that matched the ones being worn a handful of miles away by his two bosses.

＊＊＊＊＊＊

After exiting Paul's vehicle at the crime scene, Bobby Ray dispatched Elmendorf and Vane to the Kangaroo Express gas station so they could properly seize the important evidence that Wilson and Griffin had come across.

With that task taken care of, and as Bobby Ray began contacting several of his detectives who were spread out across the county working on various leads; calling them, as well as Tommy Scozz, so they could start heading back to the scene, Paul went inside the damaged home to view the area where the last shell casing had been found. Once inside, two of Elmendorf's evidence techs showed him the location where they now believed the shooter had been standing when he fired his weapon.

Once the others had returned, Paul, with Bobby Ray handing out the next round of assignments, put the next part of Payne's surveillance together after briefing everyone on what had taken place.

"We're going to keep our guy under constant surveillance for the next few days. We are going to watch him closely until we get the DNA results back on what we seized today. Hopefully when SLED compares the DNA on those items to the DNA they found on the other butts we seized from the area where the shed once stood they'll match. For now, make sure you're in touch with each other on anything Payne does that gets your suspicions aroused."

As Paul continued on with his comments, Bobby Ray's cell received a text message. It was one that confirmed Zercie and one of his assistants would be at the scene the following morning.

"OK, folks, tomorrow's Friday." Paul said as he read the message displayed on Bobby Ray's phone. "You all have your assignments through Monday. We'll adjust our plans accordingly based on Payne's actions, but for now just work on what Bobby Ray and I have assigned you to do. Please keep both of us updated on anything unusual. Oh, yeah, there's one more thing I want each of you to know about." Paul then took a few moments to explain the firearms testing that was scheduled to occur the following morning in the living room of the victims' residence. When he finished, and as the others moved off to get back to work, he made a suggestion to Bobby Ray.

"Best you get a couple of your folks to start telling the neighbors about what's happening here tomorrow. We don't want them hearing shots being fired here again and then flooding your Dispatch Center with 911 calls. Better let your patrol supervisors know about it also. I'll have Stine get word to our homeowner as well."

The surveillance that continued on their suspect for the remainder of the day was everything but exciting for the cops assigned to follow Payne. The same proved to be the case on Friday as the detectives assigned to follow him spent most of the day watching him mow several lawns in the communities of North Litchfield and Pawleys Island. None were close to where the murders had occurred.

The only excitement came on Friday night when Payne went out to unwind from a busy week of mowing lawns after first coming home to get cleaned up. Heavy evening traffic along Restaurant Row in Murrells Inlet had allowed him to escape the eyes of the primary surveillance team for over an hour. It took some time, but his empty pick-up truck was later found parked in one of the gravel parking lots along the west side of Highway 17. Like many other area residents, he had parked there so he could easily move about the several popular restaurants that backed up to the scenic inlet.

It was just after midnight when Brandau and Baughman, the two detectives assigned as the night's back-up surveillance team, followed their suspect as he walked somewhat unsteadily back to his truck. Out of concern for other motorists in the area, they were soon forced to make a decision on whether to allow their obviously inebriated suspect to drive or not. It would be a stop that a uniformed deputy who was supporting the surveillance would have to make so their cover, and the surveillance, was not blown. Electing to follow Payne for a short distance to see if he was capable of driving without endangering the safety of others, they soon determined he was safe to do so. In less than fifteen minutes, the two detectives watched from a distance as their suspect safely navigated his pick-up down the quiet street leading to his driveway.

* * * * * *

While the surveillance of their suspect's activities had proved to be less than exciting on Thursday and Friday, what Detectives Edwards and Stine would see take place late on Saturday afternoon would quickly get not only their attention, but that of Paul and Bobby Ray's as well. It would also get the attention of many others assigned to the investigation.

Twenty-Eight

A Day Off

With the surveillance details for the weekend all planned out, and with Stine and Edwards, along with their partners and a couple of other GCSD detectives, beginning the process of conducting covert interviews regarding Payne's background, Paul finally gave into Donna's mounting pressure by agreeing to take a Saturday off. While he knew all aspects of the investigation were in good hands during his brief absence, and despite knowing the firearms testing at the victims' residence had gone well the day before, he still felt the need to be present at the scene. It was not because he felt it necessary to micro-manage every aspect of the investigation, but rather it was a sense of needing to be there due to Small's absence. Like most managers, he did not like the fact that several of the detectives working that day had limited investigative experience in cases like this one.

"I guess that's why we all have cell phones these days," Paul thought as he began loading the back of his truck with two coolers of food and drinks. Donna had stuffed both of them with a variety of sandwiches, snacks, and drinks for their day out on the Waccamaw River. While it was not quite enough to feed an army, the amount of food his wife packed caused Paul to wonder if Donna had invited several others to join them for the day. "This is ridiculous," he said to himself as he slid the last cooler into his truck.

Glancing at his watch after securing the coolers, Paul saw they had close to an hour before Bobby Ray and his wife were scheduled to meet them at the marina where Paul's boat was moored.

Despite having more than enough time to accomplish what still needed to be done, Paul yelled to his wife from the doorway of the garage. "Let's get a move on, Donna! I need to get some gas for the boat, and I'd like to have these coolers stowed on board before Bobby Ray gets there." Looking back at his truck, he again shook his head at the amount of food and drinks his wife had prepared for the day. "Maybe she thinks we're going to be marooned on some deserted island or something like that."

* * * * * *

Later that afternoon, at close to six, Paul turned the *Donna Lynn 2* around on the Waccamaw River to begin the trip back to the marina. The four of them had enjoyed their relaxing day together, venturing as far north as the Calabash area of North Carolina. They had stopped twice during the day, once just south of Little River, South Carolina so they could enjoy lunch while moored adjacent to a small sandbar on the western side of the slow moving water, and the second time so Donna and Bobby Ray's wife could use the facilities at Barefoot Landing, in North Myrtle Beach. During the day, despite several urges to do so, both

Paul and Bobby Ray had resisted calling anyone for an update on the status of the surveillance on Payne.

Once back at the marina, Paul helped Bobby Ray load his Ford Expedition with the heavier items he had brought along for the day. He did so to prevent any further aggravation to his friend's back.

"Looks like I'm carrying your ass again, Bobby Ray. Seems that's all I do these days." Paul said as he wiped the early evening's sweat off his wet forehead. Despite the humidity that was present for most of the day, it was the first time Paul had broken a sweat as the breeze on the river had helped to overcome the day's warm temperature.

Laughing at his friend's comment, Bobby Ray cracked open two ice covered cans of Coors Light that he had retrieved from a cooler inside the back of his vehicle. As they stood in the parking lot talking, Paul enjoyed his first beer of the day. Always the safety conscious one of the bunch, he had made it a practice to never drink anything alcoholic while out on his boat. Now with the boat safely secured inside his slip, the taste of a cold beer brought him the reward he had been waiting for.

As Donna and Bobby Ray's wife finished putting the cover back on the boat, a task his wife always seemed to enjoy for some reason, Paul quickly polished off his beer. Soon a second one found its way into his hands. As he took his first hit, his cell phone rang for the first time that day. Seeing it was Stine calling, Paul answered the phone and then placed it in speaker mode so Bobby Ray could hear what was being said.

"Hey, Blake!" Paul said as he answered the phone. "Just so you know, I've got you on speaker so don't say anything too bad about Bobby Ray. He's standing right here with me."

"Thanks, boss, I appreciate the heads up! I guess I'll have to call you later with the real reason I called, won't I?" Stine cracked from the other end of the call.

"Screw you, Blake!" Bobby Ray offered between sips of his second beer.

"What's up?" Paul asked somewhat anxiously. "Everything OK?"

"Yeah, it is now. Thought I'd call you with an update seeing our surveillance has taken a break for a few minutes. Our guy's sitting inside the McDonald's on Highway 707 feeding his face right now. Darren and Jaws are watching him, and Bruce is with me in my car. We're hanging back a ways from the golden arches; we don't need the four of us to be that close to where Payne's enjoying his meal. He's in good hands for now."

"Sounds like something might have happened earlier? Is that right?" Bobby Ray asked as he dug out the last cold beer from within his cooler.

"Yeah, it did. But I think we may be onto something up here. Earlier this afternoon, when Darren and Jaws were following our guy they thought he was headed home at one point, but instead he drove over to the gun store up on 707. You know, the 707 Gun Shop . . . the one next to the 707 Indoor Shooting Range. It's kind of a combination gun store and indoor firing range that sits right along the road. You know the one I'm talking about, right?"

"Yes, we do." Paul answered for both Bobby Ray and himself.

"Well, when Bruce and I got here, we saw him unlock a large metal storage bin that he's got mounted in the back of one of his trucks. Then we watched as he took out two black plastic gun cases, along with at least three or four boxes of ammo. Darren gave me a shout after Payne had first gone inside the gun shop, so Bruce and I hustled up here to back Jaws and him up. We got here just in time to see him take the cases and ammo out of his truck."

Hearing what Stine said caused Bobby Ray to jump back into the conversation. "You two guys were supposed to be digging into Payne's background today. Darren's back-up team for the day was Doogan and Jefferson. Why weren't they there to help him out?"

Bobby Ray's question caused Stine to laugh out loud for several seconds. Doing so prevented him from speaking as he recalled what had happened earlier to the two cops his boss had asked about. Finally regaining his composure, he explained why he and his partner had been called to back Edwards up.

"Seems Doogan and Jefferson took their wives out for dinner last night at one of our world famous Tex-Mex restaurants that we have so many of around here. Early this morning, they both claimed they had a great time last night, but this afternoon seems to be a different story. They've each come down with a bad case of Montezuma's Revenge, or something like that. I'm sure you know what I mean, but those poor bastards have spent most of the day visiting every bathroom that's available along the 707 corridor."

Laughing so hard from Stine's explanation of Doogan and Jefferson's mutual problem caused Bobby Ray to spit out his mouthful of beer so it did not go down the wrong pipe. Like his friend, Paul also was finding humor in Stine's story.

"OK, OK, Blake, let's move on, shall we?" Bobby Ray said after a few more moments of laughter. Despite his best efforts, he could not help laughing at the misfortune that had beset two of his detectives. The humor he found in their misery continued on for several more seconds.

"After we saw him go inside the shooting range, Payne stayed there for close to an hour before he came back outside. When he did, he just had the two black gun cases with him. He must have gone through all of the ammo he carried inside. After he left the parking lot, Darren and Jaws stayed with him while Bruce and I went inside the range. Turns out he's not only a gun nut, but a self-envisioned lady's man as well."

At first, Paul did not completely understand what Stine meant by his last comment, and he quickly sought a clarification. After receiving it, Stine told them more about what he had found out about their suspect.

"Earlier today, I spoke to two people who know Payne quite well. In fact, both of those guys had hired him to work for their respective lawn service companies a few years back, but they each ended up firing his ass for several reasons. Among them was Payne's shitty attitude when it came to dealing with some of their customers. The way it was explained to me by both of those guys, Payne cost them both customers and cash because of his attitude, because he was rude, and because he generally did a lousy job when they sent him out to mow lawns on his own. They also told me they ultimately had to fire the idiot not only because he was hitting on some of their female customers, but because he was also doing the same thing with a few of their customer's daughters. After they canned him, Payne, according to these two guys, went out on his own and started stealing some of their customers by undercutting . . . no pun intended . . . them on their prices. Both of them have absolutely no use for him now. That's how I first found out about him being a gun nut. According to them, our guy likes to target shoot quite often."

"Makes sense based on the number of guns he's got registered." Bobby Ray offered.

"After I saw him leave the range, I was about to go inside, but then I remembered that one of the MBPD cops I know is a silent owner of the place. So I called him to find out if I was going to regret going inside and start asking questions with someone I didn't know. Obviously, I didn't want to tip our hand regarding our interest in Payne."

"Good thinking, Blake." Paul said as he waited to hear more about what Stine had found inside the indoor range.

"Well, this cop, Tommy Parker, he finally calls me back and tells me to go inside and speak to one of his partners, a guy who goes by the name of Bobby Bats. This Bobby Bats character, who's an Italian looking guy the whole way, in a good way that is, is a former NYPD cop. Besides impressing me with everything he knows about firearms, he also turned out to be a heck of a friendly guy. He told me Payne, who he thinks is a first-class asshole, shoots without fail every Saturday afternoon and every Tuesday night around seven. After he told me that, Bats tells me our guy always shoots in the last firing lane on the right, lane five it's referred to at the range. I was told if Payne gets there and that lane is being used, he'll wait until it frees up. Who knows? Hypothetically speaking, maybe the asshole is superstitious or something." Stine offered.

"Very weird, bro, very weird. Almost OCD weird if you think about it." Bobby Ray said in response to Stine's comment.

"Why's this Bobby Bats guy think Payne's an asshole?" Paul asked, intrigued by Bats' opinion of their suspect.

"For the reasons I just told you, boss, and for one more. It seems our boy Payne doesn't like to follow the house rules about cleaning up after using the range. Supposedly he never polices his brass and never takes down the paper targets he's been shooting at. Bats told me he has to have one of his employees pick the shell casings up off the floor after our guy leaves. He's apparently told Payne several times it's his responsibility to police the shooting lane when he's done, but it sounds like it falls on deaf ears." Then anticipating what Paul or Bobby Ray was going to ask him next, Stine added, "Guys, I've already got the answer to your question, so go ahead and ask it."

Paul's mouth formed a brief smile before he spoke. "What's that question you're expecting, Blake?"

"You were going to ask me what kind of rounds our guy was shooting off today, right?"

Despite knowing Stine could not see him, Paul nodded his head after hearing the correct question being recited. "OK, so what kind of rounds were they?"

"That's the only bad news I've got to tell you. Bobby Bats had already cleaned up the firing lane Payne used by the time I had a chance to talk with him about that. He dumped all of Payne's brass, along with brass he swept up from two other lanes, in a large metal drum that already contained a bunch of other brass. There's no way of knowing what caliber of rounds our guy had been firing as Bats says he never seems to use the same kind of ammo each time he uses the range. To top it off, it also seems that Mr. OCD, as you referred to him, took his empty cardboard boxes of ammunition with him when he left. He also, for whatever reason, took the plastic containers that hold the fifty rounds of ammo in each of the boxes. Who knows, maybe our guy does his own reloading and he reuses the boxes? But whatever he does, he must stuff the empty boxes inside his plastic gun case when he leaves the range because he wasn't carrying them when we saw him leave. They weren't in any of the garbage cans either."

"Perhaps." Paul offered. "Guess we'll know soon enough. Hey, what's this you said about Payne being a ladies man?"

"Just like the two lawn guys I spoke to earlier, Bats told me Payne likes to talk it up about his alleged shooting exploits with a bunch of different women who also like to shoot. He also told me Mr. OCD often brings a gal with him when he shoots; claims he's never seen our guy with the same gal twice."

"I'm sorry," Bobby Ray said, "but that's beyond weird. If I took my wife to a firing range so she could watch me shoot, she'd kill me for ruining one of her afternoons. Besides, I love my wife, but I need my own time just as my wife needs hers. Call me old fashion, but guns and wives just don't go together; same with girlfriends."

After listening to the rest of what Stine had to tell them, Paul ended the call. For the next several minutes, he and Bobby Ray stood talking in the parking lot. It was Paul who soon moved the conversation to the next important point which needed to be discussed.

"Maybe you're right about wives and girlfriends not mixing well with guns, but next Tuesday night they're going to. How about that young lady who works for you, the one who made the posters for us, she's an attractive young lady, right? Isn't that how you described her, Bobby Ray?"

"Yeah, I guess I did, but I didn't mean anything by it." Bobby Ray was clearly becoming embarrassed by Paul's recollection of how he had described Kelly Glover to him. "I could be her father for Christ sakes. I didn't mean . . ."

"Relax, Bobby Ray, relax." Paul could not help but laugh at his friend's embarrassment. "I know what you meant, but it's probably more likely that you could be her grandfather than her father. You old fart, you should be ashamed of yourself!"

Still red in the face, Bobby Ray looked to see where his wife was. Even as innocent as it was, the last thing he wanted was Judy hearing what Paul and he were discussing about a much younger co-worker of his.

"Does Mrs. Glover like to shoot at all, Bobby Ray?" Do you know if she owns any weapons or if she can even handle a gun?"

A perplexed Bobby Ray first stared at the empty can of beer he was holding before looking at Paul. "How the hell would I know the answers to any of those questions?"

"I suggest you find out real quick, Bobby Ray. Because if she doesn't know squat about guns, you've got three days to teach her everything she needs to know. You do your part, and I'll do mine, but on Tuesday night Mrs. Glover and someone else you know are going shooting at Payne's favorite indoor firing range. Understand?"

"Yeah, uh, OK, I guess."

******

Bobby Ray clearly had no idea as to what Paul was planning on taking place. He just knew it was likely another weird trap his friend was planning on setting to catch a rat. In this case, a deadly murderous rat.

Twenty-Nine

New Partners

On Sunday evening, after a quiet and relaxing dinner of grilled steak and baked sweet potatoes, Paul helped Donna carry in their dirty dishes and silverware from where they had eaten on the back deck. It had been a wonderful warm evening to enjoy a casual dinner outside. After clearing off the table, Paul finished explaining what he was asking Donna to do for him. With Lt. Small not working, and with Bobby Ray's only other female detective already assigned to a violent sexual assault investigation on the other side of the county, he told her he was desperate for a female undercover to help him.

"Oh, come on, Paul, not again. Why me?" Donna asked her husband as he placed their dirty dinner dishes in the sink. Her voice was now clearly agitated from having listened to what her husband was asking her to do.

"Because he likes pretty ladies like you, that's why." Paul said as he filled the sink with hot water and far too much green colored dish soap. In moments, the detergent's soapy bubbles were close to the top of the sink, ready to begin cascading down the front of sink's white kitchen cabinet.

"Paul!"

Donna's loud voice startled her husband as he stared out their kitchen window, oblivious to the growing number of bubbles and the quickly rising water level in the sink.

"The sink, you idiot! You've put too much soap into too much water! Shut the water off before you flood the entire house!" As upset as she was before the rising water threatened to escape from their sink, Donna was now clearly upset with her husband for two reasons.

Shutting off the water, and then pulling the stopper out of the nearly full sink of water and dirty dishes, Paul barely averted a minor household disaster from occurring.

"Honestly, Paul, I still haven't gotten over what you had me do the last time you needed my help. Sneaking into Mr. Melkin's office was bad enough, but now you're asking me to go shoot a gun. I . . . I don't know about that." Donna was busy putting a variety of condiments back in the refrigerator as her husband washed some of the grime off their dishes before placing them in the dishwasher, but her mind was clearly elsewhere.

Still smarting from the tongue-lashing his wife had given him, and from the near disaster at the sink, Paul now tried to convince Donna that she could handle what he was asking her to do. "I'll tell you what; maybe you're right about firing a gun at the range.

Maybe we can pull this off another way by utilizing your acting talents instead."

"My what?" Donna said as she closed the refrigerator door. Her part of preparing the evening meal, along with the subsequent clean-up, was now complete. She watched now as Paul finished cleaning up around the sink area.

"Listen, I'll set things up for you and Kelly to get into the gun store that's connected to the indoor range. We'll work it out so it looks like you ladies are there to purchase a handgun, you know, for self-protection. After that happens, I'll have one of the owners, Bobby Bats is his name, give you a tour of the range. By a planned coincidence, you'll just happen to do so when our guy is there shooting. That's way better than having you shoot a gun, correct?"

"Yeah . . . I guess so." Donna replied reluctantly, still not convinced she wanted to be a part of Paul's ruse. "What else are you going to make me do?"

Paul laughed when he saw the cautious look on his wife's face. The look clearly reflected the lack of confidence she was feeling. "Don't worry about this. I'll get with Bobby Ray and Bobby Bats, and work the whole thing out. It's going to go fine; you'll do great! On Tuesday night, Bobby Ray and I will give you and Kelly a quick briefing. All you two really need to do is to look your best, just like you always do."

"Kiss ass!" Donna smiled at her husband's compliment for a moment before adding, "Maybe I'll wear those tight jeans I have. I like how I look in them. Hey, I wonder if Mr. Payne likes red lipstick or not?" Then flashing a seductive look at her husband, she added, "I'll guess we'll just have to wait and see, won't we?"

Paul shook his head over his wife's comments as he wondered how someone who was so dead set against helping him only a few minutes earlier was now jumping at the chance to play the role of a middle-aged flirt. "Simply amazing," he said as he finished loading the dishwasher with some of the dishes they had used for dinner.

＊＊＊＊＊＊

During the day on Monday and Tuesday, Bobby Ray made arrangements to have the evidence that Wilson and Griffin had seized in the parking lot of the Kangaroo Express gas station transported to SLED's forensic lab. Sheriff Renda had used his limited amount of influence with SLED to have the DNA testing of the drink cup's straw, as well as the cigarette butt Payne had flicked onto the ground, shoved to the head of SLED's staggering number of cases that needed work done. Like the evidence that had been seized in this murder investigation, the evidence in all of those other cases was also waiting for a variety of forensic testing to be completed before any prosecutions could take place.

Based on Payne's activity at the indoor range on Saturday, Bobby Ray, whose back was finally starting to feel a little better with each passing day, also made arrangements to have the surveillance on their suspect continued through the end of the day on Wednesday.

On Monday morning, as Bobby Ray addressed the needs of the surveillance, Paul updated Solicitor Pascento, and two members of the solicitor's staff, on the events that had occurred since they last spoke.

"That was a stroke of good luck finding that missing shell casing, Paul. Make sure your folks know my staff and I appreciate their hard work. I'll tell them that myself when we all get together before we go to trial." Pascento said from where he sat with two of his prosecutors at the small conference table in his office.

"I'll be sure to do that. I'm sure they'll appreciate it more hearing it directly from you, but I'll tell them."

After he was finished updating the solicitor, Paul answered a few questions Pascento had. Then he told Pascento what his plans were for Tuesday evening at the indoor range. As he did, he did not mention that his wife and a civilian employee of the GCSD would be playing critical roles in what was about to transpire the following evening. As he concluded his presentation, Paul suggested the crime scene could be released back to the owner as early as Thursday morning.

"You sure on that, Paul? You feel comfortable enough doing so at this time?" It was obvious from the tone in his voice Pascento was questioning the timing of such an action.

"Yes, sir. I'm good with doing that. However, if it will make you feel better, instead of releasing it back to the owner then, I'll wait and give it back to him on Saturday morning instead. That way we'll know how things played out at the range, and we'll have a couple of days to follow up on anything that might pop up unexpectedly. If something unusual happens between now and then we'll keep the scene, but I'm pretty confident we've picked the house clean of any evidence that was there. I can have Elmendorf and Vane go over it one more time, but those guys are pretty damn good at what they do. If something was still there, they would have found it by now. That sound OK with you?"

"Yes, I like that minor change to the plan. I'd rather keep the scene for a couple of more days than have to go and tell a judge, even a friendly one at that, why we need it back after we released it. If nothing happens between now and Saturday morning, I'm good with you releasing it back to the legal owner." Pascento paused for a moment to compose a thought he had running through his head about an unrelated matter. As he did, he glanced at his watch. "Paul, just hear me out for a moment, and then I have to go. I'm due in court in less than fifteen minutes. I would like you to call me by Wednesday morning at the latest as I want an update on how you folks made out with Payne at the range. I don't have to tell you how critical that part is to our case. Sorry, but I've got to go. I'll talk to you soon. Great job so far!"

* * * * * *

On Tuesday, at precisely five-thirty pm, Paul and Bobby Ray, along with Kelly Glover, met Donna at the GCSD sub-station inside the Murrells Inlet Community Center. In the final stages of construction, most of the work which still needed to be finished inside the building was cosmetic in nature. The only part of the building not yet open to the public was the small dedicated office space that had been designated for use by the sheriff's department. Empty and unoccupied by others that evening, it was the perfect place to conduct a briefing for their two role players.

Just before beginning their briefing, Paul introduced Donna to her partner for the first time. As he did, he smiled as he complimented both of them on their appearances. "Ladies, from the looks of both of you, Mr. Payne would be quite foolish if he did not give each of you a second or third look tonight. You both look . . . uh . . . very hot!" Like Bobby Ray had felt a couple of days earlier, Paul felt somewhat uncomfortable describing Glover like that in front of his wife, but he was confident Donna understood what he meant.

"Paul, I think he's going to look right past me once he sees this pretty young blond standing there in those shorts she's wearing." After giving an approving nod to the outfit Glover was wearing, Donna then added, "This is one pretty girl you've got working for you, Bobby Ray. Does Mrs. Jenkins know how pretty Miss Kelly is?"

Donna's comment was meant to make Bobby Ray feel uncomfortable. The reddish glow that quickly surfaced on his face told Donna her objective had been accomplished. Her comment also brought an appreciative smile to her partner's face as well.

"Ladies, Bobby Ray spoke with Bobby Bats earlier this afternoon. He'll make his presence known to you as soon as you get there, and he'll also make it look like Kelly is purchasing a handgun." Looking at Glover, Paul added, "Kelly, he's going to hand you an empty plastic gun case so you can have it with you when you both tour the range area with him. Bobby Ray and I both want you to look the part, so that's why he's going to hand you the gun case. That's your prop for the evening . . . it's something for Payne to see when he looks at you. Hopefully it will help to stimulate some conversation between the three of you." Then Paul explained to Donna and Kelly what their real objective was for going to the range.

* * * * * *

After finishing their quick briefing, Paul and Bobby Ray, along with their inexperienced female undercover operatives, made the short drive to the indoor range. As they did, the two two-man surveillance teams kept close watch on Payne until they saw him walk inside the gun store.

The surveillance teams that evening were comprised of Wilson and Griffin, who were together in a light blue Toyota Tundra pick-up truck that the GCSD narcotic's unit had successfully seized from a drug dealer in an In Rem proceeding. The second team, Wilson and Griffin's back-up team for the first part of the evening, was comprised of Stine and Davis. They had trailed the Toyota in an older model Ford Taurus that was more than slightly banged up from years of being driven hard by many different drivers. Under a crinkled section of the Ford's rear bumper a Georgia license plate was displayed.

In planning the night's operation, Paul had decided that he would have Detective Edwards, someone who was not only extremely knowledgeable about firearms of most types, but also big in stature, to be inside the range prior to the arrival of Payne and the two ladies. As Donna and Kelly had their roles to play that evening, so did Edwards. One of his two assignments was to play the role of a shooting enthusiast who was at the range practicing his skills; his other was to keep a casual eye on the welfare of the investigation's two female operatives. Wearing both an NRA hat and shirt on his six foot four inch frame, and with a large Smith and Wesson brass belt buckle holding up his blue jeans, he looked every bit the part he was playing.

Part of Paul's plan also included not telling Donna and Kelly about Edwards' presence at the range that evening. He chose not to tell them as he did not want them staring at him unconsciously, or paying any sort of attention to him outside of what they would normally do to any stranger they were watching. Another part of his plan had been to arrange for Edwards to be placed in lane two inside the range; three lanes to the left of the one that Payne normally shot in. While Bobby Bats could not promise this would happen, he had told Paul earlier in the day he would do his best to keep lanes three and four open so Edwards could have a clear and unobstructed view of what was occurring across the adjoining firing lanes to his right. The last part of Paul's plan, one which Bats eagerly agreed to help with, and one Edwards would visually inspect upon first entering the range area, was to make sure the floor in the shooting area was free of any spent shell casings. For the plan to work, the range floor, especially the area around lane five, had to be free and clear of any spent shell casings prior to Payne's arrival.

At ten minutes after seven, with Edwards already in position inside the range, and with Donna and Kelly already engaged in a conversation with Bobby Bats near one of the gun shop's display cases, Payne casually strolled inside as if he did not have a care in the world. As he waited to pay his eight dollar fee for thirty minutes use of the range, Donna managed to sneak a handful of quick glances at their suspect as he stood near one of the cash registers. As he stood waiting, Payne completed his Waiver of Liability and Hold Harmless Agreement form that the range required from each user. Later, as a matter of practice, when he was about to enter the range area, his South Carolina operator's license would be clipped to the form. Bobby Bats had purposely designed the form so it could be date and time stamped for record keeping purposes to show who used the range on what specific date and for how long. It was not a form the state of South Carolina or ATF required, but rather it was one he and his partners had created to protect their investment. After creating this form, they found it made the range a safer environment to shoot in as their customers knew their presence was being recorded for posterity with each of their visits.

As Donna continued to shoot glances at Payne, someone she easily recognized from several surveillance photos she and Kelly had been shown earlier, she spied a black gun case sitting on the counter where their suspect had set it down. Next to it sat three boxes of ammunition.

"I know five sets of parents who would like to see you dead, you no-good son of a bitch!" Donna thought as she briefly stared at Payne with contempt. Their suspect, who was momentarily distracted by an assault weapon he saw displayed on a wall near the cash register, missed seeing the slightest bit of a scowl on Donna's face. Not a mean-spirited or violent person in life, she hated him for the heartache he had caused several sets of parents, ones she only knew about from reading their names in the papers. Despite being disgusted with her close proximity to an alleged killer, she showed little outward emotion. She was playing her role very well.

"Thanks, Miss Rybak, I appreciate your business. That's a great weapon you've purchased. I've sold several of them recently to ladies just like you, for the same reason you got yours. You know, for self-protection reasons."

As well as Donna was playing her role, Bobby Bats was close to winning an Emmy for his performance. Speaking loud enough so Payne could hear what he said, he remembered to use the alias Paul instructed him to use when addressing Kelly. His comments now caused their suspect to look over to where Donna and Kelly stood, but outside of a brief smile that he directed at them he said nothing.

"Sir, would it be possible for you to show me and my sister your range?" Kelly asked as she took her gun case off the counter. "I'd just like to see what it looks like before I start shooting here next week."

"Sure, no problem," Bobby Bats answered politely, "just let me get this gentleman signed in so he can use the range, and then I'll give you the grand tour. I'll grab some eye and ear protection for both of you to wear. As you're going to find out, it gets quite loud back there."

******

Fifteen minutes after Payne entered the range, Bats walked into the small area adjacent to the rear of where Bats and Edwards stood in their respective lanes. As he did, with Donna and Kelly following close behind him, he acknowledged the presence of the two shooters nearby. As required, they all were now wearing shooting glasses and ear protection. While the ear protection helped to significantly diminish the noise of any weapons being fired in the enclosed range, the eye protection was being worn to deflect any stray fragments of lead or any errant shell casings from hitting their eyes. The modern new range had been professionally designed less than three years earlier.

As they unknowingly passed by Edwards in lane two, Kelly, not familiar with how to speak loud enough amidst all of the noise caused by Edwards shooting at his target, yelled somewhat loudly as she spoke to her companions. "This is exciting! It's going to be fun shooting here." Nodding her head in agreement, Donna then flashed a smile. It was one that she hoped would be seen by Payne. Fiddling with his eye and ear protection, their target stood less than fifteen feet away from them.

As they moved past lanes three and four, Bats kept up with his role as a tour guide. He did so by pointing out the various types of targets that were available for shooters to use, and the three large turbo fans that removed smoke and the smell of gunpowder from inside the range.

"As you can see," Bats said as he pointed to one of the firing booths, "the lanes are all separated at this end by one-half inch thick bulletproof steel. Each section has several two-by-two foot sized black rubber panels layered over the steel. Not only does each booth have a small counter that prevents our shooters from straying too far forward, but the rubber panels on each of the walls are also there for another safety reason. They've been designed to catch any shell casings or bullet fragments that come from accidental discharges or ricochets."

Despite being out of their element, and knowing even less about guns, Donna and Kelly nodded at what they were hearing from Bats.

Using his left hand, Bats pointed to the far end of the firing lanes. "If you look beyond where the targets are all hanging, you can see chunks of black rubber piled up from floor to ceiling. Those chunks are ground up pieces of car and truck tires. That pile, one which stretches across the back of all the lanes, is made up of about twelve hundred tires. The chunks of rubber catch the bullets and take all of the energy out of each round that is fired into the pile. The pile was just changed out last week so the chunks are still fairly large. They should be able to take hits from about another one million rounds before the pile has to be swapped out again. Pretty neat, huh?"

"Pretty neat," a naïve Donna said rather enthusiastically.

"Ladies, I've got to get back to the store, but feel free to stay as long as you like. Just do all of us a favor, please do not remove your eye and ear protection until you leave the range." Then pointing at Payne and Edwards, Bats offered up a suggestion to his two visitors. "Take a few minutes to watch how these guys handle their weapons. I'm sure you'll pick up a couple of tips by doing so. I'll see you both before you leave."

Because of the ear protection they were each wearing for the first time, and the noise of rounds being fired close by, Donna and Kelly exchanged an awkward round of thank-you's with Bats before he moved back inside the store. As he did, Payne, who had already fired close to one full box of ammunition, fired the last six rounds in one of his magazines. He did so in rapid fire. They both watched as the ejected shell casings flew out of his pistol, striking the rubber mat on the wall to Payne's right before falling harmlessly to the floor. As they landed, Donna watched as three of the shells bounced away in different directions after striking the concrete floor that had been painted a battleship gray.

As Payne removed an empty magazine from his pistol, he saw the two ladies watching him from off to his left. Flashing a quick smile, he then turned his back to them as he deftly toyed with his weapon for a few seconds. Soon finished with what he was doing, he placed it down on the small narrow wooden counter of his shooting lane. Moving slightly to his left, he tried blocking the ability of the two visitors to see what he was doing with his weapon. But unknown to him, Donna, like her new best friend, saw Payne reach into his gun case twice. Then taking a moment to look back over his shoulder at Donna and Kelly, he loaded three magazines with bullets. Quickly, and with the skill that only an experienced shooter possessed, each of the seven round magazines were alternately inserted into his pistol, fired, and then ejected. As each empty magazine fell to the floor, it was immediately replaced with another until the rounds in all three had been fired. In the mere seconds it took to replace an empty magazine with a full one, Payne never took his eyes off his target. His proficiency both stunned and scared the range's two visitors. Finally taking her eyes off him, Donna looked to see where the ejected casings had landed after bouncing off the rubberized wall. On the floor around their shooter's feet she saw roughly one hundred empty casings.

Finished with his target practice, Payne, his ear protection slid down around his neck as Edwards had taken a break from firing his weapon, began gathering his few belongings as he secured his pistol inside its case. Having noticed that Payne had stopped shooting, Edwards purposely ceased firing so conversation between their suspect and the two ladies could flow easily and without any distraction.

Payne then spoke for the first time as he removed his shooting glasses, ones that had been tinted a bright yellow color to enhance his ability to see in the somewhat dark environment of the range.

"Evening, ladies! First time here?"

"Yes, it is." Glover answered rather cheerfully as she held up her black gun case for Payne to see. "I just purchased my first gun, I mean pistol, tonight. I'm going to start shooting here next week."

"Sounds like a plan," Payne said as he faced the two attractive and well-dressed women standing behind lane four. Their presence, like their appearance, pleased him, feeding his ego as both a shooter and a womanizer. Despite hearing what Glover had said, in his twisted mind he now believed they had come into the range to watch him fire his weapon after seeing him inside the gun store earlier. "Maybe I'll see you two here again soon. I'd be happy to give either of you a few pointers if you'd like. I can't tonight; I've got a hot date, but maybe next week or some other time in the near future."

"Hey, that's awful nice of you! My name's Kelly Rybak," Glover said using her alias for the evening. "This is my older sister, Janice."

"Nice to meet you both!" Payne said as he shook hands with two members of his favorite sex. "Bobby Bats has my cell number if you decide you want some free lessons, but I'm generally here every Saturday afternoon and then again around seven on most Tuesday evenings. Drop by sometime and we'll shoot some bad guys together." Laughing at his own joke as he started walking to the range's exit door, Payne nodded at the shredded paper target he had been shooting at. It was a picture of a male burglar, one dressed completely in black.

"Forget you!" Kelly said once Payne was out of earshot. The

sight of their suspect smiling at her had made her want to puke. "Freakin' asshole! I'd like to shoot you . . . you sick bastard!"

Edwards, who Glover had yet to meet at work, smiled to himself as he began policing the area around his lane. With Payne gone, and the ladies safe, his work was soon done. Casually he walked out of the range, leaving Donna and Kelly alone inside. Soon the two surveillance teams radioed to Paul and Bobby Ray that Edwards, like their suspect, was clear of the gun store. Payne's truck was immediately picked up in traffic by Wilson and Griffin as it headed back down Highway 707 towards Murrells Inlet.

"Quick, Donna, hurry! Let's get this done before someone comes in here!" Kelly said as she pulled two folded up GCSD clear plastic evidence bags from her pocketbook.

From the purse she had worn over her shoulder for most of the night, Donna pulled out two pairs of latex gloves and two yellow No. 2 pencils. "Put these on, Kelly, and then use the pencil like Paul showed us to pick up the empty casings. Remember what Bobby Ray said about picking them up with your fingers, that's a no-no! They may have Mr. Shithead's fingerprints on them, that's why he wants us to use the pencils."

The name Donna used to describe Payne caused Kelly to let out a loud laugh as she began dropping casing after casing into the evidence bag she was holding. Donna's next comment soon caused her to laugh even louder.

"What the hell were you thinking when you were chatting up Mr. Shithead a few minutes ago? You referred to me as your *older* sister. We both know I'm not your sister, but I'm hardly old, girl!"

"What should I have called you, Donna?" Kelly said still laughing, her bag now half-full with spent shell casings.

"I don't know. But I would have preferred either mature or experienced instead of old. I liked you up to that point, but now I'm not so sure." Donna's comeback caused both of them to enjoy another few moments of laughter as they finished the task Paul and Bobby Ray had sent them there to complete.

"Let's get out of here, Kelly. I need a drink or two after this ordeal. How about you? Paul doesn't know it, but he's buying!"

* * * * * *

Fifteen minutes later, in the same McDonald's parking lot where their suspect had parked his truck a few days earlier, Paul and Bobby Ray took possession of the shell casings that Payne had gone through in the range. Like so many previous occasions, he had again failed to clean up his area after he had finished shooting. Knowing his previous history of not doing so had caused Paul to figure out how to take possession of their suspect's spent casings so they could be examined by SLED. As Payne had again failed to clean up after himself, he had also abandoned any rightful claim to them by leaving them scattered across the range floor. Doing so clearly allowed Paul to consider them as abandoned property, property that no longer carried any legal rights of ownership or privacy.

The casings Payne left behind, just like others which other shooters occasionally left abandoned in their assigned shooting areas, were free for the taking. In this particular matter, they now became the property of the GCSD. They soon would become the temporary property of SLED, and of Mr. Kenneth Zercie, that department's expert Firearms Examiner. He would soon spend the better part of two days examining the casings that Donna and Kelly had collected.

Thirty

The Takedown

The morning after Donna and Kelly's visit to the range, the shell casings were photographed and inventoried by Elmendorf, Vane, and one of the crime scene processing techs before being transported to SLED for forensic analysis. As they were about to finish with their documentation of the casings, Paul and Bobby Ray met with them in Vane's processing area within the GCSD's main facility on North Fraser Street.

"Guys, any surprises?" Bobby Ray asked as he walked up to where Vane and Elmendorf were working.

Finished separating the casings into two separate piles, Vane barely looked up as he answered the question that had been posed to them.

"No, not really. I just thought we were dealing with one gun, that's all. Maybe I misunderstood what Paul's wife told Stine last night, but this morning he confirmed for me that she said she had only seen our suspect firing one gun at the range." Then motioning to the two separate piles, Vane said, "We've got two different calibers of casings sitting here." A nod from Elmendorf, who was standing at the far end of the stainless steel examining table, confirmed his partner's statement.

"You've got what, Dougie?" Bobby Ray asked, not sure that he had correctly heard what Vane just said.

"You heard me right, Bobby Ray." Vane said as he pointed at the larger of the two piles sitting in front of him. "This group on my left has fifty-nine shell casings that have been manufactured by Mauser; they're all 9 millimeter rounds. This group on my right has ten less; it's a pile of forty-nine .380 rounds. It's no big deal, but, like I just said, I was operating under the premise that only one gun was seen being fired last night."

With a sense of urgency, Paul quickly moved to the other side of Vane's work area and away from the conversation that was still taking place. As he did, he punched Donna's name on his phone's Favorites list. It was one of only six listed in that area on his Apple iPhone. Hearing her answer his call, Paul quickly got to the point he needed a clarification on.

"Donna, listen. This is important. Last night, how many guns did you and Kelly see Payne fire?"

"Just one. Why?" Donna curiously inquired.

"Are you sure? You never saw him take a second one out of his gun case, or possibly from a holster he might have been wearing?"

"Nope! He had one gun, that's all. I'll swear to it if I have to. He turned his back on us for a few seconds like I've already told you, but we never saw him take out a second gun. Can I ask why you're asking me about this?"

"I'll explain it later. I've got to go. Thanks, hon!" Paul disconnected the call without giving his wife a chance to speak again.

Looking down at the two separate piles of casings now in front of him, Paul thought quietly for a few moments as he weighed what little was really known about their suspect. After a few seconds, he looked at the others standing around Vane's table. To their surprise, Paul quickly moved away from the issue of why two different calibers of shell casings now existed.

"I know how I feel about Payne, but I need to know how each of you feels. Tell me, do you think we've got enough to obtain search warrants for his home and vehicles, and, perhaps most importantly, do you think he killed those kids?" Paul looked at Bobby Ray to speak first.

"No question at all, he's our guy. I'm convinced he shot those kids because he felt they had screwed him several times over by bouncing checks on him for times he had cut their lawn. I do find it funny that Payne doesn't have a criminal record; just like I find it funny that there's no record, at least one we don't know about yet, of him being an overly aggressive guy, a hothead. We know he's a rude and arrogant son of a bitch at times, but what's that count in the scheme of things we're looking at? Hell, ask the folks who work for me, I'm probably rude and arrogant at times as well, but that doesn't make me a murderer. I also like Payne because I think he's a guy with an attitude, and a guy who has some financial issues. I believe both of those concerns contributed to him flipping out that day when he shot the kids. We also know he's a gun nut, and the casings we've got sitting right here on the table are the same exact calibers to those we found at the scene. So, if you're asking me to vote, I'm all about getting a search warrant or two for this no-good bastard. Besides the warrants you've mentioned, we also need one so we can obtain his DNA and fingerprints as well. And, yeah, just in case you haven't figured out my position on our guy, I believe he killed those kids. I'm confident the DNA that SLED has already found on the cigarette butts from near the shed are going to match the DNA on that butt Payne threw on the ground at the gas station; same goes for the DNA on the straw as well. I could be wrong, but I'm also pretty damn confident that the casings in front of us are also going to be found to have the same ejector markings and the same firing pin impressions as the others we have already found, especially the one these two guys found in the basket of dried flowers. I vote that we start making arrangements for Payne to join the forty-some other inmates who are already on Death Row; that's just where his sorry-ass belongs."

Paul nodded at his friend's somewhat emphatic stance regarding their suspect's involvement in the murders. It was obvious to him, and to the others, how Bobby Ray felt. He now knew his friend's position was not much different than his own.

Like Bobby Ray, but in a more subdued, and certainly in a more analytical manner based on their roles in the investigation, both Vane and Elmendorf agreed with all of the points their boss had raised. They both believed that more than enough probable cause existed for Pascento and the courts to approve the issuance of several search warrants. Like their boss, they also believed Payne was the person responsible for each of the five deaths that had occurred.

As he finished giving his opinion, Elmendorf bemoaned the fact about one issue. "We've got his shell casings, we've got his DNA in several forms, and soon we're going to get his firearms. We will even have the opportunity, once we seize those firearms, to have them test fired. That testing will hopefully give us a perfect bullet, and a perfect shell casing, to match to each shell casing that we already have. What we don't have are any bullets in pristine condition from the crime scene, or from the victims' bodies, to match against that perfect bullet we'll retrieve from the water tank. As we all know, all of the bullets that were retrieved from the bodies were too damaged from striking various bones to be much good for use in comparison testing. I'm confident that he's our guy, but from an evidentiary point of view I just wished we had at least one bullet in good condition to compare to Payne's."

"You are absolutely correct, Don." Vane said, supporting Elmendorf's concern as he finished packaging the shell casings so they could be transported to SLED's forensic lab.

Like Bobby Ray's, each of the other comments Paul heard were ones that supported his own thoughts about Payne and the search warrants.

"OK, we're all in agreement then. Bobby Ray, I want to keep the full-court press on Payne for now. Make sure you've got enough folks detailed to his surveillance until you hear further. For as long as possible, I want to keep Wilson, Griffin, Davis, and Levesque on him; pick a couple of others, perhaps Mo and Carlson, to serve as their back-up teams. Then use whoever else you want, but let's get them talking to people Payne knows . . . his friends, his customers, whoever, but let's have them start asking questions about him. Maybe once he hears about us doing that he'll have some discomfort and do something stupid; something that will help our efforts. I'm going to call Edwards and Tommy Scozz and have them meet me at the firing range as I feel the need to go over a few things with Bobby Bats. I'll also get Stine in here to start knocking out the search warrants we're going to need. I'd like to seize some of Payne's clothing for GSR testing, but I'm not sure it's worth the effort. Besides not knowing what clothes he wore the day the murders occurred, too much time has passed since then to make the test results valid. Any first-year law student could easily mount a successful challenge regarding us seizing his clothing, and any experienced attorney worth his or her salt would likely argue that the clothing we seized had gotten mixed up with the clothing their client wore to the firing range, clothing that obviously would have had gunshot residue on them. I'm not really sure what to do about the clothing . . . tell you what; you and Blake work it out. Whatever you boys decide is good enough for me. The GSR testing, even if we could get it admitted during a trial, is not going to make or break our case. For now, I need to get up to the range. On my way, I'll call Pascento and tell him to expect several warrant applications being dumped on his desk later today. All of that sound OK with you?"

"Sounds like a plan, partner!" Bobby Ray said as he began walking back to his office.

"OK, Bobby Ray, you handle things here, and I'll get up to the range. I'll check in with you later to see what kind of progress Stine and the others are making." Turning to leave, Paul looked over at Elmendorf and Vane before walking out to his vehicle.

"Guys, get this evidence up to SLED as quick as possible. They know it's a priority for them to look at. If anyone there gives either of you any crap about starting work on this right away, you've got my permission to kick them in the ass, but if you do, do it hard!"

* * * * * *

With Edwards and Scozzafava standing in the deserted firing range with him, Paul listened as Bobby Bats told them all he knew about Payne. Moments earlier, he had told them about the policies and procedures of how the range was operated, maintained, and used.

"Bats, I know I said this already, but let me again express my personal thanks for all of the help you've given us. We're going to make sure you're recognized for your assistance when this investigation is over and done with. It's help like yours that helps cops like us solve horrific cases such as this one."

"My pleasure." Bobby Bats was now beaming over the compliment Paul directed at him. "Maybe if you guys give me an award of some kind, I'll hang it in my office some place. It will add to the class that I've already given this place!"

"Sounds good, Bats." Paul offered as he managed a small smile. "Listen, before we leave, we've just got a few more questions, OK?"

"Fire away, I'm here to help! Hey! No pun intended regarding my last comment." Bats quickly laughed at his own joke. It was one that Edwards chuckled over as well.

"Bats, just so we have this straight, you've told us that every time someone comes in to use the range, they not only have to pay to use it, but they have to sign in with you as well. Is that correct?" Despite already having a good handle on how the range was operated, Paul now sought confirmation on several minor administrative issues.

"Yep, absolutely! They sign the form to use the range or they leave, no exceptions. Not even for you guys. Never! After they sign the form, we date and time stamp it when they enter the range, and then do the same when they leave. We keep all of the signed forms in a couple of file cabinets and in a handful of boxes. I've never thrown a single one out; I've got thousands of them stored in my back room."

What Bats told them about his tight recording procedures for use of the range now pleased Paul. He now viewed that information they had been told as another means of tightening the noose around Payne's neck.

"So it sounds like you can tell us how many times Payne has used the range for the past year, correct?"

"Yep," Bats replied rather proudly, "and for the two previous years as well. He's been coming here for three years; been a pain-in-my-ass for about that long as well. Don't get me wrong, I'm glad to have his business, but the guy's generally more trouble than he's worth. Besides having to clean up after him every time he uses the range, he's probably cost me a customer or two because of his attitude at times. He's not quite the asshole he once was, probably because I've told him to knock it off about how he interacts with others while he's here, but he's gonna be persona non grata if he ever acts like a jerk again in front of any of my customers or staff."

"Interesting." Paul offered as he exchanged quick looks with Scozzafava and Edwards.

"Paul, mind if I ask Bats here a question or two?" Edwards asked.

"Ask away."

"As you already know, last night after Payne left, the ladies picked up a bunch of the casings that he had fired. One of the ladies has told us they only saw him shoot one pistol while he was here. But when our lab guys looked at the casings this morning there were two different calibers of casings mixed together. How'd that happen? Because when I got into the range just before our guy did, I made sure the floor was clean of any other casings before Payne started shooting."

"Well, that . . ." Bats was cut off by Edwards before he could offer his opinion on the different caliber of casings that had been found.

"Bats, I'm a gun guy just like you, but you obviously know more than I do." Edwards wisely said, deferring to Bats' years of working with firearms on a daily basis. "But I do have my thoughts on why the different shell casings were found on the floor by where Payne had been shooting. I'm thinking he fired a pistol last night that accommodates at least two different types of bullets. You and I both know that several guns can accept more than one caliber of bullet being fired in them. We also know that most guns can easily allow for barrels to be swapped out so they can accommodate different types of rounds, correct?"

"Yeah, sure, but I don't allow barrels to be swapped out on the range. Doing so wastes time, especially in a small range like mine that is often crowded with folks waiting to shoot, but more importantly it's for safety reasons. Too many of my shooters think they know more about firearms than they actually do. It's for safety reasons that I don't allow shooters to swap out barrels while they're on the line. Some people try and do it, but we'll catch it on the camera more often than not. Most times it looks like someone is trying to clear a squib load or something like that, that's how we usually catch them trying to swap out barrels. My range officers also do a good job watching for things like that. When someone's caught trying to swap barrels, I end up having to tell them that it's my range and my rules. You shoot the guns you bring to the line, no messing around, and no swapping barrels!"

"What does it take to swap out barrels on an automatic? Perhaps fifteen to twenty seconds?" Paul interjected into the conversation.

Bats thought for a moment before answering. When he did, he spoke with confidence. "Yeah, maybe, if you know what you're doing. Could be even less, perhaps five or six seconds if you're swapping barrels and each barrel has their own slide. But I don't see that very often here, maybe once or twice a year at most, and it didn't happen here last night."

Hearing something unexpected, the three cops stared at each other for a brief moment before Edwards followed up with the obvious response. "Why's that?"

"Because while several of Payne's firearms allow for two or three different rounds to be fired through them, none of them allow for different barrels to be swapped out. More than likely, he simply fired different caliber rounds using different magazines."

"OK, we've got that. So what about my thought of one gun firing two different rounds? Sounds like you agree with that?" Edwards cautiously asked Bats.

Looking up and down at the large cop standing a few feet in front of him, Bats asked him a specific question about what had been found by Donna and Kelly.

"What kind of markings were on the casings? By that, I don't mean the extractor markings or the firing pin impressions, I mean what calibers were they and who made them?"

Edwards looked to Paul for the correct answer as he had yet to see the casings himself.

"They were a combination of .380 casings, ones that looked like they had been reloaded by someone, and a similar number of 9 millimeter rounds that had been made by Mauser."

Bats thought for a moment before speaking. "Sounds like a Mauser, likely their HSc model . . . the *Hahn Selbstspanner Pistole* the Germans call it. Loosely translated, that means a self-cocking pistol. It's comparable to the more popular Walther PPK, and even to the Sig Sauer 38H. It's got a hammer that's somewhat exposed and, like most pistols, a double-action trigger. Mauser is a German made pistol that's mostly imported by Interarms; they're a gun company located in Alexandria, Virginia. The pistol I'm referring to has a barrel length that's just under three and a half inches long. It's an easy one to conceal. If I remember correctly, the various magazines designed for that pistol can handle three different sizes of rounds; most hold either seven or eight rounds each."

"You sound pretty confident about that particular pistol." Tommy Scozz stated, jumping into the conversation for the first time. "Why's that?"

Bats smiled at the FBI agent's comment. "Because I know Payne's got one. It's got black rubber grips on it. Most of them I see these days still have the brown wooden grips on them, but he's a serious shooter. He put rubber ones on his last year; they're easier on the hands if you do a lot of shooting like he does."

"You sure about him owning that kind of pistol?" Scozzafava asked, challenging Bats about his knowledge of what types of weapons their suspect owned.

"I'm darned sure, that's unless he sold it since last night. Shoots it here all the time, just like he did when you folks were here yesterday. In fact, it's a weapon I know he purchased about two years ago; at least, that's when I think he picked it up. Not sure where he got it, but I know it's one of his favorites."

"But he . . ." Scozzafava was cut off by Paul before he could finish with what he had to say.

"Scozz," Paul said as he glared at the FBI agent standing next to him, "we'll figure it out, OK?"

"Yeah, OK, sure thing." Scozzafava quickly understood Paul's tacit message to stop asking questions. He soon realized while Paul appreciated the help they were receiving, Bats did not need to know everything about their investigation.

"Bats, one last request." Paul said as he turned to face his new best friend. "How soon can you make us up copies of your waiver forms that Payne has signed?"

"How far back we going?" Bats asked as he scratched the side of his head.

"To the very first time he shot here. All the way back to the first one he signed. You make the copies for us, and I'll make sure the sheriff's department reimburses you for your time and effort."

"It'll take some doing, but I'll have them ready for you by Friday afternoon sometime. My folks aren't going to like having to do this, but I'll have them ready for you when you get here."

* * * * * *

As Scozzafava and Edwards went inside a local deli in Murrells Inlet to grab something for all of them to eat on the run, Paul called the Solicitor's Office. It took several minutes to update Pascento on what had occurred, but when he was done the solicitor agreed the timing was right for Payne's home and vehicles, as well as his person, to be searched.

"Call me when they're being brought up here, Paul. I'll have a judge standing by to sign them so you folks can execute them tonight."

* * * * * *

With Griffin following Payne's truck at a safe distance as their suspect began driving home shortly after seven that evening, the veteran detective used his Motorola radio to call out the direction of travel they were taking. Once it became clear that Payne was using Wachesaw Road to get to his home on Brown Bark Lane, Bobby Ray ordered the shutdown of the eastern end of Running Water Road. He did so as a means of keeping other traffic from accidently interfering with the surveillance of Payne's vehicle as it moved closer to their suspect's home. Not knowing if Payne would choose to shoot it out with his detectives as they moved in on him, he also ordered it closed so no innocent motorists got hurt.

"OK, we're approaching Brown Bark; we're passing Wacca Wache Drive as I speak. *All units stand-by!*" Griffin said as he calmly radioed his position for the last time just before turning onto the road where Payne's single level home was located.

"OK, we're two hundred yards away from his home. *Execute! Execute!*"

Bobby Ray had wisely let Griffin choose the exact moment when he wanted the other unmarked cars in Payne's neighborhood to move into position to block their suspect's direction of travel before he could reach his driveway. Reacting to Griffin's order, six unmarked GCSD vehicles, and two marked cruisers, all who had been strategically parked out of sight as their suspect drove down the road, boxed Payne's truck in less than fifty yards from his driveway.

Stunned by what was taking place, and with no avenues of escape, Payne had no other choice but to bring his truck to a complete stop. Immediately he raised his hands in the air as a combination of eight detectives and uniformed deputies approached his position with weapons drawn. Following Bobby Ray's verbal commands, he turned his truck off and threw his ring of keys to the pavement. Still following the commands he was hearing, Payne stepped from the truck with his hands raised high above his head.

"Slowly step away from your vehicle and walk towards me! Now stop and get down on your knees! Do it slowly and do it so I can see your hands at all times!" Bobby Ray ordered loud enough for Payne, as well as everyone else around him to hear, but their suspect stood still for several moments before even thinking about kneeling down. Standing there, he gauged the magnitude of what was taking place around him. Somewhat defiantly, and with his arms still high in the air, he smiled at the several guns being pointed at him

"Get down on your knees . . . do it now!" Bobby Ray barked for the second time.

Slowly Payne dropped to one knee and then to the other as he continued to take in what was happening all around him. In moments, he was down on all fours, his legs crossed over each other as he had been directed to do.

"I've got a gun under the driver's seat!" Scozzafava yelled, his blue and yellow FBI raid jacket quickly identifying who he worked for to several residents who had come out of their homes after hearing the commotion taking place on their normally quiet street. Moments later, after being assisted by two uniformed deputies, the FBI agent yelled, "Rest of the truck is clear . . . no other weapons."

Quickly handcuffed, Payne was immediately placed in the

back seat of a marked GCSD cruiser. A stainless steel cage separated the front seat from the back one. Briefly driven to the mouth of his driveway so his keys could be used to unlock the front door of his ranch style home, Payne was then read his Miranda Warnings by Wilson. Then, with Paul and Bobby Ray as witnesses, Griffin and Wilson advised their suspect why he had been stopped. After doing so, they advised him of the search warrants the court had issued for his home and grounds, his vehicles, and for his person.

"Mr. Payne, in a few minutes, you are going to be taken down to the sheriff's department in Georgetown so we can talk to you about several murders that have recently occurred. I want you to know that you are not under arrest at this time. The reason that you have been handcuffed is for your safety and for ours. As long as you behave yourself, I'll consider having the cuffs taken off shortly after we get to Georgetown. Do something stupid and they can stay on for the rest of the night as far as I'm concerned. Understand?" Wilson impatiently asked.

With a blank look on his face, Payne simply stared at Wilson, and then at the others standing outside the cruiser. Then, ignoring those close to him, he briefly watched as four heavily armed cops dressed in black fatigues entered his home. Next to it, an old wooden shed sat off to the left. As a large number of cops came and went in the driveway and front yard; his eyes remained focused on the small building. It was a place he often visited to find the peace and quiet his troubled brain frequently needed. It was also a place where he stored most of his gun supplies and did most of his reloading.

"Please . . . please don't let them find it!" Payne thought as he continued to stare at the place he often felt the most comfortable in.

As he sat in the back of the cruiser, he chose to say nothing, ignoring the handful of comments the cops directed at him. In moments, and as promised, as others began the process of executing the search warrants on his residence, the small outbuilding, and his two trucks, the suspect in five recent murders was driven back to Georgetown by Deputy Arne Kinsler. Like Bobby Ray, who was sitting next to Payne in the back seat, and like Kinsler, Paul sat quiet in the right front seat as they passed through North Litchfield and Pawleys Island. As they did, Paul quietly fingered one of the search warrants the court had issued. It was the one granting permission for Payne's DNA and fingerprints to be taken. As they made their way closer to Georgetown, Wilson and Griffin, followed by Stine and Scozzafava, continued to trail behind them in two separate vehicles.

Thirty-One

The Interview

The main Interview Room within the Georgetown County Sheriff's Department where Payne sat handcuffed to a desk was bigger than the one Cotton Horbin had been interviewed in down the hall. As for its size, it was about as large as a spacious storage room. The absence of furniture, besides the gray metal desk and three chairs that were present, made the room feel even bigger than it was. Unlike the other two chairs, Payne's chair, like the desk, was bolted to the floor. A strong antiseptic smell still lingered in the air from the cleaning the room had been given that morning.

Built into the soundproof room's acoustical panels were two unobtrusive microphones. While one helped to record for posterity what was said during interviews taking place there, the other was tied into a speaker in an adjoining room; one that allowed detectives, and sometimes others as well, to listen in to what was being said. On the wall behind where the interviewing detective sat, or sometimes stood when a moment of intimidation was needed, were two other objects. The first was a small high resolution CCTV camera that, like the microphone for the adjacent room, was plugged into a Dell PC which sat on a table in the Observation Room. The camera itself had been mounted on the wall's upper right corner. For those being interviewed, it was something that was hard not to stare at. The capabilities of both the camera and the PC allowed observing detectives the ability to not only view a suspect's facial features and nervous tics up close during an interview, but also allowed those images to be captured and stored as JPEG files. They were files the computer automatically date and time stamped for future use. The other obvious feature in the room was a two by three foot one-way mirror. Built into the wall just below and slightly to the left of where the camera was mounted, the mirror allowed detectives not directly involved in the interview to watch what took place from within the somewhat darkened interior of the Observation Room. The small mirror, one sometimes not used during interviews of suspects involved in minor crimes, added to the stress most criminals felt when they first saw the one-way piece of glass staring at them. Posted on the wall to the right of where suspects, perps, and an occasional witness or victim sat, were two computer generated signs. The wording on the first sign was printed in both English and Spanish, wording that advised everyone using the room of their Miranda Warnings. They were warnings which most cops considered a huge waste of time as the plethora of cop shows on television had caused even the youngest of elementary school children to know their constitutional rights. The second sign, one that only meant something to those who had not found themselves sitting in this room before, warned all who were present that all interviews were being captured on both audio and video tapes. Like the first one, this sign had also been printed in both languages.

After being placed in the Interview Room, Detectives Brandau and Baughman obtained Payne's DNA by way of a buccal swab. Also known as a buccal smear, the swab of their suspect's mouth was easily obtained with the use of two sterile foam tipped swabs. The swabs were immediately placed inside a dry transport tube as soon as the brief process was completed. Like some of the other evidenced seized from Payne's residence that evening, the tubes would also be sent to SLED for testing.

Walking into the Interview Room after Payne's DNA had been obtained, Wilson placed a file folder down on the desk as he again introduced Griffin and himself to their suspect. Knowing that Payne had already signed a form acknowledging he had been advised of his rights, Wilson skipped addressing that formality. As his partner stood off to the side, Wilson sat down at the desk, the camera hovering slightly above his right shoulder. Before speaking, he sat quiet for several moments digesting a phone call he had just finished with Elmendorf. The sergeant had called him about something important that had been found during the execution of the search warrants. Quickly dismissing his thoughts, he spoke to their suspect.

"Mr. Payne, you are here because my partner and I, along with several others, are investigating the recent murders of five young men in North Litchfield. Just so you know, that's part of Georgetown County, an area routinely patrolled by the Georgetown County Sheriff's Department. Do you understand that?"

Displaying an outwardly calm appearance, but nervous as one could be considering the environment he was in, Payne struggled to control both the rate of his breathing and his emotions. With eyes that slowly dialed wide open, he stared at Wilson for several seconds. Then shrugging his shoulders, he stated, "What's so hard to understand about that? Everyone knows the sheriff's department handles most things up there."

"OK, good." Wilson replied, showing as much emotion as their suspect was displaying. "Have you heard about these murders?"

"Yeah, sure, who hasn't." Payne said as he alternated looks at the two cops on the other side of the desk.

"Mr. Payne, we understand you did some work . . . yard work I understand it to be . . . for the victims. Is that right?"

"Yep, cut their grass several times for them over the past two years." Payne said as he tried hard not to stare at the camera looking down on him.

From where he sat, Wilson shot a quick look at Griffin before continuing with his line of questioning. "Ever have any problems with them? You know, any arguments or fights or anything like that?"

For the first time, Payne flinched as he sat in his chair. It was something most people likely would have missed, but not Wilson or Griffin. Like most veteran homicide detectives, they were paid to pick up on a suspect's flaws and mistakes. Each now made a mental note of what they saw; saving it to use against their suspect when the time was right.

"No, not really. I mean they bounced a check on me once, but that got taken care of within a few days. It wasn't any big deal, those things happen, you know. They made good on it and, to tell you the truth, I had forgotten about it until you just brought it up."

"How many times did they bounce a check on you, Mr. Payne? Was it once or was it more than just one time?"

Payne adjusted himself in his chair before answering Wilson's question. "No, it was just once. It was for forty dollars. Hey, I had no beef with those guys, so why are you asking about a check they bounced on me? What's that got to do with them being murdered?"

"All part of our investigation, that's all. With five dead kids on our hands, we're asking lots of questions to a lot of people these days, you included. We just have to ask the questions we have to ask, that's all." Wilson said as he tried keeping Payne calm by flashing a brief smile at him. Then the veteran detective, hoping to reduce their suspect's concerns even more about the questions being asked of him, calmly asked his next one. "This might be another one of those questions you consider strange, but it's one we have to ask. Do you smoke?"

"Yep, sure do. Bad habit I know, but I still smoke, can't seem to quit. No weed if that's where you're headed with this. Just cigarettes, Parliaments mostly. To be honest, I'm kind of nervous about being here. I could use one right about now."

Wilson nodded, and then again tried to calm Payne down; reassuring him he could have a smoke after answering a few additional questions.

"When you did work for those kids, did they ever pay you in cash?" It was a question Wilson already knew the answer to.

"No, never." Payne responded quite adamantly.

"Mr. Payne, each of our victims died from a gunshot wound to the head. Each of those shots had been fired at close range. I'm sorry, but we have to ask you this. Have you ever had any thoughts about shooting those kids? Maybe even up close and personal like?" Wilson asked, trying to rattle their suspect even more than he already was.

"What are you trying to infer with that stupid question of yours? I just told you that I didn't have any problems with those kids. So why would I waste my time thinking about wanting to kill them?"

Like his partner, Griffin heard Payne's response. Just as Wilson had, he also recognized that while their suspect had responded to the question, he had not denied ever thinking about killing his victims.

Wanting to catch Payne off guard, Wilson hit him with a question that he was sure their suspect would not see coming. As he did, Griffin, aware the question was going to be asked early in the interview, carefully watched to see what kind of reaction it would get.

"Mr. Payne, just so we have an understanding between us, I want you to know something important. Recently the Georgetown County Sheriff's Department served a search warrant on the bank you do business with. We did that so we could obtain your financial records." Like it had been intended, Wilson's question caught their suspect by surprise. It also told Payne one important point. The cops were focused on him, and likely him alone, for being involved in the recent murders in North Litchfield.

"Uh . . . OK . . . what . . . what were you looking for at the Georgetown Savings Bank? I mean, I really don't have much money in my accounts there and . . ." As he tried to finish with what he had to say, Payne sensed discomfort setting in. Besides his already dry mouth, now he could feel the palms of his hands beginning to sweat.

Wilson now applied even more pressure as he set the record straight. As he did, Paul and Bobby Ray watched from the other side of the one-way mirror.

"We're not as interested in those accounts as we are in the other one you have." Wilson said, speaking in a tone of voice that showed little emotion. "We served the warrant at the Garden City branch of the Murrells Inlet National Savings and Loan. You know . . . the bank you have a somewhat dubious business account at."

Payne now searched for a proper response to the surprise that had been thrown at him. As he did, his eyes began to show the furor that was building inside him. "How . . . how did . . . how did you find out about that account?"

"We'll talk about that later, Mr. Payne. Maybe. That's if we have time to do so." Griffin said as he stared at their obviously rattled suspect sitting a scant few feet away from where he stood.

Wilson now tried to unnerve their suspect even more. "Mr. Payne, regarding the bank account in question, and just so you're clear on this, we've studied all of your transactions since you opened that account a little more than three years ago. Do you understand that? Because we certainly don't want you to be confused while we're talking, do we?"

"Yeah, I understand what you've said." Payne said, becoming more and more disgusted at the questioning he was being subjected to.

Retrieving a copy of Payne's checking account transactions from the file he had set down on the desk, Wilson sensed their suspect's anger building. As he did, he turned the pages of documentation until he found the one he wanted. It was page seven of a nine page print-out. Then, with significant intention, he placed the report close enough so Payne could see the transaction that had been hi-lighted with a lime green hi-lighter. Next to the transaction the word *WHY?* had been written in large letters with the same color hi-lighter. For effect during the interview, it had also been circled and underlined several times. Wilson knew this transaction was the one that had gotten Detectives Baughman and Brandau's attention when they first saw it. It had been Griffin's idea to hi-light the transaction using a bright color hi-lighter. He had done so to intentionally increase Payne's stress during his interview.

"Mr. Payne, what's the purpose of this account?" Wilson asked.

"I . . . I use it on occasion to pay some bills with. I also deposit all of my customers' checks in that account."

Just like Griffin, as well as the others standing behind the one-way mirror, Wilson smiled a smile that only he could feel. "Bad answer, asshole!" He thought to himself.

Now Griffin began to pepper Payne with questions about the suspicious checking account. As he did, he pointed to the print-outs sitting on the desk. "Mr. Payne, just so we understand it correctly, after you receive a check or two from one or more of your customers, you deposit those checks into the account we're talking about, right?"

"If those bank records are for the account I have at the Murrells Inlet National Savings and Loan, then yeah, that's what I do with them. What's the big freakin' mystery about that? Did I do something illegal like or what?" By asking his own questions, Payne tried stalling for time so he could figure out where the cops' line of questioning was going, but despite doing so he came up empty."

"You said before that your customers have never paid you in cash. Is that still your answer?"

"Detective, are you accusing me of lying?" Payne asked as he nervously laughed. "No, no one has ever paid me in cash. I make them pay me by check so there's a written record of each payment being made."

"Smart move!" Wilson offered. "How about those kids who were murdered? You mowed their lawn, correct?"

Hearing the question, one that he knew he had previously answered, caused Payne to roll his eyes in frustration. He realized the cops were trying to catch him in a lie. His answer showed his displeasure with the game they were trying to play on him.

"Yeah, I do. So what? I cut quite a few lawns in the towns of North Litchfield and Pawleys Island; so do a bunch of other guys. But I don't see them here being asked these same questions." Payne's attitude was slowly beginning to deteriorate from the scrutiny he was under.

Realizing their suspect was becoming even more upset than he had been, and knowing they still needed to get as much information as they could from him before he lawyered up, Wilson chose to wait a few minutes before hitting Payne with his most important question. For now, he chose to ask him some easy questions in hopes of getting their suspect calmed down.

"Know anything about a shed that caught fire in the victims' backyard? We were told it burned to the ground a few months ago. Sounds to us like someone might have had a beef with one or more of the victims, and then got pissed off one night and set the shed on fire. You know who might have done that, Mr. Payne?"

Seeing Payne flinch for the second time caused Wilson to abandon his plan of taking it easy on their suspect. It was time to increase the pressure their suspect was feeling, but first he waited to hear Payne's answer about the shed fire.

"I heard about it catching on fire from them kids when they called me to come mow their lawn; unlike most of my customers I don't have a regular day I cut their lawn on. That was their choice when they hired me. They decided they would just call me when it needed cutting. I saw the shed's burnt shell when I showed up to cut the lawn two days later. I think it got torn down a day or two later. That's all I know about it. Don't know much more than that, and don't know why I should."

Wilson now came back at Payne. Doing so caused several drops of perspiration to start forming on their suspect's brow.

"Funny that you don't seem to know anything about the shed

being burned to the ground as I heard they found a few cigarette butts . . . Parliaments, I believe they were . . . in the mulch and pine straw around the area where it was torched. We've also been told that you've been seen smoking a few times out behind the shed after cutting the lawn. Maybe you were taking a smoke break there, or maybe you were plotting how to get even with those kids for not paying you for the work you performed? Which was it, Mr. Payne?"

"I've already told you that I had no beef with those kids. I may have had a smoke or two near the shed like you've said, but that's it. It wasn't me who set that thing on fire." Payne angrily responded.

Finished speaking, Payne, growing more frustrated by the minute, stared at the concrete floor by his feet. Wilson's statement had caused him to divert his eye contact away from the two cops for the first time. As he sat there fuming, he sensed his heart rate starting to increase and his breathing becoming much more labored. Zeke Payne knew he was feeling the stress of being a murder suspect.

"Lying son of a bitch!" Griffin thought as he glared at Payne from where he stood off to Wilson's left.

"Mr. Payne, we just want you to know those cigarette butts that were found in the area around where the shed had been, well those were the same brand as the one we saw you throw out the window of your truck the other day at a Kangaroo Express gas station. All of them have been sent to the state crime lab for DNA testing. The lab is also going to compare any DNA they find on them to the DNA you likely left on the straw that was in the cup you set down on the driveway at the same gas station. I just thought I should tell you that." Pushing most of the buttons he wanted to push, Wilson now waited to see what kind of reaction it would get from their suspect.

Feeling as if the weight of the world was now on his shoulders, Payne could feel himself losing control as sweat began to soak through his shirt.

"That's bullshit, man, you can't do that! I didn't kill those kids, and you didn't have any right to seize those items without my permission. Besides, you need a warrant to do that. I watch cop shows on television all the time, I know what my rights are!" Payne said as he angrily stood up from the chair he had been sitting in. As he did, the handcuffs, one fastened to a metal ring attached to the desk and the other to his left wrist, tore into his skin as he tried raising his left arm higher than the cuffs allowed. Ignoring the pain he felt, Payne continued to maintain his innocence for several more moments.

Trying not to laugh after hearing their suspect's comment about watching cop shows on television, Griffin did his best to play the role of a hard-ass. "Sit down, Mr. Payne, before I make you sit down. Don't get up out of that chair again, understand?"

"Screw you!" Payne's loud and obnoxious behavior was beginning to show itself due to the stress of Wilson's questions. "I'm about done answering your freakin' bullshit questions! Like I said, I know my rights. Charge me with something or let me go!"

A single knock on the door interrupted the questioning of Payne for several moments as Griffin answered it. Soon the door was closed and a package, one rolled up in butcher paper, was placed down on the desk to the left of where Wilson sat. It was something Payne could not help staring at.

Hoping to ask their suspect a few more questions before he refused to cooperate any longer, Wilson did his best to calm things down. "Mr. Payne, we're not going to accomplish anything here if we start yelling at each other. It's time for all of us to take a deep breath and calm down."

"Yeah, whatever!" Payne sarcastically uttered.

"What about weapons, firearms to be precise. Do you own any?" Wilson calmly asked. As he did, and in response to the question that had just been asked, Paul and Bobby Ray watched to see what Payne's body language was going to be. To their surprise, Payne barely reacted to the question. No facial movements and no sudden body movements were displayed to indicate any immediate stress regarding Wilson's question. Seeing the lack of a reaction from their suspect surprised the two cops watching from behind the one-way mirror.

"Yeah, I own a couple. They're all registered like they should be. I don't own any rifles, just handguns. If your people are searching my home like you told me they were going to be doing, then I guess they'll find them. If they don't, then I guess they aren't too good at what they do." Payne's wise-ass remark caused him to briefly smile, but the unfriendly expression he saw on Griffin's face quickly made it disappear.

While Wilson was confident that Payne owned more handguns than the ones he admitted to owning, he chose to let their suspect's answer go unchallenged for now. Instead, he chose to simply ask a few additional follow-up questions. "*All* of the guns in your home are registered? Is that what you're telling us, Mr. Payne? There's not one or two, perhaps a Mauser or an H&K, that are not registered like they should be? I'm just asking because I need to make sure I get your answers straight about what guns you own for my report."

Payne's eyes bounced between Wilson and Griffin before focusing down on the floor again. Weakly, he offered his next comment. "No, they're all registered. I'm totally legal."

"OK, good to hear that." Wilson said, not believing for a moment their suspect was being completely honest with them. "Let's go back to talking about the victims' house for a minute. Did you ever get invited inside? What I mean by that is, were you ever inside their house on any occasion? Perhaps it was just to have a cold drink or to get paid for mowing the lawn on one or two occasions."

Wilson's question struck a sensitive nerve with their suspect. Quickly the two cops saw Payne begin to sweat harder than he had been, his eyes wildly darting around the room as he unconsciously rubbed his sweaty palms on his pant legs.

"No, never. Those kids never invited me inside . . . never gave me a cold drink either. We weren't friendly like that."

"Mr. Payne, I'm thinking we're just about done here. Thanks for your patience. I just have a couple more quick questions. One of the things we heard about you is that you like to target shoot. Is that correct?"

"Yep."

Wilson smiled as he nodded his head at Payne's answer. Both were simply done to keep their suspect calm. Carrying a gun to work each day only because his job required him to do so, Wilson now lied to Payne. The truth was, he really had little interest in shooting, even less in owning firearms. "I enjoy shooting as well. Where do you do your shooting? Somewhere here in Georgetown or up in Surfside Beach, perhaps?"

"No, I use the range at the 707 Indoor Shooting Range, it's up on Highway 707, just over the line into Horry County. I think it's the best one around. The owner's a guy most folks know as Bobby Bats. Some folks just call him Bats for short, I guess. He's a decent guy; treats me well every time I go there. He's got himself a nice place there; like to have a place like that myself someday."

"I'll have to check it out," Wilson said as he opened his folder for the second time. Trying to find what he was looking for inside the manila folder, he asked their suspect what he thought was a rather meaningless question. "How often do you shoot there, Mr. Payne?"

"Every Saturday afternoon and every Tuesday night for the past three years or so. I like shooting, it helps relieve the stress and frustration that I often . . ." Realizing he had just said something that he probably should not have, something which likely made him look bad to everyone who heard it, Payne stopped talking for a couple of moments before finishing with what he had to say. Staring at the camera, and then at the two microphones he saw in the ceiling, he regretted what he had said about the stress in his life. It was something that Wilson quickly picked up on.

"Relax, it's OK, we know what you meant. We've all got some stress in our life which needs to be reduced by some type of an activity that relaxes us. You like shooting, if that relaxes you then keep shooting. For me, I go fishing when I feel I'm stressed out; I'm lucky because I don't live far from the Great Pee Dee River. After a short walk from my home, I've got my line in the water in less than two minutes. The moment I make that first cast I've flushed the stress from my system. I'm sure you feel the same way when you go shooting." Wilson's words were intended to reduce Payne's moments of stress. Over the course of the next several moments, he continued to try and relax their suspect. Then he hit their suspect again with something that he knew Payne would not see coming. The result was as if he had hit their suspect in the face with a piece of wood.

Sliding two photographs across the desk so their suspect could see them, Wilson then asked his next question. "Do you recognize either of these two women?"

Payne stared at each of the photos for several seconds, deliberately scanning the features he found attractive on both faces. "I'm sad to say I don't. Both are pretty gals, especially the younger one. I know I'd recognize her if I had ever seen her."

"OK, fair enough."

As Wilson reached for the next two photographs, Griffin chuckled to himself. Now he anxiously waited to see their suspect's reaction to what he was about to be shown.

"What about these two photos, Mr. Payne? Ever meet these two ladies?" Wilson asked as he pushed the second set of photos close enough to their suspect so he could get a good look at them.

The color in Payne's face quickly drained as he looked at the last two photographs. His eyes stared hard at them for a few seconds before they moved to take a glance back at the faces he had seen in the first set of photos.

"Those . . . those two women . . . their . . ."

Trying to ignore the muffled laughter he heard coming from his partner, Wilson laid it on the line for Payne.

"Mr. Payne, judging from the expression that I'm seeing on your face, I guess it's safe to say you figured out the women in both sets of photos you're looking at are the same in each set. The second set is how they both looked when you met them last night at the indoor range. You do remember talking to them, right?"

"I . . . um . . . I . . ." Payne was so flustered by the faces he saw staring back at him from the photographs that he had no response for what Wilson was asking him.

Wilson pointed at the photographs in front of Payne before he spoke again. "We sent these two women there for one reason, Mr. Payne. They were there to collect the shell casings you fired during your target practice. They did so after you left, and after you failed to pick up your brass as the range expects each shooter to do. It clearly says that on a sign posted inside the range. It's also printed on the waiver form you and everyone else sign before entering the range. When you walked out of the range and got into your truck, you forfeited all legal rights of ownership to those casings; you abandoned your property. That's just what the courts refer to it as; abandonment."

Despite his face growing redder and redder by the moment, Payne said nothing. Confused over both the pictures he had seen, and learning that the cops now had possession of not only his DNA from at least two sources, but his spent shell casings as well, he knew he was in trouble. An experienced shooter, he knew what markings could be found on his casings, and how they could easily be compared to others he had stupidly left behind on other occasions.

Sensing Payne was about to blow up, and knowing that doing so would cause their witness to lose focus and possibly say something detrimental to his cause, Wilson now took the offense. In doing so, he spoke to their suspect in a condescending manner as he began to hit their suspect with some additional news Griffin and he had learned just before walking into the Interview Room.

"Well, Mr. Payne, earlier today, just like we did with the cigarette you smoked, and the straw you drank from, we sent the shell casings I just mentioned to the lab to be analyzed. Maybe we'll find your DNA on them, or maybe we'll find your fingerprints, but one thing I know we're going to find out is that the markings on those shell casings are all going to match the markings on the casings we found inside the victims' residence. Know how I know that?"

Ignoring what Wilson had said to him, Payne sat motionless as he blankly stared at the wall in front of him. Like the cops in the room, the video camera and the two microphones no longer mattered to him.

"Before we came in here to interview you, one of our canines, a dog trained to sniff out explosives . . . gunpowder and other bad shit like that . . . took her handler right to where you had hidden your unregistered Mauser. I mean, they were barely inside the front door of your residence when they found it. In fact, they found it even before the three of us got back here; before we even started this interview. Did you really think that hiding it inside an empty cereal box in your pantry was a slick move on your part? I mean, come on, a cereal box?" Like his partner was already doing, Wilson now glared at Payne.

"I want . . . I . . ."

Payne was so stunned by what he heard about his pistol being found so easily that he could not complete the several thoughts racing through his head.

"Mr. Payne, one last question. To be honest, you've lied to us several times since we started talking here tonight. We know all about your problems with the victims bouncing several checks on you, and we also know you were inside their home on several occasions. So let's stop the lying, OK? Face it, your DNA is going to be found on most of the cigarette butts in question, and it's also going to be found on the straw. Just like we do, you also know the testing the South Carolina Law Enforcement Division is going to complete later tonight on your firearms is going to match the shell casings we've already sent them, don't you?" Wilson paused for a moment to give Payne a brief moment to comprehend what he had just been told. It was a very brief pause. "I'll tell you what, as a sign of good faith I'm going to give you one last chance to help yourself. Do you want to take advantage of that chance by correcting any of the lies you've told us or do you just want to keep drowning in the bullshit you've been trying to run past us?"

Payne's face quickly became even more flushed than it had been; tears began to roll down his face in a steady stream. For a brief couple of moments he sobbed heavily, his chest rising and falling with each sob. As he cried, he realized his brief moments of anger on a Friday afternoon had now ruined his life.

"Mr. Payne," Wilson said as their suspect sat crying, "see this record of your checking account transactions? This one transaction, the one dated the same day you killed those kids, we'd like you to tell us about it." Wilson's own voice began to fill with rage, angered by the thought of the person sitting across from him being responsible for the senseless murders of five young men. "Do you know why we'd like you to tell us about it?" It was a hypothetical question he asked, but despite that Wilson left no time for an answer to be given. Standing up, he placed both palms on the edge of the desk as he leaned closer to Payne. "I'll tell you why we'd like you to tell us about it, because it's *the only* one of all of your deposits that was made in cash. THE ONLY ONE! That deposit . . . that insignificant eighty dollar cash deposit . . . that was money you stole out of those kids' wallets the day you murdered them, wasn't it? Killing them wasn't enough for you, was it? You had to take it a step further, didn't you? You mowed their lawn that day and probably got pissed off when one or two of those kids told you they didn't have the money to pay you right away. So that's when you decided to teach them a lesson by killing them; something you had probably thought of doing on several occasions before then. I'm thinking that after you killed the first one or two of those kids, the others probably began arriving home and you realized they had likely seen your truck parked down the street. That's when you really lost it. You realized you couldn't afford to leave any witnesses behind, so you killed them all. You tied some of them up before you killed them, but either after tying them up or after you shot them you took the last few meager dollars they had in the world out of their wallets. That eighty dollars was money they owed you for one other occasion when you mowed their lawn and they hadn't paid you. It was also for what they owed you for mowing their lawn that day, the day you killed them, wasn't it? Is that how it all happened, Mr. Payne?" Wilson was nearly hoarse as he slammed the desk with his right fist, angry at Payne, and angry at himself for letting the deaths of five young men affect his emotions during such an important interview.

Now it was Griffin's turn to come at Payne. Moving closer to the desk, he began to unwrap the package he had set down only minutes earlier. As he did, he spoke to their suspect.

"We've both heard what you've told us about the victims . . . you know . . . the bullshit about not hating them . . . about never having any thoughts about shooting them . . . all of that crap." Tossing the brown butcher paper off to his left, Griffin let six large silhouette style paper targets slowly unfurl as he held them high in the air with his left hand. Each target had the black outline of a mugger on them; one armed with a handgun. Each of the targets had been perforated in the head area from fourteen to twenty bullets being fired through them. No other similar types of holes were found on any other section of the mugger's body on any of the targets.

"Mr. Payne, I'm kind of confused," Griffin said sarcastically as he deliberately held up each target one at a time. "If you never had any bad thoughts about shooting those kids, why would these targets have been found in your shed? You know, the shed where you do all of your reloading . . . and whatever else it is that you do in there."

Raising his voice after waiting for a response to his previous question, Griffin then came at Payne hard regarding a damaging observation that had been made concerning each of the targets. It was one he knew he would not get a response to. "These targets are ones you used during a few of your practice sessions at the range. My partner and I understand that part, but the part we're confused on is why you have taken the time to write the names of three of your victims on each of these targets." Griffin then slowly held up each target one at a time. As he did, he pointed out the names that had been roughly scribbled near the top of each one. A red Sharpie had been used to write the names of Carl Diggs, Tyler Johanson, and Robert Tanner near the mugger's perforated head on each of the targets. A crudely drawn arrow connected each of the names to the holes in the targets. Each bullet had been fired by someone far too angry in life; they had been fired by someone who never should have been allowed to own any kind of firearms.

Following Griffin's lead, Wilson now followed up with a comment of his own. As he did, he pointed at the paper targets still being held by his partner. "Seems awful coincidental that these bad guys we're seeing on each of these targets have only been shot in the head. Seeing those holes reminds me of the same kind of injuries that all of our victims sustained. Guess we shouldn't be surprised by that, should we? Seeing you're the one who did all of the shooting."

Through his tears, Payne silently looked at the two cops in front of him with disdain. Then he shook his head defiantly several times at how Griffin and Wilson had hammered away at him. He was shocked by how perfectly the cops had figured out nearly all that had happened that Friday afternoon. Upset and angry, he finally forced himself to say something, something Wilson had been trying to get him to say since the beginning of the interview.

"Why couldn't they just have paid me like they should have? Those kids have ruined my life; it's all their fault, not mine!" Payne sobbed as he began to shake uncontrollably for several moments before finally composing himself. Then, without a warning, he loudly yelled, "I . . . I want an attorney! I've told you two assholes too much already."

Despite hearing Payne's request for an attorney, Wilson came back at him one last time. His own emotions running too high for him to stop the interview without being able to say one more thing to their suspect; one more piece of damaging news. "You're going to need that attorney, Payne! Maybe he'll be able to tell us why the same kind of duct tape, why the same kind of rope, the very same kinds that were used to silence and tie up those young men before you shot them were found in your truck when we searched it tonight."

Payne's head dropped into his lap. He had meant to throw both of those items away. They had been angrily tossed into the cargo area of his truck that afternoon, but despite seeing them on several occasions since then he had not thrown them away as he had planned. Now his laziness, like his anger and stupidity, had given the cops something else to hold against him.

Calming down, Wilson nodded at Griffin before briefly staring at their defeated suspect. After rolling up the paper targets so they could be used as evidence in the case against their suspect, he began returning the financial sheets and the two sets of photos to his folder. As he did, Griffin opened the Interview Room door.

Immediately the doorway was filled with the presence of Stine, Scozzafava, and two uniformed deputies. In the Observation Room, Paul and Bobby Ray lingered behind for several minutes as they began the process of updating Sheriff Renda and Solicitor Pascento with the results of the interview.

After briefly consulting with Paul and Bobby Ray, Wilson and Griffin returned to the Interview Room for the final time. "Mr. Payne," Wilson said matter-of-factly, "you are under arrest for the murders of Carl Diggs, Tyler Johanson, Robert Tanner, James Robinson, and Trevor Gilmour. I think you're going to need that attorney you've requested." As he spoke to their suspect, Wilson had recited the names of each of the victims without having to read one of them. Like Griffin and the others who had worked hard on this investigation, they were names he now had etched in his mind. They were names he would never forget.

After Payne was taken away to be processed for the murders, and after other needs finally calmed down several minutes later, Scozzafava began the process of notifying five sets of parents with the news that their sons' murderer was now under arrest.

Thirty-Two

A Senseless Death

Tired from several long days of work which preceded the arrest of their suspect, as well as from the hectic day following Payne's arrest; Paul allowed himself an extra hour of sleep on Friday. Despite that, and despite a brief stop at the Waccamaw Diner for a quick breakfast, he still managed to pull into the GCSD parking lot not long after the others had. As he did, he saw Bobby Ray's Dodge Charger parked in its usual parking spot.

Walking towards the front of the building instead of entering through one of the two side entrances on the east side as he normally did, Paul saw something that caused him to suddenly stop dead in his tracks along the front sidewalk.

For several moments, Paul stood watching Dexter Robinson, one of the building's three maintenance workers, standing near the top of a sixteen foot aluminum ladder that was leaning against the front of the building. Robinson, an elderly black male in his early seventies, was carefully draping the perimeter of the building's front entrance with black bunting. As he worked, Paul saw him pause twice to take off his glasses and wipe his face with the sleeve of his green work shirt. Soon busy after his brief pauses, Robinson did not see the person who had been watching him as he moved closer to where he was working.

"Good morning, Mr. Dexter," Paul said as he stared at the project that Robinson had well in hand. "Something happen that I should know about?"

Lost in his work and his thoughts, the sound of Paul's voice startled Robinson slightly. Quickly he leaned against the ladder to recover his balance.

"Morning, Mr. Paul," Robinson said, a sad smile displayed on his face. "Ya done scared me a bit. Guess I'm not paying much attention this sad morning." He added rather mournfully as he looked down from where he stood on the ladder. Finished speaking, the elderly maintenance worker took off his glasses once more. Now it became clear to Paul that it had been tears his friend was wiping away and not sweat.

"You OK, Dexter? I mean . . . who died?" Paul said as he took another look at the black bunting, some of which now hung limply by the side of Robinson's ladder.

"I'm . . . I'm gonna miss that smile, Mr. Paul. It's almost like I done lost a family member this morning. Sad news . . . I'm . . . I'm sorry, Mr. Paul, I can't talk no more on this right now. Best y'all see Captain Bobby Ray or one of his folks; they'll tell ya more about what happened."

Paul could easily tell Robinson was clearly upset by something terrible that had happened. Not wanting to upset him further, he elected to move inside to find out what had happened. Before he did, he directed one more comment at the maintenance worker who he had developed a casual friendship with.

"Dexter, I can tell how upset you are, so be careful on that ladder, you hear? If you need to, you come down here and collect yourself until you're ready to get back up there. If something bad has already happened this morning, we don't need to add to it by hearing about you getting hurt. Please, be careful."

Still leaning against the top two rungs of the ladder, Robinson forced a weak smile as he looked down at Paul. Two quick nods of his head showed that he had heard the words of caution directed at him.

After entering the building's lobby, Paul was buzzed inside by one of the two civilian dispatchers on duty. As he began walking towards Bobby Ray's office, he took notice of how quiet and empty the normally busy hallway was. Continuing on, he also took note of the several empty offices he passed. Like the hallway, they were normally busy each morning with deputies, secretaries, and other civilian employees coming and going in a mixed flurry of activity.

"This is very strange. It's like a Sunday morning in here. No one seems to be around for some reason." Paul thought as he moved closer to Bobby Ray's office.

Approaching his friend's office, Paul finally heard voices, along with a few muffled cries, coming from the large work area that was shared by several detectives assigned to the Major Case Squad. The large area, which housed several desks and a semi-private conference room, sat adjacent to Bobby Ray's office. It was affectionately known by those who worked there as the Bull Pen.

Aware that something had happened, but not exactly sure what it was, Paul paused after taking two steps inside the Bull Pen's doorway. As he stood there, he saw Sheriff Renda speaking to a group of close to twenty of his employees. Off to Renda's side, Bobby Ray was quietly speaking with the department's Public Information Officer. Close to where the sheriff stood, several female employees sat crying in folding chairs that looked like they had been hastily set up next to each other. One of the employees he noticed crying was Kelly Glover. As two of her fellow employees did, she also dabbed at her tears with a handful of Kleenex tissues. As he glanced back at Bobby Ray, Paul noticed his friend had started walking to where he stood in the back of the room.

"I'd say good morning, Bobby Ray, but I think that would be an incorrect statement to make this morning." Paul said as he tried hearing what Renda was saying to the small cluster of employees who were still gathered around him.

"Sad day here this morning, partner." Bobby Ray said looking downwards as he rubbed his eyes. As he did, Paul could see the pain that was still present in his friend's face. Like many others, he had also shed a few tears that morning. Patiently he waited to hear more.

After glancing over at several of his co-workers who were

offering comfort to each other, Bobby Ray spoke again. As he did, he fought to choke back the tears that had once again caused his eyes to water.

"We got the news about an hour ago. We lost her, Paul."

Putting a hand on his friend's shoulder to comfort him, Paul hesitated before taking a guess at who Bobby Ray was already starting to mourn.

"Are you talking about Audrey?"

Wiping his eyes, Bobby Ray confirmed Paul's suspicion. "Yeah, partner. I'm afraid I am."

The news of Small's unexpected death quickly stunned Paul just as it had with the others that morning. Within moments, a host of mental pictures of Lt. Audrey Small flooded Paul's mind. They were pictures of not only her infectious smile, but of conversations they had shared with each other. The shock of her death hit hard.

"Bobby Ray, she was on her honeymoon. People don't normally die on their honeymoons, what . . . what happened?"

Sadly shaking his head, Bobby Ray told Paul what little information he knew. "The boss got a call earlier this morning from the cops in Lahaina; that's how we found out about her death. Seems she and her husband, along with another couple they had apparently just met, rented one of those sightseeing planes for a couple of hours so they could fly around a few of the small islands close to where they were staying. Partway through the flight their plane experienced some kind of mechanical problem. From what we're being told, the pilot barely had time to radio the airport at Lanai that he was experiencing a problem when it crashed into the ocean." Bobby Ray paused for a moment to turn his head away from Paul as he fought to compose himself. "The good news . . . the good news . . . is that the navy had several ships in the area conducting some type of exercise and one of them saw her plane as it went down. Apparently they got to the crash site fairly quickly, deployed one of their small rescue boats and found two of the bodies almost immediately. It apparently took them some time, but they later recovered Audrey's body a short distance away from the others. The pilot is still missing, but the other young lady who was also a newlywed herself survived. When they finally got the bodies back to shore, that's when the Lahaina cops found Audrey's operator's license and badge in one of her pockets. That's how they knew to call us."

Stunned by what he was being told, Paul quietly stared at his friend for several seconds, unsure of how to react or what to say. "Bobby Ray, I'm at a loss for the right words to say right now. We just saw her a few days ago, just before she left. I'm literally numb by what you've told me."

"We're all in a state of shock right now. Despite putting up a good front, Sheriff Renda is not taking the news of her death too well. He was so pleased by how the investigation played out, but now he's taking Audrey's death pretty hard. He told me earlier that he's already regretting some of things he said to her during the early parts of the investigation."

Paul nodded at what his friend said. As he did, he turned to look at Sheriff Renda. Like five sets of parents who had been grieving over the loss of their sons, Renda now sat crying with Glover and several others. But while their personal and professional loss that morning was significant, it was one which paled in comparison to the recent loss felt by each set of parents.

* * * * * *

Two hours after first learning of Small's death, Paul sat in Bobby Ray's office as he and his friend continued to try and make some sort of sense out of what had happened to their mutual friend. As they sat talking, an already strange day suddenly turned even stranger when the phone on Bobby Ray's desk interrupted the conversation they were having.

"Jenkins here." Bobby Ray said as he answered the call from Dispatch.

"Bobby Ray, its Suzanne. I'm sorry to bother you on such a difficult day, but a man just walked into lobby asking to speak with you. Are you available, or should I have him call you to make an appointment?"

Not expecting any visitors, and really not in the mood to be talking with anyone, Bobby Ray sought to find out the visitor's name before deciding if he would make the time to talk with him.

"He's an elderly male, probably in his late eighties or early nineties." Then Dispatcher Hartman told Bobby Ray the most important news she had. "He says his name is Peter Paul Payne; he says he's here to speak with you about his son being arrested the other evening. What should I tell him? Are you available or not?"

As the news of Small's death had totally been unexpected, so was the presence of Payne's father. Soon Bobby Ray, with Paul following right behind him, escorted their visitor into one of the small conference rooms within the GCSD facility. After exchanging friendly greetings with each other, Paul and Bobby Ray listened as Payne's father, a short gray haired man, began to speak. Despite knowing about his son's arrest for the murders of five young men, Peter Payne spoke calmly and respectfully to the two cops sitting across from him. It was just the opposite of how his son had acted towards them prior to his arrest.

"My boy really kill them kids like the newspapers say he done?" Payne's first question reflected the fact that the elderly man had received little in the form of a formal education.

"Yes, sir. I hate to tell you this, but we are very confident that he committed each of those murders." Bobby Ray said, confirming the news Mr. Payne had already learned about his son.

"He kill them kids himself, or did he have some help doing it? You know . . . an accomplice. I think that's what you folks call someone who helps someone else do something bad, that's what you call them, right?"

Like Bobby Ray, Paul could not help feeling sorry for the elderly man sitting across from them. From his attire, as well as from the tired look they saw on the old man's face, it was easy to see that he had led a hard and difficult life.

"Mr. Payne, we believe your son acted alone when he killed those young men. We can't tell you too much right now, but I will tell you it appears he killed them because they owed him a few bucks."

"For what? Cutting the grass or something like that?"

"I'm afraid so," Bobby Ray responded.

"How much them boys owe my son?"

Exchanging glances with Paul, Bobby Ray was at first reluctant to tell Payne's father what the amount was, but finally did so.

"They owed him eighty dollars, Mr. Payne. It was for two occasions when your son had mowed their lawn."

Payne's father's eyes welled briefly with tears upon learning why his son had killed each of the victims. Slowly he slumped forward in his chair, grabbing the small conference table in front of him for support with his right hand. Regaining his composure within a matter of moments, Peter Payne said something that Bobby Ray and Paul had not expected to hear.

"That boy's been trouble his whole life. Always been angry at the world for some damn reason I could never figure out. I probably shouldn't be telling you folks this, but his momma and I been expecting something like this to happen for years. Thing is, you don't always know when he's angry . . . seems to hide it well sometimes, but other times when he blows up, he blows up. I know my wife and I have done our best to get him some help, and while he's promised us both a thousand times that he'd change his ways, he never did."

Peter Payne, a year shy of his ninetieth birthday, sat quiet for several moments. From the news that had just been confirmed for him, and from his advanced age, his hands trembled as they now rested on his knees. What he said next caused Bobby Ray to sit up straighter than he had been. It also caused him to pay even closer attention to what his elderly visitor was saying.

"Must run in the family, I guess. The Lord knows that I've killed a few men in my time as well. I'm not proud of what I've done, but it was them or me."

Despite hearing what Mr. Payne had said, Paul did not react with the same degree of concern as his friend. Having already noticed the simple but faded tattoo on the old man's right forearm told him what Payne's words had meant. As the old man shifted in his chair, another tattoo, one slightly more elaborate than the first one, briefly appeared from under the sleeve of the shirt their visitor was wearing. Both had been crudely placed in their respective locations after a long night of drinking some sixty-five years earlier. The faded blue letters on the first tattoo simply read 'United States Marine'.

"Thanks for your service, Mr. Payne." Paul respectfully said.

The comment only drew a brief smile, and then a slight nod from the former Marine who had been lucky enough to survive three years of fighting in the Pacific many years earlier.

"Where'd you see action?"

His eyes already moist from the news he had learned about his son, Payne's eyes now overflowed with tears as he thought of how to answer the question Paul had posed to him. While not a difficult one to answer, it was a subject that he had never liked speaking about. As was the case with many other veterans he served with, the former Marine chose many years ago not to talk about the horrors he experienced while fighting in a violent war. For over thirty years he had chosen to keep those memories to himself.

"The Pacific mostly. Landed with a bunch of my buddies on a

couple of other islands as well . . . Wake being one of them, but the worst action we saw was at Iwo Jima. We landed with a bunch of other Jar Heads during the second wave that day. Killed a few Jap soldiers there, and I helped to kill a few more with my buddies. Had no choice if I wanted to make it back home."

While Paul detected a touch of pride in the former Marine's voice, it was pride for the service he had rendered when his country came calling; it was not pride in having taken another man's life. There was not a whisper of any bragging, nor a sense that he had made any special contribution to the war effort. As their visitor had said, he had simply done what was needed to be done in order to be considered a good Marine, and to survive.

Sitting quiet for several moments as they allowed Payne to compose himself, Paul noticed the old man made no effort to wipe away his tears.

"Mr. Payne, we want you to know that we appreciate what you and so many other soldiers have done for our country. Please know how much we both appreciate the sacrifices you have made." Bobby Ray said, trying to comfort their visitor.

"Thanks. Just like so many other boys did back then, I just did what I had to, that's all."

It was Paul who now got the conversation back on track. "Mr. Payne, just like you've told us about your son's anger and bad temper, so have a couple of other folks. Those were people your son used to work for. They've also told us they each lost work because of his actions. There's one thing I don't understand though. If your son has such a violent temper at times, how has he managed to avoid having an arrest record? Anger and bad tempers often lead to fighting and acts of violence. Those are acts that often lead to people being arrested."

A brief but troubled smile, one followed by a momentary frown which creased Peter Payne's brow, caused a few moments of silence to exist before Payne spoke again. "Surprised by that myself at times, seeing all the trouble that boy's caused his momma and me over the years. I got tired of his troubles years ago so I threw him out of the house. His ma wasn't too happy about me doin' that, but she knew I was right to do so."

Curious at what Peter Payne was alluding to, but not wanting to press him for details, Paul and Bobby Ray both waited for him to speak again.

"My son's anger has led to more broken noses, chipped teeth, an occasional broken jaw . . . his once . . . and several broken windshields. More than I care to recall these days. He seems to think that he can solve his problems with folks by using his fists against them at times. To answer your question, the only reason he's managed to avoid being arrested is because he ends up working out some kind of deal . . . sometimes involving my money . . . with the folks he's had a beef with. Cash seems to buy people's silence or forgiveness these days. Early on, when he was a teenager mostly, I know I had to pay to have a few windshields replaced; ones he smashed for some reason or another. I can only take a guess at how much money that boy's paid out to folks so they don't press charges against him. Perhaps that's why he still has them same problems. The law never done caught up with him like it should have, at least not until . . ."

Unconsciously, Paul nodded his head to show Payne that he understood what had been said. "I figured it must have been something like that. I'd like to ask you one more question if I may. Do you know if your son has ever shot anyone before he shot those young men?"

The sad expression on Payne's face, the same one that he had worn for most of the time he sat talking with Paul and Bobby Ray, now intensified after hearing the question asked of him.

"Not that I know of."

It was a response that did not have a great deal of confidence behind it.

As a follow-up to his question, Paul asked, "Do you know if he's ever threatened to shoot anyone?"

"I wouldn't be surprised to hear that he'd done so, but I've never heard talk of him doing so."

For the next fifteen minutes, Paul and Bobby Ray did their best to ease the pain that Peter Payne felt. As they did, Paul looked across the table at a father whose son had not only been a disappointment in life to him and his wife, but also a burden.

"Mr. Payne, the loss that our victims' parents are still feeling these days are ones that can never be repaired. Nor could the birth of another child or grandchild replace the loss they have experienced. While their sons were killed during a brutal and violent act that your son is responsible for committing, you and your wife are also experiencing a similar loss. Despite your best efforts, your son chose a different path in life to travel than the one you had planned for him. I'm sure that is hard for both of you to accept, but neither you nor your wife is to be blamed for your son's actions." Despite their son's horrendous actions, Paul felt genuinely sorry for his parents.

"Well, fellas," Peter Payne said as he stood up to leave, "if you boys have arrested my son like y'all said you have, I guess you did so for a good reason. I can't defend my son's actions like some folks do when their kids get in trouble with the law. If he killed them boys like everyone seems to think he's done, then I guess he's got to tell the court why he done it. I expect that his ma is gonna go visit him wherever it is you folks are holding him, but I ain't. No sense visiting someone I don't consider to be my son no longer." Tears again formed in the old man's eyes as he placed an old worn baseball style cap back on his head before moving towards the door.

As they walked their visitor outside, Payne paused a moment after shaking the hands of the two cops he had spent an hour talking with. "I doubt this will mean much to them, but will you fellas do me a favor? Please tell the parents of those boys that I'm sorry for what my son done. I'm . . . I'm truly sorry." Without waiting for a response, Peter Payne, a tired and defeated father, began the slow walk to where his pick-up truck sat in the parking lot. Like five other sets of parents, he had lost his son to a senseless act of violence. Despite being heartbroken over what his son had done, the old man managed to survive by living one day at a time. For the remainder of his time on earth, he would never speak his son's name again.

* * * * * *

Despite the morning's sadness, the rest of the workday proved to be a very productive one for Paul and Bobby Ray. While the new information they had learned from Peter Payne was unexpectedly helpful, it had been tempered by the news of Audrey Small's tragic death.

Shortly after they had finished meeting with Payne, information they had been waiting for arrived in the form of a phone call. It was information Peter Payne would not have been told about if it had arrived prior to Paul and Bobby Ray meeting with him. Like attorneys from opposing sides in a criminal prosecution, cops never cared much about sharing all of the cards they held with witnesses or suspects either, no matter how cooperative they were.

The call Bobby Ray took was one from SLED. Unlike the previous call he received, this time Zercie had nothing but good news to report.

The tests SLED had run on the cartridge casings found at the scene proved to be a positive match to those that were test fired from Payne's Mauser. In addition, the same test results were found to be true with the casings seized by Donna and Kelly at the indoor range they visited the night Payne had been target shooting.

Any cloud of suspicion about the different calibers of casings being found at both the scene and the indoor range were later removed due to a request Paul had made of SLED. While Bobby Bats' adamant claim about his customers not being allowed to swap out barrels on their weapons while using the range proved to be true, one other important piece of information was soon verified. The ease that Payne displayed in being able to swap out different magazines as he fired his Mauser explained why two different calibers of shell casings had been found at both the murder scene and at the range. Most likely, this had also occurred during the time their suspect had shot each of his victims.

While several of the detectives assigned to the investigation had reviewed the video tape of Payne shooting at the range, the reviews had been inconclusive. No one could say definitively if Payne could actually be seen swapping out different magazines when he had turned his back slightly and briefly blocked Donna and Kelly's view of him as he stood in his firing lane. But despite the somewhat less than ideal lighting conditions, and the furtive motives of their suspect, a subsequent enhancement of the video by SLED's Video Production Unit confirmed Payne had used several different magazines during his time at the range that evening. That enhancement, along with SLED's testing of a bullet that Edwards and Bobby Bats had dug out of a ground up chunk of tire at the range after Donna and Kelly had left, easily confirmed the different caliber of casings found at both locations matched those that had been test fired from Payne's Mauser. The same testing also showed the bullet retrieved from the range matched the badly damaged bullet that came from one of the victim's bodies. It would later prove to be forensic testing that the South Carolina courts accepted with little comment.

While the video enhancement of Payne using several different magazines was a critical piece of evidence against him, so were the results of the DNA testing. Despite the limited amount of DNA that had been found on several cigarette butts seized from the area around where the victims' shed had once stood, the typing of that DNA clearly matched the DNA samples found in Payne's saliva. Those successful typings occurred on both the straw he drank from and from the cigarette butt he discarded at the Kangaroo Express gas station.

Despite concerns first raised by Paul, and later by both Bobby Ray and Sergeant Elmendorf regarding only one badly damaged bullet being found at the scene to use for future comparison tests, the hard work of everyone assigned to the investigation, as well as the forensic testing performed by SLED, helped to build a solid case against Zeke Payne. That hard work and forensic testing, coupled with Payne's temper and anger issues, convinced Solicitor Pascento that Paul's investigation had correctly developed the sufficient amount of probable cause necessary to prosecute Payne for one of South Carolina's worst mass murders.

Thirty-Three

Justice

Three months after his arrest, Payne was back in court late one afternoon in Conway. Sitting next to his three court-appointed attorneys, he listened with little interest as Judge Patricia C. Everett heard arguments over a motion his lead attorney had filed. This particular motion, one of several filed in Payne's behalf, sought a change in venue for his upcoming murder trial. Payne's legal team believed the significant publicity the murders and their client's arrest received from several local media sources had jeopardized his ability to be judged fairly by a pool of jurors who lived within the court's geographical jurisdiction.

At four that afternoon, after nearly two hours of listening to points raised by Payne's attorney in support of his motion, and to rebuttal comments from Solicitor Pascento, as well as point of law arguments raised by both attorneys, Everett called the court to recess for the day.

"I've heard your rather lengthy arguments for and against the venue change that's been requested. I'll give each of you five minutes to summarize your thoughts tomorrow morning at 9 a.m. sharp. Don't be late, Gentlemen!" Everett said as she stared at Payne's attorney with a small scowl on her face. In moments, she was making her way out of the court.

After several minutes of conversation with his attorneys, Payne's legs and arms were secured by a combination of handcuffs, leg irons, and a belly chain. Due to a variety of threats against his life, Payne was wearing a bulletproof vest. It had been roughly placed over his head prior to being handcuffed. Like most vests, it offered protection against being shot in the chest and back.

"Let's bring him out the door on the south side of the building today, Teddy. There's less of a chance of us bumping into reporters and others who want to kill this jerk." One of the three correctional officers responsible for transporting Payne back and forth from the correctional center said to his supervisor.

Teddy Fuller, the supervisor of the three-man crew quickly agreed. "OK, I'll radio Jack to bring the van around to the other side of the parking lot. He can let the Conway cop know about the change that's gonna take place; he can follow the van in his cruiser to the side of the building. Let's just hope that no one's waiting there to greet us with a surprise when we get Payne outside. All things considered, we've been pretty lucky so far."

"Sounds good. I just want to get out of here. It's been a long day." One of the other guards muttered as he finished securing the leg irons around Payne's ankles.

While Fuller's comments caused his fellow guards to exchange brief looks with each other, neither had any real concern about any possible breaches of security. They were confident that if trouble confronted them they could handle it. Their training, along with the Conway cop assigned to the courthouse, and the combination of pepper spray and stun guns they each carried, gave them the confidence they needed.

Noticing the brief looks his partners exchanged between themselves as he finished giving the van driver his instructions, Fuller tried reassuring them. Like his friends, his confidence was very high. "Aw, come on, guys! Nothing's gonna happen. You'll see. Let's get this jerk back to his freakin' cell so we can go eat. I'm hungry!"

As the side door of the courthouse opened several minutes later, Fuller, a white male who was roughly twenty pounds overweight, stepped outside into the late afternoon sunlight to make sure the DOC prisoner van was in position to receive its passenger. Since the time of Payne's first appearance in court, this was the same procedure he performed at the end of each day. Somewhat relieved by seeing the van idling at the end of the sidewalk, and from quickly scanning the immediate area and sensing that no trouble was lurking nearby in the form of protestors or news crews, Fuller turned and nodded to his fellow guards that the coast was clear. As he turned back to start walking down the granite steps which led to where the van was parked, their prisoner was walked outside onto the small landing. Once there, Payne, as did the two guards escorting him, paused briefly to allow his eyes to adjust to the day's bright sunlight.

Moments later, with a guard on either side of him, Payne slowly started moving down the steps. Several yards in front of him,

Fuller briefly paused to make sure his prisoner had cleared the building. As his right foot prepared to touch down on the second to last step, the left side of Payne's face, from just below his left eye to just above his eyebrow, suddenly disappeared after being struck by a 7.62x51mm NATO round. Instantly he fell dead, his body tumbling to the blue slate sidewalk at the bottom of the stairs where it briefly convulsed from the shock of being hit by such a powerful round. Blood and brain matter quickly mixed together in a growing pool of blood where his lifeless body rested. Safely falling to the ground alongside their prisoner, all three guards remained motionless as they tried comprehending what had just taken place. In the nearby van, the first 911 call was just being made.

* * * * * *

Two days later, close to a half-mile from where Payne had been shot, a single shell casing, one later thought to have been fired from a long range sniper's rifle that had been made in Germany, was found on the second floor of an old abandoned house on 9th Avenue. The single casing was found on the wooden floor of what had once been one of the home's two upstairs bedrooms. Near it sat the room's only window. Investigators soon surmised the window had been intentionally left open by Payne's shooter. Found standing straight up, the casing, just like the brief note that was found next to it, had been staged for the police to find.

The computer generated note was simple and brief in its message. *"Payne's death won't bring those boys back to their parents, but it does ensure that justice has been served!"*

* * * * * *

Over the next three months, a task force of law enforcement officers from both the Horry and Georgetown County sheriff's departments, as well as investigators from SLED and the South Carolina Highway Patrol, worked to solve the murder of Zeke Payne. But unlike the investigation into the murders of five young men in North Litchfield, the investigation of Payne's death received little interest from any of the cops involved. When dealing with murderers, rapists, and child molesters, cops cared little about their suspect's rights and personal safety. They cared even less when the perps they arrested had been murdered. Soon the media, just like the cops and the public before them, lost interest as well.

It was not an investigation Paul was asked to participate in. It was also one he would have said no to.

Thirty-Four

Another Assignment

Four days after the arrest of Zeke Payne took place, Paul and Bobby Ray had lunch at Hannah's Restaurant in Murrells Inlet. Taking their first real day off in weeks, Paul had played golf that morning at Caledonia Golf and Fish Club with two of his neighbors. Wisely deciding to not risk hurting his back again, Bobby Ray had served as Paul's chauffeur for the morning as they made their way around the scenic course. While it had been a fun morning to be outside on such a glorious day, just like the day's temperature, the golf scores climbed far too high as the round went on.

While it was warm to be eating outside, the pleasant sunny day was made comfortable by a light wind being blown down the Waccamaw River from out of the north. Despite the warm temperature, they chose to have their meal outside under a large Southern Oak. The expansive tree, with its large hanging branches full of Spanish Moss, served to provide shade for all who dined on the small but comfortable patio. Nearby a large and obviously expensive houseboat sat moored to one of the main docks; its owners comfortably stretched out in deck chairs as they sat reading near the bow of the white fiberglass boat. Another boat, one smaller and far sleeker than the houseboat, was temporarily tied up to another nearby dock as its owner purchased fuel for an afternoon of fun on the river. In the back of the boat three young children, all donning bright orange life preservers, sat anxiously with their mother waiting for the fun to begin.

As they sipped on their first Jack and Coke of the day, Paul and Bobby Ray casually scanned the menu as they each wrestled with the many choices available for lunch. Doing so caused Paul's stomach to growl even louder as he had only eaten a light meal the night before and had skipped breakfast in favor of sleeping a few minutes later that morning.

"I can hear that belly of yours barking, Paul." Bobby Ray said looking up from his menu as he finished narrowing down his choices of what to have for lunch. "You better get something in there quick or that next Jack and Coke or two is really gonna mess you up. I'm thinking I'm gonna have me an Oyster Po' Boy." Closing his menu, he took a healthy swig of his drink as he caught the attention of their waitress. Holding his drink up in his right hand told her they were already in need of another round.

"That's a good choice! Think I'll have the same, Bobby Ray." Paul's face had a smile on it as he thought about his first bite of one of the restaurant's specialty sandwiches. Ordering the Oyster Po' Boy in the past, he had never been disappointed by the way the overstuffed sandwich had been prepared.

After taking another hit on his first drink, Paul allowed a few of the drink's ice cubes to flow into his mouth before setting his glass down. Chewing them, he watched as the boat that had been being fueled up pushed away from the dock. Quickly it headed upriver towards the swing bridge in Socastee. From his own trips out on the river, he had come to know this part of the Waccamaw River fairly well. While most locals, and even newcomers to the area like him, called the brownish colored river by its name, it was known to others as simply being a small section of the Intracoastal Waterway, one that ran along a good part of the eastern seaboard.

Paul's stare of what was happening out on the river was soon interrupted by their waitress setting down both their meals and their second Jack and Cokes. Already finished with his first drink, Bobby Ray handed the young teenage waitress his empty glass to take away so there was more room on the small black metal table for their plates and their second drink of the day. While Paul elected to first take a healthy bite of his sandwich, Bobby Ray chose to do the opposite. The generous swig he took of his freshly made drink quickly drained it by more than a third.

As they ate their lunch, Paul and Bobby Ray could not help but talk about the investigation they had spent so much time on over the past few weeks. As they did, they also referred back to the Melkin investigation at times, and to some of the similarities those two cases shared with each other. They both agreed that Payne, just like Richard Melkin before him, had carried far too much anger and pain in his life for many different reasons.

With his appetite soon satisfied by the locally grown oysters that had been fried to perfection, Bobby Ray pushed his plate away from him as he gingerly leaned back in his chair. He sat quietly for another moment as he allowed Paul time to polish off the small amount of potato salad that remained on his plate. As he waited, he waved off the waitress' attempt of handing them a dessert menu to look at. "No thanks, darling, but you can bring us another round of drinks. I'm not going anywhere special this afternoon and neither is he." Bobby Ray's comments caused a toothy smile to cross the face of their waitress as she removed his plate and empty drink glass from in front of him.

"Paul, you need to be in Renda's office tomorrow morning by ten. I'm not going to tell you everything so don't even try pumping me for any more information. Of course, if you want to try and pump me for some more info by buying me another one or two of these here drinks that's a different story." Bobby Ray laughed as he held up the drink that had just been set down on the table for him.

"For what? What's happening tomorrow?" Paul asked as he finished wiping his mouth with a napkin.

"Renda's got a small ceremony organized for tomorrow morning; he even invited a few of the other county sheriffs, a couple of the local police chiefs, and some media folks to be there. Just like the others who worked the Melkin case, and the one we just finished, I'm invited to. Seems Renda has the idea that someone's deserving of some special recognition for helping us solve those two cases." The smile on Bobby Ray's face quickly told Paul who that person was.

"Aw, for Pete's sake, Bobby Ray! Why's he doing this, and why isn't everyone who worked on those cases getting recognized? I'm not interested in getting any more plaques or awards. I've got a box full of stuff like that from back home. It's just sitting in my garage collecting dust. I know what I did, and I know what everyone else did, that's recognition enough, at least for me it is." Never being the type of person who relished attention being directed at him, Paul was less than pleased by the news he had just been told by his friend.

With an even bigger smile on his face now, Bobby Ray let Paul simmer for a few more seconds before speaking again. "Pretty presumptuous of you to be thinking that I was talking about you being the one Renda is gonna recognize, isn't it?"

For a brief moment, Paul thought he misunderstood who Bobby Ray had been referring to, but then realized he had not.

"Don't worry, partner, Renda's gonna recognize everyone who worked on those two investigations, but you're the one getting the biggest prize. That's what he's told me anyhow. He's even invited Audrey's parents to attend as he wants them to know how much she contributed to both cases being solved. Personally, I think that I . . ."

"Forget you, Bobby Ray!"

Paul's comment caused both of them to laugh as they finished off their last drink of the afternoon.

＊＊＊＊＊＊

Retiring to South Carolina had taken Paul to places and events he had not given a moment of thought to visiting or becoming involved in. In the short time he lived in the Palmetto State, he had helped find the missing gold and silver that once had been a part of the treasury of the Confederate States of America, and had also helped to solve two vastly different murders, both of which were horrific in nature.

In his move south, he had been far busier than he planned on being, certainly far busier in a professional sense than he could have ever imagined. Over the months that followed the Payne investigation, months which saw autumn turn to winter and then to spring, Paul and Donna spent as much time as possible travelling across several southeastern states. In late March, as the weather again began to warm in South Carolina, they returned to their normal routine of work, golf, and to enjoying as many weekends as possible on their boat.

In early April, one week after Bobby Ray informally made it known that he was giving serious thought to retiring, Paul's cell phone rang late one afternoon. The number he saw displayed on his phone was one he did not immediately recognize.

"Hello?"

"Paul, it's Bobby Ray, I need some help!"

Forced to soon make a decision that he was not prepared to make, Paul knew his answer would have an impact on how his friend was going to respond to the latest crisis he was facing.

"Donna's not going to like this, but . . ."

Abbreviations

GCSD:	Georgetown County Sheriff's Department
MBPD:	Myrtle Beach Police Department
NMBPD:	North Myrtle Beach Police Department
SLED:	South Carolina Law Enforcement Division
FBI NA:	FBI National Academy
ATF:	Bureau of Alcohol, Tobacco, Firearms and Explosives
DOC:	Department of Corrections
PIO:	Public Information Officer
NCIC:	National Crime Information Center
NIBIN:	National Integrated Ballistic Information Network
UC:	Undercover Officer
CI:	Confidential Informant
Vics:	Victims of a crime
NASDEA:	National Alliance of State Drug Enforcement Agencies
RPD:	Raleigh (NC) Police Department
WPD:	Wilmington (NC) Police Department

Peter Warren Books

---

www.readpete.com

Other novels by Peter Warren include:

The Horry County Murders

Confederate Gold and Silver

The Journey North

(Written with Roy McKinney and Edward Odom)

The Parliament Men is available in soft cover and eBook formats. The author's other books are available in hard cover, soft cover, and eBook formats.

CPSIA information can be obtained
at www.ICGtesting.com
Printed in the USA
FFOW04n0500170315
11874FF